DISCOVERY

Barbara Greig

dis cov ery

Barbara Greig

Matador
9 Priory Business Park,
Wistow Road, Kibworth Beauchamp,
Leicestershire. LE8 0RX
Tel: 0116 279 2299
Email: books@troubador.co.uk
Web: www.troubador.co.uk/matador
Twitter: @matadorbooks

ISBN 978 1838594 268

British Library Cataloguing in Publication Data.
A catalogue record for this book is available from the British Library.

Printed and bound in Great Britain by 4edge Limited
Typeset in 12pt Adobe Jenson Pro by Troubador Publishing Ltd, Leicester, UK

Matador is an imprint of Troubador Publishing Ltd

For my family

LIST OF CHARACTERS

All are fictional except those marked*

1557

Hernando Gharsia – a Morisco physician living in Caors, Pays d'Oc, France

Luis Gharsia – his grandson, a vintner and saffron producer, and lawyer

Johan Berenguer – the Gharsias' loyal servant

Ysabel Bernade – wealthy widow of Michel Bernade and Hernando Gharsia's loving companion

Guilhem Gaulbert – Ysabel's brother, vintner

Loise Gaulbert – his wife

Henri Gaulbert – his son, vintner

Marie Gaulbert – his daughter, estranged wife of Luis Gharsia

Thomas Weaver (deceased) – merchant of Bridgwater, Somerset, England

Alyce Weaver – his elder daughter, put aside by her clergyman husband, Matthew Blake, on Mary I's accession to the throne

Rufus Weaver (deceased) – his son, burnt at the stake as a Protestant martyr

Meg Weaver – his youngest child by his second wife, Margaret Mercer

Jane Blake – daughter of Alyce Weaver and Matthew Blake

Edward Mercer – merchant of Lewes, Sussex, England; brother-in-law of Thomas Weaver

Catherine Mercer – his wife

John Mercer – his son

Tom Flint – fisherman from Hastings

Wat Flint – his nephew

Lord Wentworth – Deputy of Calais*

John Highfield – Master of Ordnance at Calais*

1607

Luis Gharsia – a widower, vintner and saffron producer, retired lawyer

Thomas Gharsia – his son, a Huguenot scholar (French Protestant)

Joseph Gharsia – his second son, a physician

Elizabeth Gharsia – his daughter

Gabriel Gharsia – his grandson, son of Joseph and Ana Cavalina, a student

Pedro Torres – a Morisco expelled from Spain

Jacques Gaulbert – son of Henri Gaulbert, vintner

Helena Gaulbert – his wife

Luc Gaulbert – his son, vintner

Sara Gaulbert – Jacques's mother

Catarina – the Gharsias' maid

Samuel Champlain – French explorer and cartographer*

François Pont-Gravé – a ship's commander and explorer*

Guillaume Le Testu – a ship's captain and explorer*

First Settlers in Kebec
Etienne Brûlé*

Nicolas Marsolet*
Jean Duval*
Natel*
Bonnerme*

First Nations: Montagnais
Mashk
Wyome

First Nations: Mohawk
Matwau
Sheauga
Oheo
Aarushi

Jacob Eelkens – Dutch commander of Fort van Nassouwen*

PROLOGUE

Caors, The Pays d'Oc, December 1607

GABRIEL GHARSIA PUSHED OPEN THE DOOR, intruding on the heavy silence. The old oak, swollen with the damp, grated across the uneven slabs, grinding the rushes into dust. He stopped, inhaled the familiar musty smell which pervaded the hall during the winter months when the shutters were firmly closed against the cold rising from the river, and waited for his eyes to adjust to the dim interior. He flexed his shoulders, easing the tension caused by too long in the saddle, and revelled in the quietness, the absolute peace of being home. He raised his eyes to the lofty roof where the original beams slowly came into focus, unaltered since the day a nervous bride had stood next to Michel Bernade, almost a century before, and realised the true extent of her new husband's wealth. Gabriel's grandfather, when he had inherited the property, had refused to modernise by lowering the ceiling and adding an extra floor so the house appeared archaic when compared to those the young man knew in Paris. Nevertheless, today, Gabriel welcomed the spaciousness, tired as he was from the journey. He glanced around, stretched his back, and made his way to the small chamber where he expected to find his grandfather.

The old man woke with a start as the latch clicked and the book he had been reading slid to the floor with a thud. He blinked. His eyes, rimmed by the passing years, but still black and intense, were wary as he strained to see.

"Jibra'il?" he questioned. Confused in the moment of waking, he used the Arabic form of his grandson's name.

Gabriel suppressed the urge to correct his grandfather, which was his usual reaction. Instead, sobered by the uneasy thought that he was seeing himself in the future, if he was fortunate to live so long, Gabriel spoke softly, albeit with a touch of reproach.

"Why are you cocooned like an invalid, Papi? It is not yet noon."

The old man bristled, leant forward and regarded Gabriel keenly. "And what are you doing here?"

There was no sign of his grandfather's bewilderment now and Gabriel felt himself squirm under such scrutiny. Despite planning his explanation repeatedly on the ride from Bordèu, he was now at a loss on how to begin.

His grandfather was waiting. He increased Gabriel's discomfort by asking, "Why are you not in Paris studying? It is very foolhardy of you to travel at this time of year."

The young man chose to dissemble. "I was worried about you. I thought you might be lonely after Nonna's death."

Luis Gharsia eyed his grandson sardonically. "Your grandmother has been dead nearly a year and now you are worried about me?"

"Yes." Even to Gabriel's own ears he sounded feeble but he was genuine about his concern for his grandfather. He was older than anyone Gabriel knew and, until this visit, his grandfather seemed to have defied his age. A big man, tall and broad, Luis Gharsia had appeared indestructible but now, in the flickering light of the fire, Gabriel could see the frailty of age.

"Pass me my stick, please."

Gabriel reached for the long, beautifully crafted shepherd's staff, which had once belonged to Luis's own grandfather, and moved forward to help.

"I can manage." Luis struggled until he was upright and then rested both hands on the top of the staff. Gabriel straightened up a fraction, as despite his age, his grandfather was the taller. The old man's heart swelled with love but his face remained inscrutable. He asked again, "Why are you not in Paris?"

Gabriel met his grandfather's eyes, a mirror image of his own, and gabbled, "I am postponing my studies."

"Postponing?" Luis kept his voice level.

"Yes."

"Why, may I ask?"

The words rushed out. "I am going to New France."

The remains of a simple dinner lay congealing on their plates. Neither of them found they had much appetite. Gabriel, usually so hungry, was overcome with fatigue after the hard ride, broken only with restless nights in cheap, cold accommodation, and Luis's unease about his grandson's plans rendered his plate of mutton stew unpalatable. The meat had cooled and lay in a bed of solidifying grease. Gabriel etched a pattern through the fat with his knife. Luis watched him and waited. Feeling his grandfather's penetrating eyes appraise him, the young man responded defiantly.

"You started to travel when you were my age."

"I went to England. There is a world of difference between a voyage from Bordèu to Bridgwater and one across the ocean."

"New France is not so far. If the winds are fair the crossing can be made in a matter of weeks."

"You mean four months," corrected his grandfather.

Gabriel stopped fiddling; his eyes gleamed with excitement. "It is rumoured that there is to be an expedition to establish a settlement on the River of Canada."

"I thought there already was a settlement on the river?" queried Luis.

"Tadoussak is still just a trading post, Papi. This is to be different."

"I see," replied Luis in a voice which implied the opposite.

"Yes, this will be a permanent settlement and, as such, it will need a physician."

"But you have not finished your studies yet."

"I know enough," declared Gabriel. Then he had the grace to look sheepish. "It is only my exams which I'll lack."

"Your father will not be pleased."

Gabriel remained silent. Luis continued to study his grandson carefully. Realisation dawned. "Your father doesn't know, does he?"

Gabriel shifted uncomfortably. "I thought I would write – after I had seen you."

Luis raised a questioning eyebrow. "You should see him."

"I do not have time to travel all the way to Bologna. The expedition will leave in early spring."

"You should see your father, Gabriel. The voyage to New France is dangerous and then you will need to navigate up the river. Much could befall you."

Gabriel started to argue but Luis interrupted. "I have read Samuel Champlain's Travels. I know all about the canoes, made from birchbark, which are apt to turn over if you don't know how to handle them and I have experienced the treachery of rivers myself."

He shrugged. He had underestimated his grandfather's thirst for knowledge, and said, "I will be fine. It cannot be that hard."

Luis smiled at the confidence of youth and pointed to the debris on the plates. "I don't know about that but I do know that your aunt will not be pleased if she returns from Luzech and finds her stew has gone to waste."

When Elizabeth Gharsia came across Gabriel in her kitchen, raiding the store cupboard, two emotions surfaced: delight at seeing him and guilt that she was the recipient of his winning smile when his mother had lain crumbling within her grave for more than a decade. With his easy charm, Gabriel opened his palm to reveal a handful of almonds, grinned at her and popped them into his mouth. Elizabeth removed her travelling cloak, laid it across the back of the settle, took two strides, and embraced him tightly before he had finished chewing.

She tried to suppress her pleasure as she reached for two goblets and a pitcher of sekanjabin, the refreshing drink which her father preferred them to drink in the house. Then as she sat down wearily at the scrubbed table, Gabriel, his earlier tiredness forgotten, slid onto the bench opposite her. "It is good to see you, Aunt."

Elizabeth prepared herself. His animated face was disarming but she knew that if he was home unexpectedly there was a problem.

"Are you not pleased to see me?" he asked.

"I might be when I know why you are here."

His eyes twinkled in the candlelight. "You will never guess why I am here."

"I am sure you will tell me." Elizabeth took a sip of the sweet vinegary liquid.

Her nephew leaned back and lifted his drink. "All in good time, Aunt," he replied, his face alive with merriment, before he drained the goblet.

Elizabeth's mother had always claimed that Gabriel reminded her of her own brother, Rufus, but she believed otherwise. Since he was a small boy, she had never been able to look at him without remembering Ana Cavalina: the beautiful, charismatic girl who had stolen Joseph Gharsia's heart.

It was twenty years since the Gharsia family had made the long journey to Bologna for the sumptuous wedding. Ana's father, whose family had flourished since the city had become part of the Papal States, had spared no expense for his only daughter's nuptials. If her choice of spouse was not what he truly wished for, Giovanni Cavalina had hidden his disappointment well. He was a pragmatic man and realised it was too soon to aspire to a union with a minor member of the struggling aristocracy; instead marriage to a scholar, a physician with a proven pedigree, was a good step for a man whose grandfather had been an illiterate butcher. Giovanni had welcomed the Gharsias, entertained them lavishly and beamed with pride as he watched his daughter at her bridegroom's side.

Elizabeth, at sixteen a year younger than the bride, had watched the proceedings with a jaundiced eye. Tall and imposing like her father, she had felt large and ungainly in comparison to the exquisite Ana. The new dress, which had thrilled her when she had first stepped into the finished garment, felt too restrictive with its stiff stomacher and wired ruff. Even the beautiful embroidery on the full skirt failed to lift her spirits. Bored with watching the besotted expression on her brother's face as he made his vows to his bride, Elizabeth had contemplated the other members of her family, standing in a semi-circle at Joseph's side.

Thomas, her elder brother, stood rigid, unable to disguise his disdain of a Roman Catholic ceremony: his disapproval obvious from the set of his mouth. Not for the first time, Elizabeth wondered why her father had insisted that the whole family attend the wedding. Unlike their English mother, who wore her Protestantism more lightly, Thomas had embraced the Huguenot cause with zeal, leaving home to study in Montauban, one of the four Huguenot fortresses granted by the crown. He had seen her watching him and had scowled in response. She had suppressed the urge to pull a face and moved her eyes to her father.

As usual, Luis Gharsia had been the tallest man present, although Thomas was a close second. A striking figure with his black, silvered hair and sharp features, her father's immaculate clothing had been sober, and in her view more refined than Cavalina's. His face had an expression Elizabeth recognised; although apparently concentrating on the proceedings, she knew that his thoughts were elsewhere. Nominally Roman Catholic, her father had been schooled in Islam by his grandfather, resulting in a tolerant man who worshipped as he wanted at home, educated his children as he had been taught and condemned the oppression of people for their beliefs. Introverted, distant, and sometimes intimidating, her father had struggled to keep the family safe from the time he had rescued her mother and aunt from England, through the religious strife which plagued France and threatened to split the family, to this moment when Joseph clearly demonstrated where his loyalty lay.

Elizabeth had looked back at the bridal couple. Ana was

saying her vows. Small, slender as willow, with her lovely face framed by luxuriant dark hair, the young girl had glowed with happiness as her voice rang loud and clear around the chapel. Elizabeth had continued to stare until she, too, felt she was the subject of someone's attention. Her mother had caught her eye, a smile of empathy on her face and they had exchanged a meaningful glance. Her mother's fair skin had been mottled with the heat while her dress, although in the latest fashion with its gathered skirt and farthingale, was obviously unflattering as it had made its wearer appear short and dumpy.

After the wedding, Elizabeth had not seen Joseph and Ana until the following year when she had travelled to Bologna with her mother to see the new baby. Ana, elegant and neat despite having recently given birth, had welcomed them warmly, her beautiful face alight with the wonder of motherhood. Elizabeth had tried to channel her feelings into being helpful, continually reminding herself of the tenth commandment, but she could not deny the unsettling worm of envy. It had been worse three years later when Joseph, Ana, and Gabriel had visited the family in Caors. The radiant young woman had charmed their friends and acquaintances, entrancing many of the younger men, including Jacques, who held a special place in Elizabeth's affections.

The fateful letter had arrived on a clear March day. Ana was dead. Two weeks before her twenty-fifth birthday she had succumbed to a fever which had tortured her slight frame. Worried about the contagion and his son's safety, Joseph was already on the way to Caors with Gabriel. Could his parents take the boy until the danger was over?

"Aunt Elizabeth?"

"Yes." She took a sip of her drink.

"What were you thinking about? You were in a reverie – just like Papi can often be."

"I was not," countered Elizabeth, "I was waiting for you to tell me why you have come home. You should be in Paris and then your father expects you to continue your studies in Bologna next year."

"I am not going to Bologna." He paused for greater effect. "I am going to New France."

Elizabeth spluttered, sending droplets of liquid onto the table. Embarrassed by her clumsiness, she rubbed her hand across the worn surface with quick jerky movements. Momentarily speechless about his intentions, she experienced an unaccustomed sensation of dread, deep in the pit of her stomach. When she did speak, her objection had little to do with his medical career.

"You cannot go there. You will die."

Gabriel laughed, but on realising she was serious he took her hands in his. Her right one was sticky with sekanjabin and both shook slightly. "Do not worry. I will be fine. As I have told Papi, it is not so far. When Samuel Champlain first sailed to the New World four years ago, he arrived at Tadoussak in the March, explored, and was back in France by September. The following spring, he went again with Dugua and established a settlement at Port Royal. For two years Champlain searched for suitable sites for a permanent settlement before he returned home safely." He tried to keep the excitement out of his voice, speaking as if crossing the ocean was an everyday occurrence. He smiled at his aunt indulgently. "You see, there is no danger. Champlain has made friends with the local people, the Montagnais and the Algonquin. There is nothing to fear."

Elizabeth could not think of a reply. Gabriel continued

as he squeezed her hands, "All will be well. A new expedition is planned this spring with the intention of establishing a settlement on the great River of Canada. Du Pont, the merchant who founded Tadoussak, and Champlain plan to sail from Honfleur and they will need men with skills."

"And you are one of those men?"

"Of course," he replied emphatically. "There is always need for a physician."

Elizabeth sighed. "I don't know what to say."

"Good night," suggested Gabriel. "I am off to bed. I want an early start tomorrow."

"Why?"

"I am going to ride out to the Gaulberts' farm and see Luc," he answered with an impish grin. He leaned over to kiss her cheek. "New settlements also need men who can till the soil."

After he had left, Elizabeth sat for some time tracing the outline of knots on the table with her finger before she retrieved her cloak from the back of the settle and went in search of her father.

He was sitting in a circle of light. Expensive beeswax candles surrounded him as he sat at his desk, reading. He glanced up as she entered. "Ah, you are back, Elizabeth. Have you seen Gabriel?"

"Yes," she replied, concern clear in her voice.

"Come," said her father, "let us sit by the fire."

Elizabeth took two of the candles and placed them on the mantel while her father painstakingly rose to his feet. "I am so stiff," he commented as he inched his way along the desk.

"Here, please take my arm, Papa," Elizabeth invited, as she returned to extinguish the remaining candles. She led him to his favourite chair, asking, "What do you think?"

"I believe we are a long way from him actually going."

"You do?"

"Yes – Du Pont and Champlain will want to choose their settlers carefully. I doubt they have personally invited Gabriel."

Elizabeth thought about this. "You are right, Papa," she said, relieved.

Luis nodded in acknowledgement but did not speak. The fire crackled, a log broke, spraying sparks onto the rushes. Elizabeth jumped up and stamped them out. "Gabriel is riding over to the vineyard tomorrow. He is planning to persuade Luc Gaulbert to accompany him."

Her father digested this information but remained quiet. Elizabeth, expecting a response, peered at her father to see if he had fallen asleep. His eyes snapped open.

"I am not asleep, Elizabeth."

"Why don't you go to bed?"

"I will sit here a while longer."

"You would be more comfortable in bed, Papa."

"Don't fuss," he retorted abruptly. Elizabeth flinched.

"I am sorry, my dear." Luis could see she had taken offence. He sighed and said, "Sometimes I wonder why I have lived so long."

"Perhaps because Mama took such good care of you," Elizabeth replied, equally brusquely.

"But she is gone now," he stated sorrowfully.

"We all miss Mama," Elizabeth said, thinking none more so than her. She added pointedly, "But you have me to look after you now and I think you should go to bed."

However, Luis did not wish to go to bed. He wanted to doze in his chair, hard as it was. When he slept in his bed he fell into a deep sleep, and the dreams came. Dreams or memories, he was not sure which, but he knew they left him lonely and agitated. He saw them all: the long-dead and those who had departed more recently, and he often woke in a jumble of bedding, anxious for daylight to break.

LUIS

1557

ONE

Lewes, England, June 1557

I T WAS A BRIGHT MIDSUMMER MORNING, JUST TWO days before the solstice, when Luis Gharsia and Henri Gaulbert walked towards Edward Mercer's house. The sun already rode high in the sky and the sound of birdsong lifted Henri's spirits after the gruelling days at sea. Those they passed on the road glanced sideways at the men and then quickly looked away, as the travellers were obviously foreigners. Luis, a few steps ahead of his companion, wore an expression of ferocious concentration as his long purposeful strides covered the distance from the quay. Henri, struggling to keep up, was distracted, for although he had accompanied Luis to Bridgwater before, he had never travelled on to Lewes. To the north, he could see the distinctive towers of the castle while to the south the Sussex countryside rolled towards the coast. His eyes were everywhere, drinking in his surroundings, but he increased his pace as the house came into view.

From a modest yeoman's dwelling, Edward Mercer's home had been modified to impress. The magnificent newly glazed hall window, a testament to the merchant's success, reflected the strong sunlight, as did the small open casement adjacent to the richly carved oak door. As the two men approached, the sound of a voice raised in anger could be heard and Luis, already strained by anticipation, clenched his fists. He recognised the west-country tones of Meg Weaver, who had been taken into her uncle's household after the death of her father, Thomas Weaver of Bridgwater. Without hesitation Luis tried the door, found it unlocked, and walked in uninvited. Surprised, Henri followed closely behind.

Meg was shouting above the yapping of Catherine Mercer's lapdog, which squirmed with agitation in his mistress's arms, and the crying of a distressed child. Although she had her back to him, Luis could see the tension in Meg's sturdy frame. Her unruly mass of light brown curls bounced on her shoulders as she announced furiously, "I keep telling you, Jane cannot help it."

Catherine Mercer replied more quietly, puzzlement in her eyes as if she lacked understanding. "She is far too old to wet herself."

Luis studied Jane Blake. The child continued to wail loudly. Her distinctive face was contorted with misery; tears spilled from her eyes and streamed down her cheeks while her urine-soaked nightgown clung to her legs. Luis felt his head pounding: he registered Meg's indignation at the child's clothes not being washed and her threat to do the laundry herself. He heard Catherine Mercer reply, her voice now louder over the yelping dog.

"You will not, Margaret! You are a daughter of the house."

The hammering in Luis's head intensified. "Stop at once!" he bellowed.

Catherine Mercer froze, her dog scrambling and snapping excitedly in her arms. Jane continued sobbing, great gulping sobs as if in competition and Meg swung round, her eyes glistening with anger which did not quite mask the fear. She saw Luis. Instantly she burst into tears, too, and in three short steps she reached him. As he returned the girl's embrace Luis was aware of Catherine Mercer's disapproval, evident in the older woman's sharp intake of breath.

"Monsieur Gharsia," she said coolly, "we did not expect you so soon."

He nodded in response. "Mistress Mercer."

Catherine Mercer's eyes travelled to the satchel over Luis's shoulder, her change of attitude discernible as she realised the precious content, more valuable than gold.

Luis gently removed Meg's arms so that he could look at her. Immediately she started to babble. "The maid refused to wash Jane's clothes when I asked her. She just dries them on the line. They stink. All Jane's clothes are soiled. She keeps wetting herself. She never used to. There are no clean clothes for her to wear this morning."

"Slow down, Meg," Luis insisted. "Explain what is wrong, slowly."

The dog was still yapping; Henri could see its sharp little teeth. A new pool of urine gathered at the child's feet as the dog lunged forward in Catherine Mercer's arms. The woman looked at the little girl with distaste as the amber rivulets spread out amongst the rushes. The child increased her wailing.

Luis noticed Catherine Mercer's reaction. The pent-up stress of the previous few weeks erupted into a thunderous outburst: "Take that dog out! Get the maid to find something, anything which is warm and dry for the child. Tell her to wash the soiled clothes. Don't just stand there, woman, do it!"

Catherine Mercer stared in disbelief. Uncertain how to react, she looked to Henri for support. He ignored her, mesmerised as he was by Luis's behaviour. Luis who was always so controlled, Luis who was usually so restrained. Appreciating that she could do nothing other than obey, Catherine turned with a swish of her skirt and left, taking the offending animal with her.

The child, now distressed by Luis, was howling louder. Henri watched, intrigued, as Meg left Luis's side and embraced the girl. She spoke softly to her. "Come, Jane, this is Luis, our friend," and led the child by the hand towards them. For the first time Meg included Henri in her explanation. "She doesn't usually do it; she is just so upset."

"Why?" asked Luis, afraid of the answer. His heart lurched. Alyce would never allow her daughter to be in such a state.

Meg's eyes were huge and frightened; there was a trace of hysteria in her voice. "They have taken Alyce. Three days ago the sheriff's men came and took Alyce away."

They had been in Mercer's house for less than half an hour. By the time the maid returned with clean clothes, the scene in the hall had changed. All was peaceful. Luis and Meg were conversing in low voices while Jane, quietly sucking her thumb, was nestled next to Henri, comfortable within the crook of his arm.

Meg had been taken aback by her niece's reaction to Luis's companion. Once Catherine Mercer had departed, Henri had crouched down, addressing Jane in what Meg assumed was Occitan. His voice soothed the distraught child, the same way as he had calmed countless ewes in labour and more than one mare who had struggled to birth her foal. Jane stopped wailing; only the occasional sob escaped her lips until gradually she became silent. Meg had watched as Henri sat back and crossed his legs, regarding Jane with warm hazel eyes. She had released the child's hand as he held out his arms. The little girl walked steadily towards Henri: nervousness tinged her face as her hands touched her soaked nightdress. Henri changed to English. "What's a bit of piss," he had said as he encircled her in his arms.

Meg turned to Luis, admiration in her eyes. Although he was glad that the crying had stopped he was more preoccupied with Alyce's situation.

"Why was Alyce taken?"

"I don't know. All I can say is that when we came back from the market the sheriff's men were already here. They just took Alyce away without any explanation."

"Where is your uncle?"

"He is away on business, in London. John is with him."

The urgency in Luis's voice was marked. "Do you know where they have taken her?"

"No." Meg started to cry again.

"I'll need to find out."

Henri spoke in Occitan. "I might be able to help."

"You?" Luis's tone was dismissive.

"Yes."

"How?"

"I can go to every tavern in Lewes and listen."

"I could do that."

"No, Luis. People will recognise you and link you to Mercer. Also you will raise suspicion by not drinking."

Luis thought about what Henri proposed. It was logical but there was a problem. "You don't speak the language well enough."

"I understand more than you think. I just need to listen."

Luis translated for Meg. She regarded Henri keenly. "He will be drunk if he has a tankard in every tavern."

"No, he won't," Luis replied wryly, "Henri's capacity for alcohol is remarkable."

Meg continued to regard Henri. He responded by giving

her a rakish grin; partly through instinct because she was young and pretty but mainly to show her that he had understood her comment.

They had been in Lewes an hour. Henri left immediately, Meg took Jane away to be washed, and Luis went in search of Catherine Mercer. She was where he expected, in her solar. Struggling to remain calm, for he was sure Mercer's wife held the key to Alyce's arrest, Luis knocked impatiently, opened the door before she had answered and filled the room with his menacing presence. Frightened, Catherine Mercer stared at him, her embroidery neglected on her knee. In the past she had believed Gharsia to be of little interest, an entrepreneur on the periphery of her husband's business who demanded little attention, but now she was alarmed. Luis paused to collect himself, and Catherine, unable to cope with the intensity of vehemence in his eyes, returned to her sewing.

His voice, when he spoke, reverberated around her small chamber. "What happened when the sheriff's men came?"

"What do you mean?"

"It is a simple enough question." He clenched his hands. Catherine Mercer raised her light otherworldly eyes and met his stare. She put her embroidery to one side and the tiny dog leapt on to her lap. She proceeded to stroke and to kiss its head. Luis felt his anger rising and fought to keep his voice level; if the dog started to yap, he was afraid he might do something drastic. He changed his approach. "What did they ask?"

She was not as fey as she appeared.

"Questions?"

"Yes, questions," demanded Luis. He would not allow her to divert him.

She replied, somewhat airily, "They asked to see our Bible."

"And?"

"I showed it to them."

His eyes were hard and unforgiving. "Then why was only Alyce taken?"

Catherine Mercer answered, "I don't know." Then she stopped petting her dog and concentrated on what she was saying. "Please leave my house. You are not welcome."

Luis stood for some time without speaking. It was unnerving. She did not know what to do. When he did speak, it was intended to threaten her.

"I understand your husband and son are away. It will be a while before they return?"

She felt cornered. The solar door was open but her interrogator blocked her exit. His height and breadth seemed to fill the small room. She shouted, "Meg, Meg, please come quickly!" To Catherine's relief her niece did appear almost immediately, as she was already upstairs changing Jane.

"Yes, Aunt." Meg rushed through the door and stopped short next to Luis. Her astute mind assessed the situation. She remained where she was.

"Meg," her aunt ordered, "please show Monsieur Gharsia out."

"Why?"

"He is not welcome."

Luis explained, "The sheriff's men asked to see the family's Bible."

"That shouldn't have caused a problem. It's an old Vulgate copy," Meg replied, before comprehension made her voice sharp. "Aunt, is that all you showed them?"

Catherine Mercer did not meet her niece's eyes. Meg exclaimed, "Surely you didn't show them Alyce's Tyndale?" It was unnecessary for the woman to answer. Her demeanour told Meg exactly why Alyce had been arrested.

"What is a Tyndale Bible?"

Meg turned to face Luis. Her voice was strained. "A Bible translated into English by Tyndale. He was burnt as a heretic years ago. Alyce had a copy. Only a heretic would use one now Mary is on the throne."

A towering rage at the woman's stupidity threatened to swamp Luis. Alarmed by his expression, Meg grabbed his arm and tried to pull him from the room. For a moment he resisted and then he allowed himself to be dragged away.

Henri was back earlier than expected, sober and with news. "The vault of the Star Inn," he announced triumphantly. There was a rapid exchange in Occitan before Luis related Henri's discovery to Meg.

"It seems several people have been arrested but most drinkers were talking about a man called Woodman."

"The ironmaster," clarified Meg. "He has been taken?"

"Yes, last month. Gossip says that he was betrayed by his own father and brother. Apparently, he fled when the sheriff's men came to his home but left without his shoes. He cut himself so badly on the cinders, discarded from his ironworks, that he was captured. Henri heard other names. He can only remember one woman – Mary Groves."

"I know of her. And Henri said that they are being held in the cellar of the Star Inn?"

"Yes."

"Do you think Alyce is with them?"

"I don't know but it is somewhere to start."

Throughout the day Catherine Mercer refused to leave the

solar. Meg, suppressing her hostility towards her aunt, paid her a visit but she was waved away. In Catherine's customary vague fashion, she informed her niece that she felt unwell and was going to remain in her solar where she would take all her meals. Meg left without a backward glance and proceeded to gather up some belongings, as Luis had instructed.

Henri left the house again to spend more time exploring the town centre. He cut across the field to the High Street and made his way to the Star Inn, which he thought was situated where the High Street met Market Street. He spent some time reconnoitring, working out which was the fastest way to leave the town. Then he doubled back and went inside the inn.

Meanwhile Luis sought out the servant, Mark Baker, who was tending the garden at the back of the house. He hailed him and asked about Mercer's horses, hoping they would be at the local stables. Luck was on his side. Edward and John Mercer had sailed to London; Baker even asked Luis if he wanted the gelding brought to the house, so he could take the horse out to exercise. Luis thanked Baker but declined, explaining that he would see the ostler himself, when he was ready.

It was late afternoon by the time Henri returned, with useful information. He had acquired a thorough knowledge of the layout of the streets around the Star Inn and after having imbibed several tankards of the landlord's best ale, he had taken the opportunity to relieve himself outside. He was sure he had found the location of the entrance to the cellar but he had been unable to linger too long because he had seen two men, whom he believed to be the sheriff's, and he had not wanted to attract attention.

Meg had packed a bag of clothes for herself. Jane's were still hanging on the line but would soon be dry. She was unsure what to take for Alyce. She went downstairs to find Luis, who was talking earnestly with Henri in the hall.

"Shall I take this for Alyce?" she asked anxiously. Luis turned and saw the neat muslin parcel. He knew it contained a length of exquisite green silk. Meg continued, "I know Alyce treasures it."

Although his face remained unreadable, conflicting feelings jarred. Joy that Alyce had kept it but not used it, disappointment that there would not be a wedding because he was already married and then soaring hope that perhaps anything was possible. If he managed to save Alyce, they would all return to Caors. If Caors was no haven they would continue travelling east until they reached Istanbul. If necessary he would stand in the marketplace of the Aya Sofia and call for his father, Yusuf-al-Balansi. If Alyce lived, there was hope. The decision was made; Meg was waiting for an answer.

"Pack it," he instructed firmly.

There were two final preparations before they settled down to wait. It was imperative that nobody in the household guessed their intentions. In the early hours of the night, when the kitchen was deserted, Luis and Meg methodically set about choosing food which would travel well. When they had finished, Luis reached up to the shelf where the cook stored her knives. In an action so contrary for him, he removed a narrow-bladed one and stuck it in his belt, fastening his jerkin to conceal it. His hands were unsteady but he was determined that images of the past should not jeopardise his future. He steeled himself against any sentiment: Meg, who was holding the candle, saw the strain on his face and prayed silently and fervently that they would be successful.

Their timing had to be perfect. Early enough in the morning for the streets to be deserted, but not so early that the guards would be wary. Luis's plan was to bribe her captors to release Alyce and then they would ride the short distance to the coast, going east, and take a boat directly to Calais or

Boulogne. From there they would either take another boat to Bordèu or, if need be, travel overland to Caors. The sooner they were away from England the better.

After they left the kitchen, Luis told Meg to join Henri and Jane in the hall. Then he entered the small room Edward Mercer used to do his accounts. The candle cast shadows on the dark oak panelling as Luis placed a pouch, containing rubies, on the table. Underneath, he slotted a note; it explained that he would arrange the return of the horses but left no details of their destination. Mercer would have to be happy with that for Luis had already left the saffron under the table earlier in the day. There was no debt to be paid. Then with everything organised, Luis pulled the door shut quietly and returned to the hall to wait.

TWO

⸻

They were ready. It was time to go. The palest of dawns washed the sky although the sun had not yet risen. Luis drew back the bolt on the door to the garden and Meg slipped out, closely followed by Henri carrying a sleepy Jane. As he pushed the door shut Luis jumped at the strident call of a pheasant alerting his mate to danger and paused momentarily to still his racing heart. Meg and Henri were already some distance away, their footsteps leaving a trail across the dew-soaked grass of the orchard. One of the horses whinnied from the far corner of Mercer's property, where their mounts had been tethered overnight, out of view of the house. Luis increased his pace to catch them up, every muscle taut with anticipation.

As planned, High Street and Market Street were deserted at such an early hour. They were in luck but speed was essential. While the others waited, Luis made his way cautiously into the side alley of the inn. He stopped halfway along, pressing his back against the uneven wall, his hand nervously fingering the knife hidden under his jerkin. He had a partial view of the yard and the back entrance. In front of the latter one of the sheriff's men appeared asleep, his head lolling on his chest, his duties obviously forgotten. The other guard, Henri had seen earlier, was nowhere in sight and was probably inside.

Luis watched the man for a full two minutes before he crept across the yard, his soft leather soles making no sound on the beaten earth. The guard remained asleep. Unwilling to attack a defenceless man, Luis shook the sentry awake, smelt the reek of beer on his breath as he struggled to rise, and then felled him with a well-aimed blow. The thud as the man crumbled down seemed to echo around the enclosed yard but no-one came. Luis knelt and placed his hand across his victim's mouth to stop him calling out but the man was unconscious, so Luis hastily dragged him away from the back entrance. In his new position, propped up against the wall, his victim appeared slumped in a drunken stupor.

Satisfied, Luis slid inside. The door creaked alarmingly. A man, guarding the trapdoor to the cellar, was clearly illuminated by a lantern. He swung round and called out when he saw Luis. Scanning the area beyond the light to check if anyone else lurked in the shadows, among the beer barrels, Luis threw a handful of gold coins in the guard's direction. Mesmerised, the man watched the coins dance in the air, burnished by the lantern's beam, before they fell clinking at his feet: more gold than a sheriff's man could expect to see in his lifetime. The cold steel pricked between his ribs before his eyes had finished feasting on the Venetian ducats. A strong man himself, he could see that his assailant possessed a height and breadth he could not match. He waited, spellbound by the fortune before him.

"Open the trapdoor," Luis commanded, "and call for Alyce Blake." Feeling the guard stiffen, he applied more pressure on the knife and added, "The gold is yours if she comes with me." He allowed his captive to lean over and pull the rusted ring of the handle. The stench, a mix of excrement, urine, and unwashed bodies, drifted up from the cellar and mingled with the sweet smell of beer. Luis, feeling nauseous, clamped his lips together and swallowed. The guard shouted Alyce's name. Luis's chest constricted; he was holding his breath. The seconds seemed interminable, an agony of waiting, until Alyce climbed unsteadily up the stone staircase, each step preceded by her hand clutching the frayed rope fastened along the wall. He exhaled. She was looking towards the lantern, her eyes glassy but unfocused in its light. She did not see him. Her beloved face was pale and too thin, the skin drawn tightly across her protruding bones.

The sheriff's man reached down to help her, pulling her away from the entrance. The trapdoor fell back with a shuddering thump. Alyce stood motionless, staring at the ground. Luis willed her to notice him. She raised her eyes from the gold coins and glanced at the guard. Bewildered by the man's obvious fear her eyes travelled higher. For a moment Luis believed she did not know him and then recognition lit up her face. He found he could not think what to say. He indicated for her to stand further to one side and recovered enough composure to address the guard. "Pick them up," he ordered, pointing to the coins. The man stooped down and greedily gathered the ducats together. Luis raised his arm. Alyce flinched as Luis struck the back of the man's head and he crumpled to the ground. Quickly Luis thrust the knife under his jerkin, grabbed Alyce's hand and dragged her out into the fresh morning air.

He felt her stumble. He gathered her up, placed his arm around her for support and steered her forward. Anxiety made him tremble: he had no idea how long it would be before the guards came to and raised the alarm. The gold was intended to silence them forever but perhaps they were honest men? Early risers would soon be about. The baker would already have risen to stoke his ovens and hopefully would be too busy to glance out into the marketplace. He gripped Alyce tighter than he intended, her prominent ribs pressing against him, and forced her to move faster. He sensed her studying him but he kept his eyes firmly ahead. The others came into view, waiting for them. Meg's face, always so expressive, was alight with joy. She had seen them. Henri was preoccupied keeping Jane entertained and quiet. Luis felt a flash of exasperation; Henri should be keeping a lookout instead of talking to the child. Meg could have attended to the girl.

Alyce moved, a slight shifting of position as she leaned away from him and looked up. When they were almost across the road she staggered. He tightened his grip and, without taking his eyes off Henri, said, "To Caors," as he nudged her forward the final few steps.

There was no time for greetings. Meg was already mounted when Luis and Alyce reached the waiting group, as was Henri, with Jane seated safely between his arms. As soon as Luis was astride Mercer's gelding, with Alyce behind him, Henri tossed him the reins and urged his own horse up Market Street, riding north at a steady pace to avoid suspicion. Meg followed on the palfrey, keeping her distance but never losing sight of Henri and her niece. Luis swung the gelding round and rode east towards the river, fighting the instinct to canter. He heard Alyce utter a sound like a gasp, and explained over his shoulder, "We will meet up once we are well away from the town."

Luis could not see Alyce easily, but he felt her arms tighten around his waist as she took deep breaths, trying to expel the fetid air of the cellar from her nostrils. It was useless. The stench seemed to permeate her clothes; a layer of dirt and debris clung to the hem of her dress and her cheek pressed against Luis's back left a greasy, grimy mark on his jerkin. Receiving no response, Luis reassured her. "You will see Jane shortly, Alyce. The others will turn east once they reach open fields."

The mumbled reply was almost inaudible. The words refused to be formed clearly from a mouth deprived of water. He strained to hear: Alyce appeared to be trying to say the same sentence repeatedly, "You came for me. You came for me. You came for me," as if testing its veracity.

They met, as arranged, where the road divided, south to the nearest coast and east towards Hastings. Luis had chosen to take the less obvious route to the sea in the hope of confusing the sheriff's men but when he helped Alyce dismount, and she stood unsteadily, it was apparent that an adjustment to the plan was required. Meg, her customary exuberance tempered by the precariousness of their circumstances, led her sister to the grassy bank and gave her some water. Alyce's hands shook uncontrollably as she took the skin.

"Don't drink it all at once," Luis commanded, his voice loud among the birdsong of early morning. "Take small sips," he advised more softly, before he turned to Henri. Jane had remained at the latter's side, studying Alyce uncertainly.

Henri crouched down and suggested, "Go and sit with your mother," before he added in Occitan, "she did not leave you of her own accord."

"Come, my child," Alyce whispered through moistened lips. The little girl remained where she was. Aware of how she looked, Alyce tried to smile, her eyes full of love. "Stay where you are if you wish. It is enough for me to see you." Jane continued to stare at her mother and inched closer to Henri. He began talking earnestly with Luis about what to do. They spoke in Occitan, much to Meg's annoyance.

Luis was adamant. "Alyce is too weak to make the journey

in one day. We can only cover about five leagues at the most today, and Hastings is twice that distance."

"But the horses are fresh and in fine condition," argued Henri. "Perhaps we should go further today and have an easier day tomorrow?" He wanted to cross to France as soon as possible. Unease had taken hold of him since he and Luis had arrived in Lewes: they could be marooned now that England had declared war on her neighbour. "Surely, we should see how far Alyce, and Jane, can travel before we make a decision," he said reasonably.

Luis considered this. "I agree but we must allow for the fact that our journey will take longer. Even if we reach Hastings in good time there is no guarantee we will find a boat to take us to Dover and, once there, it might be several days before we secure a passage to Calais."

"I realise that," retorted Henri. He did not need Luis to point out the obvious.

"What are you two talking about?" Meg demanded. They both glanced over to where she was sitting at the roadside with Alyce, who was nibbling at a chunk of bread. Jane, attracted by food, had joined them at last.

By way of an answer Luis said, "We had better eat as well and be on our way." The sun was climbing in the sky and already people could be seen tending their crops.

They rode in silence, too tense to talk, as they traversed the rolling hills heading south-east. It was a morning of sunlight and shadows. High clouds scudded across a summer-blue sky, lowering the temperature noticeably when they obscured the sun. At regular intervals the travellers stopped briefly to rest and take a little food before pushing on. As the afternoon turned to evening the breeze blowing in from the sea strengthened; the clouds became more numerous, bubbling up until the flashes of sunshine lessened and then finally petered out. Under a blanket of cloud, pewter with the threat of rain, they came to a decision. It was sensible to seek shelter in Pevensey rather than sleep outdoors as planned. They would attract too much attention the next day if they appeared sodden and bedraggled when they reached Hastings.

The inn was a long, low building which Meg claimed must have been old when the Normans landed. The food was adequate and the accommodation limited, with no private chambers, so Alyce, Meg, and Jane shared one bed in the only dormitory while the men shared another. The innkeeper's wife had hung a curtain across one end of the room which could be drawn for the rare occasions she had female patrons without a husband. After she had washed and changed her clothes, Alyce lay in the enveloping darkness unable to sleep. She listened for Luis's breathing, sure that she could distinguish it from the other sounds of men settling down for the night, and then chided herself for her foolishness. Warm between Meg and Jane, she rested a hand on each of them and dared to hope that she might be safe.

They were up as the cock crowed, saddled and ready to depart before the other guests had thought about rising. Determined to reach Hastings by noon, Luis had purchased fresh bread and dried fish when he had paid for their beds the previous evening, and if luck was on their side they could set sail on the afternoon tide. It had rained all night and although the rain was clearing to a fine drizzle it still promised to be a cool, damp day, characteristic of coastal summer weather. Following the coast east, Henri looked at the waves with no appetite for a journey in a small vessel. The sky and the sea, both the colour of lead, merged together so that it was difficult to distinguish the horizon and his fears were not allayed when they arrived at Hastings and he saw the size of the fishing boats pulled up on the beach.

There were a few men sitting, mending nets, but most of the moorings were empty. Luis approached the nearest man, a weathered sailor, white-haired and well past his prime. The others watched anxiously: the conversation seemed to last too long. Eventually Luis turned back, walking quickly over the shingle, his manner positive.

"The fisherman will take us all the way to Calais," he announced triumphantly when he reached the group.

"In that?" Henri questioned in disbelief.

"Yes," replied Luis. "It is quite safe. The vessel is built for much more challenging seas than this sleeve of water. It is used to the stormy waters of the North Sea."

Henri looked doubtful. Luis continued, "We will hug the coast until Dover and then cross to Calais."

Meg and Alyce were also studying the boat dubiously. Luis was impatient. "It is a good opportunity. I had thought we would only reach Dover and then have to find another boat."

Nobody spoke. Luis met Henri's eyes and added dismissively, "It will not be as bad as the voyage we usually make to Bordèu."

Meg was about to retort pertly that Luis could not be certain about the outcome when Alyce spoke, her voice wobbling slightly as she realised the enormity of what they were about to do. "What will happen when we reach Calais?" Luis's face was so difficult to read. She wished she could speak to him without the others listening, but they were never alone.

Luis, conscious of Henri watching his every move, replied matter-of-factly, "We will make our way to Caors, either by ship or overland. Once in Caors you'll be guests of Ysabel

Bernade." Alyce glanced at Meg, who gave her an encouraging smile, and then back at Luis, hoping for some indication that he was enthusiastic about taking them. She was disappointed. Instead he said, rather shortly, "We don't have time to discuss it. That fishing boat is our best chance. We go now. Who knows how far the sheriff's men will extend their search for you?"

Henri still appeared unconvinced. Luis continued aggressively, "It is over two weeks since England declared war on France. Both sides will have ships patrolling the water. A fishing boat is safer than a merchantman, which could be attacked for plunder. Henri, take everyone and get them settled on board. I'm going to the stables to arrange for Mercer's horses to be returned. I will be back by the time you are ready to sail."

Luis strode towards the nearest buildings. Henri turned towards the sea where the fisherman, his thick white hair teased about his head by the wind, was waving vigorously. Despite his keenness to leave England, Henri's heart was heavy as he lifted Jane up and led Alyce and Meg across the beach to the boat.

Henri retched violently, voiding his stomach of the vestiges of his last meal. He waited, leaning weakly against the weathered timbers, for the next heave which would fill his mouth with bile. It was their second day on the seas and Henri felt as if the nightmare would never end. True to his word, Tom Flint, aided by his nephew, had sailed to Dover, where his passengers had stayed on board while he bought provisions and assessed the changing situation. They had made a brief stop at Rye, where the mariner had discovered that boats had been commandeered by the Crown to help patrol and defend the Channel. Galvanised by this information the fishermen agreed that it was imperative to cross to Calais immediately before the conflict escalated.

The boat yawed. Henri kept his eyes tightly shut, unable to look at the swell, and gripped the side with white knuckles. He felt a hand touch his back gently, just below his shoulder blades. Embarrassed, he did not want to turn around for, of all the passengers, he was the most affected by the boat's motion. A melodious voice commented, "There is nothing worse than seasickness." He wiped his mouth and moved gingerly. He stared at her, lost for words, and studied her face. The haunted pallor of the prisoner had almost gone, her cheeks were ruddy from the wind and spray, and her eyes, a translucent green, were full of sympathy. Henri experienced the unfamiliar emotion of admiration. He did not find her physically attractive as a woman, for she was too tall and slender for his taste, but he began to see her character. Here was a woman who had recently faced the terror of the fires, caring about him being sick.

It made him uncomfortable to be drawn to her, for the idea of the Englishwoman had tormented his sister for so long. Now Henri realised that Marie had cause to worry. Despite Alyce's marriage to her cousin it was clear that she possessed strong feelings for Luis. Her face betrayed her every time she looked at him. Alyce continued speaking, her rich Somerset tones soothing. "I find it helps to sit in the centre of the boat. It is something my father told me. Although he was a merchant who often sailed, he was always seasick." She passed him some water to rinse his mouth. "In fact, he made this journey several times. On one occasion, when he was a young man, he took advantage of the truce after the Field of the Cloth of Gold to trade in Picardy. He met my mother there."

Henri found his voice. "Your mother was French?"

Alyce nodded.

"That is why your brother's French was so good." Rufus had spoken the language like a native, but Henri had never thought to ask him why. Alyce's face clouded at the mention of her brother. "Sorry," said Henri.

"No, we must not forget him. I made myself believe that he courted a martyr's death, but after what happened to me, I am not so sure."

Henri appeared so ill at ease that Alyce continued almost cheerily, "Rufus had very happy memories of visiting your vineyard. He told us all about it, about meeting your parents and your sister." She did not achieve the result she wanted. Instead of relaxing, Henri became more edgy. A shifty expression marred his handsome features as he mumbled his response and turned away from her. Perplexed, she left him where she had found him, hanging over the side of the boat.

THREE

Calais

L ORD WENTWORTH, DEPUTY OF CALAIS, STUDIED the motley group before him. There were seven of them; four men, two women, and a child who appeared to be simple. Initially annoyed at being disturbed, Wentworth was now intrigued as to the purpose of their visit to Calais. He was most interested in the men. All able-bodied, the younger two seemed to be in their early thirties, while the others, obviously sailors with their weather-beaten faces, looked older and could be father and son.

"What brings you to Calais?" Wentworth addressed them all, but the taller of the younger men answered, in good but heavily accented English. "We are merchants from the Pays d'Oc on our way home. We thought it wise to sail to an English port now that hostilities have broken out between England and France."

Wentworth considered this explanation. "You don't normally trade through Calais?"

"No, we usually sail to Bordèu but we felt it safer to spend as little time as possible at sea."

The Deputy's eyes flicked to the rest of the group and then addressed its spokesman again. In an unhurried fashion, as if he was mulling his own question over and did not require an answer, he asked, "Why is a Spanish moor trading from the Pays d'Oc?" before adding, "Are you sure you are not a soldier?" He was suspicious of the man's disfigured face, where an ugly scar ran from eye to mouth while the opposite cheek was marred by a second smaller scar, and his muscular build. The man was much taller than average, with broad shoulders and calloused hands. "I think you are more than a merchant."

"We are vintners."

Wentworth studied the two younger men more closely. Their appearance chimed with this claim. They both had hands used to manual labour and athletic figures, while the smaller man's face was deeply bronzed, like a peasant's.

"What are your names?"

"Luis Gharsia."

"Henri Gaulbert."

"And you?" Wentworth addressed the older sailor. "You are no merchant."

"Tom Flint, my lord, and this is my nephew, Wat." The fisherman shifted from one foot to the other. "We would welcome a night or two in Calais before sailing home."

"Home?"

"Hastings, my lord."

"You were hired to bring these people over to Calais?"

"Yes, my lord."

Wentworth looked across the room to John Highfield, Master of Ordnance at Calais, who had brought the group to him. "I think we can accommodate you." The Deputy dismissed Flint with a jerk of his hand. As the fishermen walked towards the door, following Highfield, Wentworth was startled by one of the women speaking.

She was very young, no more than sixteen, with a wide engaging smile. "Thank you, Mister Flint, for bringing us safely to Calais." The old fisherman mumbled something under his breath and was gone.

"And you are?"

The girl showed no sign of being overawed by Wentworth. "My name is Margaret Weaver, and this is my sister, Alyce, and her daughter, Jane. We are the daughters of the late Thomas Weaver of Bridgwater."

Amused by the pride in her voice, Wentworth replied, "Never heard of him." He saw the older woman place a restraining hand on her sister's arm but was uncertain of its significance. On her part, Meg knew exactly what she was doing, and believed that an aristocrat like Lord Thomas Wentworth would genuinely have no knowledge of a Somerset mercantile family and their tribulations. Her stance changed. The Deputy watched as her eyes became moist. She held his gaze. "Lord Wentworth," she said in a quiet voice. He waited for her next words. Meg paused for effect. She lowered her eyes. "Lord Wentworth, my family has suffered a tragic blow," she almost whispered, before she raised them. Tears glistened but did not fall.

"A tragic blow?"

Meg appeared to struggle to compose herself. Then she spoke quickly, as if the words would cause her harm if she lingered. "My father and brother died within weeks of each other and then we discovered my father's business was ruined." Meg gulped prettily and a solitary tear escaped. "We were ruined."

Luis stepped forward and offered her his handkerchief. She glanced up at him, her expression one of deep gratitude. It was a fine performance. She took her time before she turned back to Wentworth. "Luis, who is an old friend of my father, is taking us to the Pays d'Oc. We are to live with his patron as companions." Meg managed to sound both thankful and pathetic. Luis prayed she would not overplay her hand. So far, she had been speaking the truth, but any more embellishment would be perilous. The reality was too dangerous to disclose. Her father had died of natural causes, but Luis feared how Wentworth would react if he knew the Weaver fortune had been confiscated by the Crown as a result of Rufus being burnt as a heretic.

The Deputy of Calais was a worried and tired man. He stroked his beard and ran his hand over his forehead where his hair was receding faster than he wanted. The outbreak of war at the beginning of the month was a disaster for the last remaining English possession on French soil. Its fortifications were in a state of disrepair and, as the territory lacked any natural defences, the port and surrounding area were very vulnerable. Despite his efforts to warn the Queen about the situation he had received no help. He had two thousand troops. They were on standby but were discontented due to lack of pay and were too few to fight off an attack by the French army. He sighed. His instinct told him that the girl was speaking the truth, but he needed to be thorough.

He surveyed the group of very different people again, one by one. It was unlikely they were working for the enemy. The Spanish were now England's allies, so he dismissed Gharsia. Gaulbert appeared to be what he claimed, a farmer, and although nominally under French sovereignty, the Pays d'Oc was historically so independent that it was an unlikely area from which to recruit a spy. The older woman, who had remained silent, was frail, perhaps hollow-eyed with grief, and was concentrating on her daughter. He studied the latter, almost convinced, for who would encumber themselves with such a child if they were gathering information for the French. But he must not fail in his duty.

"What trade was your father in?"

"My father had many ventures but most of his wealth came from exporting finished cloth."

Wentworth was satisfied with the answer as Calais had suffered long-term decline in her markets, too. He was about to ask more when the girl swayed. Henri Gaulbert acted swiftly and caught her as she elegantly crumpled towards the ground.

Meg's ruse worked. After she had been given some restorative brandy, Wentworth, who had more pressing matters to deal with, had ordered an aide to find refreshment for the travellers, with the strict instruction that Luis was to return once he had eaten.

They were led across the Place d'Armes to an old hostel next to the church. It was one of many, Calais being able to boast of providing more than two thousand beds, and although the inn was not full, there was evidence of other guests. Despite the recent outbreak of hostilities, five merchants were talking animatedly at the table by the fire and the remnants of dinner scattered several of the other tables. Luis lowered Meg onto the nearest bench. Queasy from the brandy she had been forced to drink, the girl had willingly accepted Luis's offer to carry her. Alyce and Jane joined them while Henri went in search of food.

Nobody took notice of them as they sipped the thin potage in silence, enjoying its salty warmth after days of cold food. Luis scanned the room continuously, conscious that Alyce's hand shook, clattering her spoon against the side of the bowl. The merchants remained disinterested and his eyes rested on Henri, who was regarding him closely. Luis suppressed the urge to take Alyce's hand. She looked exhausted; pallor had once more replaced the healthier glow from the sea-spray.

"You must rest," he said. "All of you." He turned to Henri. "Can you organise some beds for us? The innkeeper's wife saw us arrive with the Deputy's man so there should be no problem. However, it might be wise to speak as little as possible as there may be some who cannot recognise the difference between a Pays d'Oc accent and the enemy's."

"Where are you going?" Alyce asked, unwilling to be separated from him.

"I need to report back to Wentworth now. We must leave here as soon as possible. I think he believes us, otherwise we would not have been allowed to come into the town."

Luis found it was much harder to speak to the Deputy without an escort and dusk was falling by the time he was ushered into Wentworth's office. He was not alone. John Highfield was at his master's side, both men poring over papers spread out on the large oak desk. For a moment they ignored Luis, before Wentworth lifted his head and coolly appraised his visitor.

"If I am to believe what you say, Gharsia, and I am inclined to, how do you plan to reach your home?"

Luis considered. Realising it was ill-advised to point out that once away from Calais, Henri and he could try and pass for Frenchmen, he limited his answer to an inquiry. "Is there anyone who will sell me some horses?"

Highfield snorted in derision. "Have you any idea of the situation we are in? Calais and her Pale are surrounded by enemy territory. We can no longer look to Boulogne for help. This is the last possession in France, ours since 1347, yet our defences are woefully inadequate, our requests for reinforcements are ignored, and you ask for horses!"

Lord Thomas Wentworth raised his hand to silence

Highfield, but the Master of Ordnance responded with exasperation. "I am not saying anything Gharsia can't see for himself."

Luis watched as the two men eyed each other. There was a long pause before the Deputy repeated his question. "How do you plan to reach the Pays d'Oc?"

"I think we should travel by road as little as possible now. One of the women and the child are not strong."

The recollection of the little girl prompted Wentworth to make his decision. "I am going to let you continue your journey. I believe what you have told me." He did not add that five extra mouths to feed would be an unnecessary burden at such a critical time. "However, there are no horses for sale here. You can stay in Calais tonight but my advice to you is to travel south as fast as you can. If we are fortunate our new friends, the Spanish, will come to our aid but the French won't make it easy. If we are not so lucky we will be besieged. As you know there are already enemy ships patrolling the Channel. Either way, Calais is no place for English gentlewomen."

Luis thought quickly. They needed to travel by boat, despite the threat at sea. Without horses an overland route was impossible. Alyce and Jane would never make it. His mind raced and he was clutching at straws as he addressed Wentworth. "Would it be possible for me to speak to Tom Flint, my lord?"

The fishing boat hugged the Normandy coast: the shoreline indistinct in the darkness. Dense cloud obscured the moon, which appeared fleetingly and gave tantalising glimpses of the cliffs, while the swell of the water beneath them changed as it became shallower. When the cloud parted briefly, illuminating a sliver of sand, Tom Flint shouted with relief, but his words were lost on the wind. Luis and Henri strained their eyes as the fishermen, gesticulating vigorously, skilfully steered the boat into a sheltered bay. Luis studied the different shapes appearing in the gloom. He could just make out a jumble of what looked like huts and a couple of fishing boats creaking on their moorings.

"Quickly," ordered Tom Flint.

Standing next to Luis, Henri caught sight of a dilapidated ladder on the side of the jetty. "We have to climb that?"

"Quickly," repeated Flint. "I don't want to waste time." Wat reached for the travellers' bags.

Luis was faster. "I'll take those." He slung two of the satchels across his body, so that they rested on either hip, and reached for the ladder. "If it takes my weight we will be fine." The boat rocked disturbingly, the bags banged against his legs, and he shuddered at the black water beneath him. The sound of it lapping around the ladder followed him as he climbed tentatively, one careful step after another. When he reached the top, Flint threw him a rope, which he tied securely. Wat shinned up behind him like a monkey and checked Luis's knot with a swagger.

When they were all on the jetty, the old fisherman said, in hushed tones, "Go swiftly now. You are only a few leagues from Le Havre. We will stay here."

"Will it be safe, Mister Flint?" Meg asked, concerned.

Tom Flint fingered his beard. "I have been on this coast before; many years ago, with my brother." He nodded in the direction of the hamlet. "They will be good folk. Fishermen like us. I will tell them we were blown off course." He paused and then said earnestly, "However it is different for you. You must go now."

Luis reached under his jerkin for his money pouch and

dropped the promised gold into Flint's hand. Unable to see the Venetian ducats in mint condition, the fisherman bit each coin before pocketing them. "Let's hope this is worth it," he stated, with a rueful grin.

"Be gone!" ordered Wat. "We will wait with the boat until you are well away."

They scrambled up the cliff path: the chalky rubble shifting beneath their feet. Henri, his balance altered by Jane on his back, slipped the most and each time Alyce's heart lurched as her daughter whimpered. She whispered reassurances over her shoulder and forced herself to concentrate on Meg's determined figure in front of her. The gap between them was widening and every muscle in Alyce's body screamed as she tried to catch up. At last, she reached the top. The wind whipped around her head and tugged at her clothes, so she flopped down on the springy turf and waited for her heart to slow, as Henri clambered up the final stretch. He joined Luis and they studied the sky together, searching for stars to find their bearings. It was hopeless. The cloud cover was too thick. They would have to rely on Flint's instructions to walk with the buffeting wind on their backs.

After stopping to rest in the shelter of a copse, they reached the outskirts of Le Havre just as a summer dawn bathed the fields in soft light. Crouching in a ditch, checking for signs of life, Luis whispered to Alyce, "It is important that Jane doesn't speak. We should be able to pass for French but the sound of English being spoken will raise the alarm."

Alyce's reply was poignant. "I will try and keep her quiet. Her speech is never clear. It is her tongue, you see."

Luis addressed Henri. "Do you think you can continue to carry Jane?" Henri nodded; the child had developed affection for him whereas she was very wary of Luis. The latter continued, keeping his voice low, "When we reach the lower town, you walk with Alyce. We will attract less attention if you appear to be a family." He saw the panic in Alyce's eyes and added, "I will keep you in sight and follow with Meg."

They walked along the ditch, dry at that time of year, until they came across another field boundary and more cottages. People were stirring but nobody challenged them and soon they were rewarded by the sight of the harbour below.

It was a hive of activity. The sounds of construction filled the air; the sawing of wood, the hammering of nails, and the shouts of workmen, while the wharf was crowded with the business of loading and unloading of ships. The low sun caught the ripples in the estuary as a fleet of fishing boats rocked on their moorings.

"Busy place," commented Henri.

"Will we be able to find a passage easily?" asked Meg.

Luis turned to her. "We should be able to. There is bound to be a merchantman sailing to Bordèu. Remember, though, speak only French from now on."

FOUR

_____

Le Havre, July 1557

T HEY HAD BEEN IN LE HAVRE FOR FIVE DAYS AND on the following day they were due to sail to Bordèu. Meg, chafing at their confined accommodation, had persuaded Henri that Jane would benefit from some fresh air, as there seemed little danger on the bustling streets of the port. The group had already managed to melt into the throng of merchants, traders, sailors, and locals who filled the growing town and Luis had deemed it safe enough to acquire a private chamber for the women while Henri and he slept in the communal area.

Luis and Alyce were alone at last. There was so much to say but, now that they could speak freely, Alyce found it difficult to know where to begin. She stood at the small window of the private chamber, studying the Chapel of Notre Dame opposite. It was low, like all the buildings of the port, due to the instability of the drained marshland, but it possessed the added interest of an octagonal tower. Also, like the other buildings Alyce had noticed, it was recently built.

"Why are all the buildings new?"

Luis was leaning against the chest, the only furniture in the cramped room other than the bed, which was hardly adequate for two women and a child.

"Le Havre is a relatively new port; built because Harfleur, further up the estuary, has silted up."

"Cannot it be dredged?" Alyce asked, remembering her home town of Bridgwater where it was a continuous battle to clear the silt.

"They tried but it was easier to construct a completely new harbour."

Alyce continued staring out of the window. She observed a couple of crows circling the tower, preparing to scavenge and, without turning around, stated, "Henri is always watching us."

Luis did not respond.

"Why is that so?"

There was an uneasy silence. He tried to speak but found the words would not come. Alyce turned to face him and he could not look at her. In that moment, he hated himself.

"Luis?"

"He is watching me."

"Why?"

"Because he is my wife's brother."

It was as if the air had been sucked from the room. Alyce stared at him in disbelief. "You are married?"

"Yes."

"Does your wife know you have come for me?"

"It does not matter." His voice was bleak.

"Why does it not matter?"

"It is of no importance."

Alyce regarded Luis, the complex man she had held in her heart for so long. His face was a mask. "How can having a wife be of no importance?" she demanded.

Luis felt a surge of guilt, quickly followed by a flash of anger. He was the injured one. It was Alyce who had walked away from him and married the priest.

Alyce, her emotions still raw when she thought about her husband's abandonment, demanded again, "How can having a wife be of no importance to you, Luis?"

The acrimonious tone of her voice was disconcerting. Too ashamed of his gullibility, Luis found himself reluctant to tell her about Marie's duplicity.

"Shall I tell you about being a wife?" she continued in the same harsh tone. "For me, being a wife meant I was nothing. I was of no account. In one day I went from someone who had a husband and a home, to one who had neither. What had I done to deserve this? Nothing! What actions had I taken that led to my husband abandoning me? None! The evening Matthew Blake told me of the injunctions about married clergy was like many others, except that he simply announced that I was no longer a wife."

Alyce looked at Luis, her eyes cold. "Do you know what happened to me when I remonstrated with that worm?" Luis remained motionless. "Do you?" He shook his head. "He hit me across the face because he said I was being hysterical!" Alyce's indignation was brutal. "He said that I was being hysterical!"

Luis, realising he was holding himself stiffly, inhaled and exhaled slowly.

"Do you know what he did next?"

He took a step towards her. She moved to stop him. "He threw me in the woodshed!"

He took another step towards her. "Alyce, my love."

"No, you must hear it all," she ordered fiercely.

He gave her time to collect herself and then she continued, weary resignation replacing her fury. "I was locked in the shed all night. In the morning, the maid let me out. I challenged

Matthew when he returned from the cathedral. I said I would go, and his soul would be saved, but I wanted my dowry returned. He claimed it had not been paid according to the agreement. He gave me what little money he had and I left, taking Jane with me."

"But you found a home – Meg said you were happy with the farmer and his wife. She told me of your letters."

The sympathy in Luis's eyes reignited her fury. "Happy!" she sneered. "I had no choice. I went to Bridgwater to find Rufus. No-one knew where he was. The Hammonds let me stay for a few days, but the taint of Protestantism was too much for them. Like many, they have changed their allegiance since Mary came to the throne. The lawyer, Taylor, refused to release any of my father's money without my brother's consent. All belonged to him now. I was destitute. I had no choice but to go to the Smyths."

"I have not abandoned my wife, Alyce," Luis said, flatly. "Our marriage was based on deception. She is on the Gaulbert farm. Marie has a home and is well provided for."

Alyce wanted to learn more, but once again his expression was unfathomable. She paused to gather her thoughts. Whatever the future held for them, he needed to know what she had experienced since they were last together. "Luis, I must tell you about living with the Smyths." She had forgotten how intense his gaze could be, but she refused to be intimidated. "Gilbert Smyth and his wife, Margery, were kind in their way. She was virtually an invalid and I spent most of my time reading to her. We were welcomed as guests and Jane flourished there. My duties were not onerous."

The light flooded through the window behind her and lit up Alyce's coppery hair. She stopped speaking, feeling the revulsion rise within her. She gulped. "When I say my duties were not onerous, I tell a lie." She faltered and dropped her eyes, speaking so quietly that he had to strain to hear her. "I had to share Gilbert's bed."

She raised her eyes. He showed no emotion, but the rigidity of his stance betrayed him. It gave her the courage to reach out to him and take his hand. "Luis, my beloved Luis," she whispered. "Help me from feeling so defiled."

They had all retired early but it was evident from the noise drifting up from the street that many people were still out and about. However, the excitement about the coming day, combined with the heat trapped in the little room under the eaves, made it almost impossible to settle. Only Jane had managed it. Next to her, Alyce lay as still as she could while Meg tossed and turned, sighing loudly each time she moved.

"Stop it, Meg."

"I can't get to sleep."

"Try and lie quietly."

In answer, Meg rolled onto her side so she could face Alyce. "I am so excited about our journey tomorrow. Surely you are, too?"

"I like just the five of us, together."

"But it will be wonderful to reach Caors. Luis said that Madame Bernade will be very pleased to welcome us and we'll meet his grandfather."

Alyce was silent.

"Alyce?"

"Luis is married."

Meg pulled herself upright like a shot, threatening to wake Jane. "He can't be!"

"He is."

"To whom?"

"Henri's sister, Marie."

Meg's mind raced. "Was he married when he and I went to London to try and save Rufus?"

"Yes."

"I wonder why he never told me. It's strange, isn't it?"

Alyce, reluctant to tell Meg of the confidences she had shared with Luis that afternoon, just replied, "Yes."

Sensitive to her sister's tone, Meg asked, "Are you very upset?"

"No, why should I be?" she lied.

"Did you not hope you would be married," Meg replied bluntly, before continuing, "as Luis had always wanted?"

"I have had no hopes for so long, Meg. And now, everything has happened so quickly. Less than two weeks ago, I was expecting to die an excruciating death. I cannot suddenly think of playing the joyful wife!"

Meg slid back down the bed. "I can see that."

"Anyway, I am married, too."

"But Matthew put you aside. The royal injunctions demanded it of him."

"Or lose his living," Alyce reminded her. There was a long pause before she started speaking again. "Meg, I have struggled for some time to make sense of it all. I used to be so sure of what I believed. When Father was alive, his influence was so strong. His reformist views were convincing: we discussed the Bible for hours and I truly felt that I did no wrong in marrying Matthew. Surely if the Archbishop of Canterbury searched his conscience and took a wife, I was doing no wrong?" Alyce shifted position and lay on her back. "I was married in church by a priest. How can I be abandoned by the power of a royal injunction? I was not married by a royal injunction."

"That is true. Parliament passed the act that allowed clergy to marry but what has taken place is what we feared would happen when Edward died and was succeeded by Mary. We were certain she would try to bring back the old religious ways, and she has. She is all-powerful. It is the monarch who decides."

"She is not all-powerful," countered Alyce. "Parliament refused to pass the law to restore the monastic lands to their former owners."

"Yes, but I think that was the action of greedy men and not the influence of any religious beliefs. After all, there are many members who are Catholic."

"I think Parliament passed the Treason Act in exchange for the monastic lands being left as they are."

"Do you really believe that?" asked Meg.

"Yes, I do. And now Rufus is dead because of it."

Thoughts of her brother's death triggered Meg's memory. "When Luis and I visited Rufus in gaol, he accused Luis of not being a Roman Catholic. He said he was a follower of Islam."

Alyce turned her head towards her sister, although it was now completely dark in the room. "It is of no account to me," she said, recalling the blissful security of being encircled in his arms as they had lain together that afternoon. "He is Luis. That is enough."

Luis woke with a start. Amid the snores and grunts of his neighbours, he could hear the creak of someone quietly creeping across the floorboards towards him. He lay still, feigning sleep, and waited. The footsteps stopped. Ribbons of light, seeping through the shutters, heralded the breaking dawn but nobody had yet stirred. He sat up slowly, careful not to wake Henri, who was occupying more than his fair share of the mattress.

"Alyce?" he whispered.

She moved towards him slowly, wary of bumping into a sleeping figure. He heard the panic in her voice.

"Please come."

"What is it?"

"Jane and Meg."

Pulling on his shirt, he followed her through the array of mattresses. Henri, alert to Luis's movements, caught up with them as they reached the door of the private chamber.

"Luis?" he queried.

"Go back!" ordered Luis. "Don't leave our bags."

Henri grimaced and lifted up the two satchels he was holding with a touch of triumph. "As if I would?"

Ignoring them, Alyce pushed open the door. The room was bathed in early morning light, the shutters already fastened back. Meg and Jane lay under a sweat-soaked sheet, the child breathing with difficulty. With two steps Luis was beside the bed. He pulled back the cover and watched Jane's narrow, little chest rise and fall with startling speed. Next to her, by comparison, Meg was more settled, but her eyes shone feverishly in her flushed face.

"I am so thirsty."

Henri dropped the satchels just inside the door and made to leave immediately. Alyce, trying hard to remain calm, suggested, "I'll go and fetch some water. Henri, please can you go to the apothecary? Wake him, if need be. We want chamomile to help Jane breathe and ask him what else he advises."

Luis studied Alyce. For once, his expression reflected his thoughts.

"I am fine," she reassured him.

"You should not stay close to them. You are weak and vulnerable."

"You cannot ask me that. I will not abandon my daughter and my sister."

"I am not asking you to abandon them; just to keep your distance."

She scorned his advice. "I will go and get the water and come back and sit with them."

Luis acquiesced as there was no point arguing. "Bring enough so we can sponge them down as well."

Alyce glanced at the bed, momentarily reluctant to leave, and uttered sadly, "It is in God's hands."

As soon as she had gone, Luis placed his hand on Meg's forehead and then on Jane's. The fever was not as high as he expected. He gently brushed the child's hair back from her face, but she did not respond and open her eyes. Instead her panting increased, and she whimpered between the laboured breaths. Meg reached out and clutched his hand.

"Everywhere hurts, Luis. It is as if I have a hammer in my head."

"Alyce and Henri will be back soon. You will feel better with some water and a tonic." He stroked the back of Meg's clammy hand and then turned it over and felt her racing pulse. Totally helpless, except for making the girls more comfortable, Luis tried to recall his grandfather's views. Surely there was more to be done than administering herbs? He dismissed the wilder remedies, derived from folklore, and wished he had talked to Henri about blood-letting before he had rushed off to the apothecary's.

Alyce returned with a pitcher of water, fresh from the well, and two cups. Meg, supported by Luis, managed to drink but Jane could not be roused enough to swallow. With sickening dread, Luis recalled Hernando's words when he had told his grandfather of Alyce's daughter. "Such children die young as they are weak. I have never seen an adult with those distinctive features." His eyes met Alyce's and he had to look away as they discussed what to do.

Henri arrived back, panting from exertion and dripping with perspiration. He opened the bag from the apothecary to reveal several herbal concoctions and a jar containing leeches. "We need to bleed Meg and Jane. The apothecary says the fever is the result of too much blood."

Alyce looked from Henri to Luis. "What shall we do? You said that they shouldn't necessarily be bled, Luis."

"I am no physician, nor am I an apothecary. My opinion was based on my grandfather's. Sometimes, he felt it did no good to weaken a patient more. I cannot make the decision."

Henri, who had the advantage of speaking directly with the apothecary, said urgently, "We must do something. I can see a change in them already." He was correct. Meg's breathing had started to mirror Jane's and the little girl seemed to have slipped into unconsciousness. "The apothecary says we must not let them sleep."

Alyce grabbed the jar of leeches and started to place them on her daughter's limbs. Luis propped Meg up with the bolster and encouraged her to drink some more while she watched him with glassy eyes.

The day dragged on. The sun rose higher in the sky and when it reached its zenith, Henri left for the docks. The captain of the cog bound for Bordèu that day would have five fewer passengers. Luis went in search of the innkeeper's wife to request some food but Alyce refused anything except for the occasional drink of water.

"You must eat," Luis exhorted.

"I cannot," she replied. "I fear she will die."

Luis looked at the small figure on the bed, saw the sheen of sweat and followed each tortured breath in the knowledge that Jane was losing her battle against the devastating sickness.

He had heard that many victims succumbed quickly, usually dying within twenty-four hours, but he had never witnessed it. He knew that some did survive the pestilence and prayed fervently that both girls would have the strength to fight, but deep in his heart he struggled to hope. They had managed to keep Meg awake so far but Jane was unresponsive.

Just after sunset, when the twilight started to leach the colour from the sky, turning the world grey, Jane took a last shuddering breath and was silent.

FIVE

Caors, Late August 1557

LUIS PLACED HIS HAND ON YSABEL'S GATE AND savoured a sense of homecoming so strong it threatened to unman him. He felt the prick of tears, suppressed them with the skill honed in his early childhood, and turned away from Alyce and Meg. He had left this house with such hopes, determined to bring the Weavers to safety, but any expectations had vanished with the sound of Alyce keening for her child. She stood behind him, the same woman he had always loved, but now forever changed: an empty shell, who had needed to be restrained as the small coffin was laid in the ground, who had shown no joy at Meg's recovery, and who had tolerated the hardships of the journey with a passivity which increasingly worried Luis. His presence seemed an irrelevance to her, so withdrawn was she that he felt she could fade away and join her daughter.

He pushed open the gate, and invited Alyce and Meg to enter, for once wishing Henri had remained with them and had not disembarked from the barge at Douelle. The imposing house, built around two sides of the courtyard, stood three storeys high, topped with an open colonnade. Meg looked up and saw a small, plump figure at the top of the stone staircase leading to the first floor. She held out her hand to Alyce but, on getting no response, took her sister's arm and led her towards their new home.

Ysabel Bernade's cheery welcome died on her lips when she saw the depleted group. There was no child. She noted Alyce's demeanour, Meg's weariness, and the strain etched clearly on Luis's face. Her heart went out to him. This was not as it should be; it was not as they had planned. When he reached the top of the steps, Ysabel embraced Luis briefly and then ushered the trio into the house in silence. The large hall was cool after the heat of the day, the scent of fresh herbs wafted up as they walked across newly laid rushes, and dust motes danced in the streams of light from the windows set high in the walls. Meg stopped, studied the lofty ceiling, and liked what she saw.

Ysabel carried on walking, leading Alyce and Meg up a second staircase at the back of the hall. The third floor had been recently partitioned into separate bedchambers. There was a room for each of them and Ysabel was relieved she had assumed Jane would sleep in her mother's bed and had not made up a truckle bed. She glanced at Alyce. The woman was in enough distress without the agonising reminder of an empty bed. Hesitant about what to say, Ysabel immediately announced that she would leave them to settle in and then she went in search of Luis.

She found him in the garden, sitting in the evening sun. She joined him wordlessly and they sat together soaking up the warmth radiating from the old stones at their backs. Ysabel waited for some time for Luis to speak.

"Jane is dead. She died in Le Havre. It was so quick."

"The sweating sickness?"

"I believe so."

She rested her hand on his. "Do you want to tell me about it?"

"There is nothing much to tell."

Ysabel nodded. She could bide her time. He would talk to her about the journey when he was ready. She thought about Alyce, her eyes full of sadness, unpacking her few belongings in her new chamber and about her sister, Meg, who had looked around with interest, despite her recent trials.

They sat together in silent companionship until the cigales stopped singing and their chorus was replaced by nightjars calling in the dark. The air became chillier. Ysabel rose, stiff from sitting so long but reluctant to return indoors. It was not often that she and Luis spent time alone together. As she stretched, placing her hands on her lower back, she caught the murmuring of voices, too distant to be clearly audible. It was late for visitors. The only explanation was that Hernando and Johan had somehow heard of Luis's return and had decided not to wait any longer to see him.

A short time later, Luis stood with his shoulder resting against the mantel and watched his grandfather being charmed by Meg Weaver. They had gathered round the small fire as a focal point, rather than for its heat, for although the large hall was cool after the fierce summer sun of the day, it was still comfortable. Alyce had made a brief appearance but as soon as was polite, she had excused herself, pleading exhaustion from the journey. However, her sister had shown no sign of following her example. Meg was enjoying herself, her fatigue forgotten. It was as if she had shaken off the trauma of the last few weeks and the old Meg had returned. Any initial shyness on her part had swiftly passed and it appeared that Hernando, too, had settled down for a convivial evening. Jane had not been mentioned and Luis realised his grandfather had no reason to suspect that the child was not safely abed. Loath to spoil the atmosphere, Luis held his peace and Ysabel, following his lead, did likewise. Both knew how grief could come in waves, overwhelming in its intensity, and Meg deserved an evening's respite.

She was admiring Hernando's stick, beautifully crafted by Johan: a reflection of his affection for his master. The tool of the Pyrenean shepherd and rather out of place in the city, it had been Hernando's trusty companion in recent months and the physician was now never seen without it. "You are very fortunate to have such a possession, Monsieur Gharsia," Meg stated with a disarming directness, before she turned to Johan. "And you, Monsieur Berenguer, are very talented."

"Just call me Johan," he replied, obviously pleased with the compliment. "However, I must wish you all a good evening for I am needed elsewhere." He turned to Luis and, without any words being exchanged, they both knew that Hernando would be safely escorted back to the small house on the corner of the Place St Urcisse before he became overtired.

"Where is he going?" Meg asked, before Johan had managed to close the door behind him.

"The tavern – his evenings are his own."

Ysabel, unsure of how much the girl knew of the Gharsias' unusual living arrangements, diverted the conversation. "Would you like to stay and sup with us, Hernando? We are eating very simply tonight."

Luis, Meg, and Hernando devoured their bread and cheese with relish but Ysabel ate sparingly, unable to shake off her melancholy. Alyce's loss had reawakened Ysabel's own grief and her mind had wandered away from the conversation.

"Ysabel, are you listening?"

"Sorry, Hernando. What did you say?"

Meg spoke up. "Madame Bernade, I was asking Luis's grandfather whether he remembered the letter I wrote to Luis, in his care, when I was a child."

Meg eyed Hernando and smiled mischievously. "I addressed you as 'Eminent Physician and Grandfather.'" The old man inched slightly straighter. "Was I correct to do so?" she asked.

"It is some time since I taught at the university but I still use my skills."

She scanned the three faces in the room, assessing their possible reaction. Her focus rested on Luis. "The letter urged you to come quickly as Parliament had passed the act allowing clergy to marry." There was an awkward pause. Luis remained silent. Meg became flustered: she had miscalculated but, nevertheless, she continued, "It is a shame it took so long to arrive and you were too late." Luis's glance was reproachful. Her head down, Meg missed Ysabel's worried frown, and Hernando's raised eyebrow. She felt the tears welling up and gulped. Raising her eyes, she addressed Hernando. "I have seen Luis use the skills he learnt from you many times. I remember how he told me to make sure the midwife had clean hands when she attended Alyce for Jane's birth."

Triggered by the memory, Meg began to sob. She could almost feel her new-born niece in her arms, for the midwife had given the baby to Meg while she had ministered to Alyce. Luis watched the girl with disquiet: she rarely shed tears. The enormity of what the Weavers had experienced, and the dilemma which faced him, now he was home, appeared impossible to surmount. Ysabel reached out and took Meg's hand. "Come," she said gently, "it is time to go to bed." As they walked towards the stairs, Ysabel turned to Luis and her words echoed his concern. "You must go and see the Gaulberts tomorrow."

Sleep had been elusive during the short night, so Luis was up and dressed before Johan had stirred. It had been very late when Hernando and Luis had finally retired: both much affected by their discussion of Jane's death. The physician had reassured Luis that all that could be done to save the child, had been done. Luis must not blame himself for the child's death because the sickness could have struck in England, just as devastatingly as in France. He had taken some comfort from his grandfather's opinion but he had still spent a troubled night, disturbed by images of Jane's suffering coupled with anxiety about his return to the farm.

After quickly breaking his fast, Luis made good progress. The track by the river was baked hard by the summer heat and it was too early for many to be about their business. His spirits rose as the rising sun warmed his back, dispersed the mist hanging above the cool, green water, and lit row upon row of vines, heavy with deep, black fruit, as they radiated up the hillside from the valley floor. Luis slowed his pace when he reached Douelle and headed south. Reluctant to see Marie, he tried to order his thoughts and work out how his predicament could be solved and, sooner than he expected, he saw the farmhouse.

It basked in the sun. A solid structure, of grey sandstone, with its characteristic turret; its windows already shuttered against the expected heat. Luis tethered the horse and looked for signs of life. All was quiet. He ignored the flight of steps, leading to the living quarters, and went through the double doors of the barn below. He had guessed correctly: Guilhem Gaulbert was working there, preparing for the imminent harvest. In a few weeks, the grapes would be ready to pick. Luis stood still, inhaling the potent smell of wine-soaked oak and earth. He waited for the vintner to turn around but Guilhem continued checking the press, his back firmly towards Luis.

"You have returned."

"Yes."

"Henri has told us about the Weaver women."

Luis wished the older man would stop his task and face him. "What has he said?"

"That they are to live with my sister. Is that true?"

"Yes."

Guilhem turned around slowly. There was no friendly welcome. His eyes were hard in his usually amiable face. He studied Luis. "What about my daughter?"

"She will continue to live here."

"And you? Where will you be? Marie is your wife."

"I will divide my time between my grandfather's and here, as I have always done."

Guilhem's face softened. "You are reconciled with Marie?"

"No."

Disappointment made Guilhem harsh. "You have treated my daughter badly – rushing off without a word and bringing two Englishwomen back with you – one of whom you wished to marry!" It was as Luis anticipated. Marie had been economical with the truth. He let the vintner continue. "I will not have my daughter the subject of gossip in this valley."

"I do not intend to create any gossip. When I am here, I will sleep in the attic. No-one will know unless one of you is indiscreet."

"I cannot pretend that I am happy with this. I had such hopes when you and Marie married."

"I am sorry," Luis replied genuinely.

Guilhem rubbed the back of his head. "You are like a son to me. I have taught you all I know."

"For that, I will always be grateful. I want to continue to

work with you. I will fulfil the responsibility of a husband. I will provide for Marie but things cannot be as they were."

"Is there no hope of a reconciliation?"

"None."

"Surely," Guilhem said, almost affectionately, "you can forgive Marie. You are not the first man to be duped into marriage by a swelling belly."

Luis did not deign to answer. Marie's deception had been so much more than her father realised. Guilhem shrugged. He had promised his daughter that he would try to persuade Luis but it was clearly impossible. He felt a flash of irritation with her for creating the situation, quickly followed by pity. However much she loved the man, Luis Gharsia could not be convinced. Guilhem shrugged again.

Luis pointed to the press. "Is it ready?"

"Yes, everything is ready. We have to hope the weather stays fair with just enough rain. Too much and the grapes will swell and split their skins."

Amused, Luis's face relaxed for the first time. Guilhem was telling him what he had known since he was a child. The older man laughed. "Why am I saying this?" It was Luis's turn to shrug. Guilhem walked over to the far side of the barn. "Come, Luis," he said. "Let us taste this." He drew some wine from the barrel. "Tell me what you think?"

Someone was saying her name softly. "Alyce? Alyce? Are you awake?" She opened her eyes. Meg's face was so close it was difficult to focus. She closed her eyes, seeking oblivion, and felt the whisper of her sister's lips touch her cheek. "You must get up. Madame Bernade is waiting downstairs with a delicious breakfast. We must be polite guests."

The need to be civil penetrated Alyce's despair and forced her out of bed. Meg retrieved the clothes from the bottom of the bed where they had lain, carelessly discarded, from the previous night and tried to shake the creases from them. Handing them to Alyce, she crossed the room and flung open the shutters. Strong sunshine flooded the room. Alyce winced and screwed up her eyes. "It is so bright!"

"It is late." Meg leaned out of the window. Beneath her, on the other side of a road, a river, green and deep, flowed majestically on its journey to the sea. To her right she could see carts trundling across the bridge on their way into the city and when she looked up, white fluffy clouds were drifting across the periwinkle sky. She glanced back over her shoulder. Alyce was dressing listlessly. "Come, Alyce," she said as she left the window. "Let me help with the fastenings and your hair."

Ysabel was waiting for them in the small room adjacent to the hall. Her husband, Michel, had used it to do his accounts but, over the many years since his death, she had transformed it into a cosy room for both eating and working. A table was laid with fresh bread, cheese, ham, and fruit. Meg espied the bowl of early plums with glee before she noticed the rest of the room. A chest for books rested against one wall, while a large cupboard filled most of another. A window, with very uneven glass, was partially open, revealing a glimpse of the garden. The fresh scent of greenery hung on the slight breeze.

Unfamiliar with accommodating strangers as guests, Ysabel found she was momentarily nervous in her own home. "Please eat," she bade. "I thought you might enjoy more breakfast than usual."

As they both took a seat, Alyce replied with quiet thanks while Meg's face showed her delight. They ate in silence, except to respond to Ysabel's offer of different foods. Searching for something to say, the latter asked, "Would you like to see the city?"

"I think that would be a good idea." Meg turned to her sister. "Don't you, Alyce?" she asked, biting enthusiastically into a large plum. The juice dripped down her chin and splattered her dress. She waited for Alyce's reprimand, which never came: neither did Alyce respond to her question. Meg pulled a rueful face and enquired, "Madame Bernade, when do you think Luis will return from the Gaulberts?"

"I don't know. He didn't say. He will need to check the vines."

"And see his wife?"

Ysabel studied Meg. The girl's blue eyes were guileless. "Yes, Meg, Marie will be at the farm."

"I wish Luis had taken me with him. I would have liked to have seen Henri again." Meg paused. "And to see the vines."

There was a heart-wrenching moan. Alyce sobbed, "I am sorry. I cannot eat this." Pushing her plate, where most of her breakfast remained, away from her, she rose from the table and rushed out of the room. Meg made to follow her but Ysabel placed a cautionary hand on the girl's arm.

"Leave her for a while. There is nothing we can say which will comfort her." She thought rapidly. "Meg, would you like to see the city now? I need some purchases from the apothecary. Could you go for me? Ramon will accompany you."

"Ramon?"

"Yes, he has been with me for more years than I can count. He was my husband's servant but stayed with me after Michel died. He was with me when I met Hernando and Luis in Auch. I was returning from Compostela, having visited the shrine of St Jacques, and Ramon, and my maid, Lisette, were my companions throughout the journey." Ysabel smiled at Meg. "He was a very young man then."

Meg weighed up the suggestion. Shafts of sunlight spilled through the window; suddenly, she desperately wanted to escape from Alyce's consuming sorrow. The decision was easy. "I would like that very much."

After Meg had left, Ysabel slowly climbed the stairs to Alyce's chamber. She knocked lightly and, when there was no answer, gradually pushed the door open. Alyce lay curled up on the bed, exhausted, her grief temporarily spent. Ysabel stood beside the bed, the familiar emptiness resurfacing.

"My daughter died, too."

Alyce opened her eyes but remained motionless. Ysabel rested her hand on the coverlet to steady herself.

"It was a long time ago, but the pain is still there, deep inside my heart. I cannot tell you that you will recover but I can say that your burden will become easier. You will laugh again and see the beauty in the sunrise."

Their eyes met. Ysabel reached out and stroked Alyce's hair back from her forehead. She continued the soothing movement as she said, "If Jehanne had lived, she would have been about your age."

Alyce's mouth trembled. The tears started to flow, silently streaking her face. She reached out for Ysabel's free hand, clasped it, and the words escaped her lips like treachery. "I fear I am with child."

GABRIEL

1608

SIX

Tadoussak, New France, June 1608

H E WAS NEARLY THERE. GABRIEL COULD HARDLY contain his excitement. It welled up from deep inside him, tingled along his sinews, and settled on his face in a broad smile. He turned to locate Luc but his friend was lost amongst the throng of men eager to catch a glimpse of their destination. Gabriel saw his own joy reflected on their faces. Tadoussak at last! Carefully selected, most of the new settlers were highly valued for their skills in the building trades, and Gabriel, despite his optimism, had only managed to obtain a place as a lackey. The expedition already had a qualified physician and Samuel Champlain had no need for another. However, Gabriel's size, and Luc's knowledge of the land, had guaranteed them a berth and in return for agreeing to stay in New France for two years, they were to receive an annual salary.

As the navire rounded the wooded promontory to enter the shallower waters of the harbour, the captain, Le Testu, shouted for the leadsmen to take their positions and sound the depth. Seconds later, the crew erupted unexpectedly with angry protestation and their voices reverberated across the bay.

"What's the matter?" Luc had pushed his way to Gabriel's side. There were several ships straining on their anchors in the bay, but all eyes were drawn to a Basque whaler which had obviously taken possession of the expedition's sister ship, the *Lévrier*. That navire, under Pont-Gravé's command, had left Honfleur the week before Champlain's ship, and had made good time, only to run into trouble at Tadoussak.

The Basque captain, who identified himself as Martin Darretche, had a loud rough voice which carried easily. "You cannot enter the harbour except by force. Your fellow commander, Pont-Gravé, attacked us, accusing us of trading furs without a licence. We have defended ourselves. The commander is wounded and is our prisoner. We have captured the cannon and arms of the *Lévrier*. We will return them when you agree to leave."

All smiles faded on the settlers' faces: it was not the arrival they had expected. A dangerous mood rippled through the men. They had been at sea for three months and their anticipation had been rising during the previous three weeks as the navire navigated the mighty River of Canada. Some of the men were already chafing at Champlain's authoritarian leadership. As skilled craftsmen, used to a measure of independence, several found it difficult to adjust to the rigid regime they found themselves in aboard ship. Gabriel watched with interest as Champlain and Le Testu began an earnest discussion. He edged closer. Snatches of conversation could be heard. The expedition lacked the arms to fight the Basques; Pont-Gravé should never have attacked; Champlain had the upper hand as he was there on the authority of the King of France. Gabriel sighed with relief when the two men decided that the only solution was to parley. Champlain filled him with confidence. The leader's high forehead and his eyes, set wide apart, spoke of intelligence and trustworthiness, while his commanding presence allayed any fears that the dream of a permanent settlement would turn to dust.

Champlain used his diplomatic skills to good effect. The Basques were ready to negotiate and an agreement was reached with Darretche. Already faced with a second French ship and hearing another was on its way, the Basque leader soon realised they would be outnumbered. The traders admitted they were in the wrong although they justified their actions by emphasising their genuine fear that the arrival of the French would affect their livelihood. Champlain reassured the Basques that their fears were unfounded: there would be no interference in the whaling industry. Any other issues could not be solved in New France but needed to be referred to the courts at home. The Basques were content and the French navire slowly inched its way into the harbour, taking care to avoid the sand bar which sliced the bay in two, and dropped anchor next to the whaler.

Perched above the beach Gabriel had a perfect view. The water, deep blue and as smooth as a millpond, swept in an arc beneath him and, on the shore, Gabriel could watch the developing activity at the trading post. Constructed eight years previously, when the successful fur trader, Pierre de Chauvin, had tried to establish a permanent settlement, the cabin was already showing signs of deterioration. Its high, steeply angled roof, designed to cope with heavy snow, nestled over planks which were already worn and split. A shiver ran down Gabriel's spine as he remembered being told about the colonists who had remained to experience that first winter. Of the sixteen men who had stayed only five had survived, after being taken in by the native people, the Montagnais.

When Samuel Champlain had visited, three years later, he had written about the Montagnais on his return and Gabriel recalled his grandfather referring to the book. Champlain had described the tribe as forest-dwellers and, now he was in Canada, Gabriel could understand the term. All around him were trees: fir, birch, and cypress stretched as far as the eye could see. The men milling around the trading post were truly dwellers of the forest and they had arrived at the coast to barter their furs.

He left his vantage point and made his way towards the group, joining a cluster of settlers who had also gravitated towards them. Negotiations were soon in full swing with the aid of interpreters. While the Montagnais were showing Champlain their pelts, Gabriel heard a voice offering an explanation. He turned slightly to look back over his left shoulder: the youth, Etienne Brûlé, was just behind him.

"They are the best furs from the far north country."

"How do you know?"

The boy tapped the side of his nose and grinned cheekily at Gabriel.

"How do you know?" Gabriel repeated, with a touch of irritation.

Etienne, who looked no more than fifteen years old, had just arrived on the navire with Gabriel, yet he seemed very well-informed. He admitted, "I have been talking to the Basques."

"You should be careful. They are no friends of ours."

The boy shrugged, narrowing his eyes. "You can see the lustrous quality from here."

The skins were piled high on sleds, making it difficult to identify them. Gabriel thought he recognised beaver, now so valuable due to the growing demand of the hat industry in Europe, but not the others. Etienne, following Gabriel's gaze and eager to impart his knowledge, announced, "I can see beaver, marten, lynx, otter, and white fox."

"You can't tell from this distance," replied Gabriel accusingly.

The boy grinned again. "Can't I?" he challenged.

Gabriel moved further away and studied the Montagnais rather than their furs. The men were all lean and strongly muscled and, although not as tall as himself, they were taller than many of the settlers. Their black hair shone in the sun, the result, Gabriel suspected, of being coated in grease. It was drawn back from their faces, tied in a horse's tail at the back of their heads, and adorned with a single feather. All of the men wore hide breechcloths which hung down front and back: some had leggings beneath but most were bare-legged. Gabriel presumed that as June progressed, and the weather became warmer, all would only wear the breechcloth. He glanced down at the men's feet. They were bare.

The negotiations were becoming more animated. The youth had rejoined Gabriel. "Champlain had better not cross the Montagnais."

Gabriel raised an eyebrow at the boy's warning. "Why?"

"They control the fur trade here. They act as middlemen, buying the pelts from the nations who live in the north and then sell them here in Tadoussak. There is a great sea many, many, leagues from here."

Gabriel strained his ears. Champlain was asking about the land where the pelts originated. The Montagnais were gesticulating vigorously: they would show the French the lower reaches of the cold Saguenay River which flowed into the bay at Tadoussak but no further. Gabriel wondered what it would be like to travel far to the north, to see places no other Frenchman had seen, and to come back with enough skins to become a very rich man. As he was considering such a scenario, the persistent sound of hammering intruded on his thoughts. He decided to go in search of Luc. His friend had been assigned to help the carpenters fit out the river barque which would be used to travel further upstream to Kebec, which was to be their destination.

On the last day of June, the barque was ready to leave. Gabriel and Luc climbed aboard together, the latter with a touch of pride. Although not a time-served carpenter, Luc's woodworking skills, the result of years of making and mending on the farm, had been recognised. He pointed out the dry berthing spaces, and Gabriel found himself feeling less of an asset to the venture than his friend. Luc also had the advantage of being a cultivator and had already struck up a friendship with Martin Béguin, the gardener Champlain had persuaded to travel to Canada. To his chagrin, Gabriel, his usual confidence temporarily deserting him, had not made contact with the expedition's surgeon and was still fulfilling the role of general lackey.

They sailed up the Great River at a sedate pace, keeping close to the banks, which enabled Champlain to learn more about the new terrain, but there were mumbled mutterings about danger by some of the men. Gabriel and Luc kept their opinions to themselves as the small craft negotiated shoals and eddies, often narrowly missing submerged rocks. At times, Champlain disembarked to sketch the various plants that grew along the shores and both young men took advantage of dry land to stretch their legs. They did not go far, as the banks of the river were impenetrable. The land was as it was at Tadoussak, apparently endless hills covered with pine, spruce, and birch. On one occasion, the combination of winds and treacherous currents caused the barque to run aground, resulting in Champlain naming the place Malle Baye.

Shortly after her misadventure the barque reached the Île d'Orleans, an island Champlain knew from his previous visit. When the settlers disembarked to allow their leader to continue his meticulous research, Gabriel and Luc experienced very different emotions.

"This is a place where a man could have a good life."

Gabriel knew what Luc meant. The island appeared reminiscent of their region of France. There was open woodland, with oaks and nut trees, so unlike the crowded forest they had seen so much of recently. The land was fertile, the soil rich, and Luc exclaimed in delight when he espied the wild vines. Gabriel studied the vista before him and tried to push away the creeping doubt, questioning why he had embarked on this adventure. He wanted more than to see a place which was just like home. "We are not stopping here," he stated sharply.

Surprised, Luc answered, "I know. We go on to Kebec, the place where the waters narrow."

They had been at Kebec nearly a month: each day filled with relentless labour. As soon as the settlers had arrived, Champlain had organised the men to clear the land and build. One group set about felling the trees while another sawed the logs into planks. Luc was part of the latter group while Gabriel dug. He dug out cellars to keep provisions and dug out ditches to protect the *habitation*, as Champlain named their new home, until he had blisters on top of blisters, and his hands bled. He had sacrificed one of his shirts and bound the linen strips around his palms. Every morning his back cried out in protest and every night he fell into an exhausted sleep, only to find morning arrived too quickly. His first waking thought never varied; all he could think about were ways in which he could join the fourth group, who continually sailed back and forth to Tadoussak to bring supplies.

Champlain had shared his ideas about what they would build. Of paramount importance was a storehouse, secure from the weather and the animals, which would contain their provisions for the coming winter and be used for trade in the future. Next the men needed shelter. He had thought carefully about the design. There would be three buildings, all interconnected. One would be for the men, Champlain would have his own, facing south across the river, and the third would house a forge and workshops. Two storeys high, the buildings would be perched on the promontory with an excellent view of the river.

Notwithstanding the supplies arriving from Tadoussak and those which had been brought from France, the food was poor and the mutterings of discontent increased as each day passed. An uneasy atmosphere hung over the new settlement and although Gabriel and Luc kept their own counsel, they were aware of deep discord. A small gaggle of men, mostly made up of a locksmith, Jean Duval, and his three cronies, moved among the settlers, tapping into the resentment felt over Champlain's hard regime.

It was midday, the time to take a short break, and Gabriel and Luc had wandered in the direction of some shrubs which bore sweet, bluish berries. The Montagnais had shown the settlers these plants in Tadoussak but few of the Frenchmen chose to supplement their meagre diet with them. Luc, however, could not eat enough of the juicy fruit while Gabriel with his bound hands found them difficult to pick. They were well out of earshot of the other men.

"I think something serious is afoot," said Luc, keeping his voice low.

"That is no surprise. We can't keep working like this." Gabriel studied the berries Luc had poured into his hand, blue against the bloodstained bandages. Each night his soft student's palms were unrecognisable when he sparingly applied the salve he had brought from home.

Luc, who, with his farmer's hands, had fared much better, was sympathetic but realistic. "We have to work this hard. It is a race against time."

"I know," replied Gabriel, despondently.

Luc looked around to check that they were still alone. "What would we do if there was a mutiny?"

"We should support Champlain. There is no-one else who could lead us."

"Despite your hands?" Luc asked, with a hint of humour.

"Yes, despite my hands."

"I agree."

"Champlain is our leader. He has the king's backing. Goodness knows what would happen under someone else."

There was a commotion below them. A river barque had docked. Its captain, Le Testu, started shouting orders and the cargo was swiftly unloaded. "That is what I want to do," Gabriel admitted, as they started to make their way back. "I want to sail up and down the river with a bit of loading and unloading at each end."

It was pitch black. Someone was shouting. Gabriel's back

screamed complaint as he forced himself upright. Luc was already pulling his breeches on.

"What is it?"

"We are to assemble outside."

Gabriel stumbled alongside Luc, coming to an abrupt halt. Champlain was standing in the shadow of a lantern, accompanied by Le Testu and some of his men. The light reflected off their weapons, glinting as the men shifted their weight.

Champlain's voice rang out, strong and sure. Gabriel listened, his heart hammering. Duval and his cronies had been placed in irons, suspected of a plot to kill the expedition's leader. All settlers were to be questioned that night. If they spoke the truth they would be pardoned, if not, they were to be put to death. Gabriel felt sweat dampen his armpits, and the palms of his hands, which stung inside the bandages. He glanced sideways at Luc but his friend's face was in darkness. They were trapped: they had known there was discontent but had done nothing. He uttered a silent prayer to God and waited for his turn to be interrogated.

When the time came, Gabriel told the truth and hoped for the best. He had known about Duval mongering discontent, but he had dismissed it as the grumblings of a few, and he had no knowledge of an assassination plot. Luc did likewise. Champlain took his time assessing the two young men before him. He knew they were inseparable and of the same age, yet the taller of the two looked older. He was a big man, tall and broad-shouldered, with slightly dusky skin and eyes as black as any native of Canada. There was an air of nobility about his face, with its aquiline nose and sharp angles, and when he spoke, it was with the vocabulary of an educated man. Champlain noticed his hands bound with bandages. Gharsia was obviously not used to manual labour. His companion, by comparison, had the worn hands of a worker yet, in his slightness, Gaulbert appeared little more than a youth. His honest face, with clear hazel eyes under a shock of chestnut hair, looked incapable of deceit. Champlain let them sweat for a few minutes and then waved them away.

The rumours were flying when Gabriel and Luc climbed thankfully into their hammocks. As usual, Etienne Brûlé was talking.

"What do you really know?" asked Luc.

The boy's face shone in the glow of a single candle. "The locksmith, Natel, betrayed Duval to Le Testu, who went straight to Champlain."

Gabriel was sceptical. "How do you know this?"

Etienne gave him a disparaging look. "The man has servants, doesn't he?"

"What did Champlain do?" Another youth, Nicolas Marsolet, had joined them.

Etienne liked nothing better than an audience. "When he and Le Testu knew the identity of the leaders, they arranged for a sailor to lure the conspirators with the promise of drink. Once on board Le Testu's vessel they were seized by his men."

Nicolas asked, "What will happen next?"

Etienne paused, as if to give the matter some thought. He moderated his voice for effect. "I hear that they are to be tried."

It was the day of the trial. Champlain had sailed to Tadoussak and returned with Pont-Gravé, whose wounds were almost healed. The two officers, with Le Testu and the expedition's surgeon, Bonnerme, were to form a tribunal. To ensure fairness the trial was to be held in public. Gabriel and Luc took their places near the back, the former content, for once, about his lowly status. They were not called on to testify but many were and in the face of such overwhelming evidence, Duval confessed and begged for mercy, but to no avail. All four men were condemned to death. Duval was to be executed immediately but the tribunal recommended that the other three be taken back to France, by Pont-Gravé, to have their sentences reviewed there.

On the second day of August, Duval was hung, strangled, and then beheaded. His head was displayed on a pike in Kebec for all to see: a salutary lesson of the folly of mutiny. Most of the settlers averted their eyes as they went about their daily tasks but Gabriel, the medical student, watched with interest as the flesh was pecked away over time, revealing the clean contours of the skull.

SEVEN

UTUMN, WITH HER SHORTER DAYS AND CHILLIER nights, crept up on Kebec. Increasing numbers of Montagnais arrived on the opposite bank, to fish for eels as they ran up the river. Everyone took part and, for a time, food was plentiful: there was much feasting on the fresh eels and the remainder were dried for the coming winter. In preparation for the following year, the settlers continued planting wheat, rye, and vines throughout October, despite the threat of frost. Gabriel was still digging, his hands protected by their bandages, but he was happier working in the garden. The soil was good, rich, and friable. He and Luc toiled contentedly side by side throughout the day and, at night, created coats out of fur ready to brave the biting wind of winter.

In November heavy snow fell, swirling on the fierce winds, raising the river levels, and unnerving the French. One night, towards the middle of the month, Gabriel lay listening to the wind. It battered the planks of their new home, whistled through the crevices, and rattled the door. It almost drowned out the sound of someone moaning in pain. He was not the only man ill. Many had suddenly started to suffer, both colonists and Montagnais.

Luc was still awake. "What do you think has caused the flux?" he asked, raising his voice above the wind. He always believed that Gabriel, as a medical student, should know everything about illness.

"They have eaten something rotten," replied his friend, confidently. Gabriel's own conjecture had been reinforced earlier that day when Etienne Brûlé had informed him that Champlain had been reported as saying that the cause was probably badly cooked eels.

"I hope we don't get it."

"We must make sure our food is properly cooked."

The moaning became worse. Gabriel, inwardly cursing, hauled himself off his cot and padded towards the fire. He took a spill from the mantel, held it in the embers, and lit a candle. Immediately, the rank smell of tallow mingled with the reek of vomit. He added some more logs to the fire, waited to see whether they caught, and then turned to the nearest cot. Lifting the candle high, Gabriel studied the locksmith, Natel. He was lying on his side, clutching his abdomen, his legs drawn up in agony. His fever was high, his skin and lips dry, and by the stench of his bedding, he had lost all control of his bowels. Gabriel wiped the poor man's brow, gave him a drink of water, and then pulled the blankets back over Natel's shivering body. There was nothing more to be done. There was no clean bedding and even if there had been, it would soon be soiled. Gabriel thought about emptying the pail of vomit but that, too, would soon be used and the roar of the wind was a strong disincentive to venture outside, so he returned to the fire, blew out the candle, and then made his way back to his bed. Once there, he pulled the covers over his head to muffle the distressing sound of Natel, as well as the wailing of the wind.

As the winter progressed thirteen men died of dysentery, including Natel. The weather turned dry with air so sharp it hurt to breathe: the cold intensifying without the insulating blanket of snow. Living conditions inside the *habitation* plummeted to a new low. Christmas came and went, with very little to celebrate, and one January day, as he watched the thick ice on the river, Gabriel thought longingly of his grandfather and aunt, and of the warmth and comfort of home. He felt he would never see Caors again. Fresh food was no longer available. Although they had some salted meat and fish to supplement their bread and beans, it was difficult to hunt. Moose, easier to catch in the deep snow, were elusive in the drier conditions and Gabriel missed the meat, which reminded him of beef. The Montagnais were also badly affected by the failure of the moose hunt and that of the beaver: the earlier wet weather had raised river levels, making the lodges inaccessible.

January dragged on into February, the harshest of months. The days passed slowly; lethargy descended on the French. Depression followed, and worrying symptoms appeared. Some of the colonists noticed blue-red spots on their skin, often on their shins, which grew, forming larger marks where the hair twisted and broke away. These men were short-tempered. Arguments broke out, and the fear in the settlement was tangible. Gabriel and Luc kept themselves apart as much as possible and checked their skin repeatedly.

On one particularly bitter day, the Montagnais, on the south side of the river, gathered together and called to the French. They were starving. They had no food reserves. In a desperate attempt to seek aid, they launched their birchbark canoes. Light and swift in the right conditions, the fragile canoes were no match for the river. It was high, the current strong, and the canoes snapped like twigs as they collided with the immense ice floes which hurtled downstream. Men, women, and children were tossed like chaff into the water as they called out in terror. Some managed to cling to the ice floes, others did not. The settlers watched in helpless horror until the current forced some of the ice to the shore and the survivors scrambled to safety.

Champlain instructed all those who were able-bodied to help. Fires were built, and bread and beans were distributed. The ravenous Montagnais ate hungrily, and Gabriel, who had approached a couple, cautioned them. "You must only eat a small amount and take your time." He mimed tearing tiny pieces from the loaf and chewing it very slowly. The male Montagnais showed no sign of understanding: his sunken eyes met Gabriel's, and then shifted away. The woman had averted her eyes completely. She stared, expressionless, at her feet, mechanically forcing the food into her mouth.

Suddenly, there was a shout. Some of the Montagnais had found two carcasses the French had discarded as carrion. The putrid bodies of a dog, and a sow, were seized upon with glee. The men dragged them back to their fire and started to cook them. Luc watched in disbelief. "They will be ill if they eat that," he said, as he walked towards Gabriel. The latter agreed but the starving men could not be dissuaded. They continued to watch helplessly until Luc remembered to relay Champlain's latest order. "We are to help them build their wigwams."

His attention caught, Gabriel's companion stood up with difficulty. He had been a mighty warrior, a great hunter, but now he was emasculated by his inability to feed his family. He could hardly look at his wife, and she had not looked at him since the death of their child. He studied the two men before him; he needed them. Humiliated, he lacked the strength to build a shelter for his wife: he could not even find the energy to remove his sodden mantle. The fire had now taken hold; flames leapt, logs crackled, and sparks danced in the icy air so, with great effort, he removed his cloak. He stood tall, his weakened legs shaking, and tried to ignore his rebellious gut. Just before he regurgitated the bread and beans, he pointed to himself, and said, "Mashk."

Gabriel and Luc diplomatically ignored the pile of sick. They pointed to themselves and said their names. Mashk crouched down, and then stood up, and snarled. The Frenchmen were taken aback. "Bear," explained Mashk, as he swayed. Gabriel rushed forward, and caught him, firmly supporting him until he reached the ground. Luc glanced at the woman. She showed no sign of emotion. She had stopped eating but refused to raise her head. Of indeterminate age, due to emaciation she appeared as an old woman, her face etched with loss. Luc glanced back at Mashk, who was watching him, and pointed to the woman. "Wyome," said Mashk, so quietly that Luc barely heard.

The initial feeding over, it was time to construct the shelters for the Montagnais. Champlain provided the bark for the temporary, conical shelters which could be easily erected. Gabriel and Luc started to work, with Mashk giving instructions, while his wife remained immobile, huddled in her furs, next to the fire. First, the men made a framework of tapered saplings, which they covered with rolls of birchbark, shingled on from bottom to top. Luc then carefully sewed the bark to the framework with spruce root lacings, while Gabriel cut logs to lie against the bark to make it secure against the strong winds.

Inside the wigwam, Mashk's birchbark torch cast eerie shadows. Above them, through the smoke hole, the wintry sky was fading to a shimmering pink, and the temperature was dropping further. Their breath condensed as they surveyed their efforts. As instructed, Gabriel had made a sapling loop around the circumference of the wigwam and they had laid a pole across it from one side to the other. It passed over the central hearth, where Luc started a fire. Mashk regarded the pole dolefully. Under normal circumstances, meat and fish could be smoked using the crosspiece but now all it could be used for was to dry their clothing. He turned to the Frenchmen and mimed eating, as Gabriel had earlier.

"Atim," he said.

"Atim?" queried Gabriel.

"Dog," Mashk answered. Then he mimed eating his cloak.

"You ate dogs and animal skin?"

"Yes," Mashk replied in French, again.

"You understand French."

"Many, many moons ago, two young warriors travelled to your country. They were made welcome. They met your king, Henri."

Luc spoke for the first time. "They came back. Are they with you?"

"No."

Gabriel's spirits rose. It did not matter. He felt a bubble of excitement, long forgotten over the gruelling winter. Mashk could understand French. They could converse. He would teach Gabriel the native language and with that knowledge, Gabriel's possibilities for adventure seemed infinite. Determined to start immediately, he said, "Mashk, if you grew corn, you would have food over the winter."

The response was a look of withering disdain, highlighted by the flickering torch. Gabriel continued, regardless. "Your neighbours, the Algonquin, Huron, and Iroquois, all grow corn, beans, and squash, and do not suffer like the Montagnais."

Mashk drew himself up to his full height. "We are hunters," he said proudly.

Gabriel was inclined to pursue the matter further but decided it was better not to antagonise Mashk. However, the latter was not finished. He spoke very deliberately. "Very bad year – eel run not good. Wet weather so no beaver: no thick snow – no moose."

"What is your name for moose?" queried Gabriel.

"Mush."

Above them, the sky darkened. The first stars appeared in the cloudless, indigo sky. A hoot, from the trees on the edge of the settlement, echoed in the still air, and Gabriel said, "Owl."

Mashk studied him, a flicker of amusement playing around his mouth, and responded, "Uhu."

Gabriel's face broke into a wide grin. It was a long time until spring and the distraction of learning a new language was so very attractive.

The new settlement limped on through March and into April. Scurvy took more victims. Everyone came to fear the blue-red spots, the yellowing eyes, and the loosening teeth. Gabriel checked himself, and Luc, every day. They felt weary but they were clear of the worst symptoms. A malaise covered both the French and the Montagnais. As death followed death, Champlain directed the surgeon Bonnerme to do autopsies to discover whether the settlers at Kebec were affected like those in earlier settlements. Disaster struck, the surgeon himself became very ill and shortly afterwards he died. By the time the first fish of the season ran in the Great River, seven Frenchmen had been lost to scurvy. Of the original twenty-eight colonists, only eight had survived and four of those were very poorly.

Now shad swam upstream, so plentiful that there were more than could be eaten. The world turned green and the sun warmed the bones of those who were left. Gabriel and Luc, ill but not dying, offered prayers of thanksgiving as the shoals glistened in the sunlit water. They feasted on shad roe, eaten in Luc's case with dried French bacon. Spring, with all her magnificence, had arrived at last.

At the beginning of June, the Montagnais told of seeing a boat downstream, heading for Kebec. Gabriel, his health somewhat restored, ran to the water's edge and watched the ship's progress. At that moment, she was the most beautiful craft he had ever seen: a small shallop, open-decked and low in the water, with the French ensign fluttering in the breeze. He watched as she sailed past the Île d'Orleans, named by Jacques Cartier in the previous century, and came to dock at the landing place beneath Kebec's promontory.

The young French captain, who sprang ashore first, was Pont-Gravé's son-in-law, Godet des Marais. He was followed by a group of strong French sailors who immediately started to unload provisions. The news was good: Pont-Gravé was back in Tadoussak with more men and supplies.

Champlain appointed Godet des Marais commander of Kebec in his place and sailed back to Tadoussak. What happened there was later described, to Gabriel and Luc, by Etienne Brûlé, who had also survived the devastating winter. He came upon them working in the garden. They chose to ignore him at first, concentrating on their tasks.

"Pont-Gravé is to replace Champlain as commander in Kebec. Champlain is to return to France at the end of the summer," announced Etienne, his voice full of importance.

"Why?" Luc demanded.

The youth shrugged. "Perhaps he could use a rest?"

"I could do with a rest," grumbled Gabriel. The relentless work had started again. The *habitation* needed completing, the crops required continuous attention and, although preferable to the idleness of winter, there was still a depressing monotony to their days.

He added, "We are not privy to our leaders' thoughts."

Etienne nodded. "I can tell you something else," he said. Gabriel and Luc waited, studied boredom on their faces. He paused for effect, as he often did. "We are going against the Mohawk."

Gabriel experienced a frisson of anticipation; Luc was more cautious.

"When?" asked Gabriel, as Luc asked, simultaneously, "Why?"

The Mohawk, renowned as skilful warriors, were the deadly enemy of the Montagnais, and the Algonquin and Huron nations who lived further west.

Etienne chose to answer Luc. "Last year, Champlain met many times with the leaders of the tribes. He promised to help them against the Iroquois League, of whom the Mohawks are the greatest problem. If the nations of the Great River are attacked, Champlain will fight with them. He has tried to make peace with the Iroquois but it has failed. They are attacking up and down the valley."

"What has it to do with us?" The thought of fighting horrified Luc.

Etienne always had an answer. "I heard Champlain say that peace is needed along the Great River for us to flourish. If there is always war, there will be no trading security. Trade is why we are here."

"If we join the Montagnais and their friends against the Mohawk, we will always be in danger from them."

"Not if we beat them," retorted Etienne.

Gabriel, who had remained silent during the last exchange, commented, "We do have the weapons to defeat them – the arquebus."

Luc turned on him. "Would you kill a man who is so poorly armed against you?"

Nonplussed, Gabriel answered quickly, "I would if I had to," but in his heart, he was uncertain. Nevertheless, he was resolute that he would be chosen to travel into the land of the Iroquois. "Anyway, when is this to be?" he asked, repeating his earlier question. He was already aware of feverish activity. For almost two weeks the shallop had been busy ferrying men and supplies for Kebec.

However, it was when he saw several trained arquebusiers among the new arrivals that Gabriel knew what Etienne had said was true. They had certainly not arrived to help complete the *habitation*.

EIGHT

O N A SPARKLING SUMMER'S DAY, WHEN THE
impossible seemed attainable, Mashk revelled in his
swelling optimism. They were ready to leave. He walked
towards Gabriel and experienced a measure of affinity. The
hunger for action was clear in the Frenchman's eyes, only
partially masked by the cloud of disappointment. He was
not to accompany them. The great leader, Champlain, was to
take only twenty of his men compared to many Montagnais
warriors. Mashk studied the vessel, which the French called a
shallop, dubiously: it would not withstand the rapids awaiting
the war party on the River of the Iroquois. His eyes travelled
to the French soldiers, their metal helmets and breastplates
shining in the sun, and he fingered his own slat armour. It was
adequate against arrows but would be useless against guns.
He smiled to himself. The Mohawks, the fiercest Iroquois
fighters, had no idea of their fate.

Gabriel raised his arm in greeting, heartened by the
difference between the warrior before him and the emaciated
man who had accepted his help in February. Although still
thin, Mashk stood tall in his war attire, his face and body
daubed in red pigment. A deer-hide quiver, filled with arrows

adorned with feathered fledging, hung over his shoulder, and a ball-headed club swung loosely in his right hand. The embedded pieces of stone at its tip glistened, ready to slash the enemy before it crushed their skulls. He wore armour tied at his neck and waist to protect his upper body, and a padded helmet, fashioned from thick hide, dangled from his left hand. They had come to know each other well enough for Gabriel to show his admiration.

"A mighty brave."

Mashk pulled himself fractionally more upright. "I will stow my armour and weapons in the canoe until we reach the land of the Mohawk."

"You welcome the chance to fight your enemy." It was a statement not a question.

Mashk's eyes shone with the prospect of what lay ahead. He would return glorious, the victor of so many enemy scalps that Wyome would turn her eyes toward him once again. The drums were beating, the rhythm pulsed through his body, and he turned for one last look at his wife. She appeared indifferent, standing next to the smaller Frenchman, Luc. Mashk turned away, met Gabriel's eyes, and nodded in acknowledgement as the latter spoke. "I wish I was going with you. Take care of yourself."

He paddled hard, pleased to be in the same canoe as Kitchi, named for his bravery. Over his shoulder, flanking him, Mashk was aware of Rowtag and Ahanu straining to keep level. They would not be able to sustain such a pace but it allowed them to make a spectacle as they left Kebec. They followed the French shallop, with Champlain plainly visible on the deck, through a deep channel on the south side of the river and then, beyond the settlement, the river widened between its thickly forested banks. The water was alive with fish: a good omen as the war party would need to supplement the cornmeal securely stored in the canoes. The hunters, who accompanied the warriors, were equipped with small, light-weight fishnets and special arrows designed to stun waterfowl. They would not go short of food.

"Look!" shouted Matwau, who was kneeling behind Mashk.

"There is no need to make a noise." Kitchi's reprimand was barbed, for although Matwau had been with the Montagnais for many years, he was originally Mohawk, captured as a child and assimilated into the tribe. It was always best to keep him close.

Matwau, refusing to be intimidated, scoffed scornfully. "Do you think I am betraying us to the enemy?" Then he laughed. "Where is the enemy? Are the Mohawk coming to attack us here?"

In front of them, lining the shore, Mashk could see up to three hundred warriors. Their allies, the Huron, and the Algonquin of the Petite-Nation, had come to meet Champlain. They must have heard of the war party and had come to learn more. The Montagnais stopped paddling and watched with interest as Champlain went ashore and approached the two leaders, easily identified by their headdress.

"Iroquet of the Petite-Nation," explained Kitchi, pointing to the larger imposing figure.

"Who is the other one?" asked Mashk, who had not travelled as far west as Kitchi.

"Ochasteguin of the Huron."

From their position in the canoe, the three braves had a good view of the Frenchman smoking ceremonial pipes with the two chiefs. This lasted some time before Iroquet and

Ochasteguin came back to the shallop with Champlain. There was more ceremonial smoking. Hundreds of warriors remained on the water's edge, watching, and Mashk wished he could go ashore. Longing to stretch his legs, he was very relieved when the chiefs stood up and declared that Champlain would help them defeat their enemy, the Iroquois. However, there was still more discussion followed by Champlain demonstrating the power of the French. Mashk watched, mesmerised, as Champlain lit a length of cord, touched the arquebus, and fired.

Mashk and his companions did not flinch as they had seen the wonder before, but most had not. After the shock of the explosion had calmed, mutterings rippled through the ranks of the warriors on the bank like a wave. Such a weapon must have great orenda, great spiritual power. Champlain spoke loudly so that all could hear. He professed that the French had come as fighters, armed and ready, and not as traders. Then he invited all the warriors to come to Kebec as his guests.

Kitchi was furious. "Why must we paddle all the way back downstream? We need to strike at the Mohawk now." Mashk agreed but they were in the minority.

So, it was that a magnificent flotilla of over a hundred canoes, carrying nearly four hundred warriors, followed Champlain back to Kebec, and even Matwau and Kitchi eventually became caught up with the excitement.

To Mashk's frustration, the festivities began. He watched with mixed feelings as the great chief, Champlain, welcomed two more boatloads of Frenchmen from Tadoussak, led by Pont-Gravé. The latter's loud, booming voice could be heard throughout the settlement, and Mashk seemed to cross paths with the larger than life figure every time he tried to seek out Gabriel. He had promised to recount every detail of his experience to the young colonist but it was the third day of the celebrations before they had a chance to speak.

During a break in the ritual dancing, Luc observed from afar as his friend and Mashk conversed earnestly: the brave gesticulating wildly, equally matched by Gabriel. Curious, he was about to join them when the two men fell silent and walked in the direction of Mashk's wigwam. For a moment, he contemplated joining them, but he supressed his feeling of exclusion, reminding himself that it was his own choice. Unlike Gabriel, he had no desire to accompany Champlain and his allies on their campaign to defeat the Iroquois, or to hear about Mashk's exploits.

Much later, when the dancing had recommenced, Luc noticed Mashk but could not see Gabriel. Unperturbed, as they spent less time together than when they had first arrived in Kebec, he concentrated on the dance. The girls and women had formed a large circle. Behind each one stood a warrior. They all began to move and sing in unison, lifting one foot before stamping it down, and then repeating the action with the other foot. The beat of the drum was hypnotic and Luc watched, riveted, as the dancers moved their bodies in a series of gestures, all the while remaining on the same spot.

Then out of the corner of his eye, Luc became aware of Mashk and another brave making their way round the outside of the circle. He blinked, double-checked, and was certain: without the characteristic gait, Gabriel would have been unrecognisable.

"Have you lost control of your senses?" Luc demanded, as the two men came nearer him.

Gabriel's face split into a wide grin. "It is the perfect solution."

"Why?"

"I cannot go to war as a Frenchman, as Champlain has his soldiers. However, I can go with Mashk in his canoe. Look around you, Luc. There are hundreds of warriors here. Who is going to see me?"

Luc studied his friend. He had known Gabriel all his life but the man before him was a stranger. Mashk (or perhaps Wyome, as Luc had not seen her among the dancers) had tied Gabriel's hair away from his face, fastening it on the back of his head with a leather strip. It was plastered with bear grease to keep it in place while the rest of his hair hung loose past his shoulders. It was short for a Montagnais, but longer than the colonists usually wore theirs, despite the recent tendency to be lax about hair trimming. His black eyes danced in a face painted red for war, and what dusky skin was left uncovered by the ochre pigment was not that far from Mashk's own tone.

"I'll be fitted out with armour and weapons when we are ready to leave."

Foreboding gripped Luc, as he ran his eyes from the feather which adorned Gabriel's hair, past the breechcloth, to the soft leather moccasins on his feet. "You cannot go."

"I can," replied Gabriel. "The sagamore has given his permission."

"You will stand out. All the other Montagnais are barefoot."

Gabriel laughed. "Who will notice my feet?"

Mashk also responded. "If the terrain is too rough we will also cover our feet and Gabriel's will harden as time passes."

"Just like your hands." Fear for Gabriel, and for himself being abandoned, made Luc malicious. "You look ridiculous," he announced.

Mashk's face darkened, unobserved by Luc. Gabriel shrugged. He had not seen himself but he did not care what

Luc thought. All the assurances that they would stick together were temporarily forgotten, for the greatest of adventures was about to begin.

Ribbons of rose streaked the sky as the great armada of canoes set off. Gabriel's leaving of Luc had been acrimonious, with harsh words spoken by both. As he settled into the rhythm of paddling, his friend's last words thrummed in his head. *How can a physician, as you claim to be, fight an enemy who has personally done you no harm? How can you cleave a man's skull in half or take his scalp?* Gabriel had turned away, impatient with the indignation on Luc's face, and had followed Mashk without a backward glance. He had missed Luc's final well-wishing, and never witnessed his friend's desolation as Luc watched the spectacle until it disappeared.

Gabriel was placed between Kitchi and Matwau, with Mashk at the rear. The canoe, despite being eight paces long and a pace wide in the centre, was significantly more crowded with four men, their armour, and their supplies aboard. It was more difficult to manoeuvre and Kitchi shouted brusque instructions to Gabriel, to avoid capsizing. The latter eyed the ribs of white cedar strengthening the birchbark and recalled an earlier conversation with his grandfather, who had read Champlain's description of the canoes in the explorer's book about New France. It was as if his grandfather was there, in the canoe, reminding him of their lightness and the need for skilful handling.

By the time they reached Sainte-Croix, where the war party had initially met the Huron and Algonquin, Gabriel's muscles were protesting, but there was a more pressing problem than an aching body. Here, against all expectation, Pont-Gravé left the expedition to return to Tadoussak, taking some of the French soldiers with him. The demeanour of Gabriel's companions changed and they murmured among themselves about lack of trust. At last, Mashk asked, "Do your chiefs think some of our warriors will attack your settlement while the chiefs are away?" Gabriel had no answer. He was no longer party to any French decisions.

They journeyed on, Champlain now with only twelve armed Frenchmen, and five days later they reached the River of the Iroquois. They stopped to rest, eating heartily of the venison, fish, and waterfowl caught by the hunters. Men sat around in groups, talking. The enormity of their actions became reality, as before them was the country of their enemies. Soon they would meet them; the Iroquois, whose fighting prowess was renowned.

Matwau bit into his meat, wiping away the juices with the back of his hand. "I can think of better things to do than chase the Mohawk."

Kitchi's eyes narrowed. "Can you?"

Matwau laughed. "You still do not think of me as one of you, after all this time."

Mashk and Kitchi exchanged glances. Gabriel leaned towards the fire and pulled some venison away from the bone. "What would you do?" he asked.

Matwau studied him, taking the measure of him. It was the first time the Frenchman had spoken to him directly. "I would not waste my time chasing the wind. I would hunt so that food would be plentiful over the winter."

"Why come then?" Gabriel was aware that not all male members of the tribe were warriors.

Matwau looked deep into Gabriel's eyes as if searching for his soul. "Do I have a choice?"

An uneasiness settled over their group. Ahanu, his cheerful face sombre for once, said, "I agree with Matwau."

Rowtag added, "Some of us must hunt. Who will provide game for the women to preserve? Look what happened last year. We must do more in the summer."

Infuriated, Kitchi stood up, glared at the circle of men, and strode away. Gabriel listened, trying to understand, as the remaining four argued animatedly until they fell silent. Mashk held up his hand, turned to Gabriel, and spoke slowly, "Ahanu and Rowtag are to return. They will share the game among all our families. We will go on to the land of the Mohawk."

Gabriel stole a glance at Matwau but his expression was unfathomable.

Many left: instead of four hundred warriors, Champlain could only rely on sixty. The great flotilla of more than a hundred canoes was reduced to twenty-four as he led the war party down the river. The current was strong, the eddies dangerous, and Gabriel struggled to keep control of his paddle, but it was more difficult for the unmanageable shallop. Once the party reached a lake and beheld a series of rapids, it was obvious to the French that the vessel had to be abandoned. The remainder of the journey would be by canoe.

Kitchi was triumphant. "I knew that boat could not pass the rapids and it is too heavy to carry."

"Look!" Mashk pointed. "The soldiers do not want to leave the shallop." Gabriel could not believe what he saw. It was true. Champlain was leaving the boat with only two men, one of whom Gabriel believed to be François Addenin, a renowned arquebusier. The other Frenchmen remained aboard. Champlain called out to the gathered braves and reassured them that he would continue on the warpath and travel with them in their canoes. Mashk nudged Gabriel. "You made a good choice. You are already with us." Gabriel kept his head down, glad their canoe was full as he did not want an eagle-eyed Champlain taking a closer look at him. Kitchi, lacking the patience to wait, started to shout instructions. They needed to disembark and carry the canoe round the rapids. Slowly they started to inch their way along the shore while the shallop started her journey back to Kebec.

The battle would commence at dawn. Gabriel sat behind Kitchi, their canoe lashed together with the others in the centre of the lake, and watched the sliver of moon ride across the sky. It was a dark night of great clarity, and he felt he could reach up and touch the stars. They shone pure and white in the inky blackness. Behind him, Matwau's slow and regular breathing spoke of sleep, but rest eluded Gabriel. Every muscle was tense. Suddenly, a piercing shriek rent the air: it was the Mohawks crying scorn on their enemies. Noise erupted all around him as the northern tribes replied with equally stinging words. Matwau woke up and mumbled something unintelligible under his breath.

Much to their surprise, the northern tribes had come across the Mohawks earlier that night. The latter, also astounded, had retreated, aware that their thick, elm canoes, although strong, were no match for their foes' birchbark ones. The slow clumsy Iroquois boats were at a great disadvantage if engagement was to take place on the water. Kitchi had immediately ordered to make for the middle of the lake while the Mohawks returned to shore, landing between two distinctive promontories. Matwau had leaned forward and whispered in Gabriel's ear, "This is a magical place. Ticoneroga – where the two waters meet."

They settled to sit out the night, the songs of the Mohawk,

accompanied by the sounds of felling wood, floated across the water. The enemy was constructing a fort, much the same as the Montagnais had done on their route down the lake, which Champlain had named after himself. The journey had taken two weeks, due to the full moon. When they had arrived, it hung high in the sky, its great silver orb illuminating the water and all who travelled on its glistening surface, so they had camped in the upper reaches of the lake until it was safe to move.

Then they had advanced at night, and when daylight came, they had walked deep into the woods. Too near the enemy to make fire, they had eaten cold corncake and then tried to sleep. The medicine men, who had accompanied the war party, interpreted their dreams, and the warriors had planned meticulously, arranging and re-arranging sticks on the ground to represent battle tactics.

It was time. A fight to the death had already been agreed. Envoys from the northern tribes had crossed to the shore during the night. The Mohawks were determined to defend their territory. Before the first rays would light the eastern horizon, the signal was given to make for land. Gabriel eased his stiff body, rolling his shoulders, and flexing his legs. He grabbed his paddle, ready to glide silently across the black water.

NINE

G ABRIEL WAITED WITH THE MAIN BODY OF THE war party, positioned next to Matwau, with Mashk behind him. Kitchi had been chosen to be part of the advance group, who used their honed hunting skills to approach the enemy fort. All eyes were fixed on the wooden structure and in the dawn light, a lone Mohawk scout crept out, only to be felled by a Montagnais arrow. Immediately, up to two hundred fully armed warriors flooded out from behind the barricade.

The battle commenced. On the open ground, between the trees and the lakeshore, both sides lined up in close formation. Gabriel became aware of thirst, his tongue overlarge in his dry mouth. There were about two hundred paces between him and the Iroquois and with each step the gap was shortening. At the head of the enemy, he could see two chiefs, distinguished by their headgear of three high feathers. Soon, there were only fifty paces between the two sides and Gabriel started to panic. All around him, the warriors were calling for Champlain. "Where is he?" Gabriel asked himself. "Where are the other Frenchmen?" Suddenly, the Montagnais ranks parted and Champlain stepped through.

Gabriel watched as Champlain advanced alone, until he

was only thirty paces from the Mohawks, his armour dazzling in the rising sun. The enemy stood transfixed. However, recovering quickly, one of the chiefs raised his bow: in answer, Champlain took aim. The assembled Iroquois responded by drawing their bowstrings. The shot rang out, deafening. For a moment, Gabriel's view was obscured by a great cloud of white smoke. Then an almighty shout filled the air around him: the two Mohawk chiefs lay dead, while a third warrior had injuries so severe, he was sure to die.

Although very frightened, the Mohawks retaliated. Arrows rained down on Gabriel. He felt the impact as they struck his armour and one glancing blow knocked off his helmet. Rather than struggle to find it, he concentrated on firing, trying to keep in time with Matwau. Totally absorbed, he was oblivious to Addenin and his companion, crouching in the cover of the trees. Gunfire thundered in the air again. The two Frenchmen used their arquebuses to deadly effect, as did Champlain, who reloaded. A third chief was killed and the attack on their flank was so unexpected that the Mohawk formation floundered and fell apart. The warriors ran towards the forest, hotly pursued. The battle was over almost before it had begun.

Gabriel hung back, helping Mashk, who had a flesh wound: an arrow had grazed the top of his arm. Although not serious, the cut was bleeding profusely and, on the brave's order, Gabriel was applying force to a handful of moss to stem the flow. Around them lay about fifty dead Mohawk fighters yet none had been lost among the Montagnais, Algonquin, and Huron. There were some warriors, like Mashk, nursing wounds but none appeared serious.

After only three hours, the victors were climbing into their canoes, having looted the Mohawk camp, and having celebrated their success with ritual feasting and dancing. The spirits of the living, and of the dead, had been appeased, and the eleven Mohawk captives firmly bound. The war party headed north, paddling quickly, eager to put some distance between it and the enemy: for the Iroquois would soon regroup and prepare to attack.

They paddled until nightfall, having covered upwards of forty-five leagues, and made camp on the eastern shore of the lake. Exhausted, Gabriel wished only to sleep, but his companions were determined to wreak vengeance on the unfortunate captives. He watched, horrified, as they chose one and began their systematic torture. Warriors were invited, in turn, to burn the captive's back. Gabriel slunk away to the farthest shadows, appalled that he might be handed a flaming brand.

The Mohawk braved his ordeal stoically, even after his tormentors tore out his nails and applied fire to the ends of his fingers. Unable to stomach the sight any longer, Gabriel turned away, moving nearer the trees. He heard the poor man's screams as he was scalped, had hot gum poured on his head, and his hands cut off. He heard Champlain refuse his allies' offer to participate and was flooded with relief when they finally accepted the Frenchman's offer to dispatch the dying man. At the sound of the arquebus firing, Gabriel opened his eyes. The Mohawk was dead but it was not the end.

A small group ripped open the body. They threw the entrails into the water before cutting off the victim's head, arms, and legs. The scalp was flayed and kept as a trophy to take home. Gabriel was distressed to see Mashk lift the scalp high, his face lit with triumph. Another warrior, one Gabriel did not know, took the Mohawk's heart and cut it into several pieces. With his legs shaking and already queasy, Gabriel finally vomited violently. He bent over, holding his abdomen, while the other captives were forced to eat the pieces. Although they took the heart into their mouths, they would not swallow and the Algonquin warriors, who were guarding the captives, made them spit the pieces out and throw them into the lake.

Stunned by what he had seen, Gabriel did not notice another figure, also deep in the shadows. Matwau was only a couple of paces away. He moved quickly, grabbing Gabriel from behind, and with alarming speed he unsheathed his knife with one hand, while silencing Gabriel with the other.

The deep azure sky, reflected in Tadoussak Bay, was almost cloudless, and the light breeze which ruffled Luc's hair augured well for the beginning of Champlain's voyage back to France. The young man's longing to sail home immobilised him and rendered all rational thought impossible: for Gabriel had not returned with the war party. Desolate and alone, Luc watched Champlain's vessel disappear round the headland, his eyes fixed on the ship's wake until it was no longer discernible, and the still water magnified his sense of loss.

A sharp slap on the back startled him. Luc turned to see Etienne Brûlé's cheerful face, his eyes full of sympathy. "What are you going to do?"

"I have no idea." He had tried to keep Gabriel's disappearance to himself, expecting his friend to appear any time, and now it was too late to inform Champlain. Uncertain how the new governor, Jean de Godet du Parc, would react, Luc was trapped by indecision. He knew he needed to seek out Mashk but lacked the courage to visit the Montagnais village. The sight of the war party on its return, the canoes proudly carrying the decorated scalps of the enemy displayed on sticks, had filled Luc with dismay and he was unwilling to approach the warrior alone.

As if reading Luc's thoughts, Etienne announced, "I will go to the village with you."

"You will?"

"Yes," Etienne replied, with a touch of superiority. "Gabriel wasn't the only man who has been learning their language."

It was only a short distance to the summer camp and they were there before Luc could change his mind. As they drew nearer, they saw Wyome sitting outside of her wigwam, preparing fish. She stopped her task and waited, her face impassive. Luc spoke first. "Mashk?"

Slowly, and with great dignity, Wyome rose and pulled back the hide covering the entrance. Luc stepped into the dim interior, followed by Etienne, and immediately Mashk sprang up, his movement releasing the pungent scent of the spruce branches which cushioned his bed. He had been sleeping, his body craving the rest vital for healing his wound. He eyed his visitors suspiciously and Etienne was quick to put the brave at ease. "I see you carry the mark of battle." Mashk silently acknowledged the comment, his eyes never leaving Luc. It was unnerving. Etienne continued speaking in the language of the Montagnais. "You have won great honour. You have vanquished the Mohawk."

Mashk, his eyes shining, inclined his head towards Wyome. Feeling increasingly uncomfortable, Luc watched the silent exchange. Wyome slipped outside and when she returned, she stood directly in front of Luc. She indicated that he should take the object in her hands. Luc glanced down, his stomach heaved, but he dared not refuse. Gingerly, he took the Mohawk scalp, the black long hair still attached, and did not know what to say.

Etienne came to the rescue. "A magnificent trophy," he said. "We are glad to see the achievement of our Montagnais brother." He paused for a moment, giving the scalp his full attention before he added, "We come to honour you, but also to learn about our friend, Gabriel."

Mashk's face darkened, his eyes became hard, and he began gesturing excitedly. His words, when he spoke, were completely meaningless to Luc, who turned to Etienne for help.

"Is Gabriel alive?"

"He was."

"Where is he then?"

"He has disappeared with the Iroquois, Matwau."

Luc was aghast. "Willingly?"

"I don't know."

"Ask Mashk for more details."

There was a quick exchange with Mashk becoming even more animated. Etienne explained, "Mashk doesn't know. He didn't see them leave."

"Then how does he know they are together?"

"He believes that Matwau has taken the opportunity to return to his people."

Mashk, who had understood the Frenchmen's conversation, mimed the taking of a prisoner.

Icy fingers of fear gripped Luc. "He believes Gabriel is a captive?"

"Yes."

"But why would this warrior take Gabriel?" Luc appealed to Mashk, who spoke in French for the first time.

"White man will bring Matwau honour. Much honour. He has captured a Frenchman. The French have the magic weapons which can kill two chiefs instantly."

"What will the Iroquois do to him?" asked Luc, trying to keep his voice steady, as he looked at the pitiable prize in his hands.

Gabriel ran, his own ragged pants pounding in his ears. The sound obliterated all others as he struggled through the gloaming. He did not hear the snap of twigs beneath his feet, nor the gentle lap of the water, nor Matwau, running silently behind him, but he knew the warrior was there. Although stronger and fitter than he had been as a student in Paris, Gabriel could never outrun the brave, whose long legs effortlessly covered the leagues.

He lost track of time. As the twilight deepened, he could no longer see and he stumbled. Matwau yanked him up by the hair and tried to push him onwards. Using the last dregs of energy, Gabriel swung round to face his captor, uttering between gasps.

"Kill me now and have done with it."

A slow smile played around Matwau's lips but it was invisible in the darkness. "I am not going to kill you yet."

"Where are you taking me?" Each word laboured as Gabriel fought for breath.

"Home."

Gabriel was bending over, his hands on his thighs. His heart was slowing, now the physical exertion had stopped, but it was still racing. He tried to think coherently but the ability had deserted him: he could only articulate his need to stop. Matwau looked around, assessing the terrain. "Go," he said, shoving Gabriel towards the thicker trees. Spent, Gabriel staggered, falling against the first trunk he reached. Matwau settled down next to him, the knife still unsheathed. The Mohawk waited several minutes before he placed his knife on the ground, furthest away from Gabriel, and reached into the leather pouch slung across his chest. He had come prepared. Gabriel, too tired to eat, waved the offered dried moose away, and surrendered to exhausted sleep. Matwau remained sitting bolt upright, methodically chewing the leathery strip, and dreaming of the praise he would receive when he returned to his village with a captive Frenchman.

They travelled for three days, heading south, the blue water of Lake Champlain their constant companion. Gabriel had given up all thoughts of fleeing, for Matwau, always alert, was superior in every way. The reasons why escape was impossible played in a continuous loop as Gabriel ran: his captor could run faster, he was armed, he had the food, and although game was plentiful, Gabriel lacked the means to survive on fresh food. Not for the first time, he questioned his sanity on embarking on such an adventure. Luc had been correct. It had been madness to go on the warpath. Now, all Gabriel could do was bide his time and wait for an opportunity.

It was nearing noon when Matwau suddenly halted. He stood perfectly still; his attention caught.

"Quickly," he said, pushing Gabriel towards the trees.

They crouched in the undergrowth, the shade a welcome relief from the hot sun shining in a sky of perfect blue, and waited. Gabriel, relieved to have stopped running, took deep breaths, filling his lungs completely with the scent of pine. He shifted, trying to ease his muscles, and Matwau remonstrated, placing a finger to his lips. Gradually, Gabriel became aware of the approach of men, walking with caution, their feet almost soundlessly treading across the forest floor. Only the scuttling of small rodents and the call of a startled bird betrayed the four men, who were soon clearly visible. A hunting party, armed with arrows and spears, the men moved as one in case a stray turkey crossed their path. Gabriel knew they would wait until dusk to hunt in earnest, so he prayed for the group to pass by quickly. His legs were aching and a tickle in his throat threatened a coughing fit. Matwau placed his hand firmly on his captive's shoulder, applying such force that Gabriel feared his legs would buckle completely.

Gabriel's prayer was answered. As silently as they had approached, the hunters disappeared. Matwau waited long enough to be certain of safety, before ordering Gabriel to stand up. "Go," he said.

"I need to eat."

"We must move away from here."

"Enemy?" asked Gabriel, pointing to where the hunting party had disappeared into the trees.

"No."

"Mohawk?"

"Seneca."

"If those men are your allies, why must we leave?"

"You are *my* prisoner!" Matwau thumped his closed fist against his chest.

Gabriel watched him closely, realisation dawning. "You are worried about returning home."

Matwau's eyes narrowed. "Go," he ordered.

Gabriel started to walk away from the shelter of the forest, towards the twinkling water. He was curious. "Where is home?"

"Towards the setting sun."

Surprised Matwau had answered, Gabriel decided to continue. "How long have you lived with the Montagnais?"

"Eleven summers."

Gabriel calculated; the Mohawk must have been a boy of about twelve when he was captured. A long time to be away but he had obviously been treated well. Matwau's skin was smooth, his body revealed no scars, and his glossy hair spoke of health. It hung in a thick black curtain down his back. Encouraged by his civility, Gabriel looked over his shoulder at Matwau, and asked, "How far is it?"

"One or two more sunsets."

"How will you find your village?" Gabriel was thinking of the temporary Montagnais villages.

"It will be where it was."

"How do you know?"

"The Mohawk find a good place to settle. We live there for up to twenty summers. I can remember our village being built." Matwau met Gabriel's eyes and repeated more forcefully, "It will be where it was." Then he added, "We grow beans, squash, and corn."

Gabriel turned his attention to his feet, conscious of the uneven ground, but he could hear Matwau clearly as he had raised his voice. "We are not foolish like the Montagnais who boast they are great warriors and hunters, but don't grow enough to feed their families over the winter. We are the greatest nation, the greatest warriors but we also farm, as well as hunt, to keep starvation at bay."

Two sunsets had passed and at first light they set off. As the journey neared its end they travelled at an even faster pace. Matwau's excitement, tinged with apprehension, increased as he recognised the familiar terrain. The lake was now behind them to the north, and he knew that once he reached the river, he would almost be home. Continuing south, they made good speed, the hills of his home, green and welcoming, clearly visible to the west.

Once at the river, Matwau prepared to cross with feverish haste while Gabriel regarded the water warily. Although much shallower than when the river was swollen by the winter snow, it was, nevertheless, in his estimation, too fast-flowing. "Surely we are not going to cross here!" Matwau did not respond. It was unnecessary. His answer was to remove the long fibrous belt, wrapped several times around his waist, which held up his breechcloth. He indicated for Gabriel to do likewise and then, using both belts, Matwau made a longer rope. He tied one end round his waist and the other around Gabriel, securing them tightly. He stuffed the breechcloths into his satchel and started to wade into the water, giving Gabriel no choice but to follow.

The water was icy, despite the warm summer's day, but Matwau showed no signs of discomfort. He waded purposefully towards the opposite bank, pulling Gabriel behind him. The current became stronger, it swept Gabriel off his feet, and only Matwau's fast reaction prevented him from going under. The Mohawk started swimming, his strong strokes sliced through the water, and Gabriel struggled to keep up. The rope went taut, as the swell caught Gabriel a second time, and for one heart-stopping moment the water sucked him down. Feeling the drag, Matwau heaved on the line, his own feet finally finding purchase on the riverbed. The Frenchman was too valuable a trophy to lose at this stage and Matwau half-carried his gasping prize to the bank.

Once there, Matwau allowed a brief stop, to rest, before dressing. Then he forced Gabriel to start running. Matwau was nearly home. It was as if he had wings, and Gabriel, irritated by the slap of his wet breechcloth against his thighs, demanded that he slow down, but to no avail. By the time the late afternoon sun bathed the surrounding fields of corn in golden light, they could see the village, large and palisaded, with longhouses laid out in rows.

A shout heralded their arrival, followed immediately by a crowd gathering. Matwau's tension was tangible. Gabriel fought the fear fomenting within him. His eyes swept the crowd and his terror subsided slightly when he realised most faces were female, or very young or old male. The crowd advanced, staring. An eerie silence fell as the women at the front stopped after a few paces. They peeled away to either side, leaving one woman isolated. Gabriel blinked, his eyes stinging from salty sweat, but he did not dare wipe his brow.

The woman was elderly. Silver hair hung limply to her

waist and her face was etched with sadness. As Gabriel watched, silent tears coursed down the creases of her cheeks. She uttered what sounded like a moan as she walked up to Matwau. "Nawat," she said, her voice breaking with emotion.

"I am Nawat." Matwau's expression softened as the old woman reached out to him. "An-nah," he whispered. "Mother."

TEN

A SINGLE BLOOD-CURDLING WAIL PIERCED THE AIR and was taken up by the surrounding women and girls until the noise was deafening. Gabriel fought the urge to cover his ears and concentrated on stilling his hammering heart. All eyes were on him; eyes full of such venom that he felt he was facing death. Desperate, he scanned the layout of the village, his body posed for flight.

"Don't do it." Matwau's voice, low and urgent, was barely audible. "Do not show fear."

Gabriel stared at his captor in astonishment, trying to assess the man's motives. Images of the tortured captive Mohawk leapt, unwanted, into his mind and if he had not been so terrified, Gabriel might have laughed at the absurdity of it all. He had up to a hundred females baying for his blood and Matwau was issuing orders, advising him not to run. Gabriel continued staring, widening his eyes further. Matwau repeated, "Your only chance is not to show fear."

"Why are they wailing?"

"I have told my mother of my father's death at the hands of the Montagnais."

"I am a Frenchman," Gabriel pointed out, hopefully.

"Someone must pay."

"Who will decide?"

"My mother."

The wailing had reached a feverish crescendo when the women suddenly ceased, taking their cue from the widow. She walked forward and stopped directly in front of Gabriel. She had to crane her head to look up into his eyes. Hers were black pebbles, hard and uncompromising, in the soft folds of her face. She indicated that he must kneel, which he did with as much dignity as he could muster, trying to present a strong, calm demeanour. Reaching out and feeling the muscles at the top of his arms, honed from relentless physical labour since he had arrived in New France, she then prodded and poked him further. She forced open his mouth, with surprising force, and inspected his teeth. After a pause for considered thought, she turned to Matwau. Without any words being spoken, Matwau nodded in agreement.

The old woman gestured to Gabriel that he should stand. Taking him by both arms she turned him around to face the assembled crowd. Her voice rang out, clear and startlingly deep for such a small woman. The crowd's response was loud and animated. Drums began to beat. Gabriel felt his chest might explode. Matwau waited a moment, enjoying his power, before he relented. "My mother is to take you into her household to replace my father."

Relief flooded through Gabriel, to be instantly replaced by questions which jostled in the chaos of his emotions. He suppressed them all. It was enough, for the time being, that he was not going to die. He would see another sunrise.

A medley of sounds and smells assaulted Gabriel's senses as he entered the longhouse, his eyes taking some time to adjust to the dark smoky interior. He followed Matwau's mother closely as she made her way towards the central hearth, skirting around the other occupants they passed as they slowly progressed. He was aware of, rather than saw, separate living spaces on either side of the fires where the activity of living had recommenced after the excitement of the afternoon.

By the time they halted, after a good twenty paces, Gabriel could see that the central aisle was about three paces wide. He turned slightly and looked over his shoulder, past Matwau. The line of fires behind him was about the same length as that in front of him. Shafts of sunlight pooled onto the beaten earth; the skin coverings drawn back from the ventilation holes to maximise the light. Due to her status, Matwau's mother occupied the chamber nearest the central hearth. She lifted the hide covering, which would afford them some privacy, and invited Matwau and Gabriel to sit.

Bringing them bowls of thick corn soup, flavoured with fish, the old woman fussed over the two young men with as much care as any devoted mother. They ate heartily, enjoying the novelty of warm food after weeks of being on the move. She watched them avidly for some time, before addressing Gabriel. Leaning over, she prodded his chest with one of her thin fingers and then tapped her own chest. "Sheauga."

Matwau answered for him. "Gabriel."

She repeated the name several times, rolling the unfamiliar syllables around her mouth. Speaking her thoughts, she asked, "What does it mean?"

Her son was about to explain that the white man did not use names as they did, when a figure silently slipped into the chamber. Gabriel did not notice, as he had turned his attention to the small loaves of bread Sheauga had placed between them. Freshly baked, the bread appeared to contain a mixture of dried fruit and nuts. He took a loaf, pulled it apart, and was about to take a bite. A voice, soft and musical, cut through his concentration. "Man Unknown."

Oheo chuckled as the white man's head jerked up. The piece of bread in his hand forgotten, he bit down on his own tongue and then tried, unsuccessfully, not to wince. Her grandmother's eyes flashed, a warning even Oheo dared not ignore. She steadied her merriment and appraised the young white man. He appeared to be of a similar age to her uncle, who had miraculously returned after being missing for as long as she could remember. She had missed the clamour of the men's arrival as she had been bathing in the river following her time in the menstrual hut. Her sister, Aarushi, had sought her out, full of the news, and had urged her to make haste. It was such an unusual occurrence for a new man to be taken into her family unit, even more so as he was to take her grandmother's husband's place, that Oheo rushed her ablutions and ran to the longhouse, leaving Aarushi struggling to catch up.

Oheo was disappointed. She had expected the white man to be more fascinating. The man eating her grandmother's soup bore no resemblance to the white men of her imagination. Iroquois traders, who had travelled further east, had returned with tales of men with eyes the colour of the summer sky, yet the man before her returned her scrutiny with eyes as black as her own. There was also no evidence of the corn-coloured hair as his, under the bear grease, appeared as dark as that of any Mohawk brave. Her disenchantment made her sharp.

"Do not be too comfortable, Man Unknown."

Gabriel failed to understand but there was no mistaking the hostility of her tone. He turned to Matwau for clarification, who spoke more slowly. "Before the tribe adopts you, you need to prove your valour to the women."

Gabriel raised an eyebrow, a gesture which did not go unnoticed by Oheo. This white man who was not a white man, for even his skin was darker than she expected, was far too confident, in her opinion. She fixed him with a haughty stare. "You have to endure the trial if you are to be worthy of the Mohawk."

Gabriel accompanied Matwau, feeling like a lamb being led to slaughter. Even though he had been in the village for three days and had been welcomed, he still faced uncertainty. Matwau had explained to him that without a display of his bravery, he would not be fully adopted into the tribe. Too confused to argue, for he had believed himself safe, Gabriel drew on every vestige of courage.

His heart sank when he saw the crowd. The women and children of the village all carried whips fashioned from strips of hide. Gabriel's dismay increased as they formed two parallel lines. Upwards of a hundred pairs of eyes turned towards him and he was fighting his treacherous fear when Sheauga appeared at his side. "You must run between the whips."

Gabriel focused on the end of the avenue, obliterating the two threatening rows from his vision. He calculated that his only chance was to run faster than he had ever run in his life and to use his arms to protect his face and chest. His back would have to bear the brunt of the lashes. His medical knowledge told him that the bear grease which covered his body, liberally applied by Matwau the previous evening, would afford him some protection but he knew that by the end of the ordeal his back and arms would be cut to ribbons. He steeled himself to begin, knowing that if he fell from exhaustion he might be tortured to death.

Amidst the shouting, the crack of the whips, and the unimaginable agony, Gabriel stumbled. Once, twice, and then a third time. His vision blurred, his legs began to buckle, but he refused to go down. Consumed by the need to survive the searing pain, he did not see the end of the lines and he ran eight more paces before he registered that the whipping had stopped. Staggering forward, on the point of collapse, his fall was broken by the solid form of Matwau. The brave's words penetrated Gabriel's torment. "Stand tall." With the utmost effort Gabriel stayed on his feet, each step excruciating as he walked back to the longhouse with the sound of jubilation echoing in his ears.

Back in her chamber, Sheauga bathed his broken flesh. On the worst of the wounds, she applied poultices made from the crushed roots of the violet. She held a cup of strong willow bark tea to his lips and forced him to swallow the bitter liquid. "It will help the pain," she said, as she helped him to lie down.

He lay on his front for four days, drifting in a dreamlike state. He was back home in Caors, his grandfather as clear as if he was in the longhouse with him. He was in Paris, drinking with his friends, the enjoyment always tinged with guilt that his grandfather would disapprove. He was a child again, playing hide and seek with his grandmother, her eyes full of mischief. A cool hand felt his forehead and he was transported back to Bologna. He was six years old and in bed with a fever. His beloved mama, dead now for so many years, was leaning over him, concern on her lovely face. He blinked, the face came into focus and, instead of Sheauga, who was usually there, he looked directly into Oheo's eyes. She was so close he could smell the juniper needles she used in the infusion to rinse her hair. It was too much effort to speak, his eyelids drooped, and Oheo was gone, once again to be replaced by an image of his mother before he slipped into the blissful oblivion of sleep.

On the eighth day, he tried to haul himself up into a sitting position and the agony made him catch his breath. He drank the willow bark tea as instructed, he endured the discomfort while Sheauga changed his poultices, and he looked for any sign of Oheo, but to no avail. Sheauga was sympathetic. "It will take time," she assured him. "It will take time."

Racked with pain, he lay back down to wait out the long days it would take to heal.

Gabriel sat outside the longhouse, with his back towards the soothing warmth of the afternoon sun, idly tracing patterns with a stick on the ground. The hot days of high summer had passed, to be replaced by the kinder days of autumn. Debilitated, but no longer in pain, he fought to contain his frustration, for the sharp chill in the mornings told of the approaching cold weather. He would never survive the journey back to Kebec and the thought of another winter, this time with the Mohawk, filled him with dread. Yet he had no choice.

Bored, he flung the stick away and surveyed what he could see of the village. It was a hive of quiet activity. The hunting parties, who had dispersed to temporary camps, were returning laden with their spoils. The previous day, some of the men had come back with three moose and now a group of women were preparing the meat, ready to be hung in the bark-lined storage huts. He could see Aarushi among the older women, her sharp knife cutting through an impressive haunch. He had hoped to get a glimpse of Oheo but she was out in the fields, helping with the harvest. The corn and the squash were safely gathered in, but the knobbly tubers, which the women dug out of the earth, could be harvested anytime if the ground was not frozen. He looked forward to eating them as he enjoyed their nutty flavour.

Her task completed, Aarushi rose and walked towards him, limping badly. Broken in an accident when she was a child, her left leg had healed bent and shorter than the right one, despite

the best efforts of the medicine man who had packed the leg
with sphagnum moss and then had immobilised it with bark
splints bound by hide. She considered herself lucky as, when
the splints were removed, she could walk, only troubled by
discomfort when the northern winds brought the intense cold.
However, unable to be as active as the other girls, Aarushi
spent her time preparing and cooking food, and Sheauga had
chosen her to help tend to Gabriel.

"Do you need anything?" she asked, as she sat down
awkwardly next to him.

"No, thank you," he replied, without looking at her.

Aarushi followed his gaze. She had noticed that he had
a habit of staring into the distance, focusing on nothing in
particular. Slightly nervous, she took a deep breath and asked,
"Is Man Unknown the true meaning of Gabriel?" It was what
she had wanted to know, ever since Oheo had explained his
name, that first afternoon in the longhouse.

Torn between gaining favour with Oheo, by giving her
credit for his naming, and telling the truth, Gabriel took his
time to answer. "No, my name means God's messenger."

"God?"

"Yes, God – Allah."

Her forehead puckered with puzzlement.

Gabriel elucidated. "The Creator of all things."

Aarushi continued to watch him intently.

"Who is your Creator?" he prompted.

Pleased to have his attention, Aarushi launched into a
long explanation. "Long, long ago, before the earth was made,
the Sky People lived on an island in the sky. One day, one of
the women told her husband she was expecting twins. He was
furious and pulled up the tree in the centre of the island. It was
the tree of light as there was no sun. The tree left a big hole
and the woman could see the water below. As she was looking,

her husband pushed her and she fell from the sky. The animals who lived in the water helped her, especially Little Toad. They spread mud on the back of Big Turtle so that the woman could walk on land."

She stopped to check that Gabriel was following, curious to see how he responded to the actions of the husband. He did not comment so she stood up and mimed a sprinkling action with her arms. "The woman created the stars. Then she made the sun and the moon."

Gabriel considered this. "A woman created the sun, moon, and stars?"

Aarushi nodded, enjoying the moment, for it was rare for her to have an audience.

"What happened to the twins?"

"The woman gave birth to two male children. One, called Sapling, was tender-hearted and compassionate. He created all that was good. His brother, Flint, had a heart as cold as his name. He was responsible for all that was bad. The two sons fought and Flint destroyed much that was good on the earth. Finally, Flint was defeated but he cannot die. He lives on Big Turtle's back and his anger erupts from the earth."

Aarushi sat back down again. Suddenly self-conscious, she looked sideways at Gabriel. Searching for something to say, she asked, "Do you know of Sapling and Flint?"

"No – but I know about good and evil."

They sat in silence. The sun was sinking rapidly, the temperature was falling, and soon it would be dusk. In the distance, the sound of chattering could be heard as the women returned from the fields. In a few minutes, they would be back at the longhouses. It might be some time before Gabriel had another opportunity.

"Aarushi, what does your name mean?"

"First ray of the sun."

He smiled at her. "That is beautiful." Happiness lit Aarushi's face.

He tried to sound nonchalant. "What does Oheo mean?"

"Beautiful one," replied Aarushi, as some of her delight drained away.

Gabriel had yet to finish. "Why does Matwau's mother call him Nawat?" he asked, although he thought he had already worked out the answer.

"It is his name – left-handed one. You must have noticed that."

Of course, he had, but Gabriel's purpose was not to have a conversation about names. He had planned to bring up Sheauga casually. Now his back was healing, he wanted to assess just how much he was expected to replace Matwau's father. "Aarushi, why is Matwau's mother so elderly?" he asked, judging that she would answer truthfully.

"In our tribe, it is the custom for young warriors to be married to older women. When my grandmother took her second husband she was twice his age. She was over forty summers when she gave birth to Nawat. He was a surprise child."

"Do young men not marry young women?"

Aarushi wondered why he had not understood. "No, Gabriel," she answered, speaking slowly. "Young maidens marry older men, sometimes as old as sixty summers."

He studied his feet. It was what he had come to believe, by observing the tribe. Aarushi explained, "It is our way. It ensures wisdom is passed down from the old to the young."

It was too late to say more as the women were almost upon them. He could not stop himself seeking out Oheo, who was talking animatedly with two other maidens. She caught him looking, tilted her chin, and studiously ignored him as she walked past.

ELEVEN

THE WORLD WAS WHITE. SOME DAYS THE SUN shone so brightly on the glistening carpet that Gabriel's eyes hurt, despite his attempts to shade his eyes. On others, metallic clouds, heavy with the next fall of snow, totally obliterated the sun, and he experienced a crushing sensation as if the sky was purposefully bearing down on him. It was these days which heightened his longing for France, increasing his desire to be walking the streets of Paris, after a day at the university, or sharing a meal with friends, or even spending a quiet evening in Caors with his grandfather and aunt.

It was mid-afternoon. The women of the family were sewing by the fire, not the beadwork which needed greater light but vital garment making. As usual, Gabriel's eyes were drawn to Oheo. He studied her for some time, her beautiful face illuminated by the flames as she pulled the bone needle deftly through the leather. He was feeling increasingly frustrated; torn between his admiration of her and his desire to flee. If he tried to analyse why he resented her attitude, he could find no answer. He knew he did not want to remain with the Mohawk and even if he wished it, there was no chance of becoming her husband. Aarushi had explained the Mohawk tradition clearly: Oheo was destined for an older warrior. In Paris, his charisma had attracted a bevy of admirers, resulting in more than one disappointed heart, and in Caors, the daughters of the mercantile elite preened themselves in readiness when they heard Luis Gharsia's grandson was home from university. However, in the longhouse of the Mohawk, he was ignored.

The heat was soporific, the air dense with smoke, and the smell of many people living together. Dominating all other odours was the ubiquitous smell of wet fur and hide, hanging over lines to dry, which mingled with the distinctive aroma of moose meat being boiled. Gabriel flexed, stretched his shoulders and decided to go in search of Matwau. The brave, despite his mother's joy at his return, had been quickly married and now lived with his wife in her longhouse. Gabriel had been surprised at the speed of the arrangement. Sheauga, as the head of her family, had chosen Genesee, the daughter of another family matron. It was a good choice in Gabriel's view for, although, the bride was older than her groom, her skin was still smooth and her black hair shone. He had observed the proceedings, as Sheauga's husband, at close quarters. The day after the marriage had been announced, Genesee's mother, and her friends, had brought her to Sheauga's hearth. Matwau (for he had insisted on keeping his Montagnais name as a badge of honour) had been waiting, resplendent in decorated buckskin. Genesee, adorned with many shell beads around her neck, had presented him with freshly baked cornbread as proof of her wifely skills. Matwau had received the gift solemnly, and had given his bride a haunch of venison in return, to assure her that he was a fine hunter. The ceremony was followed by feasting and dancing, which had increased Gabriel's feeling of exclusion. He was the husband of an old woman, who fortunately did not expect the marriage to be consummated, but who controlled every aspect of his life. So much for his grand adventure.

He reached for his winter mantle, aware that Sheauga was watching him. He inclined his head in acknowledgement and then made his way outside. Several pairs of eyes followed him but no comment was made. It was customary for Man Unknown to become weary of the confines of the longhouse and to seek the freedom of the open sky. In winter, the Mohawk only ventured outdoors to gather fuel, or to hunt, if stocks were dwindling.

The stillness was tangible. Beams of silver light, from a low white sun, streamed through the gossamer clouds, giving an eeriness to the dark trees which circled the village. The snow creaked under his wide shoes, leaving only the faintest of impressions, as he took his time reaching Matwau's home. Gabriel stopped at the entrance and breathed deeply, the sharpness of the air hurting his lungs. He stood, reluctant to abandon the fresh air, but soon the cold could be felt catching his neck where he had failed to fasten his cloak tightly enough.

Carefully following the etiquette he had observed, Gabriel asked permission before entering the longhouse and before passing each hearth and fire. He kept his eyes fixed firmly forward, conscious of the need not to violate any privacy, and soon saw that most people appeared to be gathered round the central hearth. The storytelling was in full swing. Gabriel stopped to listen, using the opportunity to ascertain whether Matwau was there. He scanned the rapt faces; both young and old, man and woman, who were enjoying the tale but Matwau was not one of them.

He skirted the large group and continued until he reached the chamber where the brave lived with Genesee's family.

"Matwau," he called softly. He could hear people hastily

moving. Suddenly, the hide partition was flung impatiently to one side, to reveal Matwau dressed only in his breechcloth.

"Yes?" he asked sharply.

Over Matwau's left shoulder, Gabriel could see Genesee, her hair in disarray, sitting very upright on one of the beds. She held a bear skin tightly in front of her.

Embarrassment, followed swiftly by envy, washed over him and he was glad the dim light would mask his hot cheeks.

"Nothing."

"Nothing!" demanded Matwau.

"Nothing," Gabriel repeated, as he turned to go.

Matwau grabbed his arm. "Wait!" he said. "I will see you outside shortly. I need to talk to you."

In the short time Gabriel had been in the longhouse, the sky had changed. Pearl-grey clouds were now tinged with pink, bleeding into violet, and the sun had sunk behind the trees. Uncertain how long Matwau would be, he decided to collect some fuel. It would be a useful activity and would keep him moving.

Bending to pick up a dead branch, fallen from one of the old oaks on the outskirts of the village, Gabriel became aware that he was not alone. He left the branch on the ground and slowly straightened; his ears pricked to identify the sound. Conscious for the need to be watchful for game, he regretted leaving his bow in the longhouse, for he was now an accurate archer, though nowhere as proficient as the seasoned Mohawk hunters. He waited, his hand ready to unsheathe his knife.

Ears strained, he listened as the sounds became louder. He decided to creep forward, using the trees as camouflage, and before long, he reached a clearing. On the edge, farthest from him, was the small figure of Aarushi, weighed down by a large basket of firewood on her back. She turned towards him, her face lively with a wide, welcoming smile. "I knew it was you."

"Why?"

"No Mohawk would make so much noise."

Deflated, for he had believed his approach to be one of stealth, Gabriel retorted, "I heard you from way beyond the old oak."

Aarushi grinned. "I think not. I believe you were near the big old oak when you realised I was here."

She was correct. He shrugged, then bowing low he acknowledged her superiority. "I beg you to help me be a better tracker."

She laughed. "I think it is impossible."

"Why?"

"You are a Frenchman."

"Cannot a Frenchman learn to be as good as the Mohawk?"

"Perhaps, if he lives among them long enough?"

There was an awkward silence. Gabriel, unnerved by Aarushi's perception, was unsure how to proceed. Deciding deflection was best, he said, "Why are you out here, alone?"

She was serious, her eyes no longer dancing with the pleasure of their exchange. "It is necessary to make myself valuable."

"You are valuable. I see how hard you work."

"I want to be indispensable."

Gabriel's glance briefly flicked to her damaged leg, hidden by her bulky furs. Their eyes locked: there was no need for further explanation.

Hating the look of pity in his eyes, Aarushi demanded, "And why are you out here, alone?" although she knew the answer. She had observed his restlessness, his inability to settle during the tedious winter days in the longhouse, and his obsession with Oheo. She feared for him, telling herself that only she knew, because she watched him so covertly. Perhaps now was the time to speak?

"Gabriel, you must not follow Oheo with your eyes."

His head whipped up as if he had been struck and she realised he was about to deny his action. She looked up at him, for he was so much taller than her, and he seemed focused on some distant point. "Do not tell me I am mistaken. I have seen you." He turned his head towards her then, searching her face for a reason why the conversation should have taken such a turn, but he could not read it. "It is dangerous," she said, keeping her voice low despite them being alone.

"I don't seem to be able to stop myself."

"You must try. You know she will be married soon."

"I know."

"You must be careful. It will not go well for you if you go against our customs. My grandmother would not tolerate it."

He did not appear to be listening. "Why does Oheo ignore me?"

Aarushi thought carefully, before she said, "You are of no interest to her."

He retaliated. "I remember that when I was recovering from the whipping, she attended to me with great kindness."

A stone of sadness lodged in Aarushi's heart. All the hours she had nursed him were as nought. In his weakened, delirious state, he had believed she was Oheo. Struggling against her disillusionment, Aarushi explained, "When my sister first heard of the arrival of a white man, she was very excited. She rushed from the river to see you but you were not like the white men of the tales. Some of our traders have seen men with eyes bluer than the sky, and hair more golden than the ripest corn. Such a man would be a great prize." She spoke the last sentence with great emphasis, determined that he would understand. Then she moved away from him and began to gather more wood.

"Give me that!" he ordered, pointing to the basket on her back. It was almost full; a large burden for so slight a frame.

"I can manage."

"The light is fading rapidly. Don't be so stubborn."

Aarushi studied the sky. The beautiful shades of rose and violet had gone, to be replaced by the palest grey as the light leached away. Soon it would darken to the deepest indigo. The wood was heavy, her back ached, and her leg pained her more than she would ever admit. She longed to pass the basket to Gabriel but she did not let him take it. Instead, she said, "You can walk back with me."

"If I walk back with you, I might as well carry the wood."

It made sense. It was what she really wanted to do. She started to slip her arm out of the first strap. "You haven't told me why you are out in the woods. I don't see a basket for the fuel."

"I am waiting for Matwau. He wants to speak to me."

Immediately, Aarushi pulled the strap back onto her shoulder. "I'll carry it," she said firmly, in response to Gabriel's raised eyebrows, and she set off at as fast a pace as she could achieve. He followed, matching his stride to hers, and soon they had left the trees.

Matwau was coming towards them. He addressed Gabriel. "There you are. I couldn't find you anywhere."

Aarushi carried on walking, her limp more pronounced than usual. Gabriel suppressed the urge to run after her and help: she would not thank him. He turned to Matwau. "She would not let me carry the wood."

The brave regarded him closely. "You do her no good by fussing over her."

Stung, Gabriel asked sharply, "Why cannot I help someone who is carrying such a load?"

"She must prove she is strong."

"And why is that?"

"It is what I must speak to you about. War will come once the weather improves. The Mohawk have always been great warriors, equal to any foe, but the Frenchmen and their guns have changed that. If we are attacked near here, we must flee. We must move quickly."

"What will happen to Aarushi?" He did not want to hear the answer.

"If she cannot keep up, she will be left behind."

"Come," said Matwau, hurrying back in the direction of the council house. "They will have gathered already."

"Now?"

"Yes, the elders are meeting to discuss what we will do once spring arrives."

"Whatever you do, it will be difficult. As you say, you do not have guns."

Gabriel felt, rather than saw, Matwau's eyes boring into him. "Do not speak of 'you'. Speak of 'we'. You are one of us now."

Gabriel kept his tone light, almost jovial, to cover his disquiet. "Skilled as I am I will not make up for the lack of guns."

Matwau responded likewise. "I agree." Then he chuckled and teased, "A man who blushes when he sees a warrior has been pleasuring his wife, is not much of a brave!"

Gabriel did not deign to respond. Matwau increased his pace. Spindrift snow had started to swirl down from the gathered cloud and the temperature was dropping sharply. He called over his shoulder, trying to bait his companion. "What do Frenchmen do in the long winter days?" Still Gabriel did not rise so Matwau shouted, "We will triumph. If we call on our brothers of the Five Nations!"

"The Five Nations?"

"Our brothers; the Seneca, the Oneida, the Cayuga, and the Onondaga."

"I have heard of this league."

"Yes, we are all Iroquoian tribes."

"I did not see them at Ticoneroga."

"We thought we did not need our brothers."

Gabriel's interest was piqued. "Who leads the alliance?"

"We all talk together and if we cannot agree, the Onondaga help us to come to a decision."

"Are there representatives from the other tribes here, today?" Gabriel asked, although he doubted it due to the weather.

"No, we are just going to discuss amongst ourselves."

The snow was falling more heavily and had started to coat their mantles by the time the two men approached the council house situated at the far end of the village. Their shoes sank into the soft, fresh fall as they crossed the dance ground and the wind, which had strengthened, whipped around their faces, stinging their cheeks.

A welcome wall of warmth met them as they entered. Gabriel, who had previously never been admitted to the house, was impressed by its size. There was space for many people to sit, much of it unoccupied as only the villagers were meeting. All of them were centred around the council fire and the ceremonial pipe was about to be lit. They were just in time: the sachem threw Gabriel an unfathomable look as the young Frenchman took his place next to Matwau.

The pipe was passed around, each man taking his time. Gabriel leaned to one side, round the brave seated in front of him, to watch as the wampum strings were removed from a box fashioned from birchbark. One of the wampum interpreters, fingering the white and purple shells, recited the recent record of the Mohawk contact with the French. Heads shook as the defeat at Ticoneroga was described and cries for revenge rang around the hut.

The discussion became increasingly animated and Gabriel lost the thread of the argument. His command of the Mohawk language was inadequate in such circumstances but he had understood enough to know that the decision to go on the warpath had been taken. What was now being discussed was the finer detail. He concentrated on his own dilemma and let the talking wash over him. Escape was paramount, as the idea of fighting his own people was abhorrent. However, if he was to escape, and survive, he needed to be much further north, nearer the Great River of Canada, or he would become lost in the wilderness. He must choose his moment carefully.

He was so preoccupied with his own situation that it was a couple of minutes before he realised that the debate had stopped. The sachem was telling a story, his voice low and gravelly with age. "We must be confident, my warriors, for we are Mohawk. Remember Daganawida who was like a god. He saved Hiawatha and told the grief-stricken brave that he wanted to bring all the Iroquois together. Daganawida and Hiawatha planted a mighty tree. Its roots pointed to the land of the cold wind, to the land of the warm wind, to the rising sun, and to the setting sun." The old man pointed in each direction with great deliberation. He sat, deep in thought, studying the fire. There was no sound in the house except for the sighing of the logs in the hearth, and the cries of the wind, as it sought to gain entry. The sachem lifted his head and Gabriel felt he was looking directly at him. "Remember, the eagle sat on top of the tree and screamed a warning if any of the Five Nations were in danger. Do not fear, my warriors, for the eagle will protect you."

Gabriel, feeling progressively more uncomfortable and understanding enough to catch the last line, wondered if the eagle would protect him, too, for the fighting season was inexorably creeping nearer.

ELIZABETH

1610

TWELVE

Caors, March 1610

L UIS BRIEFLY CLOSED HIS EYES AND RESTED HIS head against the south wall of the garden. He tried to empty his mind of all thoughts in favour of listening to the sounds of spring and, although no longer as acute as it once was, his hearing was still good for someone his age. Insects buzzed and birds sang, all stirred to action by the warm March sunshine, and he knew that if he opened his eyes he would see a couple of finches, near his feet, busy collecting material for their nest. They had made repeated forays, regardless of his presence, to collect dried grass and moss. However, Luis's efforts were in vain as he could not stop himself fretting, and he welcomed the sound of approaching footsteps.

"Papa, Papa?"

Luis's eyes snapped open and he smiled. "I am still alive, Elizabeth."

His daughter, conscious of the fact that for one heart-stopping moment she had believed he had slipped away, returned his smile, albeit rather weakly. Covering her discomfort with concern, Elizabeth asked, "Are you warm enough?"

Luis nodded and patted the seat. "Please don't fuss. Sit with me awhile."

She did as she was bid, thinking of all the tasks she could be doing, rather than sitting idly in the sun.

"Have the Gaulberts heard anything?"

"No, Papa, you know they would have sent word if they had." Elizabeth braced herself for the conversation which was a daily occurrence.

"Apparently, Champlain returned last October."

"Yes, Papa."

"And still we know nothing about our boys."

"Perhaps there was no time for them to give Champlain a missive?" Elizabeth had difficulty in imagining what life must be like in New France but she doubted whether delivering letters home was Champlain's main priority.

Luis deliberated on this, as he did each day. "Gabriel would know how much we worry about him."

Elizabeth took his clenched fist and stroked the fingers straight. "Remember, we decided not to be anxious yet. We know that Gabriel, and Luc, signed a contract for two years as they sent a message just before they sailed."

"I know. You don't need to talk to me as if I lack wit!"

Elizabeth sighed inwardly, prayed for patience, and attempted to divert her father. "The first buds are appearing everywhere, Papa. Look at the plum tree. I believe they are much bigger than yesterday."

Luis regarded the burgeoning tree and experienced a lurch of longing for his vines. He knew they were well-tended, as Jacques Gaulbert was a devoted vintner, but the urge to check for himself was overwhelming. Had Jacques managed the winter pruning for the second year without Luc? Would he be able to cope with the removal of all the buds except one on each stem? And, even more of a concern, how would Jacques manage if there was a late frost and fires needed to be lit to save the blossom? He turned to Elizabeth. "I must go and see Jacques."

"Papa, you know the Gaulberts have no news," she replied, trying to keep her voice level.

"No, not about the boys. I want to see my vines."

Reluctant to keep reminding her father of his great age, Elizabeth chose procrastination. "Let us wait a little while. The vines will still be mainly bare."

The year progressed. At the beginning of April, Jacques Gaulbert called to see if the Gharsias had heard anything about the adventurers. He left disappointed and Elizabeth, standing at the door, watched his crestfallen figure until it disappeared from view, recognising the same despondency which enveloped them all.

May, Elizabeth's favourite month, heralded the warmth of summer and renewed her father's insistence that he visit the vineyard. He argued ceaselessly: the coming longer days would make the journey easier and if they took the wagon, he should not be too uncomfortable in the back. Elizabeth continued to procrastinate but she knew she would not be able to avoid Luis's wishes much longer. However, in the middle of the month, she returned from the market with news which drove all other thoughts away.

"Papa, Papa," she called, as she rushed breathlessly into his room. Luis was still abed, the hour being early, awake but not ready to face the day.

"What is it?" he asked urgently, as he struggled to sit up.

"King Henri is dead!"

The news was too momentous to be easily understood. "King Henri is dead?"

"Yes."

They looked at each other in horror. Elizabeth rushed on. "He has been killed by treachery. Stabbed in a frantic attack by a Catholic."

Luis's face was drained of colour. "Has the conflict started again?"

"I do not know. The rumour in the market square is that the assassin, Ravaillac, was working alone. Even after being tortured with molten lead and boiling oil, he has named no-one else. It is said that four horses pulled him apart."

"The young king is only nine years old. Who will rule?" He pulled himself higher up the bed and leant back against the pillow.

"And what will happen to the Huguenots now?"

"Who knows! We have only had twelve years of peace since the Edict of Nantes. Their fortified towns are very unpopular in Paris. They are vulnerable without the protection of King Henri. They might even have their rights rescinded."

"Papa, I fear for Thomas."

Her father nodded. "It will do him no harm to keep his head down for a while."

As a Morisco, Luis had schooled all the Gharsia children in his ancestors' faith, and with a Protestant mother, all three had grown up in an atmosphere of unusual tolerance. Nominally Catholic, the family had kept a low profile during the religious wars until Thomas had stepped out of line. An angry young man, the eldest of the Gharsias had left the family home to settle in Montauban, one of the Huguenot strongholds and, although not estranged, the family saw less of him as the years passed. The sorrow gradually faded, to be replaced by a feeling of relief, and an acceptance that the family was safer without him.

"Surely, the persecution won't start again, Papa?" Luis detected a slight tremor in his daughter's voice.

"It might. The Huguenots are still strong in our area but it is forbidden to preach their views in Paris. I don't think the reformist ideas have spread as much as the Huguenots hoped, despite Thomas's best efforts!" Luis flung back the covers, making Elizabeth jump. "Nothing can be done about it today," he said, heatedly. "And I am too old to live through it all again." He looked at the brightness filtering through the shutters and slowly swung his legs over the side of the bed. "I think I will break my fast in the garden. Come, give me a hand, my dear."

The sun, ablaze with orange light, slipped towards the horizon but the heat, fierce for early summer, continued to linger in the narrow streets and crowded houses of the city. Feeling stifled by the heavy air, Elizabeth made her way across the courtyard, her soft leather shoes making little sound on the beaten earth. The gate creaked as she pushed it open, disturbing the small rodents who rustled among the undergrowth at the side of the track. A few steps took her to the riverbank where she paused. Leaning forward and inhaling deeply, she filled her lungs with the verdant dampness, so characteristic of the Olt, hoping for some respite from the heat. Although the water level was low, the river was still navigable and a late barge, its lanterns casting an eerie glow, sailed sedately past her.

Loath to return to the house, Elizabeth watched the vessel until it was out of sight. She wrapped her arms around herself, not for warmth on such a hot night but for comfort. Her father was dying; of that, she was sure. He had suddenly become less interested in the process of living: he had appeared to have given up all hope of seeing Gabriel again, and the death of the king had affected him badly. The last couple of weeks had seen him keeping to his bed more often, which was so out of character. The thought of losing him tightened her chest, threatened to suffocate her, and consumed her so completely that the horsemen were upon her without her realising.

One of the horses shied, as startled by Elizabeth as she was by him. She glanced up to be greeted by an achingly familiar silhouette. Her elder brother, Thomas, towered above her, etched against the night sky, while behind him, a smaller horse and rider almost hid in the shadows. Thomas spoke sharply. "What are you doing skulking around outside? You frightened the horses."

Elizabeth bit back her retort and moved to see her brother's companion more easily. As she did so, the man seemed to sink further into the saddle. She returned her attention to Thomas. "It is a long time since we last saw you."

Thomas acknowledged her comment with a slight movement of his head. She waited for him to speak but she could not elicit an apology for his lengthy absence. It seemed that they would remain on the riverside with only the sigh of the water, and the breathing of the horses, to break the silence when Elizabeth capitulated first. "You had better come in."

As Thomas strode across the hall, after he had stabled the horses, Elizabeth had the uncanny feeling that she was a small child once more and that the man before her was her father. She could see the same height and broad shoulders, although Thomas's complexion was not so dark. His eyes lighted on the food she had hastily brought from the kitchen and then shifted to his companion.

"Are all the shutters closed?"

"The shutters?"

"It is a simple enough question, Bess."

Elizabeth ignored his use of the hated derivative. "Yes, of course," she replied tartly. "How else would we keep the house cool?"

Thomas appraised her, a glimmer of a smile playing around his lips. He admitted, "I had forgotten how forthright you can be."

In the blink of an eye, Elizabeth responded, "I have not forgotten how rude you can be."

Thomas's expression hardened, all trace of amusement gone. "We do not want the neighbours to see." He turned to his companion, who appeared to be lurking on the dark edge of the cavernous room. "Pedro, come and meet my little sister, who has spent all her life in comfort and warmth, hiding behind the popish religion."

Elizabeth, refusing to be riled and with a benign expression planted on her face, stepped forward to greet the stranger. He remained where he was, anxious about his welcome, his hands firmly clasped together. Nobody moved. Elizabeth spoke softly. "Please come into the light. You must eat and then rest."

Thomas's loud voice echoed up to the rafters. "This is Pedro Torres. A man without a country."

Elizabeth ignored him and addressed Pedro Torres. "Come, eat some bread and cheese."

The man walked towards the large table set along one side of the wall. The family usually ate in the parlour but Elizabeth felt the cosy room to be inappropriate for two men who had obviously been on the road for some time. The acrid odour of unwashed bodies caught at the back of Elizabeth's throat and she had the great urge to pinch her nose but instead she pointed to the bowl of water, and the towel, next to the food. "Please, wash your hands."

The stranger spoke for the first time, his French thickened by a strong Spanish accent. "Thank you."

She watched as he carefully soaped his hands, noting his slight frame, bordering on emaciation, and his profile, which possessed the haunted, hungry look of a man who had survived on too little food for too long. Thomas, as contrary as ever, grabbed the nearest chunk of bread with a large, dirty hand and bit down heartily. "You will find, Pedro, that the occupants of this house are very good at washing."

The silence was dragging out but Elizabeth lacked the energy to keep trying to be civil. Her eyes wandered to the far end of the hall where the stranger had immediately fallen asleep on a bed of rushes and blankets. She almost envied him. Thomas followed her glance.

"Not the guest chamber for this traveller?"

Experiencing a touch of guilt, Elizabeth defended her decision. "I will make up the guest bed tomorrow. He could not sleep there as he is."

"What about me?" challenged Thomas.

"What stink you take into your own room is up to you."

He studied her for a while, then he shrugged. "I will swim in the morning so that no stench offends your delicate nostrils."

"It is only as it should be."

Thomas was about to retaliate but changed his mind. "How is the old man? Is he abed?"

Elizabeth stiffened, always saddened and annoyed, in equal measure, when he spoke of their father in such a way. She moved on quickly to more neutral ground.

"What is his story?" she asked, nodding towards the recumbent figure breathing steadily on the other side of the room.

"He is a Morisco."

"I gathered as much." To Elizabeth, the stranger's ancestry was clear in his features and colouring.

"Where did you meet him?"

"In Marsilha. Pedro was destitute. Did you know that within two weeks of King Henri's assassination, the Moriscos, who had taken refuge in that port, were no longer welcome? Suddenly they were spies for Spain and the authorities confiscated their money!"

Elizabeth's eyes widened in surprise. "Spies for Spain, that is ridiculous. I thought they might be safe in France."

"No, most of the Moriscos who came to the Mediterranean coast are now sailing to Algiers, following the thousands already expelled from Spain last year."

"Why does Pedro not want to go with them?"

"He has no family, no ties. He wants to make his way to the Netherlands but he is in no state to do so."

"You are helping him?"

"It is the least I can do." Thomas's gaze was intent. "I do have some awareness of my heritage."

Elizabeth smiled at him with genuine warmth. "You will stay here awhile? Father will be pleased."

He did not return her smile. "I plan to leave Pedro here to recover but I must go to Montauban immediately. Storm clouds are gathering now that we Huguenots have lost our protector."

THIRTEEN

Thomas stayed for three strained days and then left for Montauban, promising to return within the month. The household seemed to give a collective sigh of relief, even Pedro Torres, who owed him so much, and especially Elizabeth, who resented her brother's negative effect on their father. Luis himself, after the first hesitant exchanges, appeared invigorated by Thomas's visit and began to rise from his bed to converse with their guest.

Each evening, after supper, Luis and Pedro would talk while Elizabeth busied herself with household tasks: a necessity as the Gharsias lived without servants. Often she wished it otherwise, but as their safety relied on secrecy, no-one could be trusted to live in. She could remember a time when Johan had shouldered the heavy work, until he became too old and decided to return to his home in the Pyrenees, and then her mother had taken control, efficiently ensuring that Islamic practices continued in their house.

She had just arrived from the kitchen, with a new jug of sekanjabin, when she caught snatches of conversation. The two men immediately ceased talking. The expression on Pedro's face reminded Elizabeth of a guilty child while

Luis stared at his daughter defiantly as she placed the jug down with a thud. Elizabeth addressed Pedro, who was all too aware of her displeasure. "Monsieur Torres, are you particularly interested in vines?" She fixed him with her penetrating gaze and he shifted uncomfortably. The formal address, instead of his given name, reinforced his perception that he had seriously erred when he only wanted to be helpful. Floundering, he started to explain himself but was stopped by Luis.

"Elizabeth, I have wonderful news."

Her attention diverted, Pedro watched as Elizabeth transferred her disapproval to her father. "I overheard some of your conversation."

"Is it not good?" asked Luis, his face lit with a broad smile as he held out his goblet to be refilled with the sweet, vinegary liquid.

Elizabeth inhaled deeply, waited moments, and then exhaled slowly. "I fear it is too much for you, Papa," she stated, making no move to reach for the jug.

"Nonsense. It will be fine if Pedro comes with us."

Elizabeth turned on their guest. "Monsieur Torres, do you drink wine?"

His answer was as she expected. "No," he said, without looking at her directly.

"Yet you want to visit a vineyard?"

He raised his weary eyes. "I want to be of service to your father."

Her expression softened slightly. "Do you think it is safe for Pedro to be seen out and about?"

Luis waved his goblet. Elizabeth relented and replenished it. "Do you?" she asked again.

Luis took a sip of the refreshing drink. "Yes," he replied firmly. "But we will need to be cautious. It is no secret that

Thomas embraced the Huguenot cause long ago and now the king is dead the situation might deteriorate. However, we have always shown ourselves to be loyal to the Roman Catholic Church. Elizabeth, you must take Pedro with you to the next service. If we try to hide him it will only raise suspicions. Someone may have seen him arrive with Thomas. Soon we will take the cart and visit the Gaulberts, for all to see. It is early days. Any directives from Paris will take months to reach us and even then, I doubt anyone will view Pedro as a Spanish spy. The authorities in Marsilha probably acted so quickly out of fear. The port is vulnerable because of its position. Also, there are so many fleeing Moriscos and they have long been suspected of aiding the Turks."

To hear his host speak of his stay in terms of months, filled the exhausted Pedro Torres with such emotion that he struggled to compose himself. Torn between wiping away the tears welling in his eyes or letting them fall, in the hope that his reaction would go unnoticed, the refugee decided to keep perfectly still. Luis continued speaking but Elizabeth's quick eyes missed nothing. "I think we should go to the Gaulberts next week, my dear, and my decision is final."

"Yes, Papa."

Luis looked at her keenly, surprised at her acquiescence. "On that happy thought, I am going to retire to my room." He stood up with difficulty, using the arms of the chair to lever himself up and said, "We must be thankful for progress and be glad that armed chairs are now commonplace."

It was such an inconsequential comment for her father to make that Elizabeth wondered if he, too, had noticed their guest's reaction. Not knowing how to respond, she simply said, "Yes."

When Elizabeth returned, after helping her father to his room, Pedro had regained his composure. He was waiting by the fireplace, ready to wish Elizabeth a hasty goodnight. She moved towards the hearth and started to snuff out the candles on the mantel, leaving only the pool of light from the wall-sconce. Their faces were in dark shadow.

"Was it so bad?" she asked.

"Not in the beginning," he replied bluntly, reluctant to say more.

She waited for him to elucidate but no further clarification was forthcoming. "Why was that so?" she asked somewhat magisterially.

Emasculated by his harrowing experience, Pedro felt cowed by the woman before him. He could not see her expression, but he felt her imposing presence, and faced with such tenacity, he recognised that some explanation was required before he could sink into the soft mattress which awaited him. Now clean and deloused, he had been invited to use the small bedroom overlooking the garden. He chose his words carefully.

"I come from Avila, in Castile, where we have lived since the time of my grandfather's father. My family made the decision not to keep ourselves apart and we have Christian friends who were ready to help us avoid deportation. It has been much harder for the more recent arrivals who came to Castile, after being driven from Granada, following the failure of the Alpujarras Revolt."

"My father has told me about that – it was about the time I was born."

Pedro nodded; he was of a similar age. "My father told me of it, too. The banning of Arabic, and Arabic names, inflamed the Moriscos in the south and when it was decreed that their children were to be taken away to be taught by priests, rebellion broke out."

It was more information but not enough for Elizabeth. "Then why were you in Marsilha if you had friends who would hide you?"

"I needed to visit my mother's family in Aragon. At the end of last year, we heard of the fate of the Moriscos of Valencia. They were taken to the ports and shipped to North Africa. There have been rumours of terrible injustices. They were only allowed to take what they could carry, they had to pay their own fares and once at sea, it is said, some were thrown overboard by unscrupulous sailors." He stopped and took a deep breath. Again, he had the feeling that she was waiting for more, so, conscious of his status as a guest, he continued. "We feared that the Moriscos of Aragon would be next. It was to be. At the start of this year the expulsion began there. Some were put on boats, sailing from Alfaques, while others were forced to cross the Pyrenees. I accompanied my aunt and cousin on the land route. They have no husbands to protect them."

"Where are they now?"

"God willing, they are in Algiers."

"Why didn't you go with them if they needed protection?"

Shame washed over Pedro. "They were frightened by the change of heart of the authorities in Marsilha. After the assassination of the king our money was confiscated. We had nothing except for the jewellery my aunt had sewn into the hem of her chemise. It was just enough to pay for passage for two as some needed to be kept for when they reached Algiers."

"Will they be safe?" As soon as the words left her lips, Elizabeth realised the foolishness of her question. "I apologise. I should not have asked you this, for you cannot answer it."

"It is true. I fear for them."

"But you truly could not go with them?"

"I could not. We barely made the fare for the two women." He paused, perhaps reliving the last time he had seen his mother's sister, and her daughter. "My aunt decided to take the risk and cross the sea now rather than wait. It could be only the start of persecution in Marsilha. She argued that they had a better chance of safety in Algiers."

"You were left destitute." It was a statement, not a question.

"Yes, until your brother came across me, weak and desperate with hunger."

Elizabeth wanted to ask more, especially about his reasons for wanting to continue travelling rather than returning home, but she could hear the weariness in his voice. Thomas had said Torres had no family or ties, but he obviously did. She walked towards the remaining candle, now almost burnt down, and taking another one from the adjacent shelf, held it in the flame until it, too, was lit. She gave the new candle to Pedro, bringing his face into sharp relief. He blinked in the sudden light, his eyes sunken and tired, and his cheeks etched with the sorrow of all he had seen. She pitched her voice soft and low. "I will pray for them."

He reached the door, lifted the latch, and then looked back. "Why did your brother help me?"

It was Elizabeth's turn for explanation. "When my father was a very small boy, he fled over the Pyrenees with his grandfather. They were helped by a stranger. She was Ysabel Bernade. It changed their life." Her eyes scanned the room. "This was her house."

Luis rose as the first soft light crept around the edge of the shutters, promising one of his favourite dawns, and by the time he had washed and prayed, the pale blue sky, fingered with rose, was deepening to cerulean. He dressed himself with difficulty, determined that Elizabeth would not fuss and decree that he was in no fit state to travel. When he had finished he unlocked the chest adjacent to the window. What he needed was already at the top; his first prayer mat. He lifted it out carefully and then reached in and found the Qur'an which his grandfather had given him. It was not his only copy, but it was his most treasured. He laid it next to the prayer mat and studied them thoughtfully.

Luis had decided. He would give them to Pedro Torres, a man who had lost everything. From what he had observed, he believed the Castilian to be an honourable man, loyal and trustworthy, and perfect for what Luis had in mind. Feeling content, he sat on the edge of the bed and waited for Elizabeth to come and help him down the stairs. He was hungry and ready to break his fast, but most of all he was excited.

They were ready to leave. Pedro, wearing Gabriel's shirt and trousers, altered to fit by Elizabeth, appeared clean and presentable as he waited patiently by the cart. Luis weighed up his daughter as she walked towards them. Despite her disapproval of the venture, Elizabeth could not hide her pleasure at the prospect of an excursion on such a beautiful day and his heart swelled with love as she approached with a spring in her step. Luis turned to Pedro, and noticed that he, too, was watching her. She wore her years lightly: the sun lit her thick auburn hair, devoid of any grey, and played across her creamy skin. Her dark eyes, their intensity heightened by the contrast with her pale face, were assessing her father, deciding whether to abandon the trip, or not.

"You cannot forbid me to go."

"I do not wish to, Papa. I only question the wisdom of such a journey."

"Look at this," invited Luis, pointing to the cart.

Under his host's instructions, Pedro had attached a sheet

from one side of the cart to the other. Elizabeth peered underneath and saw a layer of sheepskins. "I see you have thought of everything."

"I will be very comfortable. If it becomes too hot for me on the seat, I will lie in the back."

There was no option but for Elizabeth to climb aboard, next to Luis, and take the reins. Pedro climbed in the back and with an expert flick of the reins, they were off.

The cart trundled along the road which hugged the south bank of the Olt, swinging westwards as the river flowed towards the Atlantic. Progress was slow, much slower than if they had been able to ride, and at one point Luis feared they would never reach their destination. The sun climbed higher in the sky: one hour passed, then another, and a third, until eventually the farmhouse came into view. They had been travelling through vines for most of the journey and Pedro, now sitting next to Elizabeth while Luis rested on the sheepskins, could pick out the pendulous bunches of grapes, still hard and green, as the vines striped the entire valley. The house was the same as others they had passed: a two-storey building of grey sandstone with the customary outside staircase to the upper floor. The roof was of lauzes, large flat stones, laid at a gentle angle before rising sharply to the ridge. At one end, there was a large chimney, and at the other, a turret.

"At last!" said Elizabeth as she started to turn the cart onto the Gaulberts' track.

"Stop!" ordered Luis.

"Why?"

"I want to go to my vines."

Taken aback, Elizabeth answered, "We need to tell them we are here first."

"You go on to the house, my dear. Pedro will take me to the far fields."

Elizabeth gave Pedro a fixed stare. He shrugged his shoulders, indicating ignorance. Luis's voice came from the back of the cart. "You will accompany me, Pedro?"

He fought the urge to squirm under her direct gaze and replied, more heartily than he felt, "Of course."

"Jump down then, Elizabeth," Luis instructed. "Go to the farmhouse and we'll follow later. The Gaulberts will understand."

Elizabeth, somewhat outmanoeuvred, climbed down with as near a flounce as she could manage; unusual for her as she had always believed such behaviour unseemly in a statuesque woman.

The cart bumped over the hard, baked earth as Pedro negotiated the tracks connecting the fields and Luis gritted his teeth against the repetitive jostling. He had pulled himself upright and, hanging on to the side of the cart for purchase, he feasted his eyes on the landscape. As they climbed slightly, a breeze whispered across the vines, bringing some respite from the heat, and a skylark sang, high above them, filling the air with the sound of midsummer.

"How far now?" asked Pedro.

"Just a little way further – on the left."

Pedro found himself at the entrance to a large field, planted with vines running north to south. At the end of the first row, a rose bush, twisted and gnarled with age, stood guarding the crop.

"Help me down, Pedro, so that I may rest next to the rose." The grass on the field's perimeter was already starting to lose its spring green. Soon it would be parched and straw-like as June turned into July, but there was still enough softness for

Luis to be comfortable. They sat, side by side, inhaling the scent from the riot of pale pink flowers.

Luis was silent for so long that his companion wondered whether the old man wanted to be left alone but as they were so far from the farmhouse, Pedro deemed it unwise. Reluctant to be the first to speak, the Castilian waited patiently, listening to the bees buzzing on the blooms, and just as he was starting to feel dozy, Luis spoke. "They are beautiful, are they not?" Wondering whether the old man was referring to the flowers or the vines, Pedro answered in the affirmative.

They continued to sit, once more in silence, until Pedro became restless, shuffling and fidgeting as he changed position. He drew his legs up and wrapped his arms around them, resting his head on his knees; he straightened his legs, leaned back and placed his hands behind his head; he turned to the side for a different view of the field, until Luis said, "Go and stretch your legs. I will be fine sitting here."

He walked a circuit of the field, and then another, and still the old man sat, deep in contemplation. By this time, Pedro was hungry. After the third lap he stopped, sure that Elizabeth would want them back at the house, and addressed Luis. The old man did not respond. Thinking he was asleep, for his head was bowed, Pedro said, more loudly, "Monsieur Gharsia." Luis raised his head but his eyes looked beyond the younger man. A quiet sigh escaped his lips, and as Pedro moved closer he heard a single word as he caught the old man in his arms.

"Alyce."

FOURTEEN

Elizabeth was incandescent with rage. "What do you mean – you think he is dead!" She could hardly focus and failed to register Pedro's obvious distress. His breathing was laboured and rivulets of sweat coursed down his face, mixing with the tears over which he had no control. He had run as fast as he could from the far field, much faster than a cart could travel, and had blundered into the Gaulberts' farmhouse while Elizabeth had been passing the time with Helena Gaulbert and her mother-in-law, Sara. The door being open, she had heard him first, thundering up the outside steps, and her heart had lurched: something was seriously amiss. She had already been on her feet when he crossed the threshold.

"You have left him when you only *think* he is dead!" she remonstrated again.

He tried to clarify but he lacked the breath for any more words. In his anxiety, he had chosen them unwisely for he knew Luis Gharsia was dead: he had waited long enough to be sure before he had decided to run back to the house. He looked at Helena, his eyes imploring her to help. "Where is he?" she asked. He told her, between ragged breaths, as he leant over and rested his hands on his thighs. "I will get Jacques from the barn," she announced to the room, as Elizabeth pushed past Pedro and started down the staircase. Immediately, Helena followed, her clogs clattering on the stone as she hurried to catch up. He was left, too exhausted to return with them, in the company of Jacques Gaulbert's tiny, ancient mother. The old woman rose from the table with impressive agility and placed a reassuring hand halfway down his back.

Elizabeth ran, her high emotion giving flight to her feet. Jacques struggled to keep up, and soon Helena was so far behind that she abandoned running in preference for a steady walk. As she ran, Elizabeth was shouting in anguish. "Why did I let him come? Oh, why did I let him come!" Jacques did not reply, knowing there was no answer he could give, but he kept pace with her and was at her side when she reached the field.

Her father was lying on his back with his arms carefully folded. His eyes were closed, and he wore a look of contentment on his face so deep that Elizabeth stopped abruptly. The air was heady with the scent of roses and alive with the buzzing of bees intermittently joined by the clicking of cigales. With a single strangled sob, she dropped on her knees beside him. Taking his hand, still warm, she lifted it to her lips and then placed it on the side of her face. She held it there as it cooled, until Jacques lightly touched her shoulder and said, "Come, we must take him home."

He waited some minutes longer, before he turned to Helena, and to Pedro, who had finally recovered enough to join them. "Let us lift Luis into the cart, together." He gently took Elizabeth's hand and returned Luis's arm to its original position. "Helena, I will go back to Caors with Elizabeth."

"I will come, too," she said.

Pedro surprised them both by saying, "It is good of you to offer but Elizabeth and I can make the necessary preparations."

Helena was about to insist when Jacques, recalling what his father had once told him about Luis, astonished his wife by agreeing with the stranger. "In that case, I will come alone and return tomorrow morning." He gave Helena a warm smile. "It will give me peace of mind if you stay with Mother."

They reached Caors as the heat of the afternoon settled into a balmy evening and the bustle of the city had slowed down. The business of the day had been accomplished: merchants and street-traders were returning home, following in the footsteps of the goodwives who had departed earlier, laden with produce from the market. Urchins were foraging, picking through the debris discarded by the stallholders and as they passed the cathedral, a group of pilgrims was making its way up the steps. Jacques drove the cart slowly, with Pedro at his side, while Elizabeth, her face a picture of abject grief, sat with her father in the back. Acquaintances stared as they passed but she was beyond neighbourly courtesy.

Throughout the journey, Pedro had glanced over his shoulder repeatedly only to be faced with a wall of resentment, which he felt was unwarranted, and by the time they pulled up outside Luis Gharsia's imposing house, the Castilian had come to a decision. He jumped down to open the gate, his eyes travelling up the height of the building to the gallery on the top floor, and felt a stab of regret. He waited to speak until they had carried Luis into the hall and laid him on the long table. Addressing Elizabeth, he said, "I am sorry for any wrongdoing on my part. I will leave as soon as I have fulfilled my promise to your father."

"What promise?"

"Please wait."

Elizabeth and Jacques tracked the sound of Pedro's tread as he creaked across the floor above. "Who *is* he?" asked Jacques.

"He arrived with Thomas," she replied, somewhat airily.

Pedro descended the stairs, his arms full. Elizabeth was still registering the articles he carried when he began to give orders. "Monsieur Gaulbert, please go to the church and explain that we need to bury Luis Gharsia tomorrow. As it is summer there should be no questions about the haste. Elizabeth, please heat some water as I need to wash your father. We have already lost too many hours."

She recognised her father's Qur'an and prayer mat as Pedro carefully placed them down. The items appeared to have given their guest new authority. She bristled. "I will help wash Papa."

"No, Elizabeth, it is not your place," he said firmly, as he unwrapped a length of new white linen. "Monsieur Gaulbert, please hurry."

Jacques refused to budge. "It is too much for you to do, alone."

Elizabeth glared from one man to the other. "What about me?"

Jacques ignored her, speaking only to Pedro. "You can trust me. When I was a child I overheard my parents talking about Luis so I asked my father about him later. I was sworn to secrecy but I have known, for a very long time, that he practised Islam."

"Thank you. I can manage the washing but will need help to enshroud the body."

"I will be back as soon as possible."

They were alone but Elizabeth could not bring herself to talk to him. She marched into the kitchen, where Pedro could imagine her stoking the fire forcefully, before she went to the well. He took his time and appeared just as she was winding the bucket up. She refused to acknowledge him. A persistent throb sat behind her eyes and her skull felt too tight. He leant across and reached for the bucket. "Here, let me take that." She was about to refuse but changed her mind and stepped to the side. Encouraged, Pedro explained, "I only did what was asked of me." Elizabeth experienced a slight shift in her ire and she met his eyes for the first time since he had staggered into the farmhouse. He continued, "Your father was a man, not a child to be coddled."

His heart sank as her eyes hardened. "If you hadn't come he would still be alive."

"He would have found another way to see his vines."

"How do you know?"

Pedro recoiled from the viciousness in her voice but he was no longer cowed by her. Gaining confidence from his mission to help Luis, he retorted, "Elizabeth – you saw his face!"

After heating the water, Elizabeth returned to the garden, usually her place of solace, but she could not still the rising tide of resentment. Resentment that her father had ignored her advice; animosity towards Pedro because he had colluded with Luis; further umbrage towards the Castilian because he had excluded her from helping with the funeral ritual, and finally, underneath all the layers, aching hurt that her father had formed an attachment to their guest in so short a time and had given Pedro two of his most precious possessions. She raked over the days since Torres had arrived, dismissing the renewed interest Luis appeared to have in life, and concentrating instead on what she saw as the newcomer's deviousness.

The light faded, millions of stars dotted a sapphire sky

dominated by a pearly moon, and the hum of insects dwindled to the occasional buzz until they, too, became quiet. Only the moths kept her company, attracted to her warmth, their ghostly wings sporadically touching her face. Lost in thought, she did not bat them away. Eventually Jacques came to find her. She looked up at him and asked, bitterly, "Are you not needed inside?"

His weariness was palpable as Jacques lowered himself down next to her. He took her hand and held it between his two, large calloused ones and rested his back against the stone wall. Residual heat warmed his aching muscles, a welcome relief. Time passed. Inside the house Pedro was reciting the prayer for the dead. Elizabeth and Jacques continued to sit in silence. In the distance, the faint rumble of thunder could be heard and gusts of wind began to buffet the trees, promising a storm. Jacques studied the sky and sniffed the air. "Rain is coming."

He stood up, pulling Elizabeth with him. They walked together until they reached the house, their eyes adjusting to the glow of the lantern thoughtfully left by Pedro at the back door. Elizabeth, feeling comforted by her friend's calm presence, squeezed his hand. "You always were a man of few words." A wry smile played around his mouth and his eyes crinkled in deep grooves, honed by long hours in the sun. A wave of affection for him swept through Elizabeth, dissipating some of her rancour. "Thank you," she said.

The sun had just started its ascent when Jacques and Pedro returned from burying Luis. With a quick goodbye Jacques took his leave, refusing to accept Elizabeth's offer to cover the cost of hiring a horse. By chance, he had met a neighbour who was passing Douelle and would drop him off. Jacques was happy to then walk the few leagues from the main road to his farm.

Shortly after the vintner had departed, Pedro appeared in the kitchen. As Elizabeth glanced up she realised that he was carrying the old satchel given to him by Thomas. Pathetically empty, it perhaps held a change of clothes but nothing more. "What do you think you are doing?" she demanded.

The man who faced her was not the wretched, half-starved vagrant who had arrived earlier in the month. Although still painfully thin, he was on the road to recovery. His cheeks had fleshed out slightly and his eyes appeared less sunken, but most noticeable was his stance. His bearing possessed a noble quality which appeared natural and was in no way linked to social status. He looked her straight in the eye. "I am leaving."

Flummoxed, Elizabeth retorted, "You cannot."

"It is what you wish."

Although a night's rest had given Elizabeth some time for reflection, her antagonism had not yet fully abated. Nevertheless, she could not watch him go. "You must stay."

"Why?"

Reluctant to explain, and unconfident of her own motives, she answered, "Thomas will expect you to be here."

"Thomas?"

"Yes, he is due to return soon – he said he would be back within the month."

"It is not seemly for me to be alone with you."

Knowing she did not want to be unaccompanied in the house, Elizabeth's reply flew off her tongue. "I will say you are a relative."

He could not hide his disbelief. "A relative?"

"Yes, you are dark like my father. You could pass for kin."

Pedro considered her for some time. She lifted the bowl

she had used to rinse the breakfast plates, ready to throw out the water, and walked to the door. He spoke to her back. "I did not exclude you from caring for your father. He asked me to ensure he was buried according to Islamic rites. You know women cannot be present."

"And now you have fulfilled this obligation, you are leaving?"

"Yes."

She glimpsed over her shoulder and flung out the words. "You were a gift from Allah, then?"

"No," he said, patiently. "I am here through misfortune. The misfortune of my people – of whom your father was one."

Feeling chastised, she asked facetiously, "And it was just by chance that my father died while you were here?"

"I think he chose to die while I was here."

"You think people can *choose* to die?"

"Yes – if they are dying already. Your father was very old. He was clinging on to life so he could see his vines again."

Elizabeth whipped round and took two steps towards him, the water sloshing perilously in the bowl. "No, you are wrong!" she exclaimed triumphantly. "My father was clinging on to see his grandson again."

Pedro held his ground. "That may be so, but he also wanted to visit his vines and the rose seemed to be very important to him."

"Did he say so?"

"He didn't have to."

"Did my father say *anything* before he died?"

"Yes."

"What did he say?"

"Alyce."

"That is where you are wrong again. Why would he say that name? You must have misheard!"

She turned and walked out the door. Through the doorway Pedro could see her, stomping her way to the vegetable patch. She threw the water in a forceful arc and then marched back to him.

Her colour was high and her black eyes flashed. "Alyce was not my mother's name!"

It was decided. Pedro Torres would stay, at least until Thomas returned. Elizabeth, unused to living alone, found that she appreciated his presence. The large house, with its cavernous hall and its echoes, creaks, and groans, made her jittery and she began to seek out the Castilian. He was often in the small parlour, which her father had used as a study, his nose in one of Luis's many books. She would poke her head around the door, check he was there, and then continue with the task of the moment. Sometimes he would look up and acknowledge her, other times he appeared so engrossed that his attention remained firmly on the book. It was an uneasy truce, but it was a truce.

That morning Elizabeth felt strong enough to enter her father's room, untouched since his death. It faced east; sunlight streamed through the window, dust motes dancing in its beam. She ran her eyes over the room, taking in the bed, the chest, and finally, Luis's slippers, abandoned in haste, by the edge of the bed. She picked them up and cradled them. Tears, which had been slow to fall, started to flow. At first a trickle but soon a torrent until eventually, wrung out, she sniffed, wiped them away with the back of one hand, and placed the slippers neatly, side by side, on the floor.

She walked over to the chest. She tried to lift the lid, believing it to be locked, but to her surprise it rose easily.

Kneeling, Elizabeth began to sort through the contents. There were unexpectedly few. She removed each item in turn, examined it, and then laid it next to her. After half an hour, for she did not hurry, there was: a scallop shell; an old Venetian mirror, the silver tarnished and worn; a glass perfume bottle; two books, one of which was the Qur'an and the other a collection of poetry, in whose pages she found a dried, pressed rose, and a leather pouch, hard and dry, from which spilled six rubies and a gold crucifix. At the bottom of the chest there was a length of green silk wrapped in linen for protection. Elizabeth almost missed the letter, hidden as it was amongst the material. Yellowed with age, the thick paper had become brittle and with shaking hands she unfolded it and started to read.

My Dearest Love

If you are reading this I am gone. My great fear has come to pass. I pray our child lives. Our son. For I feel as I carry the babe within me, that he is a boy. You must guard your good name. Maintain the deceit. Name him Thomas for my father and Blake for my husband. Do not weep for me, my Dearest Luis, for I am with God and you have given me such Love

By your loving

Alyce

Pedro heard the sobs as he walked past the room to his own. Nervously, he retraced his steps and eased the door open. Surrounded by an array of objects, Elizabeth was sitting back on her heels, rocking to and fro. He approached her gingerly. To touch her was unthinkable so he crouched down next to her. The movement caused her to lift her head and she held up the sheet of paper. Instinctively, he stretched out to take it but she snatched it out of his reach and clasped it to her chest, its contents too intimate to share. Gulping she said, "I do not know my own father. He is a man unbeknown to me." Pedro looked at her questioningly. "It is from Alyce," she said, between sobs.

"Who is Alyce?"

"I'm not sure. I thought I knew who she was but now I do not."

FIFTEEN

By the River of the Iroquois, June 1610

WHILST ELIZABETH'S WORLD WAS CHANGING irrevocably, Gabriel, barricaded inside a roughly constructed fort with a hundred Mohawk warriors, was facing his own challenges. He was on watch with Matwau, peering through a gap in the tree trunks. Their defence had proved to be strong as they had already repulsed one attack from the Montagnais and Algonquin, killing several Montagnais braves. In the heat of the battle, Gabriel had refused to look closely at the enemy as he feared his resolve might crumble if he came face to face with Mashk, or even Kitchi, Ahanu, or Rowtag. However, he was saved the predicament as none of the dead resembled his former companions. He wondered whether they would recognise him, and with what consequences, as a second attack was sure to come.

The air was alive with insects, disturbed when the Mohawks had entered the dense woods bordering the Iroquois River and had felled the strongest trees, laying one trunk on top of the other to make a circle. Clouds of gnats and mosquitoes swarmed around their heads and Gabriel, thankful for the copious amounts of bear grease he had applied over his entire body, was continually swatting them away. A stray moth was among them, perhaps tricked by the gloom. It landed on his shoulder so he batted it away, too. "Don't do that," ordered Matwau.

Bewildered, Gabriel looked at his companion. "Why not?" he asked, covering his mouth with his hand as the mosquitoes were so profuse.

"It is a messenger from the spirit world."

Gabriel had lived among the Mohawk long enough to know that Matwau was sincere in his belief. "A messenger?"

"Yes, a ghost is around."

The moth refused to be deterred and flew back onto Gabriel's head, just above his ear. Instinctively, he raised his hand and stepped away. The moth followed.

"It is a messenger from a ghost." Matwau regarded him keenly. "How do you feel?"

"Why?"

"If it is a good ghost you will feel warm."

"And a bad one?"

"Makes you cold."

Fear, a sour taste in his mouth and a hollow in the pit of his stomach, had been Gabriel's constant companion since they had erected the barricade. There was no room for other emotions. He refused to answer Matwau and the Mohawk, used to the Frenchman's foreignness, let it lie.

They returned to shouting insults at the enemy who were gathered some way off, but soon Gabriel's worst nightmare was realised. Through the gap in the branches Samuel Champlain came into view, with four arquebusiers, all resplendent in breastplates, backplates, and helmets. Matwau and the other braves had seen, too. One word rippled through the ranks of the besieged Mohawks. "Thundersticks."

When the French commander fired, the warriors around Gabriel threw themselves on the ground but recovered quickly. Jumping up, they unleashed a hail of arrows, normally deadly with their sharp, stone arrowheads: one hit Champlain and pierced the side of his neck. Gabriel held his breath but Champlain bravely pulled the arrow out and continued fighting. The arquebusiers advanced further, faced with little effective opposition as they had triple-loaded their weapons, and the barrage was intense. If they sustained the attack, the soldiers would soon be able to rest their guns on the barricade's logs and fire directly at the crowd of warriors inside. It would be carnage.

Gabriel had no option but to hold his ground, shooting arrows in tandem with Matwau, in the knowledge that although his arrows would do little harm to his armoured countrymen, he was, in fact, fighting for his life. Suddenly, the arquebusiers appeared to stall. Champlain was giving instructions to his allies. Using their shields for protection, some of the fighters started to creep forward. Others used their shields to provide cover for their fellow warriors as they started to cut down more trees. "They aim to breach our barricade," said Gabriel, almost to himself. Matwau nodded in acknowledgement, but carried on his assault, his head forward. The French soldiers were not firing so repeatedly. *Perhaps they are running out of ammunition?* thought Gabriel, but it was a hope in vain. More distant shots could be heard, and another group of men could be seen coming from the direction of the Great River of Canada. Frenchmen, not soldiers, but who also carried guns. "Traders!" shouted Gabriel.

More Mohawks fell as the shots penetrated the fort. Gabriel watched in despair as Champlain and his allies moved forward, flanked by the gunmen. The Mohawk warriors were helpless against such power and the end was inevitable.

The enemy stormed the wooden defences, twenty or thirty of them, and breached the fort. Chaos ensued. All around Gabriel, men were fleeing. Many were mown down as they tried to escape. He ran for cover among the trees. He stopped, curled into a ball in the dense undergrowth and pulled more camouflage over himself. Others kept running towards the water, but many were caught on the soft swampy riverside and most perished. He kept very still, the sounds of death filling the air, until night began to fall and all was quiet. It was time to make a decision.

As he lay hidden, Gabriel considered his possibilities. He had the chance to escape the Mohawk. First of all, he could present himself to Champlain, as a Frenchman, in the expectation that his story would be believed, and return to Kebec. This did have its dangers. Before attempting to make contact, he needed to reach the river and wash off his war paint so that he was not attacked before he reached the French commander. The terrain bordering the river was hazardous and he could easily be picked off by one of the enemy arrows even as he was crossing the swampy ground. Also, after a year away from the colony, he was ambivalent about whether he truly wished to return. Would he be expected to labour for an extra year to fulfil his contract? Alternatively, he could try and make contact with the French traders and throw his lot in with them. They had survived the fighting unscathed as far as Gabriel had seen from his hiding place, and in the aftermath of the battle they had been joined by more men of the same ilk. The latter had come for easy pickings and Gabriel had heard the northern tribes jeering them as the Frenchmen helped themselves to the blood stained beaver skins of the dead. He baulked at joining such a group.

Gabriel's mind jumped from one choice to the next. He eased position slightly and deliberated on his next idea. He could try and make his own way back, perhaps to Tadoussak. It would be a perilous, foolhardy enterprise but it might just work. He knew where he was now, unlike when he was first captured. He had joined the scouting party, with Matwau, when they had first decided to build the fort. He was only one league away from the Great River of Canada. However, after he had given the idea some thought, Gabriel realised the impracticality of such a plan. He would need a canoe, the rapids would be impossible to navigate alone, and he would likely die. The thought of the canoe brought the Montagnais to mind. Perhaps if he would see Mashk, or some of the others, among the victors, he could appeal to them for help. The ideas played in a continuous loop, including the hairbrained one of paddling down the Great River alone, until it was fully dark. The night was moonless, the perfect time for going on the warpath, and for escaping. Gradually, Gabriel eased back the undergrowth, stretched his cramped body, and set out to explore.

He made no sound as he crept to the end of the trees. He thought Matwau would be proud of him, as would Aarushi. She flashed through his consciousness unexpectedly, and he could clearly recall the stricken expression on her face as he departed with the other warriors. They had become good friends, perhaps his closest friend in the village, as Matwau had spent more time with his wife during the winter. Oheo had continued to fascinate Gabriel, with her beauty and indifference, but she was also even more distant, particularly after her marriage in the spring. To his chagrin, she had been coupled with an older warrior, but one still imposing in his forties and he, too, had been a member of the war party. Oheo had stood next to Aarushi as the men had departed but all he could discern in the older girl's face was pride in her husband. If there was affection, Gabriel never witnessed it.

Pushing all thoughts of the past away, he made his way along the edge of the forest, taking care to remain concealed. Parched with thirst, his first task was to reach the creek which flowed into the nearby River of the Iroquois. Then he followed the creek for some time, away from its outlet, until he arrived at the point where he could trust the fast-flowing water. With enormous relief, he cupped his hands and drank copiously until he had taken his fill. Hunger gnawed at his stomach and he knew that the sweet blue berries grew abundantly on the bushes bordering the water but in the darkness they were too indistinct to be picked.

He froze. Some distance behind him a noisy rustling could be heard. Reaching for his knife, he turned around slowly. It was too loud to be a man, unless it was a Frenchman stumbling around in the dark, and, by the sound, it was a large animal. He peered into the darkness, his heart knocking against his breastbone. Although he had hunted with the Mohawk, and killed both elk and moose with his bow, he had never killed a bear, especially only armed with a knife. He waited, for minutes which seemed like hours, as the animal continued snuffling its way towards him, making for the stream.

He needed to act quickly. He took two steps backwards, swivelled on his heels, and entered the water. It was surprisingly cold for a warm June night. He had passed this way earlier with the scouting party and he hoped he had remembered the depth accurately. Already the water was gushing through his legs at knee height and the temperature made him catch his breath. He stopped to listen, filtering out the other sounds of the night; the hoot of an owl, the plop of some water rodent, and the sniffing of tiny creatures. He waited. The rustling began to appear quieter and there was a definite whooshing of the bushes as the animal hastily retreated. The bear, for Gabriel believed he had recognised its potent scent, must have been more frightened of him. He stayed as long as he could stand the cold before he returned to the bank. There was no sign of the animal so he stripped and washed himself thoroughly, removing all traces of Mohawk paint.

Darkness was brief at the summer solstice and day was already breaking when he arrived back at the Iroquois River. He saw the French shallop moored with several of the birchbark canoes favoured by Champlain's allies. For one wild moment, Gabriel considered stealing one but just as he was having a silent conversation with himself, the French commander came into view, his neck neatly bandaged. It was his chance to reveal himself. However, as he watched, Champlain disembarked in great haste, accompanied by the four arquebusiers, so he followed them at a safe distance.

The sight which greeted him was horrific. The first of fifteen Mohawk captives was about to be tortured. It was a brave from Matwau's wife's family, a young man of no more than twenty summers. He was tied to a rough stake and his torturers were in the process of igniting birchbark torches. Gabriel scanned the clearing, his eyes lighting on the other restrained prisoners being forced to watch. Matwau was there, his face inscrutable under its coat of war paint and blood. He was holding himself very erect, his poise one of disdain.

Gabriel slunk further back among the trees and closed his eyes as the captors repeatedly burnt the victim, each time increasing his suffering by throwing water over the dying Mohawk. The victory whoops of the torturers mingled with the poor man's agonised cries as they danced gleefully around him. Gabriel clamped his hands over his ears but the harrowing sound was too strong. Champlain, too, was shocked, and he intervened, trying, as he had once before, to curb the torture. Gabriel prised his eyes open and waited, with bated breath, following each gesticulation. After some discussion, one of the Algonquin untied Matwau and pushed him towards Champlain, who appeared to thank his ally before leading the Mohawk away. Traumatised, Gabriel retraced his steps. He crept back to his den, his hunger forgotten, and pulling the bushes over his head, he curled into a ball.

He lost all clarity of thought. Notions jostled but there was always one constant. He could not abandon Matwau. The brave, once they had arrived in the Mohawk village, had protected him and in a contradictory way, Gabriel owed Matwau his life. He was sure Champlain meant the Mohawk no harm and had probably requested a hostage in the hope of cultivating an emissary for peace. Therefore, the most logical action was to go to the commander and explain everything, but the possible danger of leaving his hideout while the victors' blood was up continued to keep him immobile within his hiding place.

He must have slept many hours because the half-light of a midsummer night was already intensifying when he crawled out of his den. Desperate again for a drink, he very cautiously started to make his way back towards the creek, praying there were no bears in the vicinity. All was quiet, the torture had ceased. The Mohawk braves who had suffered were dead, and those still alive would be taken back to the villages to face a more gruesome death, or, if they were fortunate, to be enslaved. Gabriel inched his way through the trees, guided by the sound of gurgling water, until he was within throwing distance of a drink. Breathing a sigh of relief, he ran softly across the soft turf and dropped to his knees.

Thirstily gulping the water from his cupped hands, Gabriel's guard was down. A strong arm throttled him from behind and yanked him backwards onto the earth. He tried to fight back, thrashing his arms, arching his back, and drumming his legs, but to no avail. Consciousness was slipping away when a familiar voice scoffed in his ear. "Foolish one!" The whisper was so low, Gabriel felt he had imagined it, but he had not. The iron grip relaxed and Gabriel swallowed. It hurt. Unable to speak, and with great effort, he pulled himself up until he was sitting with his hands clasped around his legs, his head on his knees.

Matwau walked around and crouched in front of him. "Like this!" he hissed, as he mimed drinking with one cupped hand while he continually kept watch. Their eyes met and in the fading light, Gabriel registered the Mohawk's wide grin, his teeth very white in his battle-dirty face. Blood, now dried, had oozed from a nasty gash on Matwau's forehead and caked the left-hand side of his head, his arms were a criss-cross of scrapes and scratches, his eyes possessed a feverish intensity, but the smile held warmth. He clasped Matwau's proffered hand and allowed himself to be hauled to standing.

"How did you escape?" Gabriel rasped.

"I am Matwau."

"Nonsense!" Gabriel presumed Champlain had unbound him, to reassure him, and his friend had acted instinctively. He had fled.

"Why are you here and not with the Frenchman?"

There was a difficult moment. The two men stood side by side, Gabriel reluctant to commit himself and admit his fear, and Matwau waiting for an answer. The latter moved first and knelt by the water, drinking with all his senses alert. Above them the night sky was darkening and Gabriel could no longer read his companion's expression. Still kneeling, the Mohawk asked, "What will you do?"

Wary of giving an inflammatory answer, he replied, "I am thinking." It was the truth.

"The others are lost."

Unsure which others were being referred to, Gabriel suggested, "The prisoners?"

"Yes."

Gabriel nodded. There had been a hundred warriors in the fort and the survivors could probably be counted on one hand.

Matwau rose and took hold of Gabriel by the shoulders. "Why did you not go to the Frenchman?" When Gabriel did not answer, he increased his pressure, firmly but without threat. "You are my brother?" If he wanted affirmation, Matwau was to be disappointed. Gabriel did not respond so Matwau released him, and, spreading his arms wide, stated, "I am here."

Indecision had rendered Gabriel silent. He looked over Matwau's shoulder in the direction of the shallop.

"Go!" Matwau spat out the word. "Go back to Kebec! Go across the great sea to France! I have no need of you!"

"Where are you going?"

"I must return to my village. I cannot save the captives alone."

Gabriel nodded. "Of course."

"We are defeated. The Mohawk are no longer feared. The white man with his thundersticks has joined our enemy. We cannot prevail. Our enemies will attack our villages."

"Will you move on?"

"We will try and defend first, but we are so weak."

Images flashed through Gabriel's mind. "What will happen to the women?"

"They will be taken. You know that."

"All of them?"

"No, the old and the weak will die."

"Aarushi?" To Gabriel's surprise, the name had slipped from his lips.

"They will not want a cripple."

Matwau gave Gabriel little time to ponder on his words. Glancing at the sky, he announced, "I go now," as he turned in the direction where the Mohawk canoes had been hidden. "You go to France."

Gabriel paused only fleetingly, before he ran after him.

SIXTEEN

THE DEFEATED WARRIORS MADE GOOD PROGRESS AS they retreated south as, despite his injury, Matwau ran so swiftly that Gabriel struggled to keep up. Initially, they wove between the trees which edged the Iroquois River until, after a couple of leagues, they reached the concealed Mohawk canoes. Unfastening one, they eased it out into the water and were soon paddling silently under the night-blue sky, but in what seemed a matter of minutes the first rays of light were washing the horizon, forcing them to stop and take cover.

They waited out the bright summer's day deep in the shade, eating berries and resting. Both men longed for meat but to hunt would have caused too much noise so they tried to ignore their rumbling bellies and take what sleep they could. All was quiet as, unknown to them, the victors had retired to an island in the Great River of Canada where they were planning to spend three days celebrating and feasting. Two insignificant Mohawk fighters were no longer of any concern.

As soon as darkness fell, Matwau and Gabriel set off again. A sliver of moon cast no light as they paddled towards Lake Champlain, where they would be able to rest for longer and recover their strength. So far on the journey, Matwau's attitude towards Gabriel had shifted significantly. The Mohawk did not take command, as usual, but consulted his companion, discussing schedules and tactics. On his part, Gabriel, still surprised at his own reaction, reassured himself that another year in the New World would make little difference. Now, no longer a captive, he could hopefully leave at a suitable time and return to Kebec, and thence to France. If all went well, they would cover the length of Lake Champlain in less than three days and then within the week they would see the mighty river, beyond which lay the land of the Mohawk.

Thoughts of home crept unbidden into Gabriel's mind as he paddled. He tried to concentrate on Matwau's back as the brave skilfully broke the surface of the lake, as still as a millpond on the warm, windless night, but the memories came anyway. Against a soundless backdrop, except for the occasional howls of a wolf from the dense forest bordering the lake, a jumble of images played behind his eyes; his grandfather and aunt standing by the gate as they waved him goodbye; the friends he had left in Paris; his father, always busy, always distracted; his grandmother, dead these last few years, laughing at something he had said, and, finally, Luc's devastated face as he had watched Gabriel leave with the war party. He pushed the pictures away. They could wait. He was needed elsewhere. However, a thought crept back: his grandfather could not wait. He was too old.

The memory of the moth and Matwau's reaction unsettled Gabriel. He believed there was no substance to the notion that the insects were messengers from the spirit world yet Matwau's influence was strong and Gabriel could not shake off a feeling of foreboding. In response to his morbid thought, he pulled his paddle too vigorously, breaking the surface noisily, and eliciting a ferocious glare from Matwau. He mimed his apologies, swore to himself, and put all thoughts of France from his mind.

Against all expectations an idyllic scene welcomed the two men as they approached the village. Late evening sun cross-lit the bounteous crops of beans, corn, and squash adjacent to the settlement. Children, their responsibilities accomplished for the day, were playing. The excited shouts of the tribal youths rang on the clear air as the boys raced across the open meadow, enthralled in a game of little brother of war. Gabriel paused, as much to recover from running as to watch, taking in the activity. He had seen the game many times before, being played by both sexes, yet that day all the players were male, between ten and fourteen summers. He was witnessing the future fighting strength of the village. From experience of playing, Gabriel had soon learnt that there were no rules, with jostling and elbowing being readily permitted. The boys were careering across the meadow, each one wielding a stick as long as a man's arm, with a basket at the end, webbed from fine rawhide in the manner of snowshoes. They were pushing and shoving each other, running at speed, to take possession of the leather ball, and, as he watched, a great whoop erupted as one team successfully out manoeuvred their rivals to land the ball between two sticks at the side of the meadow.

With one last look at the game Gabriel made his way further into the village, now some distance behind Matwau, who was impatient to reach the elders. Delicious aromas of cooking rose from the cauldrons as the evening meal was being prepared. Some of the women were attending to this while others were preparing the dyestuffs they had harvested.

Gabriel had been surprised at the variety of colours used by the tribe when he had first arrived: blue from beech bark; yellow from the branches of hazel; violet from the bark of the white maple, and from the roots laid out on the ground, he knew the women would produce a rich red and a deep green. He scanned the women, searching for Oheo and Aarushi, expecting them to be there but he was disappointed. There was no sign of his wife, Sheauga, either. The women stared at him and then returned to their tasks.

He skirted a circle of smaller children playing the bundle and stick game. One girl, older than the others, was being so successful that she monopolised the bundle, repeatedly piercing one of the holes in the moose hide. Several of the faces in the group wore a bored expression, tired of waiting for their turn. Gabriel dropped down onto his haunches and held out his hand. The dexterous child studied him, weighing up whether to refuse or not. However, the Man Unknown possessed such an exotic quality that she eventually passed the bundle to him. He tossed the strip of hide into the air and simultaneously tried to pierce one of the holes. He missed. There was an aghast silence: six pairs of eyes fixed on him. He tried again. He missed. He laughed and shrugged his shoulders; he was more exhausted than he realised. The children exchanged surreptitious sideways glances before their attention was caught by Aarushi coming up behind Gabriel. "Let me show you."

She took the bundle of cedar sticks from him and held it upright so that the sharp pointed stick hung down on its fibrous string. "Like this," she explained, holding the stick between her thumb and forefinger. She flicked her wrist, piercing each of the seven holes in turn with remarkable speed. The children cheered. Gabriel stood up and made a mock bow.

"I am in awe of your great skill."

Aarushi's face was alive with delight. "It was the way you held the stick." She was about to say more when he interrupted.

"How did *you* manage to be so talented?" he questioned, teasingly.

A shadow crossed over her face and Gabriel could have kicked himself for his insensitivity. Her crippled leg was more noticeable in the summer when she wore the simple hide robe, strapped at the shoulder. Always marginalised as an observer, she could never have skipped and jumped, or lifted up her heels and run like the wind. If he apologised it would make matters worse so he simply said, "It is good to see you."

The genuineness in his voice made her smile once more. "It is good to see you, too."

They left the children to their game. Aarushi walked slowly, determined to enjoy Gabriel's company. She did not ask him about the war party as the elders would report back after Matwau had spoken to them. They walked in silence until they reached the entrance of the longhouse and she turned to him and said, "My grandmother is near death." Her words were so unexpected that it took a moment for them to register. The brevity of the sentence, without any preamble or emotion, was so stark that he wondered if he had misheard but rather than question her, he followed Aarushi through the door.

As his eyes adjusted to the dimness of the interior, after the brightness of the summer's evening, Gabriel experienced a sense of oppressive quietness. There was little sign of life as most of the inhabitants were either outside or lying dead by the River of the Iroquois. When he reached his chamber Sheauga was prostrate on a bed of bearskins and her desiccated face, visible above the thick blanket which covered her, was almost unrecognisable. If he had not heard the faint rattle which accompanied each laboured breath, he would have believed he was looking at a corpse.

Totally adrift about how to conduct himself, Gabriel felt beads of sweat gathering at his temples and under his arms. He rubbed his wet palms on his breechcloth before running a hand across his forehead. Aarushi came to his rescue, as she always did. She touched Sheauga's shoulder as she beckoned him forward. "Grandmother – look, your husband has returned." There was no response. Gabriel looked at the four women attending Sheauga but only focused on the two younger ones; Oheo and Matwau's wife, Genesee.

Oheo stood up. "Where are the other braves? I did not hear the war party return."

When Gabriel did not answer, Genesee also rose, her face drained of all colour. "Matwau?"

"Matwau is here. We returned together."

Oheo's eyes narrowed. "The rest of the war party?"

"I do not know," he replied, holding her gaze.

One of the older women interrupted. "We must wait for the sachem to speak to us."

"Yes," agreed Genesee, as she picked up a damp cloth to wipe Sheauga's brow.

Gabriel was shocked by the drastic change in Matwau's mother since he had last seen her. "What ails her?" he asked, avoiding the use of the word 'wife' as he had never reconciled himself to their relationship. Sheauga, for her part, had expected him to hunt and provide for her but had never demanded that he share her bed.

Aarushi answered. "Fifteen moons ago my grandmother cut herself badly when she fell. Despite washing the cut immediately with juniper lotion and applying sap to the wound, each day her fever took hold more fiercely." Gabriel could think of nothing to say. He had no true affection for Sheauga and could only mourn her passing in the general terms of a life ending. The old woman appeared peaceful, there was no restlessness about her, no plucking of the covers with agitated hands which he had observed once before, at home, and no worry about the hereafter as Aarushi had explained to him that the Mohawk believed death was not to be feared. Sheauga's spirit would be met by her spiritual guardians who would lead her along the path of the stars to the Great Spirit. One clear winter's night when they had studied the stars together, Aarushi had pointed out the path and Gabriel had studied the milky band of light, and at that moment, as they had stood side by side in the bitingly cold crystal air, he had wanted to believe what Aarushi had said was true.

The drum started beating, saving Gabriel from his embarrassed silence. With wordless communication Oheo, Genesee, and Aarushi left the dying woman's bedside and walked sedately down the central aisle of the longhouse. Gabriel followed. He glanced back and saw the two older women remaining, their faces expressionless.

Outside, most of the members of the village were gathering on the dance ground. The women had temporarily stopped cooking and dyeing, the youths had thrown down their rackets, and the triumphant girl, clutching the bundle and stick proprietarily to her chest, led the smaller children towards the assembled group. It was a pitiable collection of people in terms of strength as it consisted mainly of women and children and old men. There were no warriors except for Matwau and Gabriel. All eyes were on the sachem as he started to recite the story of the defeat at the hands of the Algonquin, Huron, and Montagnais who had been shamefully aided by the white men with their thundersticks. At the mention of the French, the crowd turned as one to look at Gabriel, but the sachem held up his hand to still any reaction. He described the exploits of Matwau, emphasising the warrior's valour and his good fortune in meeting Gabriel by the creek, before extolling the latter's loyalty in fighting next to his Mohawk brother. Together, the men had been stronger and had journeyed swiftly in order to warn the village.

When the sachem told of the loss of so many braves one woman started to wail. The heart-wrenching sound was intensified as the other squaws joined in until the great wave of sound echoed around the dance ground. Those who had lost loved ones tore at their clothes and it appeared to Gabriel that no woman was left untouched, until he checked more closely and realised that Genesee and Aarushi were standing very still, as were those young women married to men too old to fight. The sachem cautioned all the assembled. Now was not the time for mourning. The village must wait and carefully discuss what to do next. More warriors might yet return and the older boys, who were skilled in scouting, would be sent out to see if any men lay injured, unable to return home unaided.

Meanwhile there was much to be done. The beans were ready to harvest and needed to be shelled and dried; the continuous picking and preserving of berries must not be interrupted and soon it would be time to harvest the corn. All the women must turn their minds to these endeavours. Cornmeal had to be produced, enough to last the winter, to make soups and cornbread as without the younger men, hunting would be more difficult. The village faced a crisis, not just from the loss of human life but from its potentially devastating effects.

That night as Gabriel lay on his bed, placed outside of the chamber he usually shared with Sheauga, he could hear Oheo and Aarushi conversing quietly as they watched over their grandmother. Oheo was angry in her grief. "Why does my husband not return?"

"You have heard what our uncle has reported. Most of

our warriors were killed. They were helpless against the thundersticks."

"I wish to see one of these weapons."

"Why?"

"Do you not think it is strange, Sister – only two braves have returned. One who has lived with the enemy for many summers and one who is a white man?"

Gabriel could imagine Aarushi's reaction. Her dark almond-shaped eyes would widen with disbelief and then a small furrow would appear between her eyes. He strained to hear her reply but he could not quite catch her words through the thick hide curtain. However, Oheo's response was clearly audible. "You always champion him. I have seen you in his company, talking and laughing."

Aarushi's voice rose slightly. "I like him."

"But can he be trusted?"

There was a considerable pause before Aarushi said, "I believe so. I also believe Matwau is true in his return to us. We have heard of these thundersticks before. They killed three chiefs and many others at Ticonderoga."

"Yes – and what will happen here if the white men come?"

"Do you think they will come?"

"The French are firmly allied to our enemies. We will have to fight them again."

"But we have no warriors."

The fear in Aarushi's voice penetrated the hide curtain and Gabriel knew that sleep would elude him that night.

Three more warriors did return before the new moon but for two of them their fighting days were over. One, an older man nearing the age when he would no longer go on the war path, had twisted his ankle badly whilst fleeing. He had been accompanied by a young brave, with much potential, who had struggled home with a broken arm. Although the bone would mend, his skill with the bow and arrow would never be the same. The third man, who was found wandering deliriously by the scouts, died of his wounds within the week.

His was not the only death. As the slenderest silver crescent rose in the indigo sky, Sheauga took her final breath, surrounded by her family. She was prepared immediately and then dressed in her finest robe of soft hide, intricately patterned and fringed, before being carried on a bier to the enclosure of the dead. She was placed on a platform, under which Matwau ceremoniously lit a fire which would burn for several days.

Each night, the women of the family mourned as Sheauga's spirit wandered, their wailing loud and protracted. On the tenth day, the fire was extinguished as her spirit had reached the end of her journey and the celebrations began. Gabriel heard tales of Sheauga's life, of her husbands and children, and of the great hope that, one day, her son, Nawat, would return to his home. At the mention of his name, Matwau stood up and started to dance. Others joined him until all who could were dancing.

The rhythm of the drums, the stamping of feet on the compressed earth, and the crackling of the fire as the sparks flew high into the sky made Gabriel's blood sing. Dancing next to Matwau, they exchanged triumphant glances: the hypnotic beat continued to thrum though his veins; he had survived; he was in the New World, living his adventure; he was young, and as he was turning he caught sight of a figure on the edge of the circle. Their eyes met across the flames and Gabriel knew he was where he wanted to be.

SEVENTEEN

Caors, September 1610

Thomas had been home less than twenty-four hours and they were arguing. Elizabeth, determined to have her own way, would not listen while her brother, against custom, kept his voice level and his reasoning rational. "I would strongly advise that you do not go alone to see the Gaulberts."

"That is ridiculous. I have gone unattended many times!"

"Times have changed since the assassination in May. There is unrest."

"Not here in Caors."

"No – but you have to cover several leagues beyond the city." Thomas was trying to be patient. "I cannot understand why you do not want me to come with you?"

Elizabeth, who had planned her visit for the last week, was vexed at being thwarted. Her purpose was to speak to Sara Gaulbert, the only person who could help answer Elizabeth's questions, the one person still living who had known her father as a young man and who might be able to shed light on where Alyce fitted in the family history. She did not want

Thomas's looming presence to deter any confidences she might elicit from the old woman. Curbing her frustration, she enquired, "Surely, you have much to do here?" Her tone was so conciliatory that Thomas looked at her keenly. She continued, almost meekly, "I waited for you to return so that you could go to the notary and settle Papa's affairs."

Thomas took a moment to think, running his hand over his thick greying hair. Elizabeth reminded him of his duty as the eldest son. "True," he said, before adding, "I cannot stay long."

"What a surprise!" she retorted caustically, unable to maintain her semblance of docility. "That is decided then. I will go alone tomorrow. You must implement Papa's wishes."

Reluctant to acquiesce, Thomas contemplated the perfect solution. "Pedro can accompany you." He ignored his sister's outraged face. "After two months of good food he almost looks as if he could knock any cutpurse on the head." A slow smile transformed his face. "Yes, Pedro can go with you and I will sort out father's affairs."

Elizabeth, recognising defeat, agreed, although she wanted the last word. "Tell him to be ready at break of day. I need to make the most of my time."

The ride was uneventful despite Thomas's concerns. On waking, Elizabeth had found Pedro dressed and ready to leave, although the first glimmer of light was yet to appear. Conversation had been patchy, with Elizabeth responding in monosyllables when he had pointed out anything of interest on the route until, eventually, he had fallen silent. The thick dew which laced the side of the track soon evaporated, followed by the mist which hung over the river, and by mid-morning, when they arrived at the farmhouse, the sun shone with the intensity of summer.

Pedro hung back as he climbed the stone steps of the farmhouse. Every movement Elizabeth made screamed tension: he could see it in the set of her shoulders, the rigidity of her back, the clenching of her hands, and in the firmly compressed lips which gave her face an unbecoming harshness. Once inside, instead of accepting Sara's invitation to sit and take some refreshment, he quickly quenched his thirst with a cup of water and left in search of Jacques. Elizabeth hardly registered his departure.

Sara was alone. The need to ask questions immediately was paramount as Helena could return at any moment but Elizabeth was troubled about where to start. Unable to sit and relax, she paced about the spacious room, while Sara slowly gathered together some goats' cheese and a couple of early apples, until the old woman asked, "What ails you, Elizabeth?" and invited her to the table.

Tracing the pattern of knots on the scrubbed oak, Elizabeth rushed her words and refused to meet Sara's eyes. "What do you know about Alyce?"

If she was disconcerted Sara concealed it well, although she took her time to answer. "Why do you ask?"

This was a question to be deflected. Elizabeth raised her head and met Sara's inquisitive eyes. Jacques's mother had always reminded her of a bird as Sara was tiny, with a habit of holding her head on one side when she spoke. Despite her age her eyes were keen brown pebbles in a kind, wrinkled face and they watched Elizabeth intently as she replied nonchalantly, "I was just looking through some of my father's papers."

Sara's head nodded once, twice, and then three times before she stated, "She was your father's great love."

Elizabeth was struggling to keep her composure. "How can you say that?"

Aware of her visitor's stricken expression, Sara chose her words carefully. "I first met your father when I was a young wife. My husband, Samuel, treated him. He had been wounded in the leg by an arrow."

Elizabeth's dark eyes widened. "Where was this?"

"In Bordèu – in the year of the rebellion against the salt tax. One of the rebels had shot Luis."

"I did not know you had been married before." The statement was one of many thoughts buzzing in Elizabeth's brain.

She watched Sara's face. The old woman's lips curled slightly and she shook her head. "It was when I first met my Henri."

"Why were they in Bordèu?" Elizabeth demanded sharply. She had no interest in romantic reminiscences.

Sara jerked slightly, taken aback by the younger woman's manner. She wondered what Luis's daughter had found in his papers and took her time, once again, to answer. "They were on their way to England with their wine. It was stored in Samuel's cousin's warehouse – that is how we came to meet them." Sara paused and added, "Your father was going to be betrothed."

Elizabeth's voice squeaked, "To Alyce?"

"Yes."

"What went wrong?"

"Luis was too hurt to travel and then the rebels took over the city. They destroyed the warehouses – the wine was gone. As the summer progressed the situation deteriorated. In the August, the governor was murdered. Many, many people lost their lives. Eventually the king's forces defeated the rebels but it was November before Henri and your father could leave. It was too late to sail to England then." Sara gauged Elizabeth's reaction and waited, giving her time to digest the information, before she continued. "The following year I saw them again but your father was too late. Alyce was betrothed to someone else, a distant cousin, I believe."

"And that is how it ended?"

"No, years later Luis brought both Weaver sisters to Caors. You must know this."

Elizabeth ignored Sara's last comment. "She came here?"

"Yes – but your father was married by then."

"To my mother?"

"No."

"To whom?" Elizabeth demanded fiercely, leaning forward across the table.

"Marie, Henri's sister."

Elizabeth's voice rose an octave. "I did not know my father had two wives."

"There are many things children do not know about their parents."

Elizabeth sat back and mulled over Sara's words. "Were there any children from that marriage?" she asked eventually.

"No, I believe Marie could not have any children. Luis was her second husband and there were no children from her first marriage."

So much learnt in so short a time rendered Elizabeth speechless for several slow minutes until she leaned forward and asked, "What else can you tell me?"

However, Sara was tiring. "I only know what I saw. Your father was like a man possessed when he could not travel to England in 1548."

"But... my mother?" Elizabeth's eyes shone with tears and Sara regretted her directness.

"I am sorry – it is what I observed. The rest Henri told me." She looked at Elizabeth's forlorn face and said more gently, "It was all so long ago."

"But how will I find out the truth?"

"Whatever that is."

"It was not your father who died with a name on his lips which was not his wife's," Elizabeth snapped, her pitiful mien replaced by indignation.

Footsteps could be heard ascending the steps. The door was ajar and soon Helena would rush in and interrupt. Sara experienced a surge of sympathy for the confused woman at her table. She reached across and took Elizabeth's hand between her old gnarled fingers.

"Have you looked through your mother's things?"

Elizabeth shook her head, her eyes glistening with unshed tears. Luis had kept her mother's personal possessions in a chest except for the pieces of jewellery he had given his daughter.

Sara stroked Elizabeth's hand and said, just as her daughter-in-law crossed the threshold, "Look for them. I know your mother kept a journal. She spoke to me about it more than once. It might answer some of your questions."

It was the middle of the afternoon when Elizabeth and Pedro rode away from the farmhouse. They had stayed longer than Elizabeth had wished, eating with the family at noon when Jacques and Pedro had returned from the fields. The vintner had decided that the grapes were almost ready to be harvested: everything was in place. The vats and barrels were clean, the itinerant workers had arrived, and the weather was favourable. The conversation was all about wine-making until it eventually moved to Luc, and then to Gabriel.

Pedro had listened attentively while the Gaulberts and Elizabeth lamented the lack of news about their loved ones.

He had observed Helena's clumsiness in cutting the bread, her hands shaking, and Jacques's concern as he took the knife and started attacking the loaf with a vigorous, sawing motion. Sara, next to Helena, had rested her hand on her daughter-in-law's lower arm and left it there, a warm, comforting presence. Pedro had swallowed and looked away, fighting the desire to be part of a family, to know that back home in Avila people were worrying about him. He had glanced at Elizabeth and was surprised to see her studying him as if he was one of the curiosities that men of science were beginning to collect. Unsettled, he had lowered his eyes and returned to his meal, eating with studied concentration.

They were halfway home when they felt the first fat drops of rain, harbingers of the torrent to come. Dense purple-bellied clouds, blowing from the west, obscured the sun and caused Pedro to glance over his shoulder with alarm. Elizabeth did likewise: the fall in temperature was drastic. Worryingly they were too far from the farm to turn back and Caors was a good hour's ride ahead. "Is there anywhere to shelter?" asked Pedro, scanning the countryside in the gathering gloom. A flash of lightning forked across the sky, rapidly followed by a clap of thunder so loud that Elizabeth's reply was lost. The wind whipped away her words, to join the swirling leaves, so she pointed to a stand of oak trees. "I had hoped for a better shelter," shouted her companion as he regarded the tossing branches, but Elizabeth had already urged her horse off the track.

The heavens opened just as Pedro reached her. After swiftly dismounting, they stood for some time, side by side, as curtains of rain surrounded them, the noise making it difficult to talk. With a quick, furious action Elizabeth wrapped her cloak more tightly around herself and stared at the wall of water. "Why are you so angry?" Pedro asked, raising his voice above the beating rain. Elizabeth's response was an exasperated sniff; his question unworthy of an answer. "Truly," he said, "I want to know why you are fuming."

"Can you not see the rain?" Elizabeth demanded, sweeping her arm in an arc.

"It is only rain, Elizabeth," he said matter-of-factly.

Reading his lips, she shouted, "And thunder and lightning!"

"Yes, but it will pass."

"People have been killed, struck down when they sheltered under a tree."

"A single tree, yes – but not a clump of trees. We would be very unlucky to die."

She stamped her feet and turned away from him. The storm was now directly overhead. The sky was alive with light, the thunder was deafening, and the rain stotted on the stony ground, splashing and soaking Elizabeth's hem even though she had stepped further under the cover of the branches. The weight of water began to drip through the leaves and Pedro, seeing Elizabeth shivering, removed his cloak and wrapped it around her shoulders. She flinched as if she had been stung. He stepped back and held up his hands. "I only thought you needed it."

She watched him warily. He met her gaze, their eyes level. "It was a kind gesture," she admitted reluctantly, pushing away the twinge of guilt which had surfaced. Surprisingly, he laughed.

"I do not see what there is to laugh about."

"I apologise."

Elizabeth raised her chin, bestowing her most haughty look on him. He laughed again, at the absurdity of the situation, and said, "It is not even my cloak. It belongs to your nephew in the New World. I have nothing except the kindness your family has shown me."

Unsure whether she was being chastised, Elizabeth remained silent, but her guilt resurfaced. Although much recovered, the man before her still bore the signs of deprivation, obvious on close inspection. His frame was that of a much sturdier man, but it was still devoid of enough flesh to cover it and his eyes and hair lacked the rich lustre to which she, with her comfortable life, had become accustomed. He saw the changing expression in her eyes and bristled. He did not want pity. He laughed again and shrugged. "I am sure your nephew would not want his aunt to develop a fever from being caught in a storm." If he had hoped to raise a smile, it was not to be. He became serious. "I do not know why you are so angry with your father or why today's meeting with Sara Gaulbert failed to bring you peace but I do know, from my experience, that you must let go of the past or it will consume you."

She lowered her head slightly, her black eyes once again glistening with angry tears. He waited patiently, curious about her response. When it came, her words echoed her enveloping emptiness. "My father, my Papa whom I loved greatly, is no longer known to me. It makes his loss even more unbearable."

Thomas was waiting impatiently when they finally reached home, weary and soaked to the skin. Pedro hastily excused himself, on the pretext of needing to change his clothes, but Thomas blocked Elizabeth's route to her chamber and indicated that she should enter the parlour. "There is a good fire there," he said, in a tone which invited no argument, and Elizabeth, too tired for her usual sparring, meekly acquiesced.

Rather than sit, she stood in front of the flames.

Thomas was correct: he had built a roaring fire which crackled and sparked as it devoured the dry wood. "What is it?" she asked.

"Did you know of this?" Thomas held up an old parchment covered with small neat handwriting in French.

Elizabeth twisted towards him briefly, careful not to lose any warmth. "No."

"It was written by our father and left with the notary."

"What does it say?"

Thomas replied without looking at the document. "In the event of Father's incapacity or death, the farm and saffron fields he inherited from Ysabel Bernade are to go to Alyce Blake or, if she predeceases our father, to Margaret Weaver, on the understanding that the latter is to provide for her niece, Jane Blake. A trustworthy envoy must travel, on alternative years, to someone called Mercer with the spice or directly to Alyce Blake or Margaret Weaver."

Elizabeth had not recovered from the tumult caused by Sara Gaulbert that morning and Thomas's demeanour was not conducive to clear thought. "Well?" he said.

"When is it dated?"

"January 1556."

Sara's words from earlier that day resonated, slipping from Elizabeth's lips. "Such a long time ago."

"What kind of answer is that? I want to know what you think."

Elizabeth wanted to shout that she did not want to hear about Alyce Blake but instead she held her peace and said, "Does it change Father's will?"

"No," replied Thomas shortly. "They are all dead."

Elizabeth changed position and faced into the room. She lifted the back of her skirt slightly so she could feel the warmth on her heels. "Why concern yourself about it then?"

"I am *not* worried. I just think it is strange. Why did he do it?"

"We will probably never know." Elizabeth was calculating as she spoke. "It was some years before Papa married Mama?"

"Yes, but he obviously knew of her then." Thomas mused as he put the document down on the table and picked up an envelope. He joined her by the fire. "The contents of this letter are surprising, too."

Elizabeth's heart lurched when she saw her father's handwriting, spidery with age. She had found the letter in his book chest, with the instruction that it be opened on his death, and she had given it, still sealed, to Thomas when he had returned home. "What does it say?"

"It talks about these two pouches. They were in a casket under a floorboard in his chamber."

For the first time Elizabeth noticed the pouches on the table. They looked very old, the leather dried and cracked. She walked over to them and picked up the larger one. It was heavy with the weight of coins. She examined the other one, which was lighter, and she started to open it, pulling at the brittle thongs.

"Stop!" shouted Thomas.

Startled, she swung around. "Why?"

Her brother ran his fingers through his hair absently and eyed her quizzically. "You will never guess."

"I am far too weary to play games, Thomas."

"You must not open it because, dear sister, these pouches and their contents have been bequeathed to Pedro Torres!"

EIGHTEEN

Despite being weary, Elizabeth did not go to bed after she had taken her leave of Thomas. Waiting until she heard his heavy footsteps pass her chamber, she crept out of her room in the direction of her father's. She paused momentarily outside Pedro's door and wondered if he was asleep and if he had helped himself to some cold mutton from the kitchen before retiring for the night. Once again, she experienced a niggle of guilt as she had done earlier in the day; she should have invited him to eat some supper instead of acquiescing to Thomas's demand.

On reaching Luis's chamber, Elizabeth lifted the latch tentatively and was rewarded by the faintest of clicks as it was released. She eased the door open. Shafts of silvery light flooded the room and through the open shutters Elizabeth caught a glimpse of the full moon, riding high in a cloudless sky now that the storm had passed. Leaving the shutters open, she padded towards the bedside table and positioned the candle to give maximum light. Its yellow glow fused with the moonlight, producing an eeriness which somewhat unnerved her. Glancing around the room, to check that she was alone, Elizabeth chided herself for being fanciful.

The chest, one of two which held her father's books, was locked. Thwarted, she took her time to think where he might have put the key. She scanned the room, puzzled over why the chest was locked, for the books had been freely available when her father was alive. The volumes, although valuable, many of which had been collected by her father's grandfather, Hernando Gharsia, were only known to the family and to friends at the university. Her eyes alighted on the other chest in the room, the one where she had found the letter. It was worth a second look.

As before, she removed the items one by one except for the letter which was now concealed in her own jewellery casket: a piece of paper so momentous that no-one must see it, especially Thomas. However, unlike the previous occasion when she just laid it to one side, Elizabeth untied the bundle of silk. It rippled from her hands, a cascade of sea-green, the colour given depth by the ghostly light. The material was old and creased with dirt at the edges where the linen cover had slipped open but enough could be salvaged to fashion an exquisite dress. She ran her hand across the silk. *Why did her father have it in his possession? Why had her mother never used it? Or told Elizabeth about it?*

Returning to the task in hand, Elizabeth retrieved the candle from the table and held it low over the open chest, revealing the base and all four corners. There was no key. Disappointed, she returned her father's treasures, ensuring that the silk was well-wrapped within the linen, and was about to take a last look around the chamber when Thomas's deep bass boomed from the threshold. "What do you think you are doing?"

She swung round to face him, the candle-holder shaking in her hand. "You gave me such a fright!"

Thomas made a dismissive gesture. "It is your own fault – creeping like a thief in the night."

Elizabeth did not retaliate, which immediately aroused her brother's suspicions. Instead, she continued to stare at him, her eyes huge and defensive in the flickering flame. "Well?" he demanded.

"I wanted to look in Papa's book chest."

"What for?"

"A book," she replied lamely. She could tell he did not believe her, so she challenged him. "Why is the chest locked?"

"The contents are very valuable."

"I know, but I can't remember Papa ever locking it."

"I am the head of the household now."

"You have the key?"

"Yes."

"Why have you locked the chest?"

"We have a guest in the house."

Elizabeth surprised herself by rushing to the Castilian's defence. "Pedro would never steal from us."

"How can you be certain? I see you have given him access to the books in the parlour. He might wonder what others we have."

"Pedro would not steal. I have come to know him while you have been away."

"Perhaps that is so, but you know that our father has many books in his possession unsuitable for a faithful Roman Catholic."

"Pedro would not betray us either. He is a Morisco. Papa gave him his Qur'an."

"He did?"

"Yes."

"True, I think it unlikely he would betray us, but we must protect ourselves, and our assets."

"Assets?" Realisation dawned on Elizabeth. "You cannot think of selling some of Papa's books!"

"I might if money is short."

"But we have the vineyard, the saffron, and our trade."

"I was not talking about us."

"Oh Thomas," Elizabeth warned. "You must not support the Huguenot cause now. It is too dangerous."

"Nonsense! Now is the time to arm, to be ready for any attack from the new king. I plan to set off for Uzès the day after tomorrow to see what preparations that city is making. Then I will return to Montauban."

There was no point in arguing, Thomas was, as he had said, the head of the family. Elizabeth walked towards the door. "I think I will go to bed."

"What about the book you were looking for?"

"It can wait. I am tired."

She reached the threshold, came to a halt and waited for Thomas to move. Raising the candle, she looked directly into his eyes but did not speak. He paused long enough to make her feel uncomfortable and then stepped to the side. "You can ask me for the key anytime."

After a disturbed night, when images of her father's death intertwined with the events of the previous day, Elizabeth fell into a deep sleep just before dawn. On awaking, the resultant grogginess made her headachy and irritable. She drank two cups of water from the pitcher on the bedside table, collected her thoughts, and waited for her ill-temper to dissipate. Bright light already filtered through the cracks in the shutters, urging her to leave her bed, so she rose, pushed back the shutters and opened the window fractionally. The rush of cool air was invigorating; her ears were assaulted by the sounds of the city; carts trundling over the Pont Neuf, drovers marshalling their beasts on the way to market, church bells chiming the hour, and from the courtyard below two voices penetrated her bleary consciousness.

Thomas's confident tones were easily audible. "What do you think?" Pedro's reply would be less distinct, so Elizabeth inched the window open further but he did not reply immediately. As habitual, her brother was curt. "I asked you what you thought."

"You have given me much to consider."

"Do not take too long. I leave tomorrow."

Intrigued, Elizabeth refastened the window, dressed quickly, and made her way downstairs, all the while mulling over Thomas's words. However, when she checked the courtyard it was empty, as was the parlour, and the kitchen, so her opportunity to satisfy her curiosity did not arise until later in the day. Thomas had disappeared on some unspecified mission of his own and he was still absent from home when, unable to wait any longer, Elizabeth ambushed Pedro as he left his chamber. "You have kept yourself very private today."

He gathered himself, refusing to be riled by her haughty, accusatory manner. "I had a decision to make which needed deliberation."

"Have you made it?"

"I am not sure."

"Why?"

"It depends on you." Any answer he might have given her could not have astonished her more.

"Me!"

"Yes, you."

For a moment, recalling the feel of his hands as he had wrapped his cloak around her, Elizabeth thought he might have formed an attachment to her but then dismissed the thought as ridiculous. "In what way?"

"Your brother has asked me to stay here as steward in his absence."

Indignation rose like bile, sharp and sour, rendering Elizabeth speechless.

Pedro studied her warily, disappointment washing over him. "I see you disapprove of your brother's request."

"Disapprove," she hissed. "Disapproval comes nowhere near how I feel!" Her eyes flashed, her colour heightened, and her hands were shaking. Pedro braced himself for the onslaught, but when it came its venom exceeded anything he anticipated. "I am a helpless woman, am I? Widows manage the businesses of their dead husbands but I, a daughter and a sister, am nothing! My brother is leaving to join his beloved Huguenots and I am told that some beggar he picked up in Marshila is to run his affairs!"

He looked at her with such sadness that a tiny chink of remorse surfaced in Elizabeth, to be hastily supressed. Spinning on his heels, Pedro re-entered his room. He closed the door almost silently, a reprimand stinging in its calmness.

He sat on his bed until the sound of Elizabeth's footfall on the staircase receded and then he descended himself. Bangs, thumps, and thuds emanated from the kitchen as the mistress of the house expended her temper on innocent utensils, and if he had not been so hurt, Pedro would have found her outlet amusing. As it was, his main concern was to leave the house and put some space between them.

Walking briskly away from the river, Pedro struck out for the centre of the city. The Place St Jacques was bustling with merchants, making the most of business opportunities before the autumn days turned to winter and rendered travelling and trading less agreeable. He wove in between knots of people without breaking pace, a man moving quickly but with nowhere to go. He traversed the city until he found himself at the Pont Valentré, joining the steady stream of people returning to their homes after a day at the market. He walked alongside a goodwife, her empty basket evidence of a successful day selling her goats' cheese. The woman glanced sideways at him and hung back, wary of the agitated foreigner unaccompanied on the bridge.

Once over the river Pedro stopped abruptly, almost colliding with a pedlar jangling with wares hanging from his pack. He looked up at the expanse of sky; a skein of geese, in perfect formation, flew majestically overhead, setting off in search of a winter home and, as the scurrying clouds parted, bathing him in autumn warmth, Pedro came to a decision. It was late in the season to travel on to the Netherlands and, as he had not fully recovered his strength, he would accept Thomas Gharsia's offer and wait out the winter in Caors. Any nascent admiration he felt for Elizabeth Gharsia would be quashed and all his effort would be channelled into managing his employer's affairs.

Thomas returned home while his guest was striding back across the Pont Valentré. He found Elizabeth in the kitchen, her colour still high and her indignation unabated, kneading dough with such vigour that beads of perspiration shone on her face. Thomas was taken aback. "You look heated, Sister."

Elizabeth's glare was venomous for the second time that day and her question was fired through clenched lips. "Why have you asked Pedro Torres to be your steward?"

"Is it not obvious?"

"Not to me!"

"He needs to work, and he was a steward on a large estate in Castile."

Elizabeth had been ignorant of this fact. For a moment, she wondered why she had never asked him about Castile, but it was only for a moment. "Oh, I see," she said. "The perfect solution for *you*."

Alerted by her sarcasm that something was amiss, Thomas appraised his sister more carefully. Surprised to see a film of moisture gathering in her eyes, he was reminded that he had never really understood her. An age gap of fifteen years, his conversion to the Huguenot cause, and his subsequent departure to Montauban had meant that they had never been close, but her reaction today was totally beyond his comprehension. "I believe it to be a good idea. I am needed elsewhere, and you cannot oversee all of our father's ventures."

"Why not? For years Papa has had people in place to manage for him. Look at what Jacques does."

"Jacques Gaulbert is struggling without Luc and our vines will be the first to suffer if we neglect our interests. And what will happen to our saffron production once Jean Canac can no longer manage it? He is not getting any younger!" Thomas watched Elizabeth's hands as she punched the dough. "Surely you want to help Pedro?" He continued, "I believe a man who risked everything to get his aunt and cousin to safety, without thought for his predicament, is worthy of our faith in him."

"But you do not trust him enough to leave the book chest unlocked?"

Thomas had the grace to look embarrassed. "Perhaps it is not a question of trust but one of my responsibility as the head of the household. I need to protect father's possessions from everyone."

Including me, thought Elizabeth. She paused and wiped the flour from her hands. "It is your duty to stay here."

"No, Bess, it is my duty to see that we Huguenots survive.

You know full well that the Edict of Nantes which gave us our freedom of worship and our protection was solely dependent on King Henri. He agreed to pay the salaries of our pastors and to permit us to garrison our towns. Without him, we face an uncertain future. The Catholic faction can easily dominate at court and a boy king always augurs ill. The reformist cause is greater than our personal differences. I leave tomorrow, and I want Torres to stay here and act on my behalf." Elizabeth began to speak but Thomas held up his hand. "There will be no more discussion. If Torres accepts my offer, as I hope he will, he can live here. If that disagrees with you, you can go to Joseph in Bologna."

"Bologna! Bologna! I cannot go to Bologna."

"Why not? Joseph will welcome you."

"I need to be here."

"Why such urgency?"

"I must be here – for Gabriel." The sympathy on her brother's face was harder to stomach than his intransigence. She lowered her eyes and two fat tears plopped onto the pommelled dough. "For when he comes home."

When Pedro returned to the house he felt ambushed once again, but on this occasion his accoster was Thomas Gharsia. The big man loomed from the dimness of the far side of the hall and he did not break stride as he demanded, "Have you an answer for me?"

"I do – but I prefer not to discuss it here." Pedro glanced around, expecting Elizabeth to appear, like a legendary fury.

Thomas led him into the small parlour where Luis had kept all the accounts. A newly lit fire burnt fitfully in the hearth but gave little warmth, and Pedro shivered involuntarily. He accepted Thomas's invitation to sit and waited for his host to settle himself behind the desk.

"What is your answer?"

"I will accept your offer, but I must be honest with you." Thomas gestured for Pedro to continue. "I will stay until a more settled time. I understand your desire to return to Montauban as soon as possible. You want my help as I needed yours in Marshila. I wish to repay your kindness."

"Thank you."

"I have not finished."

Thomas straightened slightly in his high-back chair, curious about the Castilian's tone. Pedro did likewise but more to ease his shirt from sticking to his skin. Now he was stationary, after such vigorous walking, his sweat was cooling and becoming uncomfortable. Thomas studied Pedro's earnest face and wondered what was coming next. "I am listening."

"I will stay for no more than one year. My plan has always been to reach the Netherlands. I intend to go to the rebel provinces in the north – to Amsterdam, where I have heard that there are opportunities for a man who will work hard."

"True," replied Thomas. "There is wealth there, and more tolerance."

"Yes, I will stay and guard your interests as if they were my own. I can live frugally but wish to accrue enough money to take me to Holland. I will also need somewhere to live."

"You can continue to live here. It is well-established in the city that you are kin."

"Your sister would not wish it."

"I am the head of the family. She will do as I say. It makes no sense to rent elsewhere." Thomas noted Pedro's dubious expression and added, "I will rest more easily if you are here with Elizabeth."

There was no alternative but to consent. Pedro reminded himself that it was a large house, before he said, "I agree to comply with your wishes." He was already an expert at being unobtrusive.

Thomas's shoulders relaxed, he briefly allowed a smile to brighten his face, and then he became serious again. "I almost neglected to tell you that my father, against usual practice, has bequeathed all of our saffron production and trade to Elizabeth. He had some peculiar notion that it is beneficial for a woman to have independent means. You will need to help her. She will be difficult at first, but I trust in your abilities."

Thomas slid a document across the desk. "This is a contract stating that I appoint you as my steward to act on my behalf in my absence. Before we both sign it, I have something to give you."

Pedro examined the two pouches. They were very old, the leather dried and cracked. One, he could tell, was heavy with coin while the other was full of small stones which clacked and clinked as he moved his hand. "They are for me?"

"Yes, my father wished you to have them. They are to help those who need to flee. If I am not mistaken, you can now easily reach Amsterdam and survive."

Pedro eased open the coin bag. Inside, he could see Venetian ducats, the gold as shiny as the day they were minted: more gold than he had seen in his life. He raised his eyes in wonderment. "How can this be?"

"My father was often a mystery to me."

"I cannot take them."

"And I cannot go against his wishes."

Silence fell, a log on the paltry fire shifted and sighed, and Thomas rose from the desk. He stood next to the wood basket as if debating whether to replenish the fire, and then rested his hand on the mantel and stared into the crumbling embers for some time. Pedro remained seated, the open pouch resting on his lap. Eventually, Thomas stated, "You could leave now – you have the means to go."

"I gave you my word. I will stay."

Thomas's reply was heartfelt. "Thank you. Let us sign and seal our agreement. I can depart tomorrow a reassured man."

NINETEEN

A S THE LIGHT WAS FADING ON A DAMP NOVEMBER afternoon, Pedro briefly stopped in his task of painstakingly checking the Gharsia accounts. He eased his neck, taut from sitting too long, and turned his head towards the window to catch the last weak rays of the sun. The north wind, which had brought the rain south across the mountains, was rattling the shutters and buffeting against the glass. Elizabeth should have returned, laden with purchases from the haberdasher, as it would soon be dark. He pushed himself up from the desk and went in search of Catarina, the maid Thomas had insisted on hiring. Crossing the hall, he almost bumped into her, a bundle of new candles in her hand. Reaching out to take them, Pedro was startled by a loud thumping on the front door. "I'll go, Catarina, you see to the candles."

A young man, whippet-thin, stood on the doorstep. His weather-beaten face spoke of an outdoor life and his hazel eyes, chestnut hair, and handsome features told Pedro that he was face to face with Luc Gaulbert. The resemblance to his father was marked, both in appearance and voice. "Good afternoon, is Mistress Gharsia at home?"

"No – but I am sure she will return soon." Pedro held the door open wide. "I am Pedro Torres."

Luc nodded. "My father has told me of you. I am Luc Gaulbert."

"Come in. Elizabeth should be here any minute."

They sat either side of the hearth in the small parlour the Gharsias used in the winter when the hall was too cold and draughty. The fire was burning brightly, the candles flickered in the wall-sconces and as Catarina had closed the shutters, the room was cheery and inviting. Luc refused the offer of refreshment, preferring to wait until Elizabeth returned, so the two men eyed each other awkwardly until Pedro took the lead and asked, "When did you arrive back from New France?"

"I arrived at Honfleur in the last week of September."

"You had a good crossing?"

"No, it was slow – fifty days." Pedro was trying to calculate how long it would take to reach Caors from Honfleur when Luc announced, "I was not well, otherwise I would have come earlier."

The reprimand slipped off Pedro's lips. "You could have sent word. Elizabeth is keen to have news of her nephew."

Luc's response was ominous. "I wish to speak to Mistress Gharsia in person. I will say no more until she arrives."

Luis's prized clock noisily measured the minutes and still Elizabeth did not return. Eventually, the lack of conversation became so oppressive that Pedro could contain himself no longer. "If you cannot tell me news of Gabriel, at least tell me about New France."

Before he began, Luc appraised the Gharsias' kinsman. He noted his clothes, which were of a cut and style more appropriate for Paris than a small city in the Pays d'Oc, and which closely resembled those he had seen Gabriel wear. The older man was leaning forward in his seat, his penetrating eyes alight with interest, and Luc recognised the thirst for adventure he had witnessed many times over the last two years. Unable to organise his thoughts, he said, "There is too much to tell. I don't know where to begin."

"Is it a bountiful land, ripe for cultivation, with good soil and plentiful game?"

"Parts are – but there are many trees, which makes travelling difficult except by boat. Also, it depends on the season. The winters can be very harsh – many perished in the first winter." Luc registered Pedro's reaction and quickly continued, "No, not Gabriel. We both survived. The second winter was mild by comparison."

"And the summers?"

"Warm, perhaps not as hot as here." Luc dropped his eyes and studied his feet, reluctant to elaborate.

Pedro glanced at the clock, increasingly concerned about Elizabeth's absence. In the few weeks since Thomas's departure they had settled into a distant but cordial relationship which Pedro found oddly depressing. He missed Elizabeth's vitality, the fieriness which simmered beneath her calm exterior, and even her haughtiness, which he was beginning to realise masked a caring heart. She had begun to act with an alien meekness around him and although she did not apologise for her stinging outburst, she did channel her energy into making his stay comfortable, albeit without any overt warmth.

After Thomas had left, Catarina, recommended by the family's lawyer, had been hired almost immediately to help Elizabeth. Recently widowed and in urgent need of a position, the young woman had swiftly decided that the large house on the bank of the River Olt was a more desirable option than living with her brother, his peevish wife, and their four children. Although possessing no experience as a servant, Catarina had taken to her new role. The work was not onerous, as Mistress Gharsia continued to do much of the day-to-day running of the household herself and Monsieur Torres was a polite gentleman who spent most of his time poring over books.

A good half-hour after the visitor had arrived, Catarina knocked on the winter parlour door and, on entering, found Monsieur Torres and the young man sitting in obstinate silence. After receiving Pedro's request for some almond cakes and sekanjabin, she hastily retreated to the comfort of the kitchen. While waiting for her to return, Pedro decided to try once more to engage the taciturn young man in conversation. "I believe such an adventure might suit me."

Whether it was the naïve eagerness on the older man's face, or his own pent-up tension, Luc could not tell, but the dam of his emotions had been breached. His voice rose with each word uttered. "You cannot begin to know what it was like. The unrelenting labour; the race against the first winter; the numbing cold; the disease, and the stench of the dying!" He was on his feet, shouting now. "Then the people – the mutineers, the Basque whalers, and the soldiers who came in the spring – were like nobody I had ever encountered."

Pedro, unable to remain seated in the presence of such distress, stood up and touched the distraught man lightly on the arm. Luc wheeled round, his eyes blazing. "And the Indians – what they do to their enemies – how they torture them – it is unspeakable!"

The Inquisition's methods against heretics in his own country, including some of Pedro's family, came to mind but the Castilian refrained from making a comparison. Luc was shaking, clutching his arms around himself so Pedro said calmly, hoping to soothe him, "You have suffered. I am sorry to have upset you."

"Two years – two years I endured! I have earned every

sous of my seventy-five livres a hundred times over. But do you know what the worst was?"

"No," Pedro replied.

"I was abandoned! I was abandoned!"

"By whom?" He had to ask although he feared the answer. Luc spat out the name. "Gabriel Gharsia."

The door opened. Both men remained facing each other, expecting Catarina. There was a sharp intake of breath immediately followed by a strangled exclamation. "Luc!"

The clock had chimed midnight, the candles had burnt to stubs, and the only light came from the fire but still Elizabeth would not move. Hours had passed since Luc had retired to Thomas's chamber, fortified by the brandy Catarina had discovered at the back of the sideboard. Kept by Elizabeth's mother for medicinal purposes only, the bottle was old and infrequently used, but its contents were unspoiled. The rich, amber liquid in Elizabeth's glass remained untouched, glowing in the firelight. She sat where she had collapsed, her buckled legs lacking the will to push upwards, straighten, and walk to her bed.

Earlier, Luc had blurted out the truth, sparing no thought for her feelings, in a manner totally at odds with what he had planned. The sight of her devastated face as she swooned brought him to his senses. Ashamed, he had started to weep, the great wracking sobs of a broken man, reflecting all he had borne. Elizabeth had stared at him, dry-eyed. Pedro, crouching next to her and ignoring Luc, had taken her cold clammy hands in his. "Take slow, deep breaths. In – out, in – out, in – out," he ordered.

Catarina, returning with the refreshments, had found her

mistress on the floor in front of the fire, a sheen of sweat on her ghostly-pale face. Agitated and upset, her young visitor was sitting to her right, trying to control himself, his face still moist with tell-tale tears. Monsieur Torres had looked up with such appeal in his eyes that Catarina had immediately placed the tray on the table and retreated in search of a stronger drink.

Pedro glanced at the clock: only five minutes had elapsed since the striking of the hour. "Elizabeth," he said, forcefully, "you cannot sit here all night."

Her glassy-eyed stare alarmed him. "I do not comprehend why Gabriel did what he did."

Pedro could feel his patience waning; the continuous loop of conversation had run all evening, and there was no explanation or comfort that he could offer. "You must go to bed. It is very late."

"Tell me again what Luc said about Gabriel."

"The summer before last, Samuel Champlain joined with his Indian allies to fight their enemy, the Iroquois. The campaign was a great success but after the battle, while everyone was celebrating, Gabriel disappeared." Each time he gave it, the explanation grew shorter.

"And Luc believes Gabriel was taken prisoner by a renegade."

"Yes."

"Do you think he is dead?"

Pedro struggled to keep his voice level. The persistent pounding behind his eyes had intensified, and he had no answer. "He could be a hostage," he said, not for the first time that evening.

"It is fifteen months since he was taken." He waited for Elizabeth to continue, as he knew she would. "We have heard nothing."

"New France is an untamed place – a wilderness. It would be very difficult to send a message."

"Why did he leave Luc? Why did he disguise himself as an Indian?" Pedro did not reply. He leaned forward and took the glass from her. He stood up and placed it very carefully on the table as if it was an object of great value. He appeared to be contemplating it.

"You think he is dead, don't you?" Elizabeth asked, yet again.

"I do not know." He moved towards her and firmly clasped her hands. "Come to your bed. I will ask Catarina to give you something to help you sleep."

She allowed him to pull her up. "Surely, I would feel it here, if he was dead," she whispered as she touched her heart. Her eyes met his, her face crumpled. He encircled her in his arms and, against all expectation, she rested her head in the crook of his neck.

The next morning, a mist-wrapped autumnal sun was high in the sky by the time Pedro entered the kitchen in search of some breakfast and found Jacques Gaulbert sitting at the table with Luc. "I did not realise it was so late."

Jacques smiled contritely, his eyes feasting on his son. "I am an early visitor. I left at first light – Luc's mother is eager to have him back home."

"There is no need for such ado, Father. I had arranged a ride back." Moving along the bench to make room, Luc turned to Pedro and said, "I apologise for my behaviour yesterday. I was overwrought."

"Do not worry, Son. Elizabeth will understand."

"Where is she?" Pedro asked, reaching out to tear a chunk of bread from the loaf.

"Catarina says she wishes to stay in her room," replied Jacques. "Terrible business this, about Gabriel. What was the lad thinking of?"

Pedro put his hand to his forehead where the remnants of yesterday's pounding were still lingering. "Is there anything else you can tell us, Luc?"

The young man's eyes slid to his father and then focused back on Pedro. "There is, but I cannot say it is the truth."

Pedro had caught the silent exchange. "What is it?"

Luc paused before he started to speak. "In June, this year, Samuel Champlain and his allies fought another battle. Afterwards, back in Kebec, one of the Montagnais warriors who had been there with Champlain told me that he thought he had seen Gabriel fighting with the Mohawk."

"The Mohawk?"

"One of the Iroquois peoples."

"How certain was this warrior? It must be nigh impossible to pick one man out in a battle."

"It was when the Mohawk were fleeing – their fort had been breached and most of them were slaughtered. However, a few of them escaped and headed for the river. It was the way the man ran which made Mashk believe it was Gabriel. He was some distance away though."

Jacques asked, "If it was Gabriel, why didn't he surrender to Champlain?"

Luc agreed. "He could have been saved."

"You said nothing to the authorities?"

Luc shook his head, reluctant to be questioned further. "There was no proof."

"So, Gabriel has just disappeared?" Pedro looked at him with such scrutiny that Luc squirmed. "And you set sail for home, in August."

"You don't realise how difficult it would be to find anyone."

"True," Pedro admitted.

Jacques came to his son's defence. "I believe this sighting is very questionable. I do not think Elizabeth needs to hear of it."

Upstairs, Elizabeth was having difficulty shaking off the effects of valerian. More than once she had turned over and slipped into oblivion, safe from the images of Gabriel which played across her mind. Her nephew dressed as an Indian, although she had no idea of how he would truly look; Gabriel being put to death by the Iroquois, his body tossed aside as a thing of no value; Gabriel lost and alone in the wilderness: each scenario vivid in the detail of her imagination. Jumbled with these was Luc's distorted face as he had blurted out his news, and Pedro's, full of concern, as he had leant over and taken her hands. Her mind had veered away from the end of the evening, when she had been encircled in his arms. Too significant a gesture to be ignored, it alarmed her, so she fought to suppress the memory. Yet, part of her yearned to relive the sensation: now her father was gone she was rarely touched, and it was a very long time since she had been embraced.

Eventually, she forced herself upright and scanned the familiar room. In the muted light, which escaped around the shutters, she could make out the press, on the opposite wall, where she stored her clothes. She studied it, trying to bring some reasoning to her muddled brain. Suddenly inspired, she was galvanised into action. She washed hastily and tugged on her chemise, dress, and stockings without any regard for her appearance. She deftly braided her hair and wound it into a knot on the back of her head. Teasing free some tendrils, to soften the angles of her face, Elizabeth briefly glanced in the mirror. She looked respectable enough in the unlikely event that visitors might call. Finally, she grabbed her thick shawl: it would be cold in her father's room as no fire had been lit there since his death.

The shutters clattered noisily as she flung them back with more force than she had intended. Weak sunshine picked out the film of dust coating the furniture and gave her enough light to search through her father's clothes-press. Previously, unable to face the task, she had left his clothes untouched and now his shirts, breeches, and doublets lay as neatly stacked as the day she had placed them there herself. She began to remove each article of clothing carefully until she reached the bottom of the press, where the old clothes her father had refused to discard were stored in the hope they might, one day, be useful.

Elizabeth reached beneath them and touched something solid. Heart thumping, she curled her fingers around the object and pulled it up through the rumpled clothes. It was a thin book, with thick quality pages, bound in fine calfskin. She held her breath as she randomly opened it. Her mother's rushed, untidy handwriting raced across the yellowing pages and then, flicking to the first page, she saw her mother's name, neatly written and accompanied by the date '1564': the year Joseph was born. Her hands shaking, Elizabeth carefully placed the journal down and returned to the press. She grabbed impatiently at the garments, tossing them heedlessly on the floor and there, at the very bottom of the press, was a pile of books of different sizes, neatly stacked with the largest first.

She quickly established that the storage order was not chronological, so she glanced at each book and then made a semi-circle of them on the floor, positioned according to year. Soon it became obvious that it would take some time to organise them because her mother had sometimes used one volume for two or more years and, as time had passed, the entries were more infrequent and haphazard. However, she was certain she had identified the first volume. Opening it gingerly, her lively, mischievous mother leapt from the pages, so vividly that Elizabeth's chest tightened. Fighting back the emotion which threatened to swamp her, she made herself concentrate on the words, and began to read slowly, as she had not spoken English since her mother's death.

It was too cold to stay in her father's chamber for long, so Elizabeth returned the good clothes to the press, in case Thomas wanted any, and gathered the old ones up and placed them in a heap on the bed. She would dispose of them later. For a moment she was undecided whether to take all the journals with her to her room or to leave them where they were. Nobody used the room, so the books could be left on the floor until she had more time to arrange them. Taking only the one she had started reading, Elizabeth made her way to her chamber, her soft leather slippers making no sound on the worn floorboards.

She climbed onto the bed and made a nest of pillows for her back. Too excited to eat, she would abandon breakfast, try and supress all morbid thoughts about Gabriel, and spend the morning with her mother.

MEG

1557

TWENTY

The fifteenth day of September 1557

I, MARGARET WEAVER, UNDERTAKE TO WRITE IN good faith everything which betides me. This day there is joy in my fingers. Alyce and I are in Caors dwelling with Madame Bernade. She has shown us such kindness. This journal is a gift from her for my birthday. I am sixteen this day and heartily glad that I am not in Lewes with my uncle. I did not wish to be married to the blockhead son of a glassmaker because I displeased my aunt. Verily, I am happy but for Alyce. Her heart is heavy. Two months have passed since the sweating sickness took poor Jane, and Alyce is so very doleful. Nevertheless, I think she is with child. She often vomits and keeps to her room. Madame Bernade is very solicitous of her and I am kept somewhat separate. They talk in hushed voices and think their murmurings do not reach my ears. This makes me melancholy but me thinks Alyce will tell me in her own time.

I have made a friend of Ramon who has served Madame Bernade loyally since he was a very young man. On the morrow he is accompanying me to see Luis who is harvesting his grapes. Since our arrival in Caors Alyce and I have seen little of Luis as he has been busy with his enterprises. I will take him to task as he is neglecting Alyce. At this time of the year, it is customary for Madame Bernade to visit the vineyard as she sayst it is her favourite season, but she is to remain with Alyce. It will be pleasant for me to see Henri again and to see his sister, Marie, the wife of Luis. It will be interesting to meet her.

The sixteenth day of September 1557

It is eleven of the clock and all are abed, but I am unable to sleep. The experience of encountering Marie Gharsia proveth too diverting. I will recount my day before I retire, leaving out nought.

We left as the sun rose on a balmy morning and made goodly progress. Ramon was an attentive companion, pointing out sundry things, and the many leagues passed quickly. The countryside differs from Somersetshire in that all the slopes are covered with row upon row of vines. The leaves are dressed in divers colours and the deep black grapes hang low, ripe for picking. The farmhouse is of grey stone with a turret at one end. An outside staircase leads from the yard to the upper floor where the family live. Ramon hammered on the door, but none answered. The door was unlocked so he pushed it open and shouted that we had arrived. I turned and looked out over the yard. A man appeared from the barn opposite. He is slight of stature, his chestnut hair sprinkled liberally with grey. He greeted Ramon warmly and commanded us to go with him.

After introductions, we did not enter the barn. Monsieur Gaulbert explained that the grapes were being pressed. It is necessary to press the grapes on the day they are harvested. I asked to witness the pressing but could not on account of the men being naked. We were taken to the fields where there was much busyness. It was a marvellous thing to behold. The sunshine, the divers colours, and all the people working. I soon espied Luis for he is so tall. My heart leapt when he came towards us and I stammered out a greeting for he did not look like the Luis I know. He wore a smock over his trousers and wooden clogs on his feet. In all the years we have been friends he has always worn boots of the finest leather. His dark countenance was lit by a smile, one he bestows on me when my actions amuse him. I need to remind him that I am no longer a child, but I forgot myself and was so pleased to see him that I embraced him merrily.

Notwithstanding my joy, Luis suddenly unclasped me for there at his shoulder appeared an angry wife. Her glowering could not disguise a personage of great comeliness and she turned her vehement eyes on me. I faltered under such scrutiny but then I met her stare full on. I tossed my hair: plain brown it may be, but I knew the sunlight would catch the waves as they bounced on my shoulders. Her eyes were ablaze and if they had not been so full of maliciousness, her countenance would have been pleasing for she has a good complexion. She commanded Luis to step away from me which he did. This vexed me for I have always greeted him fondly since I was a child. He recovered swiftly and sayst to his wife: Marie, this is Margaret Weaver from England.

Madame Gharsia continued to look at me most cruelly, disliking my friendship with Luis. I was most uncomfortable, but I smiled without restraint to show her that her ire did me no harm. Then she sayst something in Occitan, so swiftly that I did not understand. Time went by without any more words until Henri appeared. I was mightily pleased to see him, and him, me. Presently we sat down at the side of the field and I ate a small portion of victuals. I could not eat more as Madame Gharsia still fixed me with her gimlet eye. Me thinks she is jealous, which is foolish. I am not Alyce. It is my sister who is the thorn in her flesh.

Henri was good company and we made remembrance of our journey from England, speaking not of Jane but of carefree things, until Luis scowled at us and demanded of Henri that they return to work. After they had left, Madame Gharsia made herself agreeable, being exceedingly pleasant, and asked me to accompany her back to the house. I was perturbed by this change, as well I might. Ramon took himself off to the pressing and all I could do was follow Madame Gharsia up the staircase to the living space.

Inside, I met Madame Loise Gaulbert who appeared to care little for me. She made a poor welcome and then went to feed the hens. I sat nervously on a stool while Marie Gharsia was a bombard with questions. It made me recall my dear brother, Rufus, who died a martyr of the reformist cause. He would ask many questions of acquaintances. I wonder how he would ponder on my lot. Me thinks he would be mightily displeased to see me dwelling with Madame Bernade and going to mass now we have escaped our Catholic queen. But my experience proveth that you can have great friendship with those who have difference of religion. At heart Luis is a Mahometan and I do not despite him for it for he possesses a noble spirit and has great courage, as has Madame Bernade. She succoured him when he was a child all though she is a papist. But I digress. It is Madame Gharsia who interests me.

She entreated me to partake of their black wine and to drink it heartily. I fear it made my tongue loose all though it was my good fortune that I know some Occitan if spoken slowly and Madame Gharsia knows no French. She did not call Alyce by name but used the words 'thy sister' always. Me thinks I understood her questions which were most searching and surpassed politeness. She has the benefits of a wife but no love from Luis as he appears cold to her which is unlike him. I saw a tear gather in her eye and began to see that her natural inclination is to be a good wife but her husband looketh elsewhere. There is nought to be done as Luis gave his heart to Alyce before he married Marie Gaulbert and he is steadfast. Madame Gharsia asketh me to make merry with her and be her friend. I will think on this and be vigilant for I suspect some plotting of mischief. I wonder what she has done to make Luis so cold.

I was heartily pleased when Ramon came to the house for our return to Caors. We went to the fields to bid our farewell and I privily admonished Luis for neglecting Alyce while Ramon was speaking to Henri. He took my admonition and sought my understanding. He has much to concern him. He persuaded me to take great care of Alyce until he has more time. I did not tell him of my fear that Alyce may be with child.

The journey back was long. The candle has burnt low. My eyes are tired, and my bed awaits.

Chortling, Elizabeth laid the journal carefully on the bed, face down, and took some time to recover herself. The sudden change in her mother's account, from being fully immersed in her task to losing all interest instantly, was so characteristic that Elizabeth had initially laughed out loud. Now as her reaction ebbed from amusement to nostalgia, Elizabeth recalled her first memory of her mother. It came to her without difficulty as she had cited it often, despite derision from Thomas who continually claimed that the event, and her role in it, had been described to her so many times that she had begun to believe that she could remember the detail.

It was her fourth birthday and as a treat the whole family had attended a performance by visiting players. Her father had lifted her onto his shoulders for a better view and she had perched high above the gathering crowd. Her mother, whose excitement at the coming entertainment was palpable, had stood close to them on one side while on the other side Thomas had simmered moodily at the forced activity. The whereabouts of Joseph had always been hard to pinpoint, in her mind, although he must have been present.

The acrobats had leapt and somersaulted, the jugglers had mesmerised with their colourful clubs, and the fools had warmed up the crowd when the pageant wagon had trundled into position. It was early afternoon and a good proportion of the audience were noisy, already fuelled by wine. However, a hush descended as the first two players descended. They were dressed as a king and a queen. The latter, a pretty boy devoid of any sign of beard, sported an extravagant wig of honey-brown curls while his companion was richly attired in the latest fashion with elaborate doublet and two-tone breeches. The two began to argue, the woman haranguing her partner, who cowered beneath her vitriol. Behind the performing couple a massacre with great loss of life began to be mimed by the rest of the troupe.

As the crowd had cheered her father had placed a cautionary hand on Thomas's shoulder. Despite this, Thomas had hissed loudly. "They mock the Huguenots. They make light of the Day of St Bartholomew – they reduce Henri of Navarre to a cringing coward."

"Shh," her father had ordered, for the people in front of them had peered round, their faces threatening.

"Shame on you all!" Thomas had shouted, refusing to be silenced. More people turned away from the spectacle towards him, some incensed by the youth's words, others by his interruption of the play. He had glared at them with all the outrage of his nineteen years, protesting vehemently. "We have been granted an amnesty. We are not to be mocked and belittled!"

One old man who was nearest to the family tried to calm him, "Now, lad, it is only a bit of fun," but Thomas was fuming, dangerously so.

She had felt the rigidity in her father's shoulders as he moved his head, looking for a suitable exit from the crowd. Attracted by the players, many people had travelled into the city from the outlaying area, bringing with them their very conservative religious views. The educated mercantile elite and the scholars of the university, who might view Thomas's reaction as youthful rebellion, were seriously outnumbered by illiterate agricultural workers who abhorred any change to their established customs. Many of them still scattered stolen blessed bread, secreted in their mouths during mass, on their newly planted crops.

Before her father could move, her mother roughly tugged off one of her new shoes, her birthday present. Incensed, she had wailed loudly and looked down to meet her mother's eyes. Startlingly blue, they had stared up at her with wide innocence before her mother shouted, "Please make way for my daughter. We need to leave. Please make way. Cannot you see she is distressed?" Positioning herself in front of Thomas, with the dainty shoe concealed in her hand, her mother had pushed through the crowd with Elizabeth and her father following closely behind Thomas. Enjoying making so much noise, she had continued to wail until tears rolled down her cheeks. Grumbling volubly, people had parted, and the family had inched away from the suspicious and unnerving looks.

It had been at this point that Joseph's absence was realised. Her father had swiftly lowered her down from his shoulders and had ordered her mother to seek refuge in his office, a short distance away, while he went in search of the errant boy. Thomas had started to complain but had been quickly silenced by their mother and the three of them had hastily made their way to the building her father had shared with Martin Ebrart.

Disinterested in such diversions as travelling players, the lawyer had been busy working. However, he laid down his quill with enthusiasm and had set about being sociable. Eager to tell of her birthday treat, she had regaled her father's partner with the events of the afternoon, emphasising her own role in helping her family to escape the crowd. The lawyer had listened carefully, eyeing each member of the family in turn, before resting judgementally on Thomas. A sermon, on the need to keep one's religious views private, had followed and for once Thomas did not retaliate. Even he would not challenge his father's former teacher and senior partner.

Her mother, who had played down both her own quick-witted thinking and the potential seriousness of the incident, had bestowed on Martin her warmest of smiles and had enquired if he had any refreshments. Certain of a negative answer, she had been heartened when the lawyer delved into his desk drawer and retrieved some dusty peppermints which he kept for freshening his breath. Thomas had regarded the offering with as much disdain as he dared but she and her mother had taken one. They had eaten them, and a second one, by the time a chastised Joseph arrived with his relieved father.

A sharp knock returned Elizabeth to the present. She tried to ignore the interruption but Catarina's voice, loud and insistent, followed a second impatient knock. The door opened before Elizabeth could gather herself together.

"You are awake." The maid's tone skimmed just below accusatory. "The sun is high in the sky and the Gaulberts have been long gone."

"The Gaulberts?"

"Yes, Jacques Gaulbert came to collect his son." Catarina, realising that her mistress was fully clothed and that the shutters had been opened, stalled momentarily and repeated, "You are awake."

"I am," replied Elizabeth. "And I am well aware of the hour."

Ignoring the rebuff, Catarina bustled across the room towards the bed. Elizabeth, still unused to having a servant, pulled herself further upright against her nest of pillows. "What do you want, Catarina?"

"The Master has sent me to see if you need breakfast."

Feeling herself at a disadvantage on the bed, Elizabeth swung her legs over the side and tried to stand up with as much dignity as she could muster. From her advantageous height she looked down at Catarina. "As I have explained to you before, Monsieur Torres is not the master of this house." She paused for emphasis, hoping that this time her maid would truly hear what she was saying. "He is my guest, my kinsman, who is staying with me to help with my father's affairs." The lie slipped off her tongue as easily as a cheery greeting, spoken so often to acquaintances, that Elizabeth herself could almost believe it. "I am mistress of this house and you must call Monsieur Torres by his name."

Catarina pursed her lips and bit back the retort flashing through her mind. "So be it. Would you like me to bring you some breakfast, Mistress?"

Elizabeth was about to decline but her fingers were itching to read more of her mother's journal and she could not do that undisturbed downstairs. "Yes, thank you, Catarina. I will stay in my chamber."

Once the maid had gone Elizabeth returned to her reminiscing. She thought about Thomas: about how difficult he had always been, pulling in the opposite direction to the family; how he had argued constantly with their father; and how on the day of her birthday treat, he had refused to acknowledge that he had endangered them all. She brought to mind her mother who, as Elizabeth had been growing up, had always tried to mediate in the hope that Thomas would temper his beliefs.

The focus on her brother led Elizabeth to pick up the journal and move to the window-seat. Instead of reading carefully, she flicked through the months following her mother's visit to the vineyard. She glimpsed details about everyday things; the book her mother was reading, a visit to the market, people she had met, and plans to visit the dressmaker, until Elizabeth came to the page she was seeking. She turned towards the window, seeking better light, and gnawing her bottom lip in concentration, Elizabeth began to read.

TWENTY-ONE

The third day of December 1557

ON THIS DAY AT ONE OF THE CLOCK AFTER WE HAD eaten heartily, excepting Alyce, and were all together, Madame Bernade bade us to enter her solar. It is a small room for so many people: myself, Monsieur Hernando Gharsia, Johan, Alyce, Luis, and Madame Bernade. Luis dominated the chamber with his height for he did not sit. He stood behind Alyce with his hands on her shoulders, his face a mask. His grandfather sat very still, waiting, and his eyes sought mine. He raised an eyebrow. Johan was restless and wanted to be elsewhere. He sat on the edge of the settle. Alyce was most quiet and watched Madame Bernade. I was certain of the purpose of our gathering, as for some time Alyce has been unwell and her dress strains evermore across her stomach. Me thinks it is tardy to tell us now.

Madame Bernade sayst quietly that we must all pledge to say nought which would harm Alyce. We must endeavour to show that the babe is the child of her husband who, if asked, we will infer is dead. I looked at Luis, but his face still showed no emotion. Alyce lifted her left hand and rested it on his.

Monsieur Gharsia sayst: When is the babe to be born?

Alyce sayst: April.

Monsieur Gharsia sayst: It is to be hoped that the child does not have black eyes and hair.

Madame Bernade sayst fierily: Hernando, thou must not jest.

There followed a disagreeance betwixt Madame Bernade and Monsieur Gharsia for he sayst that he did not jest but that he was most serious. Me thinks that we must wait until the child is born and be brazen for who in Caors knoweth that Matthew Blake is a man of fair hair and grey eyes. I looked at Alyce whose face was full of anguish at the disagreeance and sayst: What about Henri?

That is a question most thorny for Henri Gaulbert knoweth Alyce had dwelled with Uncle Mercer, in Lewes, for some time before she was arrested. All eyes turned to me. Luis sayst that he will speak to Henri if the babe is late. If not, it is best to say nought. Luis does not go to the farm so often now it is winter, and I have not seen his wife since the harvest. She never comes to Caors. He spends much time with Alyce, but it does not lighten her spirits. This will be a wretched Christmas without Jane.

Elizabeth, conscious of discomfort, stopped reading. She touched her sore lip, painful from being gnawed too vigorously, and stared through the window. She could see into the courtyard, and across the river to the far bank, where skeletal trees etched a pattern against the wintry sky. A lone crow, perched high in one of the branches, cawed incessantly, its discordant cry loud above the sound of a cart trundling across the Pont Neuf. She shivered, feeling all the tension her mother's words conveyed. The caw made her think of death; of her mother, of the child, Jane, and of all the people who had been assembled in that room, especially her father, so recently gone. Her thoughts roamed over each one; those she had known intimately and those who were just a name from the past, all of whom were now dead. Her heart clenched when she brought her parents to mind and, again, when Gabriel stole unbidden amongst them. How could she have spent time reading of the past when her nephew was lost? The future unfurled before her, devoid of those she loved, and stinging tears soon snaked silently down her cheeks.

It was some time before Elizabeth scolded herself for melancholy thoughts and rubbed her wet cheeks with a handkerchief. Gabriel could still be alive. She decided to abandon the journal for the day but as she left her chamber, instead of descending the stairs, her footsteps involuntarily guided her to her father's. Once inside, she searched for the following year's journal with almost feverish haste and soon found it. Then, despite the cold emptiness of the room, which did nothing to alleviate her despondency, Elizabeth opened the shutters and sat back among the scattered books. She skimmed through the relevant pages until she found what she sought.

The twenty-fourth day of April 1558

How can I beareth this: Alyce has perished. Luis keeps to her chamber bellowing in fury, like a wild animal, for his heart is cleaved asunder. It is horrible to hear. The babe lives. He cries lustily and Madame Bernade has acquired a wet-nurse.

I feared Alyce lacketh the strength to bring forth a child, notwithstanding the care we took of her. She knoweth how mightily she was loved and sayst so not three days since. My heart is cleaved asunder, also, for Alyce was my sister and my mother for my mother perished as did she.

Yet while I mourn Alyce I think of myself. By tragedy and happenstance my guardian is now Uncle Mercer which is intolerable. What is to become of me?

As she was reading, Elizabeth experienced such intense emotion that, for a moment, it was difficult to breathe. She stood up and walked to the window. Her father's room looked out over the long, narrow garden at the back of the house, which was presently clad in its winter drabness. Heaps of leaves, brown and brittle, lay trapped at the foot of the low hedges separating the herbs from the rest of the garden. What little colour there was came from the holly tree, its bright berries barely visible among the glossy, spiky leaves, and from an overgrown rosemary at the edge of the herb garden. As she watched, a solitary robin flew down and flitted from bush to bush, his red breast adding another flash of colour to the garden's sombre palette. She fixed her eyes on the small bird, in an effort to recover her calm, and to bring some order to the maelstrom of her thoughts. *If Thomas was her half-brother, did he know? When had their father acknowledged the baby as his? When were her parents married? What had happened to Marie, her father's first wife? Why had she, Elizabeth, never known these things?*

Totally absorbed with her tumble of thoughts, Elizabeth had ignored the cold in the room, but it was beginning to bite. She registered the discomfort in her feet first, the thin leather slippers inadequate in the unheated room, and then shivered violently. Brushing a stray hair back from her face, with a hand so cold that she rubbed it against her other one, Elizabeth decided to go in search of warmth.

As she crossed the hall a low murmuring of voices could be heard from the direction of her father's accounting room. She ignored them and made straight for the kitchen, where she found a small fire smouldering beneath the cooking-pot. At the risk of encroaching on Catarina's new domain, Elizabeth placed another two logs, one across the other, on the embers and watched with great satisfaction as they caught. Then she helped herself to some bread and cheese.

She had almost finished eating when Catarina returned, smiling and humming a lively tune. The maid stopped in her tracks. "I did not expect to find you here, Mistress."

Elizabeth nodded in acknowledgement but, feeling uncomfortable in her own kitchen, she remained silent. Unfazed by her mistress, Catarina resumed her humming and set about attending to the contents of the pot. Watching the maid stir the potage with a secret smile on her face, Elizabeth felt the creeping worm of jealousy: she had never known Catarina smile and hum after she had talked to her. "You are in good spirits today, Catarina," she stated through narrowed lips.

Catarina looked up from her stirring, about to give a pert reply, and then thought better of it. Her face sobered. "I hope I do not disturb you, Mistress. It is but a day since you heard the news of your nephew. I did not know the young man, but I did see him about the city. A fine man."

Caught off guard, Elizabeth's fragile composure faltered. She had been mulling over what Catarina and Pedro must have been talking about and not thinking about Gabriel. Mortified, she tried to speak but words failed her. Catarina took command. She filled a large goblet with the wine that Thomas Gharsia kept for his own consumption, and then added spices. Just before handing it to Elizabeth, she plunged the hot poker into the deep black liquid and said, "Here, drink this. You look mighty pale, Mistress."

"My father does not like me to drink wine."

"Your father is dead," Catarina retorted, somewhat brutally. "Drink it!"

Elizabeth took the cup, lowered her eyes, and sipped. Warmth, from both the wine and the spices, hit her stomach. She took another mouthful, and then another, and watched the dancing flames beneath the pot. Drowsiness descended, and Elizabeth was no longer deliberately avoiding eye contact with her maid: it was becoming too difficult to stay alert.

"Elizabeth!" Pedro's voice cut through her haze. She opened her eyes and he was crouching in front of her, his forehead creased with concern. He took the goblet from her and sniffed the dregs. "Have you drunk all of this?"

"Yes."

"It is wine."

"It was good," she whispered.

"I would not know," he whispered back, conscious of Catarina's presence.

She looked at him long and hard, expecting to feel some embarrassment at seeing him after the intimacy of the previous evening. None came: their exchange about the wine had been almost conspiratorial and bound them together. She experienced a flicker of recognition, a fledgling acceptance that something had shifted in their relationship, and she was glad. Uneasy about Catarina's watchful eyes, Pedro was the first to break the spell. Any hint that he was not the kinsman they claimed him to be, would do untold harm to Elizabeth's reputation. He stood up abruptly, startling Elizabeth, and addressed Catarina. "Please can you light a fire in the winter parlour now that Elizabeth is down."

Catarina, who had been studying them very closely, readily complied with Pedro's demand. However, as she left the room she glanced back, just in time to see the unguarded look on his face.

When Pedro escorted an unsteady Elizabeth into the winter parlour, a cheerful fire was already crackling in the grate and casting a circle of light in the centre of the room. He pulled a chair nearer to the heat and indicated Elizabeth to sit down. Wordlessly, she followed his command and sat staring into the flames. He remained standing, with one hand resting at the end of the mantel; dubious about leaving her but aware that she often appeared to be content with her own company. He waited, watching the firelight dance across the rich auburn strands of her hair, and thought carefully about what he was going to say. He was still thinking when she said rather flatly, "I have been reading my mother's journals."

Pedro knew her well enough not to question her about the content, so he spoke from the heart. "They have unsettled you."

His perception was a characteristic which had already endeared him to her, when she allowed it, and at that moment Elizabeth chose to acknowledge it. "Yes, very much so." She looked up from the fire and locked eyes with him, her pupils so dilated that the entire eye was a black pool of sorrow.

He fought the urge to move towards her and replied, "Leave them be, if they distress you."

"I cannot. I was going to come downstairs earlier but I found myself in my father's room."

"Your father's room?"

"Yes – I found the journals hidden amongst his clothes."

"No wonder you are so chilled."

She nodded, her eyes still on his, and then turned back to the fire. Her voice was so quiet, he had to strain to hear. "I have read about Alyce."

Recalling her reaction when he had first mentioned her father's dying words, Pedro refrained from responding. She turned back to him. "I have learnt things I never knew."

The silence hung in the air, expanding until he felt there were no words he could use. He was saved by a log splitting and spitting a shower of sparks onto the floor. He stamped on them vigorously, crushing the scorched rushes, their acrid smell filling his nostrils. He grabbed the poker and repositioned the logs. "There," he said, "that is better."

Her expression changed, and a ghost of a smile graced her lips. "Thank you."

"Do you need anything?" The ledger he had been working on would not check itself and he had an important meeting the following day.

"No, I am fine." She tried to stand but, on feeling dizzy, flopped back down again. The slap of wood was hard beneath her and it had been more uncomfortable than she wanted to admit. "On second thoughts, could you please bring me a journal from my father's room? It is the one by the window." Pedro looked sceptical. Elizabeth justified herself. "I need to know what happened next." He remained where he was. "Please," she repeated, "I cannot rest until I know what becomes of everyone."

"That may take a long time."

"Yes – especially as my mother has written in English. I have not spoken the language since she died." She glanced at the fire. The room was cosy, and it dawned on her that neither

Pedro nor Catarina would be able to look over her shoulder and understand her mother's words. "I will stay here."

"And not get chilled in an unused room."

Her smile, when it came, contained such genuine warmth that Pedro almost ran up the stairs two at a time.

After he had returned with the book and some candles to combat the already gathering gloom, Pedro left immediately. Before the latch of the door had clicked into place, Elizabeth turned to the next entry in the journal: to her surprise more than a month had lapsed since the last harrowing account.

The thirty-first day of May 1558

All is not as it should be. How can life change so mightily? Luis is gone. His grief is too great, and he cannot beareth to be here. Madame Bernade, or Ysabel as she has asked me to call her, sayst that he will return but it will be upwards of a year or more. He has gone to Constantinople, or Istanbul, as the Ottomans call it. That is where his father dwells. From there he plans to go to Mecca, a place of holy pilgrimage. There has been fierce argument as Luis wanted to go alone but his grandfather insisted that Luis ask his father, Yusuf, to accompany him. Ysabel sayst that there is mighty dislike between Hernando and Yusuf which shows how earnest he is that Luis does not travel without a companion. Also, Ysabel is worried that if Luis is away too long his grandfather may be dead by the time he returns. Yet Hernando has given Luis his blessing to go.

This is a day when my heart sighs. I yearn for Alyce, and

my friend, Luis. I am in a foreign land which is strange without them. Ysabel tries to comfort me and verily, when I am not downcast, me thinks I have been reprieved for Luis cannot take me back to Uncle Mercer if he travels in the East.

The sixteenth day of July 1558

I have neglected my journal but tonight I must recall what befell this day. Madame Marie Gharsia knocked on the door at eleven of the clock this morn and demanded that she speak to her Aunt Ysabel. I was surprised as Marie never comes to Caors. I sayst that Ysabel was at the house in Place St Urcisse, with Hernando, who is unwell. I waited for her to take her leave, but she stood so long on the doorstep that I invited her to enter. I led her through the house to the garden, where we found some shade in which to sit, as the sun was shining brightly. The seat by the wall was cool. She asked about me with great amity but all the time her eyes were on the house. We talked about Luis and the great perils and dangers which might await him and still her eyes stayed on the house.

I enquired diligently of her and sayst: What ails thee?

She sayst: Is the babe in the house?

I sayst: He is with the wet-nurse inside. It is too hot in the garden.

Then she asketh to see the child. The babe was asleep when we saw him for which I was mightily pleased, as he has eyes too black for an Englishman. Nevertheless, his skin is pale and as yet he has little hair. What he has, appears to be dark red. She studied him for too long a time.

She sayst: He resembles his father?

I did not tell a lie for I sayst: Matthew Blake was a man of pale countenance. Her eyes were suspicious but I sayst: I knew Matthew well. Then I added that I did not like him, which was the truth, and that helped allay her fears.

She sayst: What is his name? At that I felt a tightening of my heart and told her that the child was named for our father, Thomas. It was the dying wish of Alyce.

When the wet-nurse took the babe away I asketh Marie Gharsia to take some refreshment. She declined and left. Me thinks she did not come to visit her aunt but to see the babe.

TWENTY-TWO

T HAT NIGHT ELIZABETH COULD NOT SLEEP. HER racing brain rendered all rest impossible and by the early hours she admitted defeat. Rather than seek the sleeping draught which had helped her the previous evening she dressed warmly in her night robe and wrapped her outdoor cloak around her shoulders. Conscious that her feet would be the first to feel the cold, she also pulled on a pair of thick stockings before sliding her feet into her slippers, and then made her way along the silent corridor to search for the journal of 1559.

Earlier that evening, in the comfort of the winter parlour, she had finished the distressing year of 1558. She had read one heart-rending account after another: details of her mother's racking pain at the death of Alyce as anger battled with loneliness and loss, and of Ysabel's searing grief as Hernando had quietly passed away in his sleep to be discovered by an inconsolable Johan. The latter had immediately announced that he would keep the house on the corner of Place St Urcisse in readiness for the return of Luis but then he, too, would leave them. He would retrace the journey he had made as a youth, back to the Pyrenees. In his forties, he was still in possession of his health and vigour and without Hernando he felt his life lacked purpose. He would return to his sister and her husband at the inn at Gavarnie. Elizabeth paused then in her reading. Johan must have changed his mind for she had known him as a young girl and could remember him clearly.

Elizabeth had learnt of her mother's heartbreak and tribulation on her own father's, Thomas Weaver's, death. Memories, triggered by the events of 1558, had poured onto the page in her mother's distinctive writing and Elizabeth had discovered how her distraught mother had joined Alyce and her husband, Matthew Blake, in Bristol, only to be rejected by the clergyman. She had been placed into the care of her Uncle Mercer and his wife in Lewes as nobody knew how to contact her brother, Rufus. The antipathy the child felt for her new home and especially for her aunt leapt from the yellowed paper, upsetting Elizabeth reading the words half a century later.

In the final two entries of 1558, as another miserable Christmas approached, there was a glimmer of hope. Ysabel had pledged that there would always be a home for her mother in Caors as Luis had secretly guaranteed to provide for the Weaver sisters and she was more than happy to give the young woman shelter. At that point in her reading Elizabeth had once again rested the journal on her lap and a profound tenderness for her father had washed over her as she made the connection with her own recent inheritance of the saffron production. Her mother had had no reason to fear for her future as her father had already legally ensured the survival of the remaining members of the Weaver family, even before he had brought them to the Pays d'Oc.

Finally, on the shortest day of the year, news of the death of Queen Mary of England had reached Caors. She had died in the same month as her cousin, Archbishop Pole, and the two architects of the Catholic revival were no more. By eradicating King Edward's Protestant reforms, Mary, in Meg Weaver's view, was responsible for all the woes which became the Weavers. Now Mary's sister, Elizabeth, would rule and once again England would be Protestant. Her mother's joy was apparent in the words she used and the quill had clearly skimmed across the page, but, walking alongside the glee, was the utter futility of Rufus's martyrdom.

Elizabeth had closed the journal, totally wrung out, and had promised herself a breathing space, but now she was padding softly over the worn floorboards towards her father's chamber in search of the next book. As she approached it she heard a shout, followed by a scream, the unmistakable sound of a man in distress.

Pedro was dreaming but the reality was devastating. A small boat, over-packed with men, women, and children, had left Marshila under a summer sky of the clearest blue. The sea, a mirror image of the azure expanse above, had been calm but five hours into the crossing the first white caps appeared, whipped by an ominous wind. At first, they only lapped against the bow but the small craft, so low in the water, soon succumbed. The captain, his feet already wet, scanned his human cargo: weary, undernourished Moriscos who had paid handsomely to reach North Africa. He shouted to his men, who drew their weapons.

The old, the infirm, and any who would not fetch a good price in the slave markets of Algiers were thrown overboard, Pedro's aunt included. Amidst the heart-rending screams, his eyes sought those of his cousin, Juana, and her naked terror forced him to act. He could see his aunt, her arms flailing helplessly, and he had only seconds to act. Thanking Allah that he was one of the few people on the boat who could swim, Pedro dived into the water and struck out towards her.

Panicking as her water-logged clothes pulled her beneath the surface, weighed down further with the jewellery she had secreted in her hem to tide them over in Algiers, she grabbed hold of Pedro in a vice-like grip. Devoid of rational thought, she was deaf to Pedro's entreaties: he tried to release himself but to no avail. They were sinking, sinking, sinking, and he could no longer hold his breath. He opened his mouth to welcome the silky, saline death and then he became aware of the light.

Someone was holding a candle high above his head and the smell of melting wax was nectar to his battled senses. He opened his eyes slowly to see Elizabeth Gharsia peering down at him, her glorious hair tumbling loose around her face. Her voice when she spoke was loud and slightly accusatory, as if she was embarrassed by her concern. "You screamed loud enough to wake the dead." In the circumstances it was an unfortunate choice of words, but he was too relieved to find that he was alive to be offended.

Pedro pulled himself upright. His nightgown, borrowed and too big, fell away from his right shoulder and Elizabeth's gasp had escaped her lips before he had time to recover it. There was a pregnant pause. Elizabeth, with only a glimpse of his back, waited for his reaction; her eyes fixed on the place where criss-cross scars had briefly shone silver in the candlelight. She had never seen the like before, but she knew instinctively what they were. Pedro refused to meet her eyes and eventually said, almost nonchalantly, "They are very old."

"How old?"

"More than twenty years."

"You were but a youth!"

"Yes."

The silence dragged out. "Why?" she asked.

"The Holy Office."

"You were tried for heresy?"

He nodded, his eyes still averted, and stated flatly, "I was fortunate." Elizabeth placed the candle carefully on the bedside table and sat at the end of the bed directly in his line of vision. Their eyes met. "Others were not."

"Who?"

"My brother, Bartolomé."

Elizabeth kept very still, her joined hands resting in her lap. She would not pry, nor was she ready to leave him, so she continued to sit silently on the end of his bed: all thoughts of impropriety negated by the anguish in his eyes. At last, cocooned in the warm glow of the candle, he opened up to her, as images, forever seared in his mind, surfaced. "We were in Saragossa visiting my mother's family. Someone must have denounced us. We never knew who it was. The familiars of the Holy Office are everywhere acting as informers and spies. Moriscos are hunted down intensely but we thought we had been so careful."

"What happened?"

"Bartolomé and I were arrested and taken to the Inquisitor's prison. I was kept alone in a cell and never spoke to my brother again."

"You were tortured?"

"They used the strappado – but not enough to endanger my life. I did not confess. As Moriscos, Bartolomé and I were considered to have relapsed, which would mean we would burn."

"You never saw your brother again?"

"I did see him – at the auto-da-fé – that great spectacle where the accused are publicly brought before the Inquisitor. But I could not speak to him. All the condemned, including me, were seated in tiers according to the gravity of our offences. I was on a lower tier and when I saw Bartolomé being led to a higher one I knew he had confessed to practising Islam. We all wore the sambenito, but his tunic showed he had refused to recant. I could do nothing. All I could do was wait for my turn to be led to the centre of the platform, with my candle in hand, and await my sentence. I denied relapsing and was sentenced to scourging – fifty lashes. I think my brother had saved my life by swearing that I did not do as he did. I escaped prison and the galleys, which were both death sentences in their own way."

Elizabeth almost dared not ask. "What happened to your brother?"

"He was passed to the authorities to be put to death." A brittle laugh followed. "The Holy Office does not dirty its hands with executions."

"My uncle went to the flames in England, during the reign of Queen Mary. He was a Protestant."

"That explains something about your brother, Thomas. My brother did not burn. He died in prison. When the day of execution came he was burnt in effigy. I did not see it as by then I lay between life and death, but a neighbour of my aunt witnessed it."

Pedro shuddered, the recollection of his dream so vivid. "And now all the Moriscos are being expelled from the Spanish kingdoms."

"What ails you?" Elizabeth asked. Her face wore an expression he was unfamiliar with; one of genuine sympathy, and her tone possessed a gentle quality which elicited confidences.

"This night I had a terrifying dream."

"That is why you screamed?"

"Yes."

"What did you dream?"

"My aunt, and many others, were thrown overboard on the voyage to Algiers."

"You have told me rumours of such unspeakable acts."

"Yes – I fear mightily for my aunt and cousin. I did not want them to make the journey."

"It is but a nightmare."

He looked at her long and hard. "What if it is a premonition?"

She held his gaze. "Were you there in your dream?"

"Yes."

"Therefore, it cannot foretell what is to come for you are here." She almost added 'with me' but stopped herself. To conceal her thoughts Elizabeth glanced down at the coverlet and traced the outline of stitching, very aware of what she must say. "I have done you a great injustice."

"You have?"

"Yes."

Under normal circumstances Pedro would have enjoyed her discomfort but within the intimate circle of light, he was just curious. "Why?"

"I called you 'some beggar' my brother picked up in Marshila. It was unworthy of me."

He wanted to be gracious. "I was not begging but I was destitute."

Elizabeth raised her head. "I have come to know you and I apologise. My words have troubled me for some time."

Pedro wished he could prolong the moment, as her contriteness was so engaging, but he found that he did not want to toy with her. He leaned forward and took her clasped hands in his. "Do not dwell on it. You were upset."

242

"Thank you," she said softly.

Unsettled by her closeness Pedro released Elizabeth's hands and asked, "What brought you to this end of the house in the middle of the night?"

"I was on my way to my father's chamber – to find the journal for 1559."

"You have been reading through the night?"

"No – I finished reading what had happened in 1558 earlier this evening, but I could not sleep. The tragedy of it all disturbed me."

"You hope to read of happier times?"

"I want to see when my father returns."

"He went away?"

"After Alyce died he left to seek his father and then to go on pilgrimage to Mecca."

Pedro's brow puckered slightly. "In all our conversations he did not tell me he had been to Mecca."

"I did not know of these things. Much of my father's life is unbeknown to me."

"I would have liked to have talked to him about Mecca."

Elizabeth studied him closely. "Pedro, have you put the past aside?"

"Why do you ask?"

"The past troubles me. All the things I did not know."

He attempted to lighten the mood. "That is because of your nature."

"What do you mean?"

"You want to be in control – to know everything." She opened her eyes wide in mock offence and then smiled broadly. He had gambled and won.

"You have the measure of me."

"I do, Mistress Gharsia. I also know that you must let the past go."

"You have told me that before, in the storm. And you have not answered my question. Have you put the past aside?"

"I have tried although I still dislike the colours red and gold."

"Red and gold?"

"The colours which decorated the platform of the auto-da-fé."

Elizabeth looked down at the red coverlet, which appeared blood-red in the candlelight. "Oh," she said.

"Do not worry. I am a stronger man than that. I look to the future."

"To the Netherlands?"

For the first time Pedro seriously faltered in his resolve. For so long the Dutch provinces had beckoned, with their rebellious nature and hatred of Spain, that he had never contemplated an alternative, but the unusual woman sitting on his bed, wrapped in her outdoor cloak, was weaving a web which threatened to prevent him reaching his goal. He gathered himself and said, rather brusquely, "You had better go."

Hurt fleetingly misted her eyes but then she rose with all the hauteur of which she was capable and soundlessly left the room.

Elizabeth stood for a moment, outside Pedro's chamber, in a state of high dudgeon, all positive feelings towards him temporarily vanquished. *How dare the man speak to her in that authoritative manner? Who did he think he was sitting there in her father's nightshirt?* As she brought to mind the silvery scars, her ill humour ameliorated a fraction, but she firmly shut her mind to any thoughts of him. She stood poised, indecisive about what to do next, when the candle fluttered in a sudden draught and extinguished. She uttered an unladylike oath, one her brother, Thomas, regularly used, and started to feel her way back to her own room, inch by inch.

On reaching her destination one of her slippers fell off and as she manoeuvred herself through the door she stubbed her right little toe. The pain was momentarily excruciating. She hobbled and then fell, the candle and its holder scattering across the floor. She stayed where she lay and emitted a great cry, out of all proportion to her injury. Great sobs followed as Elizabeth wrestled with all of her recent discoveries. She wept for Alyce who had died in childbirth, for her father whose world had been wrecked, for her mother, a very young woman struggling to adjust, and for Gabriel who appeared to be lost forever. Finally, she succumbed to tears of self-pity, lamenting her own situation. At thirty-seven years old she was bereft of her father and mother, without a brother at home for whom she could keep house, and with no hope that she would ever welcome her nephew home. She was a woman without a role and the future loomed large before her, laced with uncertainty.

At last Elizabeth's sobbing abated. She crawled across the floor to the bed and climbed in. Her fingers trembled as she unfastened her outdoor cloak, and let it fall onto the plaited rush mat, before she slid under the covers fully clothed. She turned on her side, drew up her knees and refused to think about Pedro, but he crept into her thoughts unbidden. Once his contract terminated he would leave for the Netherlands, taking advantage of easier travelling conditions, and she would be left in this cavernous house with only an obstinate maid for company. Treacherous tears leaked from her closed eyes. She wiped them away vigorously, stretched out, and flung herself onto her back. The full moon had broken cover from the clouds and Elizabeth could see the outline of the shutters. She watched the light until she fell into an exhausted sleep.

ELIZABETH

1610–11

TWENTY-THREE

Novemeber rolled into December and Elizabeth spent many of the dark, short days immersed in her mother's journals. The pages covering the year 1559 proved sparse and sketchy with little of great interest. She learnt that the baby, Thomas, was weaned. He was growing into a lusty boy and had developed an attachment to his Aunt Meg which Ysabel was pleased to see. There were accounts of new teeth, of a worrying fever, and of the gaping hole left in Meg's life by the death of her sister and the departure of Luis. It was as if all the young woman's affection and attention were focused on the child. As the year progressed there were more descriptions of Thomas; of his first steps, of his curiosity about the world around him, and, tellingly, among these was the brief statement that the child was never taken by Ysabel to visit the Gaulberts.

As Elizabeth read about the imminent arrival of Christmas 1559 she recalled her mother's customary excitement as the festival approached. When her children were young, Meg had insisted that the family follow the traditions that the Weavers had practised in England. After the fasting of Advent, her mother had always prepared a mince pie bulging with dried fruit, mutton, and spices, and had plucked the plumpest goose the Gaulberts had raised. The Yule log was lit on Christmas Eve to burn throughout the festive days and Elizabeth had always felt sad on Twelfth Night when it was almost all over. On that night the family would exchange gifts, play games, and enjoy the pudding with the hidden coin. As a child, alight with anticipation, Elizabeth had loved the process of searching through her slice in the hope that she would be honoured with leading the evening's amusement.

A memory, shiny and bright as one of the newly minted coins, surfaced with such clarity that it threw Elizabeth off balance. Her mother had decided to start the fun with a game of Blind Man's Bluff. Excited, Elizabeth had watched her father tie the blindfold and turn her mother round and round. Laughing, Meg had lifted the cloth and peeped at Luis, her eyes ablaze with mischief, and Elizabeth had witnessed a returned look of such tenderness that she had felt the need to turn away. Thinking about that evening, a quarter of a century later, Elizabeth experienced conflicting emotions: the sobering thought that on that evening her mother was younger than she herself was now, and also that her parents had tried to fill the house with joy. Other recollections came flooding back, memories of her parents together, which calmed Elizabeth and made her speak to the empty room. "We were blessed. As a family we were blessed."

Spurred by her reminiscences, Elizabeth went in search of Pedro. He was, as usual, in the accounting room, poring over documents as if he dared not waste a single second. It was just before noon and a shaft of winter sunlight pooled onto the desk, highlighting Pedro's concentration. He finished what he was writing before he raised his head, expertly hiding his pleasure at her arrival. Elizabeth did not wait to be greeted.

"Pedro, I have decided that we must celebrate Christmas as my mother did."

Her outburst was so different from what he expected that for a moment Pedro felt wrong-footed: used to the normally despondent Elizabeth, upset by her mother's journal, he just shrugged and said, "What can I say?"

She gave him a stern look. "You could say that an English Christmas will fill you with delight!"

"How do I know it will fill me with delight if I have no experience of such an event?"

Elizabeth studied Pedro, not sure whether she was being teased. His face was unreadable. "I will make it a celebration you will not forget."

"That I do not doubt."

"There will be rich food and merriment."

"What will we eat?"

"A pudding with spiced fruit."

"A pudding with spiced fruit! That would be wondrous."

"And a goose – I must see Jacques about a goose."

"A goose! That is truly wondrous."

"You jest with me, Sir!"

Pedro allowed himself a flicker of a smile. "No, I am not." Elizabeth raised her eyebrows. "Well – only a little," he admitted. "But I look forward to Christmas. I have never eaten a pudding made with spiced fruit."

Elizabeth paused, as if she was deciding which way the conversation should progress, and then she returned his smile. "Wait until after the victuals when it is time for merriment."

Pedro's expression changed. "I cannot play the zany."

Elizabeth, enjoying the moment, agreed. "Verily, I cannot see you as the clown. You are more at home with the ledgers."

"You have the sum of me, Mistress Gharsia."

She laughed. "That I do!"

Revelling in her spontaneity, he spoke without thought. "And I am getting the measure of you even more." She stared at him intently. Immediately he became guarded. "I must finish this work before morning's end."

Aware of the sudden change of atmosphere, Elizabeth took his lead. "What worries you?"

"There are several debts outstanding. Your brother will expect them to be paid."

"Shall I look? Unlike you, I might know the people."

"Thank you," he said formally. "I will finish and then show you what I have found."

Elizabeth nodded and turned on her heel. As she lifted the door-latch, she glanced back over her shoulder. "Pedro."

"Yes."

"Although my father was always true to Islam, he did enjoy the Christmas celebrations."

He smiled at her once again and she was almost out of the door when he said, "Elizabeth."

She took a step backwards but did not turn around. "Yes, Pedro."

"If you want to go to see Jacques Gaulbert about a goose, I will accompany you."

A secret smile, not often seen, curved Elizabeth's lips. "We will see," she said. "We will see."

Their breath, and that of the horses, condensed in the cold air, and the keen wind stung their faces, yet both Elizabeth and Pedro found themselves in high spirits. Earlier than expected, the frozen earth of the farmyard glistened in the wintry sunlight as the absence of mud had meant that they had made good time. At the sound of hooves, the door at the top of the stone staircase flung open to reveal an animated Helena inviting them in. "You are here!" she called.

Elizabeth waved in return. "Yes – we have come for a goose!"

"Come on up. Pedro, take the horses to the near barn and then come and join us."

Minutes later, it was a cheerful group gathered around the Gaulberts' kitchen table. Jacques and Luc had returned from the cellar where they had been sampling their oldest vintage, made while Luc was in New France. The vintner had been eager to learn his son's opinion, and continued to relish their restored partnership, so wine-making dominated the conversation. Elizabeth, as Luis's daughter, contributed fully while Pedro was content to sit back and listen, appreciating the passionate discussion.

Helena was particularly pleased to have company, a luxury in the winter, and wanted Elizabeth to stay the night. "You will need to leave soon so that you return by daylight and we have not yet eaten."

"Pedro and I have bought victuals with us. We plan to eat on the way home."

Helena rose from the bench and opened the door, letting in an icy blast. "I think the sky is darkening already. It could snow."

Jacques snorted. "Stop your nonsense, Helena," he said affectionately. "It is too cold to snow. Be honest and ask Elizabeth to stay because you want to gossip. She is always good company." Jacques turned his handsome face towards Elizabeth, and if Pedro had not been watching so closely he would have missed the wash of blush which coloured her creamy skin. It puzzled him, for it was so unlike the woman he had come to know: acting demurely seemed alien to Elizabeth, nevertheless, a simple compliment from an old friend had her turning coy. It was a nugget of information which he would store, to help him understand the enigmatic Elizabeth.

Sara chipped in, supporting her son. "Please stay, Elizabeth. We could do with some diversion to liven these long days."

"They are short days, Mother," corrected Jacques.

"Only if you have much to occupy oneself. My eyes are too old and tired for close work."

Elizabeth looked from one to the other. She could not refuse. "Thank you," she said. "I accept your invitation." The words had left her lips before she realised she had not consulted Pedro. Treated like a servant, he refused to meet her eye, so he missed the spectacle of her floundering in her mistake. Sara did not.

"Do not worry, Monsieur Torres, you will have a warm bed for the night. You can share with Luc." As the recipient of the proffered hospitality, Pedro had no alternative but to acquiesce. He nodded in acknowledgement, and courteously accepted through narrowed lips, which did not quite mask his displeasure. "That is decided, then," the old woman announced with delight. "Elizabeth will sleep with me." She smiled at her son. "There will be time enough on the morrow to kill the goose."

The household retired early as the Gaulberts had never seen the sense of using too many candles to light the long winter evenings. Elizabeth, glad of the prospect of a warm bed rather than a cold ride home, had slid the warming-pan into Sara's bed before supper and now she offered to help the old woman undress. As soon as Jacques and Helena were out of earshot, behind their partition, Sara chuckled and whispered playfully, "Your kinsman is out of sorts." For a moment, Elizabeth was confused, which confirmed the old woman's suspicions. She added emphatically, "Your kinsman – Pedro Torres – seems upset about staying the night." Elizabeth uttered a sound, a peculiar amalgam of a cough and a nervous laugh. Sara patted her arm. "He is no kinsman, is he?" Elizabeth did not answer and concentrated on folding Sara's clothes. "You do not need to busy yourself doing that, my dear. Do not worry, your secret is safe with me."

Elizabeth replied, somewhat haughtily, "Thomas has asked Pedro to stay awhile and help with Papa's enterprises, as he cannot. My brother will be back soon. I expect him for Christmas."

"Yes, my dear." However, Sara was not going to be easily deflected. "Now he is eating well, your guest is turning into a very fine man."

"I hadn't noticed."

"You must have done. He is almost unrecognisable from the man who came with you and your father six months ago."

"I see him every day. You don't see alteration in the same way."

The old woman agreed. She knew when she was defeated. She would not be able to coax Elizabeth Gharsia into revealing more. "Come to bed quickly," she ordered, "I'm shivering."

As they lay cocooned in the bed's warmth, Elizabeth admitted, "I have been reading my mother's journals."

"You found them."

"Yes, they were among my father's clothes."

"And what did you find out?"

Elizabeth thought quickly, unwilling to disclose too much. As a means of deflection, she asked, "When did you first meet my mother?"

Sara's memory of the distant past was as sharp as if it was yesterday. "I first met Meg in Bordèu, in the spring of 1560. She was returning to England with Luis. Henri was with them – he always took the chance to leave the farm and spread his wings. They only stayed two nights. It was a very difficult time for me. My husband, Samuel, was dying. I did not know it then, but I feared for him. He was my friend and protector and I was consumed with worry about my future.

"I was sitting by Samuel's bedside – we had a bed downstairs which used to be his mother's – when they knocked on the door. It heartened Samuel mightily to see his old friends. Henri was full of life, but Luis was downcast. Your mother, although courteous, burned with indignation at being taken back to England. She fascinated me. I had never been near eyes of so intense a blue or skin so pale. Her hair did not hang straight like mine but bounced, thick and wavy, whenever she moved. It was light brown with threads of red and gold." Sara stopped abruptly. "I digress. Of course, you will remember your mother's hair. I am prattling like an old woman!"

"Yes – she used to let me brush it when I was a little girl. But please carry on, Sara."

"They managed to gain a passage quickly and left, as I said, after two nights."

"What came to pass in England?"

"That I cannot tell you. I only know what I witnessed when they returned and what Henri told me later."

Elizabeth reached out across the bed and gently touched Sara's hand. "Your husband?"

"Samuel was old enough to be my father, even older, and his health was never good. Since 1557 we had suffered. The harvests were poor, food was short in the city, and sickness was rife. By the time Henri, Luis, and Meg returned from England in the early autumn, Samuel had died. I was almost destitute. There was very little money left in Samuel's coffer. He had not worked as a physician for many months and when he had worked people struggled to pay him. My only hope was to accept the charity of Samuel's cousin, Jacob, but I knew Jacob's wife did not want an extra mouth to feed."

"What did you do?" asked Elizabeth, although she knew the answer.

"I accepted Henri Gaulbert's offer of marriage. I had always enjoyed his company and I suspected that he had admired me for some time. He had never argued when I watered down his wine and he would always accompany me when I had errands to run. Henri was a kind man, Elizabeth. A kind man is a gift. Samuel was a kind man, too."

"Did you ever regret what you did?"

"Never! I first beheld the farmhouse on a soft September evening. Its stone glowed, cross-lit from the sinking sun, and Henri took my arm and led me towards it. The space around me took my breath away. It was a different world from the Rue Judaica and the crooked, crowded streets around the Basilica of Saint Seurin. That I, Sara Milanges, should have such a home brought tears to my eyes. I worked hard and every day I thanked God that Henri Gaulbert had asked me to be his wife. Then, the children came. I lost one child in the womb, and another at birth, and I feared I would never be a mother. But then Jacques was born. And he lived. Did I ever regret taking my chance, Elizabeth? Never, never, never."

"And my father and my mother?"

"I knew something had changed as soon as I saw them. On the other occasions I had met your father he was contemplative, and often melancholic. Only once had I seen him in a lighter humour – when he was going to ask for Alyce Weaver's hand. But that ended in failure. Now I was looking at a different person. There was a calm about him and he laughed often with your mother. Meg appeared to be lit from within, beautiful in her youth and happiness. Remember, she was not yet twenty then. But there was no sign that they would marry."

"What caused the difference?"

"Two things – I believe. Henri said that there was a mighty

argument with Edward Mercer, your mother's guardian. He wanted her to marry the son of one of his acquaintances. Luis thought the young man was not worthy of Meg. Mercer told Luis that, as he was not a relation, he had no say in the matter. Meg said she would kill herself rather than marry her suitor."

"That sounds like my mother. She always liked drama. She would never have done such an evil thing!"

"Luis insisted that Meg's feelings be heeded and just when it appeared that no solution could be found, a letter arrived from Henri's aunt, Ysabel. It had taken four months to reach Lewes and it carried sad news. Your father's wife, Marie, had died of the sickness like so many others. Henri mourned his sister, but he believed he was alone in his grief. Although your father behaved with propriety, Henri could see no sign of sorrow. He did not know what Luis said to Mercer, but he thinks your father promised to provide for Meg himself. By the end of that week, the three of them were on the way back to Bordèu."

"I need to know more."

"Find the journal of 1560."

"I will as soon as I get home."

Elizabeth turned on her side with her back towards Sara. "Good night."

"Are you still awake, Elizabeth?"

"Yes."

"Be careful with what you find in the journals."

"I will."

"Good."

"Let sleeping dogs lie."

"What was that? I can't hear you so well when you are facing away from me."

"One of my mother's favourite sayings – let sleeping dogs lie."

Sara turned on her side but could not get comfortable. The niggling pain in her hip was troubling her and, after talking about the past, she felt very old. She moved position carefully, as Elizabeth was already beginning to breathe sonorously, but she could not stop herself fidgeting.

Elizabeth was vexed. "You have woken me up."

"You cannot be asleep so soon."

"I was."

There was a long pause. Elizabeth settled back down and pulled the coverlet up over her ears. She was drifting off into the most restful sleep she had experienced for some time when Sara's voice pierced her consciousness. "Is your Monsieur Torres a kind man?" Elizabeth pretended not to hear but the old woman's words curled around Elizabeth's mind until they had firmly taken root.

TWENTY-FOUR

E LIZABETH DID NOT HAVE AN OPPORTUNITY TO find the journal of 1560 as Thomas arrived the following day, Christmas Eve. Although it was late afternoon, and Catarina had already closed the shutters, Elizabeth and Pedro had only been home an hour. As usual, she greeted her brother with mixed feelings; pleasure at the familiarity of him, so like their father, and apprehension about his mood. However, tired from the long journey from Montauban, Thomas's priority was to eat, smoke his pipe in contented solitude, and then retire to bed. Elizabeth, aided by Catarina, worked late into the evening preparing the festive food and Pedro had helped too, pleasing Elizabeth by offering to pluck the goose.

Their labours were rewarded. On Christmas Day the goose was rich and succulent, the moist, minced beef pie crumbled in the mouth, and the marzipan cake at the end of the meal was a triumph of Elizabeth's culinary skills. Thomas leaned back and patted his stomach. "Bess, that was as good as any meal Mama cooked."

She chose not to rise to his bait about her name. "Thank you. I wanted to make an effort this year. It is our first without

Papa, and for the three years since Mama died we did not have the heart to celebrate."

Thomas looked at the empty chairs around the table, his sharp features tight with emotion. "It cannot be three years since Mama died."

"It is — it is near four."

Whatever Thomas was going to say, he appeared to ponder on it and then think better of it. Instead, he said, "Have you any news of that young pup, Gabriel?"

The joy of the occasion leached away. Elizabeth's last piece of marzipan cake threatened to lodge in her throat. "You don't know!"

"I don't know what?"

Elizabeth glanced at Pedro, who came to her rescue. "Luc Gaulbert is back. He visited last month to give Elizabeth news of your nephew."

Thomas eyed his sister searchingly. "I can tell by your reaction that the news was not welcome."

Elizabeth recovered some of her composure. "It is feared that he has been captured by Indians."

"But I thought Champlain was on good terms with the local people."

"He is, but these are a different tribe."

"Why did you not send word to me immediately?"

"I don't know," replied Elizabeth, which was only partially the truth. She had been too caught up with her own shock, and her mother's journals. With a jolt, she realised that she had neglected to inform her brother, Joseph, about his son. Guilt made her aggressive. "I did not know whether you were in Uzès or Montauban! What could you do anyway?"

"I could have made enquiries."

Elizabeth was dismissive. "How could you find out more than Luc knows? New France is so far away."

Thomas had the grace to be honest. "You are correct, Sister. I have few contacts of influence now."

Elizabeth looked at the remnants of the meal. Now, it was unpalatable. She started to gather up the best pewter plates and the cutlery, as Catarina was spending the day with her brother and his family. Without a word she walked out of the room. Thomas raised his eyebrows and pulled at a piece of goose while Pedro reasoned with himself over the wisdom of sharing with Thomas the suspicion that Gabriel had been fighting alongside his captors. As it was not his decision to make, he said, "Thomas, you should speak to Jacques Gaulbert. Perhaps Luc has talked more fully to his father."

Thomas popped another gobbet of meat into his mouth. "Yes, I'll talk to Jacques. Now there's a good man."

Pedro, seizing the moment, asked, "Has your family always been close to the Gaulberts?"

Thomas, luxuriating in the aftermath of a fine meal, did not appear to find the question odd. "My father and Henri Gaulbert, Jacques's father, were friends since childhood."

"Jacques has proved a worthy friend, especially when your father died."

Thomas acquiesced, nodding his head.

"Was there ever any thought of a union between the families?"

"A union?"

"Sometimes, families who are close form an alliance through marriage." Thomas shook his head in response and reached for another slice of marzipan. Pedro had ventured so far he could not stop himself. "It is perhaps possible that Jacques and Elizabeth could have made a match."

"Bess and Jacques!" hooted Thomas. "The only time Jacques showed any interest in our family was when Joseph brought his comely wife to visit. He was never away from our door!" Suddenly more incisive, Thomas added, "Why do you think Jacques and Bess would have been a decent match?"

Pedro flinched, unperceptively, under Thomas's penetrating gaze. "No reason, except that both families are involved with wine."

Thomas relaxed and chuckled. "I cannot imagine any man being brave enough to take Bess to wife!"

Pedro held his peace. Thomas continued to pick at the leftovers while his companion's heart felt for the young woman whose admiration for Jacques had been unreciprocated.

"You two are very quiet," pronounced Elizabeth as she returned from the kitchen to collect the remaining food.

"Sit down, Bess," Thomas ordered. "I have yet to finish."

She did as she was told and received a sympathetic glance from Pedro. "That was a delicious meal."

Before Elizabeth could reply, Thomas butted in. "Have you any news of the Netherlands, Pedro?"

"Not since last year's truce."

"Do you think it will last?"

"I think it has a good chance," said Pedro. "After over thirty years of struggle Spain is exhausted. She would not have recognised Dutch independence and signed a truce otherwise. The United Provinces have all the advantages, especially the province of Holland. The Dutch have a continuous source of wealth as they have already made great progress in the carrying trade. Their ships are superior in every way, the fluytships can carry more cargo, they need fewer sailors to man them, and as they are made from pine, they are cheap to build. They are an ambitious people. Their East India Company has only been established seven years but soon, I believe, it will dominate the carrying trade east of Good Hope."

Elizabeth watched his face, alive with enthusiasm, and

said, "It sounds as if the United Provinces will be prosperous now they are free of Spain."

"Yes. Trade is what matters. A man is not persecuted for his religion if he worships privately. Amsterdam flourishes, it is an exciting place for an industrious man."

Elizabeth tried to mask her disappointment about his continued interest in the Dutch: such fervour indicated a strong resolve to be part of the new country. She stood up and slowly lifted the platter littered with the debris of the goose. The day, which had already lost its gloss, had palled even further.

It was time for Thomas to leave. Twelfth Night had come and gone with none of the merriment Elizabeth had anticipated. The mood of their party of three had not been conducive to jollity so the festive season had ended somewhat despondently as she and Pedro had stripped the hall of its greenery. Thomas had excused himself on the pretext of packing for his departure the following day.

The first rays of wintry light washed the horizon as Thomas set out for Montauban. Elizabeth stood on the doorstep, her thick outdoor cloak hiding her night attire. Thomas looked at her with a hint of disapproval. "You did not need to rise from your bed to say a farewell."

"I wanted to."

Thomas stood awkwardly, waiting. His natural choice would have been to stride out towards the livery stable and to be on his way as quickly as possible, but Elizabeth's woebegone face and dejected stance stalled him. "Thank you," he said.

"For what?"

"Christmas, it reminded me of old times." Elizabeth's eyes filled with tears. "Don't weep, Bess."

"I miss them so much."

"It is life, Bess. We are born, and we die."

"I know," she whispered, as she wiped away a stray tear with the back of her hand. "I have been reading Mama's journals." The words slipped out and it was too late to retrieve them.

"Mama kept journals?"

"Yes," she admitted and then added hurriedly, "they are mostly about outings, recipes, and sundry things."

Thomas nodded, already disinterested. His sister, although relieved at this, felt the overwhelming urge to beg him to stay. "I wish you didn't have to go."

He bristled. "You know I must. I have even thought of going with Pedro to Amsterdam later in the year. The Calvinists are strong there and we Huguenots need all the friends we can get." In response, Elizabeth's tears flowed more freely. "You must understand," he continued, "that some things are bigger than family." She shook her head. He retaliated. "Mama understood," he stated defiantly.

"She did?"

"Yes, because of her brother, Rufus. I could talk to her."

"And not Papa?"

"He never understood."

"He just wanted to keep you safe, and all of us."

"We chafed against each other for as long as I can remember."

Thomas had never spoken in this way before, so Elizabeth took her chance and gently probed. "What is your first memory of Mama?"

"Being upset and Mama hugging me, surrounding me with the scent of lavender."

"She always wore that perfume."

"I must have been very young because in my memory she is kneeling." Elizabeth watched his face soften. "I carry it with me always."

"I have treasured memories, too." They looked at each other, bound together more closely than they had been for years. She kissed his cheek. "Safe journey."

He stood still a moment longer and then turned on his heel. She watched him until he was out of sight and then whispered to herself, "Let sleeping dogs lie."

After Thomas had left, Elizabeth went to the kitchen, where she found Catarina about to warm some water for her mistress's morning wash. The maid bustled around the room, huffing and puffing under her breath, behaving as if Elizabeth had deliberately arrived early in the kitchen to inconvenience her. Instead of finding the situation amusing, as Pedro usually did, Elizabeth bridled and spoke curtly, demanding that Catarina bring both water and food to her chamber.

Once there, Elizabeth regretted her reaction and chided herself. She should be more like Pedro, who would have talked amiably with Catarina and offered some assistance. He had the ability to coax the best out of the maid whereas she always appeared to do the opposite. She thought about Thomas and his comment about chafing against their father and she wondered if such friction could be avoided. She would try and be more patient, and when Catarina arrived at the door, Elizabeth was so cordial that the maid regarded her warily through narrowed eyes.

Having congratulated herself on being agreeable, Elizabeth washed and dressed hurriedly. Her breakfast could wait and in a matter of minutes she was on her way to her father's chamber. A damp, musty smell greeted her as the door swung open, and faint shafts of light, from the edges of the closed shutters, illuminated the thick film of dust which had accumulated, unnoticed, over the preceding weeks. Following the light, Elizabeth opened the shutters and then the window. Cold air flooded in, fresh and sharp, and Elizabeth breathed deeply, tasting the lingering tang of frost.

Pulling her shawl tightly around her, she left the window ajar and set about the task of finding the relevant book. It took some time, and she was becoming dispirited when she came across the journal of 1561. Following a hunch, Elizabeth smiled with delight. She was correct; her mother had included the end of the previous year in that volume.

Christmas 1560

Verily I am home for this is the place where those I love dwell. We have been returned from England for many weeks, but I have not written of my happenings. I was well wearied by my travels in body but also in spirit and am heartily glad now to be restored.

Ysabel greeted me as a daughter and Thomas, who did not remember me at first, soon followed me everywhere. He is a strong child and understands much but speaks little. It disappoints me that he has no affinity with Luis. He hides when Luis visits, as he did when Luis came back from Mecca. Luis remains in the house in Place St Urcisse with Johan who has not yet departed for the Pyrenees. Ysabel sayst not to worry about Thomas for he is young, not yet three years, and Luis is a stranger to him. We must give him time.

I did not write on my travels as I was too full of ire and never wanted a reminder of that time. Luis thought himself honourable to take me back to Uncle Mercer in Lewes, when Henri and he were delivering the saffron, but I did not want to go and cared not a flea for being honourable. Luis argued that it was safe for me to return to England now that Queen Elizabeth reigns and not the Catholic Mary. I was mightily relieved when Uncle Mercer wanted me to marry Job Beste for I could rail and rage against it. Uncle Mercer, who is a caring man at heart, not like his shrew of a wife, did not know what to do. I was saved by Marie Gharsia dying. I have said divers prayers for her and feel sadness for her as she was a troubled woman. I am also melancholy because Luis is a free man yet Alyce is dead. As soon as he heard the news about Marie, Luis made an accord with Uncle Mercer, but he will not tell me of it.

We set off for Caors without delay but when we reached Bordèu, after a voyage where we suffered great discomfort from the movement of the ship, we found Sara Milanges in dire circumstances. She dwells now with the Gaulberts and is to marry Henri when her mourning is over. Me thinks we have become friends. I have visited her on the farm oft times and she comes to see me on market day when she can.

It is late, and my candle is burnt low and I have not written about Christmas. The wind is whistling around the chimney and Thomas is snuffling in his sleep. We moved his cot into my chamber as Ysabel is getting too old to be disturbed at night. It is no trouble for me. The child is good and only wakes if he has a cold or has eaten something which upsets him. Me thinks Thomas likes it too. In the mornings he climbs into my bed. We make a tent and I tell him stories. I often look at him to see signs of Alyce. She is there in the red lights in his hair and, I believe, in his hands. Although scarcely out of babyhood he has her long slender fingers.

Engrossed, Elizabeth did not register the first knock. She

jumped as the hand rapped more loudly, twice. Pedro's voice penetrated the thick oak. "Elizabeth, are you there?"

"Yes, come in."

The icy air hit Pedro as he opened the door to find her sitting on the floor, tightly wrapped in her shawl. Around her, apparently scattered randomly, were numerous bound journals of varying sizes. His eyes swept the room. "Are they in order?"

"No," she replied. "I should spend more time sorting them but each time I become lost in my mother's words."

"I cannot read English but if the date is clear I could help."

She was about to dismiss the offer and then changed her mind. "Thank you."

"What year are you reading about now?"

"1561."

Pedro picked up the book nearest to him. It was clearly marked '1594'. He carefully placed it back on the floor and picked up the one next to it which was written two years later. "Are these in the same place as when you first discovered them, because these two go together."

"I did do some sorting, Pedro," replied Elizabeth, "just not enough!"

"I'll help you put them in decades. That should help."

"Yes."

"But first of all, I am going to close the window."

On his way back across the room Pedro scooped up what he assumed was an early journal as the cover was worn and the pages yellowed. As he opened it a flower, dry and papery, floated towards the floor. He caught it skilfully in one hand just before it landed. "Look at this," he said, as he continued towards her.

The flower, once the most exquisite violet, nestled in the centre of Pedro's large palm, its faded petals still holding some colour. Elizabeth leant forward, certain she could smell an echo of the flower's distinctive scent. She experienced an irresistible urge to reach out and touch it, but whether it was the flower itself, or Pedro's palm, which drew her hand forward she did not know.

"It is a love token," she said, her voice thick with emotion.

"A very old one," replied Pedro, as he handed the violet to Elizabeth with a bashful smile.

"Mistress Gharsia?" Catarina's voice boomed from the foot of the stairs and ambushed the moment. "I am going to the market now. Is there anything you have forgotten to ask me to get?"

Elizabeth's hackles, instantly raised, were smoothed by Pedro's understanding grin and she found herself replying calmly, "Thank you, no, I do not need anything else." She met his twinkling eyes and felt a surge of hilarity.

"She cannot help it," he said. "It is her nature."

"I cannot help it, either," admitted Elizabeth between bouts of chortling.

"Who do you think the token is from?"

"It must be my father."

Pedro handed her the book and she turned the pages carefully until she found the one stained by the pressed flower. For the first time she read aloud.

The tenth day of June 1562

This day is a day most glorious. Francesco Zametti approached me after mass. He is a pleasing young man who is the nephew of Lorenzo Zametti who taught with Hernando at the university. Ysabel was busy talking and I was standing apart with Thomas. Francesco greeted me with a bow and gave me a gift of violets. I marvelled at them as I had long suspected his intent, but this is the first time he proveth it.

When I told Ysabel and Luis, he sayst that Zametti is a young man of fair words but no substance. Seemingly, I am not to encourage him. I will not do as Luis sayst for his natural inclination is to gloom. Oft times, it is I who cheers him yet not this day. I favour Francesco Zametti and sayst to Luis that he is like an old man, albeit he be but six and thirty. He sayst that I be too pert.

Elizabeth raised her eyes to see Pedro studying her closely. "You do not understand?"

"Some words, I do."

She translated the entry, giving him the gist but quoting Meg's interchange with Luis verbatim.

Pedro nodded in approval. "I like your mother."

Elizabeth's expression made her beautiful. "So do I."

"How did they ever marry?"

"I have no idea."

"But there will be an account of it somewhere," said Pedro, as he returned his attention to the scattered books.

GABRIEL

1611

TWENTY-FIVE

Mohawk village in the valley of the Mohawk River, March 1611

A S THE THREAD OF SEASONS UNWOUND GABRIEL realised that, after three years in the New World, he was adjusting to his environment. He had not pined when the winter solstice had occurred, aching for the familiarity of a Christmas in Caors, as he had done the previous two Decembers. The dark days of January and February had passed and now, as he lay in his bed listening to the sounds of melting snow, Gabriel found himself looking forward to the spring planting. Already the snow had receded enough to expose the cornstalks left to nurture the soil after the previous year's harvest and soon the women would pull them out and sow the new crop. He had never delighted in the first days of spring when he had lived in France, either as a student in Paris or as a child growing up in Caors. He had often accompanied his grandfather to tend the vines, to pinch out all the buds except one on each stem, but it had always been a chore reluctantly performed. His thoughts roamed to his aunt, Elizabeth, and her pleasure in her herb garden, and he was a small boy again, basket in hand, as she snipped the various leaves, all the while explaining the value of each plant.

He rolled over onto his back, experiencing the full force of the dilemma which always teased him on waking. If he was to make the journey back to Kebec he would need to depart within the next few weeks, yet how could he leave? He was confident the tribe would let him go, for Matwau's honour had long been re-established and the brave would not prevent him leaving. However, the village was so depleted, so lacking in its young men, that Gabriel felt it was ignominious to desert the Mohawks. He tossed and turned under the covers, his predicament gnawing at his serenity, and, feeling constricted and over-heated, he pushed them back.

The sun had not yet risen but he could already hear someone stirring. The fire had been replenished and now the uneven soft padding of feet moved towards the food-pit where the corn kernels were stored, kept free of mould by its bluegrass lining. Without opening his eyes, he knew it was Aarushi, continually proving her value to the community by making herself indispensable. There was still a good supply of dried produce as the women had harvested the crops as usual, but it was in the provision of meat that the tribe's destruction was obvious. With so few active men it had been difficult to drive entire herds of deer into a restricted area with no escape, and the hunters had been reduced to targeting individual game.

He fought the urge to rise to help Aarushi and determined to stay in bed until the food was ready. That was an adjustment he still found hard but at last, after many warnings from Matwau, he usually acted like a Mohawk warrior. To distract himself from his dilemma and the wish to aid Aarushi, Gabriel turned his thoughts to Oheo and began to dissect every recent look and action. Since the disastrous campaign of the previous summer Oheo had gradually paid him more attention. From being initially suspicious of Gabriel and Matwau's return, when her own husband and so many others had perished, she had eventually accepted their survival as a considerable feat and acted with greater respect.

In such moments of reflection Gabriel could even delude himself that perhaps the traditional marriage arrangements of the Mohawk could be abandoned due to the dire circumstances of the village. He usually surfaced from such considerations with a jolt, for how could he be contemplating marriage and leaving the tribe simultaneously? He sat up quickly and shook his head. He must concentrate on the present. Flinging off the bedcovers, Gabriel sprang to his feet, pulled back the hide curtain and almost collided with Aarushi returning with a basket of kernels ready to grind.

As he reached out to steady her, Aarushi's face broke into her customary beaming smile. "You are ready for the day, early!"

"So are you!" he countered.

She relaxed for a moment, enjoying the exchange, when the rustle of someone rising and the flap of a curtain caused her to move away from the fire. Her face, no longer illuminated by the flames, was now masked and Gabriel was unaware of her disappointment. All he could see was Oheo coming towards him, her eyes bright with challenge. She did not stop but side-stepped him and continued, without speaking, to the sanitation pits. He needed to relieve himself, so he waited a few courteous minutes and then followed.

There was no sign of her and as it was impossible for him to have missed her, Gabriel slipped out of the longhouse. The cold air caught at his throat and filled his lungs; the contrast to the smoky, muggy, interior extreme. Oheo was a few steps from the entrance with her back to him, her eyes firmly fixed on the palisade which encircled the village. He joined her, and she spoke without looking at him. "Here comes the Frenchman with heavy feet." There was no answer to her comment. His relationship with Oheo lacked the easy banter he had developed with Aarushi and he often found himself ill at ease with their conversations. He took a step closer to her and she moved, leaving a gap of two paces between them, and then turned to face him. "Will you protect me when our enemies come?"

The question was so far removed from what he expected that Gabriel struggled for a meaningful reply. He realised that with Oheo a simple affirmative was not enough. He studied the palisade and thought about his answer. In places the timbers had deteriorated over the winter to the extent that they needed replacing and the tribe lacked the manpower to rectify the problem effectively. By way of a response, he said, "The defences need strengthening."

"You think that will save us?"

"It will help."

"What if they come with fire?"

"We will douse the flames."

She eyed him keenly. "There are not enough of us."

"There will have to be. If we plan and prepare we will have a chance."

"A tribe of women, old men, and children?"

"Yes."

Oheo shifted her gaze to the mountains. In the east, faint blue light etched their outline and a hint of rising sun could just be discerned behind the wooded summits. "They will come once the snows are gone."

"I know."

"Will you be gone with the snow, Man Unknown?"

That was another facet of his dilemma. Was he facing certain death if he chose to remain with the Mohawk? Gabriel only paused momentarily. "No, I will stay and plan."

"And fight?"

"Yes, and fight."

If he had been with Aarushi, Gabriel would have made a joke about needing to stay and test the weapons he and Matwau had fashioned all winter but with Oheo he met the ultimatum in her eyes and repeated, "Yes, and fight."

The attack came on a late spring day when the burgeoning greenery was of such beauty and variety that Aarushi's heart sang. She was in the fields with the other women planting the new season's crops. Her task was to plant beans, less back-breaking than clearing the soil, and she placed each dried bean into the warming soil with great precision. The tiniest shoots of corn could already be seen thrusting through the earth and a wave of relief washed over her: Sky Woman had heard their chant. Just before the corn planting was due, the women had performed the essential ritual, keeping time to the words with tortoiseshell rattles, asking Mother Earth to give the gift of corn to her children. Then the kernels had been planted, after being soaked in herbs to encourage germination and to discourage the birds.

As she worked Aarushi was aware of a solitary crow, perched on a nearby mound, his beady eyes watching her every move. She let him be, for he was a good sign, a sign of protection, and glanced around to reassure herself that all was well. After she finished her circles of beans she was due to sow sunflowers. Smiling to herself, she thought of those showy flowers whose seeds and oil were prized for their versatility and stood up and stretched. The sun was warm on her back and the ache in her leg, often a constant pain in winter, was more bearable. In the distance she could pick out Oheo and Genesee among the group preparing the ground for melons, cucumbers, and pumpkins, and in the far woods she knew Gabriel, Matwau, and some of the youths were setting traps.

Conscious of the threat of attack, the men of the village had organised themselves to be as ready as possible. The old and the infirm stayed within the palisade, stationed near the caches of weapons and water containers, while the able ones hunted for small animals in the surrounding woods. Some youths, those fleet of foot, had been sent out as scouts as the enemy was expected to approach by water from the west. A short advantage might be gained while the attackers made safe their canoes.

Matwau and Gabriel were constructing deadfall traps. They had almost finished camouflaging their sixth pit with logs when the former held up his hand to stop Gabriel talking. He stood poised for several seconds, every sense alert. Then he set down the final log so silently that the hackles on the back of Gabriel's neck rose. Their eyes met and Matwau indicated to Gabriel that he follow him. Straining to hear what had warned Matwau, Gabriel did not look down and caught his foot in a bass-wood cord attached to the end of a sapling, which they had set earlier. The sapling sprang back with a thwack and earned him a damning glare from his companion, who uncharacteristically noiselessly spat out the words, "Stupid Frenchman."

Mortified, Gabriel cursed himself and increased his speed. To the men's right, as they ran, Gabriel became aware of a distinct rustling in the undergrowth. It could have been an animal, until a Mohawk youth, of no more than twelve summers, stumbled into view. His face, distorted with exertion, said everything. "Huron!" he mouthed. "Huron!"

In Matwau's footsteps, Gabriel sped through the trees faster than he had ever run in his life and his lungs were screaming when the first whiff of smoke assaulted his nostrils. Unlike the ubiquitous smell of the village's camp fires, which mingled with the aroma of cooking, this smoke carried with it terror and death. They broke cover together, the youth left far behind, to witness their greatest fear. A group of Huron warriors, with a smattering of Algonquin, were stealthily approaching from the west. An advance party, it was small in numbers, but both men knew more fighters would follow.

In the blink of an eye, Gabriel scanned the scene before him. One burning arrow had already lodged in the palisade and desperate attempts were being made to douse the flames. The women were streaming in from the fields: some had abandoned their tools, but others carried them with them in the hope that they might provide some defence. In the bustle he could not identify anyone as all the women were making for the only way through the palisade, a narrow entrance the width of a single person. He tried to see if Oheo and Aarushi were among them but on finding it impossible he ran after Matwau, a fraction of a second behind him. A hail of arrows, fired above their heads, protected them and they reached the safety of the stockade just as hordes of whooping Huron poured into view.

Gabriel raced to the nearest arms cache, grabbed a handful of arrows, and pulled on chest armour. "Have you seen Aarushi?" he shouted, directing his question towards Matwau and anyone within hearing distance.

Someone shouted back, "She will be with the women by the creek helping to fill the water butts."

Gabriel spoke to Matwau who had come alongside him. "I thought she was in the fields planting this morning."

Matwau shrugged. He had other priorities than Gabriel's lame friend despite her being his kin. "She will have to take her chance with everyone else."

Torn between searching the village and doing his duty, Gabriel was forced, by the onslaught of Huron arrows, to climb to the palisade's platform and take his place next to Matwau. The numbers before them did not augur well. Many more fighters had joined the advance party. Arrow after arrow rained down upon them and the struggle to prevent the palisade being destroyed seemed untenable. Frantic activity dominated the defences: many warriors fell, including old men who were still accurate with the bow, and there were not enough youths to replace them. The women, despite their valiant efforts, could not bring the water fast enough to quench the flames and after two hours of concerted attack the defences were breached.

The first Huron fighters through the gap met a grisly end as the Mohawk concentrated their best warriors in that area. Matwau and Gabriel were among them, swinging their war clubs and hatchets to deadly effect but the superiority of the enemy numbers meant that the offensive became unstoppable. Gabriel continued to fight like a man possessed, heedless of the blood pouring from a gash on his upper arm and of the sweat running down his face until it blurred his vision, and oblivious to what was happening elsewhere in the village.

While he had been defending the first breach, the palisade had collapsed near the creek where the women were collecting the water. The attackers flooded the area, their aim to capture as many able-bodied Mohawks as they could to take as slaves, and to kill those of little use. The women's screams penetrated Gabriel's consciousness as he was felling a short, stout Huron who had been outmanoeuvred by his opponent's height. In one swift movement he removed his war club from the man's skull, then pivoted on his heels and dashed towards the creek. Matwau, who had heard the petrified cries at the same time, speedily dispatched his assailant and ran to join him.

As he approached the melee Gabriel became aware of calm and commotion. Before him, on his right, a group of women stood, sullenly silent, encircled by Huron warriors. Among them he could see Oheo and Genesee. They were not going to die but faced a long march to Huron territory. For a split second he saw, or imagined, Oheo's challenging look. On his left Aarushi was struggling to free herself from the grip of a young brave. His eyes were alight with bloodlust and he was yanking her up by the hair as her crippled leg gave way. She refused to rise, using her fists to beat him around his legs. The Huron raised his knife. Gabriel, blinded with fury, leapt with inhuman strength and swung his war club. The first blow caught the brave across the shoulders. In surprise, he momentarily loosened his grip on Aarushi but swiftly recovered. Gabriel took his chance, praying that Aarushi would stay low, and brought the club down once more.

The Huron in charge of the captured women had made an instant decision as Matwau and four Mohawk warriors surged towards them. Tired from battle, and conscious of his precious booty, he glanced at his fellow braves and saw their weariness. In a well-planned tactic, five of the guard peeled off to meet their attackers and the remaining Hurons closed ranks around the women and forced them, at a steady trot, to run away from the village towards the waiting canoes.

It was five against five, evenly matched in agility and ability. The men slashed and chopped. Muscle and sinew were rent in two. Bone was crushed. The need to stay upright was paramount. The first to fall was a Mohawk. The victorious whoop of the Huron spurred the defenders of their village. Matwau, his honour tarnished by the sight of his wife being enslaved, fought with a viciousness which enabled him to annihilate two of the enemy as a comrade crumpled beside him. All the remaining men were beginning to flag when thick acrid smoke made it difficult to breathe. The Hurons, always the greater in numbers, were torching the village: the water-soaked timbers had finally caught alight. Clouds of black smoke billowed through the air and the heat was becoming unbearable. Coughing and spluttering, Matwau swung his hatchet wildly from side to side, expecting the next blow which did not come. The remaining Hurons stole away through the smoke and he was left with his companions, bloodied and exhausted but still alive.

He stood immobile, in shock. Then he heard a voice calling his name. Moving in the direction of the sound he stumbled over bodies, the dead and the dying. The flames had leapt to the grain store and several longhouses were alight, crackling as the flames ate up the walls and thatch. As he raised his head, Matwau could see the sky above the smoke, a sky of the clearest blue where sparks danced, and a warm sun shone on him benignly. He heard his name again, spoken with such urgency that he tried to increase his pace. He stumbled again, slipping in a morass of blood and brains, and cried out, "Where are you?" An arm hooked under his and tried to pull him up. Gabriel's battle-scarred face, half-obscured by blood, dirt, and soot, loomed above him. "My brother," uttered Matwau as he rejected the help and lay flat on his back.

TWENTY-SIX

AARUSHI'S LEGS WOULD NOT STOP SHAKING. IT was as if they had a life of their own and however many times her brain told her she had been saved, her body refused to accept it. Sitting, she wrapped her arms around her traitorous limbs and tried to appear the strong Mohawk maiden she was meant to be. Gabriel had left her in the care of an elder, a man so ancient that his skin had the consistency of old hide. She fixed her eyes on his shins, which appeared devoid of flesh, the leathery membrane stretched taut over the bone, and then turned away. She would never look on bone again without recalling the sickening sound of Gabriel's club smashing into her assailant's skull.

Half of the Huron's face had caved in on contact, but the brave had not released her completely until Gabriel had severed his jugular with one deft chop of his hatchet. A torrent of blood had soaked Aarushi, mingling with the shards of bone and gobbets of flesh which clung to her hair. She could smell the Huron now. He was all around her, entering her every time she took a breath; his pungent, ferrous odour becoming one with the stinging smoke and the elder's tobacco. Someone had given the old man a pipe and he sucked on it noisily as if unconcerned about the ruination behind him.

They were downwind of the burning village, on the bank of the creek which flowed, unperturbed, towards the mighty river and then on to the sea. Upstream on the river, the Huron warriors would be paddling furiously, taking her sister and Genesee to their new life, but Aarushi's mind could not encompass such a situation so she dismissed the thought and concentrated on the water. Pricks of light twinkled on the surface and the water was so translucent that she could pick out every stone, smooth and round, on the bottom. Small fish darted, here and there, trying to find some shade, and if she bent down and scooped some water in her hands, she could surely catch one. However, she did not move but sat rigid, staring at the water, her arms like a vice around her legs.

It was how Gabriel found her a good hour later. He had taken Matwau to the dance ground where the medicine man was treating the wounded with the help of Genesee's mother, who had had the initiative to hide in the woods. She had returned, wary but unscathed, after she had heard the triumphant enemy whooping their way to the river. After having his gash dressed, Gabriel had left Matwau and had circled the village, helping the wounded and counting the dead, before retracing his steps. Briefly watching the old medicine man washing wounds with juniper and dressing them with willow bark poultices, Gabriel had recalled what he had learnt at the university in Paris but swiftly decided it was of little use in the context and made his way to where he had left Aarushi.

The words he was about to say died on his lips when he beheld her. She was sitting, facing away from the smouldering village, curled over her knees with her arms tightly wrapped around her legs. Gabriel squatted down in front of her. Very gently he touched her shoulder and, when she did not flinch, he took her hands and prised her arms open. He nodded to the elder, who seemed more concerned with smoking his pipe, and then led Aarushi away.

They walked downstream for several paces until they were shielded from view by a stand of aspens. Although not fully out, the leaves had unfurled enough to rustle in the light breeze. Gabriel stopped and inhaled, trying to clear his lungs of the astringent smoke. The resultant coughing fit provoked a reaction in Aarushi. She placed a comforting hand on his back and waited patiently for him to straighten up. Then she touched his cheek where the blood had dried. "Come," he said, and gently guided her into the middle of the creek, where the water pooled, swirling and deep.

The water flowed around Gabriel's thighs and was so deep for Aarushi that he had to hold on to her, under her arms, as she lay back and let it wash over her. "Your turn," she said, when every vestige of the Huron had been swept away. She held his hands, to steady him, while he ducked under the surface. It was an unnecessary gesture, for he was quite capable of keeping his balance, but Aarushi believed that if she let him go she might sink and allow the creek to take her and wipe away all memory of that day forever. Gabriel resurfaced and, unable to use his hands to clear the water from his face and hair, he shook his head showering her with sun-drenched droplets.

"Stop that!" The instruction rang out with all the authority and anger Matwau was experiencing. Aarushi instantly let go of Gabriel and the force of the current, considerable from the spring melt, swept her down. He grabbed her, pulled her upright, and encircled her in his arms to stop her falling again. "Stop that!" Matwau screeched, the effort tormenting his scorched throat.

Gabriel faced him and demanded quietly, with enough

menace in his voice to show he would not be intimidated, "Do you want her to drown?"

The question penetrated Matwau's fury and when he finally answered, it was with reason. "You go against all custom."

"Under the circumstances, I feel that little harm can be done in helping Aarushi."

Matwau's eyes were hard, obsidian pebbles as he narrowed them against the dazzling sun. "You are mistaken, Frenchman. It is women's work. It is at times like this that we Mohawk must follow our ways."

On reflection, it was a belief Gabriel could understand but still it rankled. Aarushi, shivering in his arms despite the increasing heat of the day, tried to wriggle free. Slowly and very deliberately, Gabriel removed his arms but remained ready to grasp her at any sign of unsteadiness. She stood for some time, getting her balance, and then, head bowed, she waded towards the shallower water. Gabriel followed, hovering, never taking his eyes from her small, proud back.

When he reached the bank, Gabriel was ready for confrontation but Matwau's rage had dissipated as quickly as it had come. With indescribable sadness etched on his face, he said, "There are so few of us now." Gabriel nodded coolly in acknowledgement and was about to join Aarushi, who was walking distractedly towards the dance ground. Matwau caught his arm. "There is to be a council. The sachem has survived." By way of answer, Gabriel turned towards the Mohawk and studied him. Close acquaintance had prepared Gabriel for the absence of any conciliatory gesture so Matwau's revelation stunned him. "We need you," he said, as he grasped Gabriel's arm with both hands. "We need you, my brother."

As the council house had been reduced to a smouldering skeleton, the sachem convened the meeting in a clearing in the woods. Gabriel took his place and studied the gathered assembly. Most of the men were old and those who were not displayed the scars of battle and were thankful to sit wearily on the hastily positioned logs. A few warriors were absent due to serious injury but overall what Gabriel could see was the sum of the male members of the village. His heart sank: whatever decisions were to be taken, they would be difficult to execute.

The sachem started speaking: his voice, usually gravelly with age, rasped with the effect of the smoke. He lamented the death of the warriors the tribe could ill afford to lose; the tragedy of the older women and the very young, cut down where they stood, and the capture of the younger women as war booty. He swore vengeance for them all. At these words, Matwau struggled up from his log, ready to interrupt. The sachem held up his hand. "We must wait until all have spoken." To Gabriel's surprise, one of the interpreters produced the wampum strings. How they had survived in their birchbark box, he could not fathom, but as nobody else seemed to show any emotion he assumed they had been hidden somewhere other than the council house.

The ceremonial pipe was passed round for each man to speak in turn. Gabriel tried to concentrate but the throbbing of his injured arm became increasingly intrusive. He touched the poultice which covered the deep cut and winced. Badly bruised, from shoulder to elbow, his arm was stiffening, as were other parts of his body. He glanced sideways at Matwau, who must be experiencing a similar reaction, but the brave showed no sign of discomfort. Every fibre of his being was tense as he sat poised for action, hating every valuable minute which was wasted while the discussion took place.

The elders spoke first, advising caution before reprisals

were carried out. The food supplies needed to be checked, the wounded cared for, and the dead mourned. There was the issue of the young scouts. Surely some of them would return. Shelters needed to be constructed as, like the council house, the longhouses were uninhabitable. Matwau's face darkened with each suggestion. It was over four hours since Genesee and the others had been taken and the trail would soon be cold. When it came to his turn to speak, Matwau was almost at breaking point. Gabriel, who could appreciate the elders' circumspection, placed a warning hand on the brave's arm. He shook it off and admonished the elders for their reluctance to act. By not acting immediately the Mohawk would lose respect, it would confirm to their enemies that the Mohawk could no longer fight, and more attackers might come for easy pickings. It was unthinkable not to leave at once. The old must stay but all those able must pursue the Huron.

The sachem listened, then turned to Gabriel and asked for his opinion. Taken aback by being consulted, Gabriel thought carefully. "I hear what the elders have said. They are wise." He paused, conscious of Matwau at his side. "I hear what Matwau has said but we are too few to separate. I would go with you alone, my brother, but what would happen to the village?"

The suppressed anger radiating from Matwau was tangible. "There will be no village without women!"

There was a murmur of agreement. The sachem decided it was an opportune time to draw the discussion to a close. "We are too few to remain. This we know. We will see to our dead and make preparations to leave. We will go to our brothers, the Onondaga, and ask for help against the Huron. We will recover our women." His words were final. The meeting was over.

Gabriel hurried to catch up with Matwau. "Why do we not join with other Mohawk villages?"

"Do you think they are in a better state than us?"

Gabriel shrugged. "But why the Onondaga?"

"They are our brothers. This you know. It is said that they have a great fortified settlement. This I have never seen but it is told that it is on the edge of a lake surrounded by good land."

They walked through the torched village towards the dance ground. Gabriel could see Aarushi with Onitario, Genesee's mother. They were squatting down with their backs to him but as the two men approached both women straightened, turned towards them and moved closer together as if they were shielding something. Matwau, his emotions still high, spurted in front of Gabriel. "What have you there?"

Onitario tried to prevent him from seeing and while the two were occupied in a tussle of wills, Gabriel glanced down. There, wrapped in a blanket, was a slumbering baby. Aarushi's eyes met his. Hers were full of wonder. "He has survived. It is Helaku. He has been spared."

"He should have died," Matwau shouted. "We cannot travel with a baby!"

"Why not?" demanded his mother-in-law.

"He has no mother."

Onitario, aware of her position as matriarch, replied with great dignity, "He has me."

Matwau looked to Gabriel for support but none came. Instead, the latter stretched down and picked up the baby, who having just passed his second spring was heavier than Gabriel expected, and passed him to Aarushi. Dozy in the first moments of waking, Helaku rested his head on her shoulder. With his warm little body moulded to hers, Aarushi had a silent exchange with Onitario. Witnessing this, Gabriel positioned himself in case Aarushi staggered but she stood firm. Matwau, sensing defeat, drifted away and Onitario followed to check on the wounded. Although Gabriel was the only one within earshot, Aarushi spoke as if she was addressing the world. "I will defend him with my life."

They were ready to depart, some to leave the village which had been their home for over twenty summers. The ten days of mourning had finished; the dead, already on their final journey, rested in the ground; the food supplies had been recovered and were now stacked ready to be loaded into the canoes. Fortunately, the enemy had not discovered these, expertly camouflaged on the riverbank, and once the villagers had walked the few leagues across country, they would be able to travel west by the river. One elder, his mind still sharp, could remember visiting the lake of the Onondaga as a youth and confidently asserted that he could lead the way.

It was a small group consisting of old men who had escaped from the Huron arrows and hatchets; Aarushi, Onitario, and three middle-aged squaws; a handful of warriors who had survived the battle; four scouts, three of whom had melted away into the woods at the sight of the Hurons and the youth who had warned Gabriel and Matwau; and Helaku, the only baby to have been spared. In all, they numbered twenty-one.

They followed the creek to the river. The strong and able-bodied walked at the front, at the back, and on the flanks, protecting the wounded and elderly in the middle. Two young warriors, Nayati and Otetiani, were pulled on hurdles as they were too injured to walk, and Aarushi carried Helaku in his cradleboard. Gabriel had almost offered to carry him but, on receiving a withering look from Aarushi, stopped himself in time. Onitario had noticed and spoke quietly to him as Aarushi set off determinedly. "Do not concern yourself. I will take the child when she tires."

Once they reached the river progress would be easier, despite having to paddle upstream. "Tenonanatche," announced the sachem when he saw the wide expanse of water. "Tenonanatche will take us to our brothers, the Onondaga." They retrieved the canoes and set to work. Matwau, Gabriel and the scouts loaded the food they had carried. It was the same as that taken on the warpath; cornmeal, dried meat, and berries which could be supplemented with small, fresh game as they travelled. After the food, they carefully stowed away the weapons, and spears for fishing.

The big elm canoes were spacious and there were more than enough but due to the nature of the group it was decided to take only four. Matwau steered the lead canoe containing the sachem, the elder who knew the way, Nayati, and one of the scouts. Gabriel followed with Aarushi and Helaku, Onitario, and another of the young scouts. The third canoe was manned by elders whose numbers would help if any of them started to flag later in the day, and the final canoe was the responsibility of Gyantwaka, a young brave who had proved himself a true warrior in the battle against the Huron. It was estimated that, with the longer days of early summer, they would reach their destination before the next full moon.

As the sun dipped towards the horizon at the end of the first day's paddling, the sachem decided to make camp, much to Matwau's chagrin. He argued that the sun was still high in the sky, which was an exaggeration, but to no avail. Being cautious and spotting a good site to moor for the night, the sachem would not listen. Gabriel, paddling close to the lead canoe, did not catch all of the exchange but the way Matwau thrust his paddle into the water and made for the riverbank spoke volumes about the brave's displeasure.

Even after they had eaten, his mood did not improve. Helaku, tired and disorientated, started to cry. Matwau's head whipped round. "Silence that child now or I will." Aarushi hastily threw some water in Helaku's face and held him close, watching her uncle over the baby's head.

He continued crying so Onitario leapt up and threw more water. "That will wash away your troubles," she said, softly. The shock of the second dousing worked and Aarushi withdrew to sit some distance away from the group.

Matwau stood up too, declaring, "That child will put us all in danger if he wails like that. We will all be killed. If he does that again, I will kill him myself."

The group began to disperse, each person readying to settle down for the night. Gabriel and Onitario were left alone. "Would Matwau really kill the child?"

Onitario did not answer Gabriel's question directly. "Aarushi is a good mother for one so young. She must keep Helaku safe."

"Why do you say she is so young?"

"She is only fifteen summers."

Gabriel was astonished. "She looks older."

"It is the pain and her struggle to do more than she should. You can see the discomfort etched on her face." Onitario studied Gabriel keenly. "Not like you. How many summers have you lived?"

For one embarrassing moment, he thought she might be thinking of him as a potential husband. Onitario read his expression and laughed. "Do not worry, Frenchman, I do not wish for a husband yet, although perhaps I will find a handsome Onondaga brave."

Gabriel grinned in response. The more he came to know Genesee's mother, the more he appreciated her. Then he became serious. "Do you think we will find our women?"

"It is good that they are alive. Usually, the Huron would kill everyone in a raid. They must have a need for women. I hope to see my Genesee again. The humiliation of losing her eats away at Matwau. That is why he is so angry. Such rage is good if it can be harnessed. He will find her. Our Onondaga brothers will help us."

Gabriel, conscious that darkness was falling, pushed himself up. Every muscle objected, after paddling for so long. "You have not answered my question," Onitario stated correctly.

"Which one?" He had lost the thread of the conversation. He was more tired than he thought.

"How many summers have you lived?"

A deluge of emotions threatened to overwhelm him: his birthday was inextricably part of his French identity, submerged by circumstance. He preferred not to think about it but Onitario was waiting. "When this summer has passed, it will be twenty-three."

TWENTY-SEVEN

T HEY ARRIVED AT THE SETTLEMENT AS THE LAST
rays of sun shadowed the fertile land. Onondaga scouts
had warned of their arrival and a reception party was ready
to greet them. Aarushi, her back aching from the weight
of Helaku, stared in wonder at the height of the palisade.
Constructed of interlocking timbers it rose higher than the
height of five men and was topped by a parapet. The gate
had already been opened and they were led straight through.
Onitario, seeing her companion's weariness, tried to take
Helaku but was rebuffed. Habitually determined to prove
her capability, Aarushi insisted on carrying the baby to their
destination: they had not walked far from the canoes and if
she could not manage that distance, her value to the tribe was
truly diminished.

It was much further to the centre of the settlement than she
expected. After the first palisade there were two more, rising
almost as high. Gabriel, on her right flank, noticed what she
did not. Each palisade they passed through had a water system
to quench any fire attack. He was near enough to Aarushi to
point out gutters and waterspouts and comment that it would
be an ingenious enemy who could conquer such defences. The

Onondaga accompanying them nodded proudly in agreement and she allowed herself a brief, luxurious moment of believing she was safe.

The Onondaga sachem, surrounded by his elders, was waiting for them outside of the council house but, as it was late, lengthy discourse was postponed until the following morning. The women and Helaku were immediately taken away to be fed and given beds while the Mohawk sachem succinctly explained their situation. The escort of Onondaga braves instantly shouted for revenge, but the sachem calmed the younger members of his tribe and reiterated that all discussions and decisions must wait for the council meeting.

Nevertheless, the following day, it did not take long for a decision to be reached. The Onondaga would give their Mohawk brothers refuge, but the elders had, at this time, no interest in a revenge raid. They could, however, provide anything a Mohawk scouting party might require. The Huron were renowned for living in large settlements, dependent on agriculture, and would be easier to find than the more nomadic tribes to the north-east. It would be a small party, consisting of Matwau, Gabriel, and Gyantwaka, who would try and locate the prisoners. No other Mohawk warriors were well enough, and the Onondaga did not want to fight so late in the season. Matwau was furious to miss the chance of a full revenge attack and Gabriel could understand his anger and frustration. Images often flooded Gabriel's mind: the old women chatting contentedly as they turned back the corn husks with a bone pin; the young people playing little brother of war; the children occupied with their bundles and sticks, and the joyous dancing of all when the tribe celebrated a success. Most of them were now slaughtered. Even the tedious, claustrophobic winter days in the longhouse acquired a rosy hue when remembered by a refugee, one who had survived against the odds.

The evening before his departure, Aarushi sought Gabriel out. He was sitting outside of his lodging enjoying a few moments of peace. He heard her coming, her soft voice murmuring to Helaku, and he opened his eyes just before she arrived.

"You are ready to go," she stated as she sat Helaku down on the ground.

"Yes."

She gave the baby a stick and he started digging. "I fear for you," she admitted to Gabriel, without looking at him.

"We will be careful."

"Would it not be better to wait until Nayati and Otetiani can accompany you?"

"There is no time to wait for their wounds to heal. It will take longer than one full moon to the next to reach the land of the Huron and then we will need to return before the leaves fall. You know how early the first snow can come." Aarushi appeared unconvinced so he continued, "Do you not want news of your sister?"

"Of course," she replied, although she still watched Helaku rather than look at Gabriel. What else could she say? It was unthinkable to confess that if it was a choice between Gabriel's safety and Oheo's, she would choose the former.

The baby started to crawl towards her. Instead of lifting him up she waited. "Watch," she instructed Gabriel. Helaku pulled himself up by hanging onto the folds of her skirt. He moved from one knee to the next, always holding on, and then he studied Gabriel with an expression of great concentration.

"Come," invited Gabriel and held out his hands. Helaku

clasped them, steadied himself, and took a step. He took another step, his face lit with triumphant delight, and Aarushi rejoiced in his achievement, as proud as any mother. Her eyes met Gabriel's and he was heartened to see some of the worried intensity fade from her face. He smiled at her warmly. "You nurture him well."

Revelling in his admiration, she smiled shyly. "By the time you return Helaku will be running."

"I do not doubt it," he replied.

Aarushi stood up. Gabriel lifted the baby and placed him in her arms. "We go at first light, so I will bid you farewell now."

She tilted her head, unable to speak, and made her way slowly back to her lodging. It was not the last she saw of him. The next morning, she watched him leave, committing every movement to memory as he crept stealthily through the palisade with Matwau and Gyantwaka.

Once clear of the palisade, the three men were met by four Onondaga scouts who led them to the edge of the lake. There, they retrieved a canoe hidden in the undergrowth, and with much gesticulating the scouts explained a route north across the eastern end of the lake where the Mohawks could take advantage of a chain of islands. On reaching the northern shore, the travellers would need to move speedily, utilising the time between one full moon and the next to their advantage.

The land of the Huron was unlike any area of the New World Gabriel had already seen. He had thought the country cultivated by the Onondaga bountiful but as he travelled further away from the lake, he beheld vast cornfields which provided excellent camouflage. Almost ripe, the corn stood at its highest and as they crept through the enveloping rows they came across the first settlement well before dawn. Fortunate that the crop needed little attention, they kept watch, each man taking a turn to reconnoitre for any signs of the Mohawk captives.

With no success they travelled on to the next settlement, a distance of little more than three leagues, easily covered before the next night. They followed the pattern of the previous night: Gabriel and Matwau waited in the corn whilst Gyantwaka prowled the circumference of the village. He returned earlier than expected, his excited demeanour raising Matwau's hopes. "You have found Genesee?"

Gyantwaka replied, looking at Gabriel, "No, but I have seen a white man."

"Where?" demanded Matwau, refusing to believe the youth.

"Just walking."

"He is not a captive?"

"He walks freely among the Hurons." Gyantwaka turned towards Gabriel again. "What is he doing at this time of night?"

Matwau's voice was laced with disdain. "The Hurons are like animals – they mate at will. Before they marry, they have many unions. He will be looking for a woman."

Gyantwaka's almond eyes grew rounder. "How do you know this?"

"Do not question me!" retorted Matwau. "The Hurons are dogs."

Gabriel, knowing Matwau's temper could flare dangerously, admonished both of them. "Be quiet!"

Matwau ignored him although he lowered his voice a fraction. "They cannot hear us from this distance."

"Maybe so, but we cannot chance it." Gabriel addressed Gyantwaka. "Show me where you last saw the white man."

"No," remonstrated Matwau. "I will go."

Gabriel knew better than to argue so he hunkered down to wait for his companions' return. It was already well past midnight and the late-summer sky had darkened to the deepest sapphire. A carpet of stars arced above him while, amongst the corn, a cacophony of rustling, snorting, and scraping told of nocturnal activity unperturbed by his presence. He shifted position continually and fought the urge to sleep. Keeping his mind active, Gabriel thought about the vulnerability of their situation, of the unlikelihood of a white man living with the Huron, and of the odds against them finding the women.

Matwau and Gyantwaka approached him unawares and Gabriel inwardly cursed his inability to be their equal. Matwau's accusation stung. "You were asleep."

"Did you see him?"

"It is a white man I have seen before."

"Where?"

"Kebec."

"You are certain?"

Matwau's tone hardened. "It was dark, but I have seen the shape of the white man before."

Two days later, after a frustrating period of surveillance, Gabriel was able to confirm Matwau's declaration. A small group of Hurons had left the village at first light and there was such a familiarity about one of them that Gabriel's heart skipped a beat. The man's hair, significantly lighter than that of his companions, fell thick and loose past his shoulders while his neat frame appeared small next to the Huron hunters. All of the men carried bows and spears.

"A hunting party," stated Gyantwaka unnecessarily.

"Did you see him?" asked Matwau.

"Yes."

"We will track them."

The trees were dense, pine and birch with a few oaks scattered here and there. They followed a creek downstream until the terrain opened up to reveal a glade patterned with dappled sunlight. Not twenty paces from them, Etienne Brûlé was trapping fish with no sign of the rest of the party. Matwau signalled for Gabriel to approach Brûlé and use the opportune moment.

Absorbed in his task, Brûlé did not hear Gabriel's approach and the latter, conscious of Matwau and Gyantwaka watching his back, crept right up to him and whispered, "Etienne."

Brûlé swung round with such force that he nearly lost his balance. He studied Gabriel with narrowed eyes, his spear held aggressively. "Gharsia?"

Gabriel, experiencing an odd mix of emotions on hearing his name, nodded. "It is I."

"What are you doing here?" Etienne glanced around suspiciously. "You are with the Mohawk?" A low call, similar to that of the hen-like birds which populated the forest, alerted Gabriel to danger and he did not answer. Another call immediately followed.

Etienne stared towards the dense trees but could see nothing. "Meet me tonight at the edge of the sunflowers," he said as Gabriel hastily retreated. A knowing smile teased around Brûlé's lips. "Listen for an owl, you will hear him three times."

As the slimmest of crescent moons rose in the dark sky Gabriel and Matwau, who had insisted on coming, concealed themselves among the sunflowers and waited for the signal. Eventually, three screeches rent the air and Matwau pushed Gabriel forward.

Etienne Brûlé eyed Matwau with suspicion, trying to determine whether Gharsia was a captive. It was difficult to judge so he looked from one man to the other and said, "Why are you here?"

Matwau had understood and replied in halting French, "We seek our women."

Brûlé addressed Gabriel. "And you, too, Gharsia?"

"Yes."

There was a long pause. Brûlé appeared to study the stars twinkling above his head.

"Can you help us?" Gabriel asked, as he continued to watch his fellow countryman, well aware of Etienne's record of gathering and imparting information in Kebec.

Matwau was more cautious. "Why you live with the Huron?"

Once again, Brûlé addressed Gabriel. "Champlain arranged it. I am to live among the Huron for a time to learn their language and their ways."

"You have seen Champlain recently?"

"Yes, this past June. There was a big meet near Montreal and he and I ran the rapids, the Grand Sault Saint-Marie, successfully." Etienne met Gabriel's eyes defiantly. "He holds me in high esteem. As you know I can already speak with the Montagnais and Algonquin in their own languages."

Gabriel assessed the young man. Still no more than twenty years old, Etienne had lost none of his irksome confidence. "How do you fare with the Huron?"

"They treat me well."

"Do you know of any Mohawk captives?"

Etienne paused once again, calculating what to say which would be to his advantage. Matwau took a step forward: Gabriel placed a cautionary hand on his chest. Etienne's eyes flicked from one man to the other, enjoying his power. "What if I have?"

"You either know or you do not know." Gabriel spoke with the superiority of the educated man and immediately regretted it as Brûlé's face took on a weasel-like expression.

"Who are you to speak so? You were just one of Champlain's lackeys."

Gabriel saw his chance. "But I am the son of a well-connected man." He waited for the impact of his words to register. "And I am the grandson of a rich man."

Brûlé sneered. "What of it?"

"I will not always be in the New World – neither might you." Gabriel increased his pressure on Matwau's chest, warning him not to react.

Etienne pondered on Gabriel's words, saw the logic, and decided to help. "I have heard of these women."

Matwau leaned forward, trying to make sense of the exchange in French. Gabriel removed his hand and shot his companion a reassuring look. He spoke more slowly so that the Mohawk could understand. "Are they here?"

"No."

"Where are they?"

"Carhagouha, I believe."

"Where?"

"A settlement several days from here."

"Will you take us?"

Etienne laughed. "And you'll just walk in and rescue them?"

Matwau hissed and uttered in Iroquois, showing that he had followed the conversation, but it was Gabriel who replied, "Of course not. We must make a plan."

"A plan," Etienne echoed mockingly.

Gabriel had forgotten how irritating the youth could be and bided his time before responding. He studied his feet and idly kicked at a lump of friable earth, ignoring the palpable tension emanating from Matwau.

Brûlé, disappointed that Gabriel had not responded to his sarcasm, changed tack. "You are in luck, gentlemen. I am in need of some adventure."

It was too dangerous for Etienne Brûlé to accompany them to Carhagouha so a rendezvous was arranged a couple of leagues south of the settlement. Gabriel, Matwau and Gyantwaka hid in the woods for three days after they had arrived and still there was no sign of the Frenchman. "He is not coming," repeated Matwau continually, until Gabriel's nerves were frayed. "We cannot trust him." Gabriel argued against him but with less conviction by the beginning of the fourth night.

Matwau was keeping watch, while his companions snatched some sleep, when he heard a man approaching. A satisfied smile stole across his usually solemn face as he silently unsheathed his knife. "Unwise man," he whispered in Brûlé's ear as he held his knife across his victim's throat. "I could kill you now."

Etienne gasped, "If you do you will never find your wife." He struggled to breathe, so tight was Matwau's right arm across his chest.

"I do not trust you."

"I have seen her."

Gabriel and Gyantwaka, now both fully awake, waited with bated breath, Gabriel's hand firmly on the younger man's arm.

"You do not know my wife."

"She is called Genesee." The pressure of Matwau's arm lessened slightly. Etienne pushed home his advantage. "She is older than you. Ten summers or more. A woman in mid-life." The arm relaxed fractionally. Etienne took a gulp of air.

"I do not believe you."

"Come with me."

"Why?" demanded Gabriel.

Etienne made what movement he could with his head and rolled his eyes to the side. Gabriel gazed into the night but could discern nothing. It was Gyantwaka who stiffened. He raised his hand to silence them and gradually they all became aware of soft footfall. Matwau turned half-circle, taking the captive Brûlé with him, so that he faced the direction of the footsteps. Two indistinct figures loomed out of the darkness, one taller than the other. There was a moment of palpable silence as Matwau registered their identity. He reluctantly released his victim, who crowed in triumph, "What did you think I have been doing all these days?"

It was Gabriel who spoke, as Matwau was lost for words. He ignored Etienne's question and said, "Genesee."

She took a step forward, leading the girl beside her. "And Degonwahdontee."

Gabriel stared at the space they had vacated. "Where is Oheo?"

Etienne answered, "She did not want to come."

"I do not believe you!" Matwau had found his voice. Etienne shrugged and invited Genesee to explain.

"It is true. We all can see Oheo's beauty. She has caught the eye of the chief's eldest son. He has already sought her out and lain with her. She is treated well and believes she will become his wife."

Genesee was about to say more when Gyantwaka interrupted her. "What of my sister and the others?"

"Your sister is dead. Many of us did not survive the journey. Those who could not keep up were killed. I do not know where anyone else is. We were separated when we reached the land of the Huron." She looked at the three men in front of her.

All bereft for different reasons. She addressed Gabriel. "I have a message for you from Oheo. She said 'Tell Man Unknown that I am now Huron. Tell him to go home. Go back across the great sea to France. There is nothing for him here' and this, I swear, is the truth."

All eyes turned momentarily to Gabriel. He stood impassively. Then Matwau, with more pressing concerns, looked towards Brûlé. There was no sign of the Frenchman. He had silently melted into the night with all the stealth worthy of the Huron amongst whom he lived. Without his help, the only alternative was to return to the Onondaga. Matwau sniffed the air. Autumn, with her unpredictability, was fast approaching. It was time to leave.

PEDRO

1611

TWENTY-EIGHT

Caors, August 1611

H
E WOKE WITH A START, HIS NIGHTSHIRT WRAPPED around his body as tight as a winding-sheet. He sat upright, trying to still his racing heart. At the end of a disturbed night, Pedro had tossed and turned in the throes of a dream so vivid that he believed himself to be awake. It was often the same dream. He was on the platform at the auto-da-fé in Saragossa, reliving the anguished moment when his eyes had locked with Bartolomé's for the last time. From that point the dream would become multi-faceted; his brother being tortured, his brother dying alone in his own filth, and even being burnt alive which Pedro knew to be untrue, yet he could not banish the scenes from his mind.

Forcing himself to remember that he was being haunted by events which had happened more than twenty years ago, Pedro doggedly set about preparing for the day. He had been spared, given the chance of life, a life which he must not waste. The sun was already well above the horizon and the water, left by Catarina, had already cooled. He washed, uncomfortable with the thought that the maid had been in his room while he slept.

Usually, he was awake when she brought the jug and recently he had become disconcerted by her familiarity. She had taken to interrupting him while he was working on the accounts, lightly knocking on the door and entering immediately, bearing a tray with sekanjabin and his favourite almond cakes. She would linger, chatting about the local news, until he cut her short politely but firmly. His attitude did not deter her. Catarina seemed to second guess his every movement and what, at first, he had believed to be the actions of an attentive servant were now becoming claustrophobic. There was no denying that Catarina was an attractive woman but she was wasting her time setting her cap at him. He repeatedly told himself that he did not want to be encumbered with a wife on his journey to the Netherlands.

As he left his chamber, dressed and ready to leave, he noticed the door to Luis's was open. He knew what he would find if he entered. Elizabeth would be sitting on the floor surrounded by the journals, now neatly arranged by himself in chronological order. One of the journals would be open on her lap, being read with such consuming concentration that she would not immediately register his presence. He would speak, reminding her that he had knocked, and she would lift her head, her face still pinched with grief for her father and nephew, and her forehead creased with anxiety as she tried to make sense of her parents' life. He would suppress the urge to kneel in front of her, to take her face in his hands, and rub his thumbs across her forehead to smooth out her frown.

Eschewing such distraction, he made for the staircase, planning to grab some bread and cheese to eat on the way, which would save both time and avoid breaking his fast watched over by Catarina. His foot was posed mid-air over the second step when Elizabeth's clear voice rang out. "Pedro, is that you?"

"Yes." He turned to see Elizabeth at her father's door.

She glanced at his clothes. "Where are you going?"

"We talked about it earlier in the week. I am going to see Jean Canac about the saffron orders. I need to discuss whether we can meet the demand."

"Oh yes," she replied distractedly.

"Do you want me for something?"

"I've been reading what my mother wrote in 1563." She glanced down at the book she was holding and her whole demeanour softened. "It will wait." She had started to share some details of the journals with him and the pleasure it had given her had taken her by surprise. She gave him a warm smile. "You had better go."

He was almost at the bottom of the staircase when she stated, so bluntly that it sounded like an accusation, "You are dressed finely for such a visit."

It was true. Earlier in the year he had availed himself of the services of a tailor whose workshop nestled among the university buildings, deliberately positioned to win the custom of the sons of the mercantile elite. Now, no longer wearing a selection of Gharsia cast-offs, Pedro had experienced an improvement in his attitude and posture and whenever he was conducting business he wore his fine but sober doublet, his breeches cut in the latest fashion, and his stylish riding boots. He assessed Elizabeth's mood carefully. "Perhaps I am going a courting."

Quick as lightning she retaliated, "I wish you good luck – more likely you will frighten the maidens with your dazzling attire."

He shrugged, humour dancing in his eyes. "I can but try."

Keeping the banter light, Elizabeth responded, "You will need to act quickly, for I believe you are due in Holland soon."

He instantly became serious. "Yes, I thought your brother would be home by now."

"So did I."

"Have you had word from him?"

"No."

It was as Pedro thought, Thomas Gharsia was being elusive and placing his steward in an awkward position. The agreement had been for one year only.

Jean Canac eyed his visitor with misgiving. Although he had met the Gharsias' new steward before, the man was not due to visit. The last thing the saffron farmer wanted was interference in his production. The old man, Luis Gharsia, had not troubled him with regular visits for several years, preferring only to meet when the proceeds from the harvest were distributed. The arrangement had suited Jean, for he had learnt early on to be uncomfortable in the presence of his landlord. His own father, having taken over the tenancy from his great-uncle, Vicent Canac, had always claimed that Gharsia's penetrating eyes had induced a feeling of guilt, as if he knew, without speaking, of the precious stamens secreted away. It was a practice which was soon abandoned but Gharsia, whose reserve, to the Canacs, bordered on incivility, was never a welcome visitor.

Canac watched Pedro Torres dismount and walk towards him. He noted the steward's attire, unlike the clothes he had worn on his last visit, and his approach, which was relaxed, calm and unhurried. The farmer waited, trying to read the steward's face, and was pleasantly surprised when Torres, after a genial greeting, announced, "I have good news."

"You had best come into the house."

It was cool and dim inside, the shutters having been closed shortly after breakfast to keep out the heat, and the smell of burnt wood hung in the air from the previous evening's fire, despite the hearth having been swept. The two men sat either side of the long table which dominated the room, while Canac's wife, Agathe, busied herself with the refreshments. The farmer could not disguise the suspicion in his voice. "What news do you have?"

"We have had many orders for the saffron already and I want to know if we are able to meet the demand."

Canac was cautious. "We can only produce what we can."

"Yes," agreed Pedro, "but production has increased steadily for the last few years."

Jean Canac studied the new steward, who had obviously come prepared. He imagined him poring over ledgers instead of dirtying his hands with God's good earth and did not comment. Instead he suppressed his disdain and said what was on his mind. "It is a strange thing to leave this farm to a woman."

If Pedro Torres was taken aback by the change of subject it was imperceptible. "Unusual, yes, but not unheard of."

"With a widow perhaps, but not a daughter when there are sons."

Pedro held his peace. It was not his place to gossip about Luis Gharsia's affairs. Jean Canac totally misinterpreted his silence. The farmer rubbed his calloused hands together and struggled to find the relevant words. Agathe interrupted his thoughts. "You are kinsman to the Gharsias?"

Pedro nodded. It was a lie often repeated. The glance exchanged between husband and wife spoke volumes. Rumour and speculation were rife in the valley, for the newcomer's heritage had not gone unnoticed. He would have laughed if he had known. One goodwife had even suggested to Agathe Canac that Pedro Torres was Luis Gharsia's bastard and that he wanted to claim the saffron production as his own. Although the lie still sat uneasily he said, "My cousin, Elizabeth, does not plan to make any changes. I am only acting as steward while her brother is away."

As relief washed over Canac's face, Pedro understood the farmer's fears. He was tempted to emphasise the temporary nature of his stewardship and explain that it was time for him to head north for Amsterdam, but the words would not form. Instead, he turned the conversation back to the harvest and accepted Agathe's offer of a cup of fresh well water.

His next visit was to the Gaulbert farm. He arrived shortly after noon to find only Sara and Luc at home. Jacques and Helena were in Luzech, visiting Helena's sister, and were not expected to return until nightfall. Masking his disappointment, Pedro sat with Sara on the stone bench, constructed long ago by Ysabel Bernade's father and strategically positioned to maximise the shade from the barn. Luc had excused himself as soon as was polite: Pedro Torres, with his searching questions about the New World, was best avoided.

"What brings you out here?" asked Sara, her head characteristically tilted on one side. Pedro shifted on the bench; it was too low for him to be comfortable. Sara, thinking her question was unwelcome, rested a gnarled hand on his arm. "You don't need to tell me."

"It's not that," he replied as he took his time, taking off his doublet. Despite the shade it was still very hot. The farmyard was a suntrap, the beaten earth dry and cracked beneath his feet.

Sara smiled at him indulgently. "Take your boots off," she said. "It is too pleasant a day for discomfort." He did as he was told and leant back against the rough stone of the barn, stretching his legs out in front of him. The lowness of the bench appeared perfect for the tiny old woman, whose face, now with eyes closed, was a picture of serenity.

"I was hoping to see Jacques to ask if he knew where I could send word to Thomas Gharsia."

"Why not ask Elizabeth?"

"She doesn't know where he is."

Sara's eyes snapped open and she looked at him keenly. "Why do you think my son will know?" Thomas Gharsia's Huguenot sympathies were dangerous.

"I thought Thomas might have had the forethought to leave his plans with him." Pedro paused. "So that Jacques could contact him if anything befell Elizabeth."

Sara mulled over his logic. "Perhaps, although I do not know of any arrangement. Thomas Gharsia has been disappearing for long stretches of time for many years."

"Yes, but Elizabeth's father was alive then."

"I do not believe Luis ever knew where his son was once he was a man grown."

"That said, it is Thomas's duty to care for his sister now."

"And not yours?"

Pedro stiffened, and Sara realised she had been too forthright. "Forgive me, I speak out of turn," she said, somewhat disingenuously, as she was weary of seeing Elizabeth and Pedro skirting around each other for the last year.

He ignored her apology. "I must leave for Amsterdam before summer ends. I have remained this late because Thomas has not returned as we had agreed. I still have time before the poor weather sets in if I take passage from Bordèu."

Sara, who very much doubted that Thomas would make an appearance, asked, "Why Amsterdam?"

"There are opportunities for a man who will work hard, and he will not be persecuted for who he is."

"Are you persecuted here?"

Pedro was slow to answer, thrown by her question, so she

continued, "I don't think you are persecuted. You have been welcomed, as was I."

"It is different for you."

"It is?"

"Yes, I am a Morisco."

Sara studied him with the wisdom of the old, her bright, birdlike eyes tender. "Did you not know that I am a Marrano?" She enjoyed the astonishment on his face as he pulled himself more upright on the bench and rested his hands on his thighs.

"I did not know."

"Yes – my forebears were Portuguese Jews but even after we were forcibly converted, we were persecuted. My parents fled to Bordèu in 1539 to escape the Inquisition. I was married to a friend of my father's before I married Henri Gaulbert." Pedro remained silent, digesting her words, so she continued speaking, the warmth of her voice soothing. "I have been safe here." She waited a moment and then added, "And I have been loved." He turned his head and looked at her but still did not speak. The old woman's voice held a touch of sadness. "Verily, I regret the lapse of my customs, but I cherish them in my heart. We have no choice."

Pedro fixed his eyes on the chickens pecking around the yard. "We have no choice," he echoed.

"Do you think it will be better in Amsterdam? You will be expected to attend church – only it will be a different church."

"I will not be imprisoned for who I am."

"Have you been imprisoned here?"

"No – but since the death of King Henri the authorities are clamping down on heresy. I saw it in Marshila, and I have seen it before. Persecution comes in waves, lapping lightly at first and then, like the weight of the incoming tide, it engulfs you."

"Are you a heretic?"

Pedro felt his chest tighten. For an instant he was back in Saragossa being interrogated. "How can you ask?" he stuttered.

"Who is to hear us?" demanded Sara, sweeping her arm around the yard. "The chickens, the birds in the trees, the insects? Luc will be in the far field by now – and he would never betray me."

"I am a Morisco." It was all that needed to be said.

"And I am a Marrano," replied Sara, her eyes alight with conspiratorial empathy. "And this is where I belong."

He had barely closed the heavy oak door when a voice rang out from the kitchen. "You are home at last. I feared you were lying in a ditch." Pedro dropped his bag and crossed the hall, simultaneously experiencing disappointment that it was not Elizabeth who had greeted him and chiding himself for being foolish. He entered the kitchen to find Catarina standing expectantly by the hearth, where a small fire flickered fitfully. Chilled by tiredness, and the fall in temperature which had come sharply as night fell, he stood next to her, enjoying the welcome warmth, and hungrily eyed the cold supper waiting for him on the table. It had been a longer day than he had anticipated.

Elizabeth swept into the room to find a cosy scene: Pedro eating, his plate piled high, with Catarina sitting opposite him, apparently idle. Both of them turned towards her, defiance flaring in the maid's eyes. Elizabeth ignored Catarina and addressed Pedro. "I am glad you are back. Come into the parlour."

"I will finish eating and then I will be there shortly."

"No, come now. Bring your food. I have been waiting to talk to you."

Pedro glanced from Elizabeth to Catarina, who was watching them closely. He took another mouthful: he was not Elizabeth Gharsia's servant, his contract was with her brother, and although he was eager to join her, he said firmly, "Please give me a few minutes, Elizabeth."

Thwarted, she turned to Catarina. "Surely, you have work to do?"

"No, Mistress, as you can see, all is in order."

It was apparent that Catarina was correct. All was tidy in the kitchen; the copper shone, the plates from the evening meal had been washed and returned to the dresser, the water pitcher was full, and the floor was swept and clean. Elizabeth tried to ignore the hint of insolence in the maid's voice which, as usual, rankled, but it was not as unsettling as seeing Pedro and Catarina sitting at the table like a contented couple. "Pedro," she said, her voice sharp. "When you are ready, I will be in the parlour."

He ate as quickly as he could and was at the parlour door in fewer than five minutes. "What is so important?"

Instead of answering, Elizabeth asked, "Why were you such a long time at the Canacs?" A valid question, as the saffron production was now hers.

"I decided to visit the Gaulberts."

"Why didn't you say you were going to the vineyard? I would have accompanied you."

"It was a whim. I finished at the Canacs early."

He expected her to be more indignant about missing a visit to the farm, and to ask more questions, but she changed the subject. "Listen carefully," she said, and started reading from her mother's journal, translating each sentence for him as she progressed.

The fifth day of March 1563

This day is the most wondrous day. Francesco Zametti and I have pledged to marry. Francesco sayst that it must be our secret as his father will not countenance such a union. My Love hopes, in time, that his uncle, Lorenzo, will speak for us but, for now, we must be circumspect. Joy maketh my heart sing and I fret not for Francesco is true and most ardent in his kisses. I could but pass little time with him as Ysabel was waiting for the purchases from the apothecary. I have promised to try and meet him on the morrow.

Pedro waited. "Is that all?"

"What do you mean, is that all?"

"It sounds like a young girl's romancing." She glared at him. He shrugged, not wanting to antagonise her further. "Although the ardent kisses trouble me," he admitted.

"And the secrecy! This extract is from March 1563. My brother, Joseph, was born the following year."

"What are you saying?"

"I am not sure."

"You must not conjecture. You must read more."

"Yes," she replied absently, "I must." Then she put the book down and concentrated on Pedro. "Why did you visit the Gaulberts?"

It was his turn to evade answering. He stood up and walked towards her. The words rushed out. "I need to go to Montauban. Thomas should have returned by now."

Her face was inscrutable, there was no sign of the sickening dread which gripped her, and her reply brooked no argument. "If you are going in search of my brother, I will accompany you."

TWENTY-NINE

Montauban, Late August

IT WAS WITH GREAT RELIEF THAT THE THREE WEARY
travellers reached the outskirts of the fortress city. The
week's journey had stretched all of their nerves to the limit;
Elizabeth, so keen to accompany Pedro, now regretted her
insistence, for he had proved distant and uncharacteristically
uncommunicative, as if she was an encumbrance; Catarina, her
temper soured by each passing league on the hired mule, had
taken her impudence within a whisper of dismissal and had
devised repeatedly to ride alongside Pedro while her mistress
brought up the rear, and Pedro, torn between the adventure
of Amsterdam and the comfort of Caors, sank into silence as
the significance of the journey robbed him of any enjoyment.

After an initial lengthy interrogation, they were allowed
through the ramparts, their passage oiled by Thomas
Gharsia's name, and clattered across the bridge to the newly
fortified quarter of Villenouvelle. Pedro glanced down to see
the water of the Tarn gilded by the setting sun and then his
eyes were drawn upward to the grand houses of the wealthy
entrepreneurs and merchants which lined the riverbank. Built

of the ubiquitous red brick of Montauban, they glowed a rich terracotta, while the late afternoon light dazzled and danced on their windows. An unfamiliar stab of envy pierced his preoccupation.

The streets were quiet as they made their way to an inn near the church of Saint-Jacques. Now no longer used for worship under the Huguenot regime, the bells were silent, as were those of the church of Saint-Louis. Instead of worshippers they were garrisoned with soldiers and used as arsenals. Everywhere Pedro could see and feel the austerity of the Huguenot consuls who ran the town. Unlike other places, Montauban was empty of those who usually gravitated towards the heart of a town: travelling players who provided a welcome distraction from everyday life; the itinerant Catholic friars in their recognisable brown robes; and even the prostitutes, if any remained in Montauban, stayed behind closed doors.

On reaching the inn, Pedro realised that the building was under surveillance. Elizabeth and Catarina were too tired to notice the two soldiers lounging in a dark corner furthest from the fire, but their presence made Pedro's skin crawl. He dropped his satchel to the floor, clasped his hands together to stop them from shaking and reminded himself that he was as far away as possible from the clutches of the Holy Office. The innkeeper, a small man who possessed more than a passing resemblance to a fox, eyed Pedro with suspicion but was happy enough to take his good coin. He bit the silver to check it was unalloyed, scanned the three travellers, and then offered them two private chambers.

After a quick, tasteless supper, during which very few words were exchanged, Pedro announced it was time to retire, as he had become increasingly troubled by the open scrutiny of the two men in the corner. He followed Elizabeth and Catarina as they climbed the rickety wooden staircase and wished them a curt goodnight. Elizabeth watched him progress down the corridor with a disquieting feeling of loss and turned to see Catarina watching closely. She pulled herself together and pushed open their chamber door.

The frowsty smell of mildew assaulted her nostrils before she lifted the candle to reveal a cramped room with an ancient box bed, a truckle bed for Catarina, and an old battered chest on which stood a bowl and jug for washing. Catarina edged past her, wrinkling her nose in disgust. She eyed the truckle bed covered with very worn, patched blankets and loudly stated, "This cannot be a private chamber." Elizabeth was too busy worrying about the lack of privacy to respond. On the journey Pedro had always managed to acquire separate chambers for the two women, with Catarina often enjoying a higher standard of accommodation than her status demanded. Her mistress, in her naivety, had wondered whether it was because he favoured the younger woman when in fact it was because Pedro had long realised that Elizabeth, who had always lived without servants, found the relationship difficult. Catarina had never crossed the divide from household servant to personal maid, as the idea of anyone helping her to dress was abhorrent to Elizabeth. Catarina picked up one of her blankets and sniffed it. "Ugh! I cannot sleep under these."

Elizabeth looked over to the covers on the box bed, which appeared to be in a better state and, desperate for sleep, she made a decision. "You can have a couple of these. It is a mild night. There are enough for both of us."

Catarina took the offered blankets with as little grace as she dared, turned her back on her mistress and began undressing. Seizing her chance, Elizabeth followed suit and slipped under the scratchy cover, still in her chemise. She was asleep in seconds, leaving Catarina to blow out the candle on the chest. However, instead of settling down, the latter waited several minutes, listening to her mistress's even breathing. Then she lifted the latch on the door and made her way stealthily along the corridor.

It was harder than she imagined. The sconces on the wall were unlit and the small flame from her candle gave little light. She steadied herself against the wall, her eyes adjusting to what illumination came from the window at the end of the corridor. It was not enough: certain that she had remembered which door Pedro had disappeared through, she now stopped, unsure on which one to tap. Defeated, she stood for some time, hoping for more brightness from the window, a combination of the guards' torches and the rising moon, but it was not to be. Eventually, she tiptoed back to her own chamber, consoling herself with the thought that there would be other nights.

The following morning dawned grey with not a patch of blue to break the monotonous sky; reflecting, in Pedro's view, the colourless essence of Montauban. As he looked out of the window even the red bricks appeared the colour of dull rust. He had risen early and found the parlour empty except for two unfamiliar soldiers silently breaking their fast. He greeted them cordially only to be faced with an indifferent stare from one of them. Conscious of his foreignness, he chose a bench a moderate distance from them: not so far away as to arouse suspicion but not so near that they would be able to hear his conversation with Elizabeth.

He waited for her, taking his time to eat his bread and cheese, and it was not long before she arrived. Now in Montauban, he realised how inappropriately dressed she was for the Huguenot fortress. In a city where sober black was the norm, she had the appearance of an exotic creature from another land. Always striking, with the contrast of her dark eyes and her pale skin, her height and her luxuriant hair, Elizabeth drew the attention of the two men. They watched her traverse the room towards him and Pedro was convinced they disapproved of her clothing, that of a wealthy merchant's daughter or sister. In preparation for meeting Thomas she had discarded her travelling clothes and wore an elegant gown of fine linen and had adorned her ears and neck with pearls.

She slid onto the bench opposite him. "Good morning."

"Good morning, Elizabeth."

"Did you sleep well, Pedro?"

"Yes, and you?"

She nodded and chewed some bread. "This is stale."

"This inn is not what I expected. It lacks much comfort, but we should only need to be here for two nights."

"That would be agreeable," said Elizabeth, heartily.

"It will save time this morning if I go to the temple to ask about Thomas while you go to the academy with Catarina. Whoever sees him can set up a meeting for us both later. Then our business will be complete. Thomas is either here or not."

"I agree."

Pedro left immediately, while Elizabeth returned to her chamber to wake Catarina. Striding past the church of Saint-Jacques, whose bell tower was now a watch tower, he could see the sentry on duty and hear the sounds of the saltpetre workshop housed in the nave. Everything in the town was militarised and there was an overwhelming atmosphere of anticipation. He soon reached the temple. The new building, only two years old, looked stark and out of place among the old, weathered brick and lacked the ornateness Pedro had become accustomed to in the churches of Castile.

He was greeted politely but warily, the elder's eyes darting from Pedro's brown face to his good quality boots and back again. At the mention of Thomas Gharsia, the Huguenot lowered his voice, almost reverentially, and confirmed that Elizabeth's brother was in town and could be found at the academy. Pedro wasted no time and left immediately. Expecting to meet Elizabeth and Catarina before they reached their destination, he hurried in the direction of the academy. The cloud was lifting, a strengthening sun warmed his back, and the knowledge that he would see Thomas that day put a spring in his step.

He was almost there when he saw a group of youths, probably students from their dress, clustered in a circle. It took a moment for him to register that within the circle was an extremely agitated woman. Pedro's ensuing emotion coalesced all his complex feelings towards Elizabeth. Towering rage, followed immediately by a wave of immense love and protectiveness, engulfed him as he saw her surrounded by the baying youths, and left him in no doubt of his affection for her. He called out, ordering the young men to stop. How dare they torment a woman? His woman, whose distraught eyes met his for an instant without recognition and then filled with tears of relief as she beheld his familiar face.

One of the youths, who was already uncomfortable with the taunting, stepped to one side, allowing a gap through which Elizabeth escaped. He took the measure of the furious man bearing down on them; a Moor, bellowing incoherently in heavily accented French but whose message was clear. Once the Catholic woman was by his side, he calmed down slightly and shouted, "What are you doing, you callow boys? You should be ashamed of yourselves. If your teachers saw you now you would be flogged. You should be flogged for bedevilling an innocent woman. You should be scourged. Call yourself students, men who learn – you are an abomination!"

All of the youths hung their heads except one. "She is

a Catholic!" he exclaimed and spat on the ground in front of Elizabeth. "Look at that bauble around her neck." Not understanding what he meant, Pedro turned and looked at Elizabeth, who very defensively covered her cross with her hand. How could he have been so foolish as to let her wear it in Montauban? How could Elizabeth be so irresponsible, for the cross, intricately wrought in gold and studded with garnets and pearls, clearly proclaimed its wearer a Catholic? It was guaranteed to inflame Huguenot sensibilities.

"It is an heirloom," Elizabeth explained, in a voice so moderated and demure that it was almost unrecognisable to Pedro. "My mother wore it and she was an English Protestant." The young man scoffed in disbelief. "Verily, I speak the truth. It was given to her by a dear friend who was a Catholic, but it is worn for remembrance now."

"You jest, Madame," he replied. "There cannot be such friendship."

Pedro was losing patience. "Do you know who this is?" he asked sharply and tucked his arm under Elizabeth's. The young man before him was beneath contempt.

"Tell me," demanded the youth, his lip curling.

"Mistress Elizabeth Gharsia."

"Gharsia?" Doubt flickered across his face.

Pedro enjoyed the moment, despite his ire. "Mistress Gharsia is Thomas Gharsia's sister."

All colour drained from the loud-mouthed youth, one of the group sniggered and nudged his nearest companion, the other two students studied their feet. Pedro glared at them, his silence now more powerful than words. The young men retreated, bowing low and mumbling apologies, frantic to escape and maintain their anonymity.

He led Elizabeth away, his arm still linked through hers, until they reached a quiet spot by the water. With each step, she felt her panic receding until she was able to notice her surroundings. "We have walked in the opposite direction to the academy."

"I thought you would wish to compose yourself."

Elizabeth, still slightly shaky, acquiesced without argument. She disengaged herself from Pedro and sat down on the bank of the Tescou just upstream from its junction with the Tarn. Leaning forward, she could see the bridge to her right, busy with mid-morning traffic, and to her left, the city's gardens spreading down to the tributary's banks. Pedro crouched down next to her and idly pulled up a piece of grass. He held it between his thumbs and blew. The high-pitched sound caused Elizabeth to swing round. Their eyes met. He grinned. "Not bad," he said.

"I am so glad you came when you did."

"So am I."

"I feel so slow-witted now. I should have carried on walking and ignored their taunts. They gathered around me because I stopped. I should have walked past them quickly and kept going. The academy was but a short distance away."

"It is easy to say that now. Where is Catarina?"

"She said she felt unwell and needed to stay abed."

"We did not bring her with us for her to stay abed!" retorted Pedro, caustically. "She was fine yesterday. You should not have been alone."

"Do not blame her. I wanted my own company, so I did not encourage her to rise."

"It is unlike you to take her side."

He sat down next to her and stretched out his legs. Elizabeth was looking directly at him, as if she was trying to decipher his expression, and he hoped his face did not betray his feelings. The closeness of her eyes revealed the clear distinction between iris and pupil and what he had thought of as black was in fact the deepest charcoal, tinted with indigo. At that moment he could drown in them.

To prevent himself becoming a laughing stock, a man with nothing declaring his love for a wealthy woman, Pedro lowered his eyes and focused on her hands, which rested on her lap. He repeated his comment. "It is unlike you to take Catarina's side."

He could feel Elizabeth's gaze on him, but he kept his eyes down even when he heard the chuckle in her voice. "It is true that I have not relished Catarina's presence in my house, but I have come to see that without her I would not have come to know you better."

And I you, he thought, his heart swelling with tenderness.

"She is a worthy chaperone. You could not have remained in our house with Thomas away."

"She is indeed!" he exclaimed, matching her mood. He stood up and gestured with his hands. "But where is she now?" he asked jokingly.

Elizabeth laughed. "We have misplaced her." She pushed herself upright, still tickled by her own humour, and put out a hand to balance. For a second, he almost reached out to her but the sound of approaching voices brought him to his senses. He kept his arms tense against his body and watched a disappointed Elizabeth compose herself, brush non-existent dirt from the back of her dress, and turn away from him.

He spoke to her rigid back. "If you are willing to go, we could seek out your brother now."

They walked away from the river, each preoccupied with their own thoughts, and the silence hung heavily between them by the time they reached the academy. It was easy to locate Thomas; he was, as expected, in the department of theology. A student, a solemn young man who treated them with great respect, took them to Thomas's study and timidly knocked on the door. There was no answer. "Knock louder," Pedro and Elizabeth said simultaneously. "Knock louder."

The door swung open to reveal Thomas in academic dress. Tall and broad-shouldered, he filled the doorway, his resemblance to their father, once again, unsettling Elizabeth. He appeared to be genuinely pleased to see them. "Bess," he boomed. "And Pedro Torres. Come in."

Thomas drew up two chairs and waited expectantly behind his desk. Pedro, having rehearsed what he was going to say, spoke first. "I have come because my contract with you has almost expired."

"Is that a problem?"

"Yes, if I am no longer contracted to work for you."

Thomas waved a dismissive hand. "I trusted you to continue."

Elizabeth broke into the conversation. "You cannot expect Pedro to work without a contract."

"I have been much occupied, Bess."

She eyed the pile of papers on the desk. "I can see."

Pedro, not wanting Thomas to lose focus, said, "I expected you back in Caors."

"I also expected you," echoed Elizabeth, which was an untruth as, in the past, Thomas had rarely returned when promised.

Thomas looked from one to the other. "I cannot see why you needed to come to Montauban."

"Perhaps I was worried about you."

"I doubt it, Bess."

Irritation rising, Pedro spoke firmly. "I signed for one year only. I need to leave for Amsterdam soon."

"Ah," Thomas responded. "What prevents you?"

"I cannot just leave Elizabeth."

"Why not?"

Flustered, Pedro groped for the relevant words. "She will be alone."

"I do not believe that is so. What is the maid's name – the one I hired?"

Elizabeth ignored them both. She stood up. "Who will do the accounts?"

"There are other stewards."

"You would not come home when Pedro leaves?"

"No, my work is too important. The threat to our independence increases each day. We must be ready. These are difficult times for Huguenots."

"I do not want another steward!" exclaimed Elizabeth, petulantly.

"Then be your own steward."

"Now you are being ridiculous!"

"That is where you are wrong, Sister. As a small boy, I remember seeing Ysabel Bernade poring over ledgers and being told to play quietly when men of business came to the house. Also, I seem to remember that when Pedro first became our steward, you objected and wanted to run Father's affairs."

Unable to argue, Elizabeth sat back down with a flounce.

Pedro addressed Thomas. "When my contract has run its course, I will go to Amsterdam, and you will replace me?"

"Yes."

"When?" Another month and the weather would make travelling more difficult.

Thomas sighed, rested his elbows on his desk, and ran his fingers through his shock of greying hair. He studied Elizabeth's sullen face, feeling the weight of his responsibilities. His eyes dropped to her neck, where a wide gold chain was just visible behind a row of pearls. He pointed and asked, incredulously, "That is not Mama's ostentatious bauble you are wearing? Even you would not be so foolish." As he was expecting her to retaliate in her usual manner, he was completely taken by surprise when she burst into tears.

Totally perplexed, for neither Elizabeth nor Pedro chose to enlighten him, Thomas capitulated. "I cannot come to Caors immediately, but I will come within the month."

Elizabeth, who had only partially registered his words, continued to weep, so Pedro rose and clasped Thomas's offered hand. Feeling some sympathy for the older man, he said, "I will take her back to the inn."

The three of them stood awkwardly, Elizabeth sniffing loudly into Pedro's handkerchief. Thomas shifted from foot to foot, disconcerted by such emotion. "I would ask you to dine with me tonight, but I have a meeting to attend."

Pedro was about to reply when Elizabeth announced, through her tears, "We go home early tomorrow. We will dine simply at the inn."

"We wish you farewell, Thomas. And I trust to see you within the month."

Thomas was back at his desk reading his correspondence before Pedro had closed the door. Elizabeth paused and waited for him. Her face was blotched, her eyes were red-rimmed, and her shoulders slumped. "Don't look at me like that!"

"Like what?"

"With such pity."

"You are incorrect, Mistress Gharsia."

"Do not walk away, Monsieur." She hurried to catch him up. He crooked his arm, she slid her arm through, and he momentarily rested his hand on hers.

"Come," he said, "let us go home."

THIRTY

THE DAY AFTER THEIR RETURN TO CAORS DAWNED brightly, with just enough chill in the air to persuade Catarina to light the fire in the parlour. She was coaxing the first flames to catch when her efforts were interrupted by an urgent knocking. She hurried across the hall, the loud noise echoing around her, and pulled open the heavy oak door to reveal a diminutive figure.

"It is early to be thundering on a person's door."

Shrewd dark eyes pinned her to the spot. "I am Sara Gaulbert and I wish to speak to your mistress."

"She is abed."

"Then wake her up!"

Her attention caught, Catarina looked past the old woman to the untethered mule, who had chosen that moment to defecate copiously in Elizabeth's yard. She watched the animal move a couple of paces to reach some grass, pulling the old battered cart behind him, and then she gave Sara the benefit of her most withering expression.

"Wake up your mistress immediately," demanded the tiny figure. "And invite me in." Sara Gaulbert would stand no insolence from an uppity servant.

Five minutes later Elizabeth appeared, a shawl quickly thrown over her night clothes. In her haste, she had forgotten her slippers and she hopped from one foot to the other as the cold penetrated from the stone flags. "What is it, Sara?"

"It is the harvest. The pickers are late." The enormity of the situation was clear on the old woman's face. Her eyes implored. "We could lose much of the crop."

"I will come." Nobody had noticed Pedro's presence. Three pairs of eyes turned towards him. For a moment he experienced the customary irritation, that he often seemed to be invisible to people, and then suppressed it as unworthy in the circumstances. How could they have known that he had risen well before dawn to ensure the ledgers were up to date before he left for Amsterdam?

"I will come," Catarina volunteered, rather too swiftly for her mistress's liking. Elizabeth raised her eyebrows in a gesture reminiscent of her father and Sara waited with interest to see how her friend would respond to the maid's impudent reaction. "I will be of more value than you. You are not used to hard labour."

Conscious that Pedro was studying her, Elizabeth clamped her lips shut on her sharp response and rephrased her answer. "It is true, that of late, I have not had the responsibility of running the household alone, but I can assure you I am capable of bringing in the harvest. When I was younger my father insisted all of us worked in the vines and I enjoyed it." She paused, felt the emotion building, and determined to continue. "It was I who taught Gabriel to cut his first bunches."

Sara looked from one woman to the other: something was afoot which was more complicated than aptitude for hard work. She stole a glance at Pedro Torres. He was staring at Elizabeth with a mixture of sympathy and amusement, while Catarina's focus was clearly on him. *Now I understand*, she thought, and studied the maid. The woman was comely enough and, on Sara's first acquaintance, she appeared spirited, which was a characteristic Sara secretly admired, but she doubted Pedro would be interested. In her opinion Pedro's admiration of Elizabeth was perceptible and Sara truly believed they would make a good match.

He caught the old woman's eye and smiled the curious half-smile she had often seen, as if his life had never allowed him to beam broadly. "You must be exhausted," he said, "rising so early to come and see us."

Sara chuckled, pleased her journey had not been wasted. "The mule needs the rest, which he can have while I break my fast with you. Then we can all leave together."

By noon they were out in the fields, except for Sara, who had retired to rest. Pedro was working on a row with Elizabeth, much to Catarina's chagrin, and he found he was revelling in the repetitive task. After filling each basket, he stretched and allowed himself a few moments to appreciate the scenery. Laden with fruit, row upon row of vines, their autumnal leaves quivering in the light breeze, unfolded up the slopes before him. He could see Luc and Helena, Jacques and Catarina, and the collection of neighbours who had rallied around to help, all methodically progressing between the rows. He had noticed that Jacques periodically glanced in the direction of the farmhouse, willing the itinerant pickers to arrive. It was true that the Gaulberts had started to harvest early but the extra hands they needed usually arrived in good time.

"Stop idling," teased Elizabeth as she, too, stretched and placed her hands on the small of her back.

Pedro retaliated in the same tone. "Who are you to call

me idle, Mistress Gharsia? My basket is full, unlike yours." He hoisted the hod onto his back, struggling slightly with the straps, and called back as he strode towards the waiting cart. "However, if you speak kindly to me I will carry your grapes, too." He turned when he reached the end of the row, pleased to see that she was still watching him.

"Pedro!" Jacques voice startled him, as the vintner was partially hidden by the increasing pile of grapes. "How about you coming to the barn to start the pressing?"

"I was helping Elizabeth."

"She will be fine. She has been harvesting grapes since she was a child."

"I will just go and tell her."

Jacques waited impatiently. *How long did it take for a man to say he was going to the press?* he asked himself, reflecting on the way Elizabeth leant forward slightly, apparently listening intently. Her affection for the Castilian was as obvious to Jacques as it was to his mother, but it was no business of his.

The cellar was cool and dark after the outside heat and it took a moment for Pedro to adjust his eyes. The huge vats and press gradually came into focus as Jacques said, "We have enough grapes for one vat and you and I will have to manage. Come on, strip off." Too busy pulling off his own shirt, the vintner did not notice Pedro stiffen and pause, torn between exposing his lacerated back and his desire to stomp the black, glistening grapes. "Come on," repeated Jacques as he clambered into the vat and, if he noticed the scars, he showed no sign of it. "We have no time to lose. All the grapes picked today need to be crushed."

The stalks were hard, digging into Pedro's feet, while the fruit burst and oozed through his toes. At first, the strange sensation was disconcerting but soon he was lost in the rhythm, and although he did not know the words, he hummed to the tune of his companion's song. He became absorbed in the physical exertion, his mind free, for once, of facts and figures, supressed emotion, and haunting memories. At the end of each verse Pedro breathed deeply, filling his lungs with the musty smell of the old stones and the earth floor, wine-soaked over decades, which mingled with the pungency of the newly crushed grapes and the sharp, woody smell of the new oak barrels Jacques had recently acquired. He experienced a moment of complete contentment and then a voice broke the spell. Both men turned towards the door.

"Not now, Mama. Pedro is here!"

Sara stayed where she was, averting her eyes. "Pierre has just been to tell us the pickers have been seen. They landed at Fumel this morning so will be here by sunset."

Her son punched the air in delight and grinned at his companion. "You can go home tomorrow." Pedro's disappointment must have shown on his face as Jacques swiftly added, "Only if you wish to."

As the last rays of light leached from the sky, Elizabeth sank thankfully into the bed next to Sara. Lying on her back, she eased her aching shoulders into a more comfortable position, an involuntary sigh escaping from her lips.

"Was it that bad?" asked Sara, settling her old bones into her half of the bed. Normally, she slept in the middle, where she had moulded a perfect hollow, and now the mattress felt strangely flat beneath her. It was the one luxury she had insisted on after her husband's death, for Henri had stoutly proclaimed over the years that there was nothing amiss with straw. The rest of the family had easily been persuaded and every mattress, except the one Pedro lay on in the attic, was feather. Even Catarina, in the kitchen, was cosy on the truckle bed.

"No, I enjoyed it, but I will suffer in the morning."

"It was good of you to come."

"I wanted to."

"Would you have come if Catarina had not offered?" asked Sara mischievously. There was a long pause: so long that Sara wondered if her companion had fallen asleep. "Elizabeth?"

"What do you mean?"

"You know what I mean. Mistress Maid has her eye on Pedro. You need to be wary, my girl."

A much longer silence followed Sara's candour. She felt Elizabeth tense, so she placed a reassuring hand on the younger woman's arm. "What troubles you?"

Elizabeth spoke very quietly, a catch in her voice. "Something happened in Montauban."

Sara waited. She increased the pressure on Elizabeth's arm slightly and moved closer to ensure she could hear. Discerning her friend's profile in the soft moonlight flooding the room, Sara whispered, "Tell me."

The words came slowly, directed towards the ceiling rather than Sara. "You remember the crucifix my mother left me, the one with the garnets and pearls?"

"Yes, it had once belonged to Ysabel Bernade."

"That is the one. I was wearing it in Montauban. I did not think."

"It was stolen?"

"No, I have it safe, but it pains me to wear it."

"Why?"

"I was on my way to the academy to see if there was any news of Thomas while Pedro went to the temple. We thought it would be quicker."

"Why was Catarina not with you?" demanded Sara.

"She was to accompany me, but a malady prevented her just after Pedro had left."

"What malady?"

"Her monthly course was troublesome."

Sara snorted loudly in response and then asked, "What happened to you?"

"A group of young men, talking, blocked the path. I thought they would move when I approached but they turned and stared at me. One of them pointed to my crucifix and started to jeer. The others followed his lead, their eyes full of malevolence." Tears began to leak from the corners of her eyes as she remembered her ordeal. She turned on her side, so she could face Sara. "I was so frightened." Her tears were flowing freely now so Sara opened her arms and held Elizabeth.

"Did they hurt you?"

"No, it was only words. They despised me for being a Catholic."

Sara chuckled. "Foolish boys, if they had known!"

Elizabeth wiped her cheeks and allowed herself a rueful smile. "Mama loved the crucifix because Ysabel had worn it, but she never forsook her Protestant beliefs. These young men were so zealous, so angry."

"As young men often are."

"Did you know that my uncle, Mama's brother, died a martyr for his beliefs in England?"

"Yes, I did. She told me that she was there, with your father."

"You must have been very close friends for her to tell you."

"We were."

Elizabeth snuggled into Sara: the old woman's arms were stronger than they appeared, and the memory came sharp and bitter-sweet. "Pedro came to my rescue."

"He did?"

"Yes."

"What did he do?"

"He berated them vehemently for being so discourteous. Some of the students became very bashful in the face of Pedro's ire as it is well known that Moriscos have given the Huguenots much support. He did not draw breath until they made an apology, their heads bowed. One youth, the leader, refused to be cowed until Pedro used my name. If I had not been so afeard I would have laughed. As soon as the villain heard 'Gharsia' he hung his head in shame, as Thomas is a man well known in Montauban."

The clouds had gathered, obscuring the moon and plunging the room into darkness. No longer able to see Elizabeth, Sara hugged her more closely and said, "What happened next?"

"After the youths had departed, Pedro was most solicitous." Elizabeth paused, conscious not to give too much information, before she elaborated. "He led me to the river, away from prying eyes, where we could walk, and I could compose myself."

Reading between the lines, Sara tried to imagine the scene. The child of her dearest friend, torn between her life of respectability and the man of whom they knew so little. "I think Monsieur Torres has stolen your heart."

Elizabeth's reply was tantalisingly quiet, almost inaudible to Sara's old ears. "What did you say?"

Leaning forward and speaking directly into Sara's right ear, she repeated, "Verily, I am lost."

"I thought so."

"I am like a young girl who yearns for what she cannot have."

"Nonsense! You are a mature woman. If you want this man you must let him know. You are a woman of wealth, he possesses nought but his good character."

"You believe Pedro to be a man of good character?"

"I do, and I have lived many years on God's earth." Sara eased her left arm slightly, it had become numb, and Elizabeth shifted so they were both more comfortable.

"I cannot speak to him."

"Why not? What have you to lose? If he leaves for the Netherlands, he will be gone soon."

"He does not care for me."

"Nonsense, again!"

"You are mistaken. The night of my encounter on the way to the academy I woke to find Catarina's bed empty. I crept to the door, peered out, and saw her coming out of Pedro's chamber."

It was not the reason Sara had expected so she thought carefully about her response. "Since her husband's death Catarina must fend for herself. She is a woman alone with no family except for her brother and his scold of a wife, who would not give her a home. She must look where she can for support and I am certain she sees Pedro as a possible husband. She will use any wile to snare him and she could easily accompany him to Amsterdam. That said, you do not know what happened. He may have rejected her. I have seen no sign of his interest."

"You have not?"

"Verily, I believe his heart is turned towards you. But is he to abstain from all women? You have not told him of your affection, you have no claims on him."

Elizabeth turned on her back and thumped the mattress either side of her making Sara jerk awkwardly. The old woman was tiring, it had been a long day, and nothing would be solved that night. "Go to sleep, Elizabeth. All will be clearer in the morning."

Listening to Sara's soft snoring, Elizabeth rejected her friend's words. All would not be clearer in the morning. Her mind was alive with memories: Pedro, dirty and emaciated, skulking in the shadows the first time she had seen him; the sensation of him wrapping Gabriel's cloak around her in the storm; his quiet concentration as he sat cross-legged on the floor of her father's chamber listening to her mother's journal, and finally, the image she usually tried to repress, Pedro enfolding her in his arms as she learnt of Gabriel's fate. She tossed and turned, each move executed with minimal impact on the sleeping Sara, until every nerve in her body screamed. Eventually, she rose and padded to the window. The clouds had dispersed to reveal a bright white moon, wreathed with wispy remnants, floating high in the sky. She shivered in the evening chill, hugged herself and rubbed her upper arms. As she did so, a treacherous thought crept in unbidden. She wondered how it would feel to fall asleep in Pedro's arms.

Directly above her, Pedro was admiring the moon's radiance from his bed. Physically exhausted from his day's harvesting, he had flopped onto the old mattress fully expecting to fall asleep immediately but had found, to his surprise, that it eluded him. It was true that the bed was uncomfortable, for the mattress had lost any volume it had once possessed, but he had slept in far worse conditions. The attic was dry, although very dusty, and best of all, he had his privacy. The choice, suggested by Jacques, between sharing Luc's bed or sleeping in the barn with the newly-arrived hired hands had been one he had been reluctant to make. One glance at Luc's glowering face had scotched that option and the thought of bedding down with twenty strangers held even less attraction. At the last minute, Jacques had remembered the attic, which contained an old bed and chest among the sundry detritus discarded over the years and would be comfortable enough on an autumn evening.

He lay on the bed, his hands behind his head, and mulled

over the day. Elizabeth came to mind, more relaxed, shedding her haughty manner like a skin, as she expertly cut the grapes. She had even looked different: her glorious rich, auburn hair covered by a simple kerchief and her pale, creamy skin blushed by exertion and the sun. He, too, felt changed by the day. It had been a long time since he had experienced such an intense feeling of fulfilment. He found he was smiling to himself, to the moon, and then to the darkness as a single cloud dimmed the silvery light.

THIRTY-ONE

T HE KNOCK AT THE DOOR WAS HESITANT, NEITHER characteristic of Elizabeth nor Catarina, and it hardly registered on Pedro's consciousness. It sounded again and Pedro, deep in the intricacies of production and profit, cursed the interruption and reluctantly stopped studying the page before him. He rubbed his eyes, gritty from close work by candlelight, and pushed himself up from Luis Gharsia's imposing desk. A blanket of despondency settled on him as he contemplated Elizabeth: he would miss this room, this house, and especially the woman who was now standing framed in the doorway.

Since their return from the harvesting she had become politely detached, which he found far more disheartening than Catarina's permanently woebegone expression. Gone was the friendship he treasured, with its easy banter and cosy conversations: it had evaporated as soon as he had announced the date of his departure. "What is it?" he asked, wearily.

She held up the book she was holding. "I have found something."

"Do you want to share it?" It was some time since they had discussed the contents of the journal.

By way of answer, Elizabeth walked into the room. She stopped when she reached the desk, appeared to consider it thoroughly, and then pulled herself onto the only place not littered with papers.

He could not help himself from exclaiming, "Are you certain you are quite comfortable?"

"There is nowhere else to sit," she retorted and for a moment there was a flash of their old comradeship.

Without commenting, Pedro sat down on his chair and waited, ignoring the urge to suggest they move to the parlour. He watched Elizabeth intently as she carefully moved the candle. The light illuminated the journal, leaving her face in shadow. "Listen," she instructed, excitement in her voice. She began to read, translating each sentence so he missed nothing.

The fourth day of August 1563

This eve, I am in high dudgeon. This morning I walked with Francesco through the Portal des Augustins away from the ramparts. He was full of ardour and we secretly conveyed ourselves towards the woods. There we lay as man and wife for surely that is to be. The trees were thick and not a person espied us. Ysabel believed me to be about my errands and as Ramon is troubled by his leg, now he is old, I was alone and quite safe in the city. My heart swelleth with joy when I am with Francesco. He is of handsome visage, possesses wit, and bestows on me divers pretty sayings and gifts as a sign of his troth.

When I returned home, Luis had visited. He was in ill humour and demanded wherefore I had left the house for he had found Ysabel and Thomas in the garden and Ramon alone in the kitchen.

I sayst: I had no need of Ramon to help me with my errands for my purchases were few.

He sayst: Where are they?

I did not answer for I had forgotten to buy them.

He sayst: Where have you been? There is earth on your dress.

I sayst: I do not have to answer to you.

At that, Luis looked mightily displeased, but I have never been afeard of him. Ysabel placed her hand on his arm to calm him.

She sayst: Luis, Meg is not a child.

He shrugged her away and fixed me with his stern eyes.

He sayst: You have been with Francesco Zametti.

I sayst: What if I have? Am I to talk to no young men? Am I to be an old maid because you do not like my suitor?

He sayst: You are a foolish girl.

I sayst with great heat: You are the fool. You are ridiculous. You shut yourself away in that house with Johan and do not go about and mix with people unless it is to do business. You do not care for your son. Alyce has been dead for five years. She would not want to see you so. You cannot talk to me about love.

He sayst: Love? You think Francesco Zametti is enamoured of you?

I sayst: We are to be wed.

I did not hear what Luis sayst in return for I walked away. Luis made to follow me but me thinks Ysabel sayst no.

The fifth day of August 1563

It is but two of the clock, yet I must gather my thoughts. Not an hour has passed since Luis came upon me in the garden.

Ysabel had retired inside with Thomas to escape the heat, but I chose to remain sitting in the shade of the old walnut tree reading one of Hernando's many books. I miss Hernando so, as I felt he was my friend and I think of him often, especially when I search in his book chest for a new volume. Me thinks, I will need to go to the house on Place St Urcisse when Luis is about on business if he remains displeased with me. Johan will let me choose a new book.

I was content with my book when Luis appeared. He stood in front of me and tried to be contrite. Luis finds it difficult to apologise and I did not make it easy for him. He was awkward.

I sayst: Sit with me in the shade for the sun is strong.

He sat next to me and stared at the wall opposite.

After some time, he sayst: I have been to the university to see Lorenzo Zametti.

I sayst: Because of me?

He sayst: I spoke harshly yesterday.

I sayst: You did.

He sayst: I promised your uncle, Mercer, that I would provide for you and pay a handsome dowry on your marriage.

I felt humbled and sayst: Thank you.

The cordiality was spoilt for he sayst: Francesco Zametti is not the husband for you.

I sayst: You have forgotten what it is to love. Cannot you remember how you loved Alyce even when you had a wife? We cannot always choose who enters our heart.

He sayst: I married Marie when I believed Alyce was lost to me. You cannot compare a woman like Alyce to Zametti. You do not know the true Zametti.

I sayst with great ire: Did you know the true Alyce? I knew her all of my life, but you came into our lives but rarely, yet you claim great knowledge. I saw more of you than Alyce did.

He sayst: I did not need time to see the essence of Alyce.

I sayst: That is what I feel for Francesco.

He leant forward and rested his elbows on his knees and looked at me with kindness. He sayst: I spoke to Lorenzo and he gave no indication that he knew of the intentions of his nephew.

I sayst with heat: You spoke of our promises to each other.

He sayst: No, but I talked in general terms.

He turned and faced me and looked at me with such warmth that my stomach knotted, and sayst: Lorenzo told me Francesco is to return to Venice next month and will not resume his studies here.

I could not speak. I turned and beat Luis on the chest with my fists. He caught them and enfolded me in his arms as he did when I was a child.

When at last I found words, I sayst: You are mistaken. You are mistaken. I hate you.

I pushed him away and ran to my chamber where my tears dampen this page of my journal.

Elizabeth passed the journal to Pedro, so he could see the old stained page. He took the book gingerly, unsure of how he should react, while Elizabeth waited patiently for him to comment. He ventured his opinion. "Surely if she was very upset by Francesco's return to Venice, she would not be able to write." Elizabeth's withering look failed to stop him continuing. "I believe your mother is in love with the idea of the young Francesco rather than the man himself."

Elizabeth's tone was a trifle too sharp for his comfort. "What makes you say that?"

Pedro cursed himself for digging the hole from which he was now trying to extricate himself. "She is still young with little experience of men. Her journals show she lives a quiet life with much time taken up by your brother, Thomas. She has no father or brother to guide her, to introduce her to suitable men and Luis appears too withdrawn to realise she is ready to be married."

"Perhaps you are correct," Elizabeth volunteered reluctantly, but his view had not surprised her as she had long been aware of his perception.

"What happens next? Does Francesco leave?" He handed the book back to Elizabeth, who started to read. The text was bolder, less faded, as if her mother had pressed hard on the page, and in more than one place the nib of the pen had scratched through the paper.

The sixth day of August 1563

This day is one of the most heinous days of my life. Francesco Zametti is the lowest worm of a man. He is a cockroach who scuttles to hide when the light shines, a turd who sticks to my shoe, slippery and evil-smelling, and when he turned his Janus smile on me today, I wanted to vomit.

I rose early this morn, my intention to challenge what Luis had said. I had gone a short distance towards the university when Luis appeared beside me.

I sayst: Go back.

He sayst: You cannot go alone. It is unseemly.

I sayst: How did you know what I intended?

He sayst with a rare smile: I know you so well. It is what I expected.

I marched on ahead, but Luis easily kept pace as his legs are so long. I was all hot and uncomfortable when I reached Lorenzo Zametti, who was in his study. He was a great friend of Hernando, as they worked together. It was Lorenzo who cut out the tumour which threatened to kill Ysabel once Hernando had applied the mask soaked in poppy juice to make her sleep.

He looked up from his desk when we entered and offered us refreshments. Luis spoke first. There was much chatter about sundry things and I became very irate that Luis had ordered me to act demurely, so I interrupted their tedious conversation.

I sayst: How is your nephew, Francesco, Monsieur Zametti?

He sayst with surprise: My nephew?

I sayst: Yes.

He sayst: Are you acquainted with my nephew?

I was about to speak when Luis sayst: On occasion, we have talked to him after Mass.

This seemed to please the physician. He sayst: My nephew is well. He is to return to his family next month. He misses them.

Then Zametti sayst: He is to be betrothed.

I spluttered into my cup. Luis caught my eye and I read a warning in his. He sayst: That must please his family greatly. We wish him well.

Lorenzo Zametti sayst to me: What ails you? Is the drink not to your satisfaction?

I sayst: I will tell you what ails me. My heart is broken.

Luis rested his hand on my shoulder as if in a comforting caress but pressed down firmly to silence me and he sayst: Meg, my dear, Lorenzo does not want to hear of such trifles.

At that point the worm slithered in, looking mightily handsome. Monsieur Zametti sayst: Here is my nephew now.

The worm refused to look at me. His uncle sayst: Francesco, do you recall Monsieur Gharsia and his ward?

He turned his eyes on me with no sign of affection and his lips formed a recreant smile.

He sayst: I believe we have met at church.

I sayst: I thought we had but now I see I was mistook. You are not the man I believed you to be.

I turned to Luis and sayst: I am unwell. Please escort me home.

I took my leave with dignity.

As we walked home I sayst: Do you expect me to weep great tears?

Luis sayst: You should not for he is a man unworthy of you.

I sayst: My heart is broken.

Luis sayst: Better a broken heart now than when you are married.

Ysabel was waiting for us by the gate. Luis refused to come in and returned to his house. I came to my chamber where I have fumed ever since.

The light has faded, and I am fatigued from this day but before I retire, I must think carefully about what Luis revealed on the way back.

As we reached the river I sayst: Why did Monsieur Zametti call me your ward? I know of no arrangement.

Luis sayst: I did not deem it necessary to tell you. A long time ago I made provision for you. It was when Rufus died and you and Alyce were left penniless. I have not legally made you my ward, but I refer to you as such to acquaintances as it explains our relationship.

I sayst: I know something of this. Ysabel hinted at some arrangement when I feared I would be abandoned when you left for Mecca.

He sayst: I would never have abandoned you.

I sayst: Much danger could have befallen you on your journey and Ysabel is old. I was worried that I would need to return to Uncle Mercer.

He sayst: I would never abandon you.

I sayst: Yet you took me back to Uncle Mercer.

He sayst: It was the honourable thing to do.

I sayst: Why?

He sayst: He is your guardian.

I sayst: Why did you bring me home again?

He sayst: Home?

I sayst: Yes, to Caors.

He looked at me, his face all closed and did not respond.

I sayst: Why would you not abandon me? Because of Alyce?

He still did not respond.

I reached for his hand and sayst: You have always been my dear friend.

Elizabeth looked up from the journal. "She does not seem too concerned about Francesco Zametti."

Pedro agreed. "It appears her pride is more hurt than her heart." He paused and then asked, "Do you know what happened next?"

"I have not read further. Do you wish for me to continue?"

Pedro nodded. Elizabeth shifted slightly, arranging herself more comfortably on the desk.

The first day of October 1563

It is past midnight and still my candle burns. I fear what thoughts will come to me if I do not write. I am ashamed and downcast. What had held such promise for me is now my shame. I have listened, when I should have not, and I have lost the esteem of the one I love most in the world. This evening after I had kissed Thomas goodnight, warm and snug in his bed, I sat in the garden the better to enjoy the end of the day. I was hidden from view by the juniper. I had been there but a short time when I heard voices. Luis had come to visit.

He sayst: It is a fine evening.

Ysabel sayst: It is warm for the season.

Luis sayst: Is Meg inside?

Ysabel sayst: Yes, she is with Thomas.

There was silence and then she sayst in a low voice: There is a matter on which I must speak. A most hurtful matter.

I strained to hear. Each word was as fire as it scorched my heart. Madame Clement had told Ysabel of my meeting with the worm, Zametti, in August. Her maid had seen me emerge from the woods with him. Me thinks the girl must be impolitic to pass on such gossip for what was she doing in the woods. I could not see Ysabel, but I knew her forehead would be creased with worry and she would be wringing her handkerchief.

She sayst: I fear Meg's reputation is ruined for Madame Clement will not be silent.

Luis sayst: Is she with child?

The sorrow in his voice distressed me and I hung my head in shame.

Ysabel sayst: No, her monthly cloths have been washed twice since then.

Luis sayst: All is not lost.

Ysabel sayst: It will still reflect badly on you, and on me.

Luis sayst: I should have taken more care of her.

Ysabel sayst: She is too spirited for her own good. Sneaking off to meet her lover.

Luis sayst: She is young. He turned her head.

Ysabel sayst: Luis, wake up. She is no longer a young girl. She should be married.

Luis sayst: Then even more should I have taken care of her.

Ysabel sayst: Luis, my dear, do not be rash.

Luis sayst: What are you afeard of?

Ysabel sayst: It is not your responsibility. It is different from Marie.

Luis sayst: What is to be done then?

Ysabel sayst: She must return to her uncle.

Luis sayst: Meg hates it there.

Ysabel sayst: You must speak to her tomorrow.

Pedro realised he was on the edge of his chair leaning forward. He was so close to Elizabeth his hair almost touched her skirt. "Is that the end of the entry?"

"Yes."

"Find the next one quickly."

"Yes, Sir," she answered teasingly, although she was equally keen to learn more.

The second day of October 1563

My hand shakes as I write, for I cannot believe what has befallen me. I was still in my chamber, having slept late after a most disturbed night, when Luis called my name from the hall. Thomas was with me, playing quietly with his chuck stones. I wrapped a shawl around my shoulders, bade the child to be good, and opened the door. Luis was alone, waiting for me.

I sayst: Have you come to take me back to England? If I had not been so mortified, I would have been amused at the surprise on his face.

He sayst: Why do you say that?

I sayst: Why do you think? I was in the garden.

I thought he would be cross, but he smiled. A genuine smile which started in his eyes and then he laughed, a deep throaty laugh. "You have been listening as you did as a child. You are incorrigible, Meg!"

"Thank you." I love it when Luis smiles. It changes his face dramatically, softening all the sharp angles of his features.

He sayst: It was not a compliment.

I sayst: I can accept it as I wish.

He sayst: You heard all the conversation in the garden?

I sayst: I heard enough.

He sayst: Ysabel thinks it is better for you to return to England where there is no stain on your reputation.

I sayst: She does, does she?

He sayst: Yes, and as you heard she is thinking of herself, and of me.

I sayst: And what do you think?

The silence was heavy in the room. Luis was no longer smiling. He sayst: I think I cannot bear for you to leave.

I sayst: I cannot bear to go.

He did not answer but looked at me for a long time. I met his eyes, for I have always loved Luis since I was a small child. So used to him now, I had stopped noticing how dark his eyes are. I sayst: What can we do?

He sayst: Will you marry me?

I sayst: I will only marry a man who loves me.

He sayst: There will always be Alyce.

I sayst: Do not worry, my dear friend, my dear love, for I have always shared you with Alyce.

He sayst: How can I not love you?

I shivered, for it was cold in the hall and I was still in my nightclothes. He took me in his arms and I knew myself loved.

Elizabeth lifted her head and blinked away the gathering tears. "They loved each other, they truly loved each other. Not the ardent love of romance but strong, unwavering love."

Pedro, disconcerted by her emotion, felt inadequate. "So it seems," he said.

"They must have married almost at once, for Joseph was born the following summer."

Pedro felt it unnecessary to comment. He watched her expression as her thoughts tumbled and found voice. "They were together for over forty years. He was lost when she died. He never thought he would outlive her. He told me once."

He stood up and took her hands in his. He did not ask whether she had laid the ghost of Alyce to rest, nor why her parents' love was so important, he just let her rest her hands in his as her tears fell. The weight which he had been carrying since he had reported Luis's dying words to her lifted and he knew he was ready to face his future.

THIRTY-TWO

Caors, October 1611

THOMAS ARRIVED, AS PROMISED, ON A MELLOW autumn day. Elizabeth was in the garden tidying the herbs ready for winter. Many were dying back while some, like the rosemary, still sported flowers. Behind her a climbing rose defied the season, scenting the air with summer as its white blooms hung limply in the still air. She worked methodically, persuading her busy hands to ignore her aching heart. Next year the neat rows would again produce a yield too great for the household: she would be without her father for a second year, it was three years since she had seen Gabriel, and Pedro would be gone too. She was brushing away treacherous tears, for they came more easily each day, when Thomas appeared, striding down the path.

"Bess, greetings! I have come as I said I would."

She looked up and beheld him with little pleasure. "Go inside. I will come shortly."

He glanced at her apprehensively and decided to ignore her wet eyes. He was tired: the journey had been trying and he was in no mood for overwrought women. "Do not fret, Sister.

I will take some refreshment, arrange my things, and then go in search of Pedro Torres. He will be eager to see me."

Elizabeth stared at her brother's retreating back and made no attempt to stop crying. Perhaps if she wept until she was exhausted, her pain would be replaced by a great emptiness which would consume her and leave no cracks through which her grief could creep? Blinking away her blinding tears, she hacked at the lavender, sending clouds of dried seed pods into the air, and then covered her face with her hands. The sharp, sweet scent undid her; her mother's favourite perfume.

Pedro, watching from the window, saw her fall to her knees. Helpless, he witnessed her torment as she rocked to and fro, and without thought, his instinct drove him to leave his work. He found her curled within herself, her hands resting on her tucked head.

"Elizabeth," he said gently.

He thought she had not heard him but eventually she lifted her head and said flatly, "Thomas is here."

"Come, Elizabeth, let me help you up."

She made no sign of moving so he crouched down next to her. "You cannot stay here weeping."

She turned her tear-ravaged face towards him. "I miss them so much."

He reached out and tentatively stroked her hair, caressed her arm, and then took her hand. "Come, stand up. There is nothing I can say to make the pain less but in time it dulls, and these moments of grief will become fewer."

She stood, her eyes almost level with his, and asked through her tears, "Did it happen to you?"

"Yes."

"With your brother?"

He nodded, took a deep breath, and his gaze remained steady. "And with my parents and my wife."

Her eyes widened. "Your wife?"

"Yes, I lost all three of them in the winter of 1599. We were weak from lack of food and they were taken by sickness."

"I did not know you had a wife."

"It was a long time ago."

"I did not know this," she repeated.

"Why should you know of my life in Castile?"

"I could have asked."

"I doubt I would have told you."

"Why?" she asked, and then shame surfaced. She had treated him cruelly at first and wariness was his second nature.

Diverted by his disclosure, her grief temporarily receded. "Were you married for long?"

"A few years."

Pedro waited. He had the impression she was struggling to compose her next question. "Ask me what you wish."

"Was it a love match?"

"No, but we did well enough together."

"And you have never married again?"

He fought the urge to avert his eyes and the lie slipped off his tongue. "I have had neither the means nor the inclination."

The blunt statement hung between them. She looked at him expectantly and he silently cursed his lack of courage. He should enfold her in his arms and affirm his love despite being unable to provide for her, but his pride stopped him. He was floundering, desperately thinking of how he could phrase his feelings, when he was saved by the heavy tread of Thomas.

"Torres, there you are! I have been searching for you. We need to speak."

Pedro made no move to leave. Thomas, totally misjudging the situation, addressed Elizabeth. "Stop prattling, Bess. Pedro is too much the gentleman to declare his boredom on the subject of gardening." His sister shot him a look of pure venom which heartened him. It was easier to cope with than tears. Pedro took a step back from Elizabeth but still showed no sign of leaving. "Torres, please can you come inside, I need to see the accounts."

Unable to ignore a direct request, Pedro obediently followed Thomas into the house, leaving Elizabeth alone with her turmoil. Her tears had dried, spent for the moment, and she walked over to the bench by the wall. She sat, lost in thought, uncertain of her reaction to Pedro's candour. All the time he had been in Caors she had imagined his life as that of a solitary man, a man of resolution striving towards his goal of reaching Amsterdam, only diverted from his path by the need to help his aunt and cousin, and by the necessity of recovering from the consequences of that action. She chided herself for her naivety, for a man nearing forty could be expected to have had a wife and the idea of Pedro having lived in contented domesticity was strangely disquieting.

Thomas sat behind the desk, giving his companion a clear message about who was in charge. Disguising a flash of irritation with busyness, Pedro crossed the room to the chest and took out the account books he had kept perfectly for the last year. He placed them on the desk in front of Thomas with a more resounding thud than he had intended. "They are all up to date."

"It is what I expected."

"Are you going to check them?"

"Later. I have decided I am too tired now. When do you leave?"

"Before the end of the week."

"All is changing. The maid Catarina has just told me she is leaving too."

"It is the first I have heard of this."

"I will need to replace her."

"Could you find a young girl, someone Elizabeth will find more biddable?"

"Bess finds Catarina disobedient?" Pedro could hear the disbelief in Thomas's voice.

"No, not disobedient. It is difficult to say. Catarina has been used to her own home. I do not think a widow is always a good servant, especially when Elizabeth has run this household without help for many years."

Thomas shrugged. "So be it. I will engage a young girl."

"How long are you staying?"

"Why do you ask?"

"I believe Elizabeth needs your company. She has been quite downcast and grieves for her father and nephew sorely."

"It is life, Torres. Our father was a very old man. She could not have expected him to live much longer. And as for that young pup, Gabriel, he seems to have brought his troubles upon himself. I did not know him well, for I had left for Montauban before he came to Caors, but he struck me as having too great an abundance of confidence and charm."

"Elizabeth does not see it that way."

"You seem mightily concerned about my sister, Pedro."

To deflect Thomas's attention, Pedro walked back to the chest. He reached to the very bottom and pulled out two old leather purses. Thomas recognised them immediately.

"You are taking your inheritance."

"I will take some of it, the gold ducats and some of the jewels."

"It is yours to take."

"You have not said how long you will stay."

"Such concern for Elizabeth does you credit, Pedro. I will stay the winter. It is getting late in the season to travel across country, as you know. I will go to Uzès in the spring."

"Good, then I will leave the day after tomorrow." Pedro stood very erect, glad now that the big man opposite him was sitting down. "I want to thank you for all you have done for me."

Thomas waved him away, his attention already on Elizabeth, brought to mind by the conversation with Pedro. As soon as the latter had left the room, he went in search of her in the garden.

He found her on the seat against the wall and sat down without ceremony before he announced, "Pedro is leaving the day after tomorrow." Elizabeth turned to face him. "By the devil, your face is mournful, Bess."

She tried to summon the energy to reply tartly but it evaded her. "There is much which causes me sorrow."

To her surprise Thomas took her hand and clasped it between his. "You take things to heart so! Do not dwell on worldly things but put your faith in God and the fate he has predestined for us."

Elizabeth had no answer. It would only inflame him to demand whether Gabriel had been predestined to be lost in New France and it was too reassuring to feel his large, strong hands encircling one of hers to risk an argument about religious doctrine. Of all her losses, it was her nephew's which troubled her the most. Her parents' demise she could understand but the idea that Gabriel, with all his vitality, would never come back into her life was unimaginable. If Thomas had known of the expensive candles she had lit in the cathedral, and the prayers she had offered for Gabriel's safety, he would have chided her for superstition, but he did not, so he squeezed her hand gently and said, "I will stay until spring."

"Thank you. The house will feel empty when Pedro goes."

"He is mightily concerned about you."

"He is?" Thomas heard the catch in her voice.

"He wants me to find a suitable maid for you when Catarina leaves."

"Catarina is leaving?"

"Yes." Thomas eyed her keenly, curious about the tightness of her voice, and the tension in her body.

"Why?"

Thomas replied airily, "Some family matter."

Elizabeth's shoulders relaxed a fraction. "I would like a young girl. Someone who needs a home and is willing to learn."

"I will start asking around tomorrow."

They sat in silence, watching the late afternoon sun cross-light the garden. Elizabeth's arm was becoming uncomfortable, so she shifted position slightly. As if on cue, Thomas released her hand and asked, "Have you been reading any more of Mama's journals?"

"Why do you ask?"

"I was just wondering."

She refused to prevaricate. "Yes."

"I might look at them."

Her intake of breath betrayed her.

"Why should you read them and not me?" he demanded. "What secrets are there, that must be kept from me?" He watched her stricken face and laughed. "I would wager I know more than you."

Stung by his tone, she took the bait as she always did when they were together. "Do you know about Alyce?"

"My mother?" He laughed again. "Close your mouth, Bess. You look as if you are catching flies!"

"'There are no flies at this time of year,' she retorted crossly and then added, more quietly, "How do you know?"

"I have known for as long as I can remember. I was five years old when Mama married Papa. It was one of the happiest days of my life. She was my world and I had lived in fear that she would be sent back to England. She told me about Alyce when she asked me to call her Mama, but I already knew she was my aunt, so I must have been told about my mother earlier."

"Did you know Papa was your father?"

"I think I knew then, we looked so similar, but Mama and Ysabel always said my father was Matthew Blake when I asked. It was only after Mama and Papa were married and Joseph was born that I began to call him Father."

"You were a family."

"I resented Joseph and my father. They stole Mama from me. The baby took all of her time and I no longer shared her bed."

Elizabeth felt for the little boy Thomas had been. "It must have been difficult for you."

"It was, but at least I knew Mama was safe in Caors."

"And eventually, I was born."

"Not before Mama lost two babies."

Elizabeth felt tears forming again. She had never heard of the babies, although she was certain they lived within the pages of the journal. When she felt stronger, she would read about them.

"Why are you crying now? You never used to be so emotional. I always thought you were like Mama and rarely cried."

Elizabeth looked at him and brushed her hand over her damp eyes. "That is true. I have just thought of an entry in her journal. She wrote about tears on the page. Pedro was correct, she was writing for effect. She was writing as a dramatic young woman."

Amazed, he asked, "You shared Mama's journal with Pedro Torres?"

"Yes."

Thomas experienced a flash of understanding. "You must hold him in some esteem to share such intimacy."

Flustered, Elizabeth replied, "I have found his company pleasing."

"What about your fury when I appointed him steward?"

"I have changed. I have come to see the value of Pedro." Thomas raised his eyebrows, a habit inherited from his father, and she hastily added, "He has taught me much about business and I see that I cannot do everything alone."

"When I go in the spring, I will hire a new steward."

"I do not want anyone to live in the house."

Thomas nodded and stretched his long legs out. Running a hand through his thick grey hair, a sign he was thinking, he stated, "Pedro is a good man."

"That he is." She betrayed herself again, as clearly as if she had blurted out her love.

With uncharacteristic discernment, her brother asked, "Have you spoken to Pedro?"

"No."

"I think you should."

It was not until the following morning that Elizabeth could speak to Pedro alone. He was packing, his meagre possessions laid out neatly on the bed, and he swung around, startled by her knock.

"The door was ajar," she said.

"Yes." He waited for her to say more, without success.

She stood for some time on the threshold and then said, "I will be back shortly."

He was transferring his clothes, and Luis's treasured Qur'an, into a satchel when Elizabeth reappeared. "I want you to take these," she said, with a touch of her old authority.

Pedro glanced up and registered the cloak and doublet. Inwardly moved, for he was certain of their ownership, he only managed to ask, "Why?"

"It is a cloak to keep you warm," she replied, holding it up to reveal the fur lining. "And the doublet is of the highest quality…"

"Of the highest quality!" he interrupted. "Why would I need a doublet of the highest quality?"

"When you reach Amsterdam you must appear to be a man of substance."

"Am I not a man of substance in my own clothes?"

He watched her as she tried to ascertain his meaning. She was hollow-eyed from lack of sleep, the contrast between her eyes and skin even more marked, and the tell-tale line had formed between her brows. "I only wanted to do my best by you. Gabriel never wore them."

His heart flipped. "I jest, Elizabeth. I jest."

She walked into the room, ready to lay Gabriel's clothes on the bed, but paused as if she was requesting his permission. "Thank you," he said, moving the satchel to one side.

Elizabeth rested her hand on the cloak almost reverentially. "He would want you to have it."

"I have some measure of the distress you feel, Elizabeth." He wanted to reach out and touch her. Instead, he placed his hand on the bedpost, his fingers idly tracing the carved wood.

At last, she raised her eyes from the cloak. He started to thank her again when she cut him short. "When did you know Catarina was leaving?"

Disconcerted by the change of subject, he rephrased her question instead of answering it. "When did I know Catarina was leaving?"

"It is a plain enough question," she said, the furrow on her forehead deepening.

"When your brother told me, yesterday."

"Catarina is not leaving with you?"

"Why on earth do you think Catarina would be going to Amsterdam with me?"

"I saw her coming from your chamber in Montauban."

Mystified, he walked around the corner of the bed. "Why would you ever think that about me?"

"She is pleasing to the eye."

"So is the butcher's wife!"

Elizabeth could hear the amusement in his voice. "I have noticed she pays you great attention," she stated tartly. "I am correct. I saw her with my own eyes in Montauban."

He took a step towards her. "Elizabeth, my door was bolted."

"She did try your door?"

Illumination struck him. He laughed, his eyes dancing. She was jealous, Elizabeth Gharsia was deeply jealous of her maid because of him. "Somebody tried the door," he admitted.

His elation was infectious. Elizabeth began to laugh, too, and her words slipped out on a wave of jubilation. "I was so afraid you were enamoured of her."

"How could you not know it is you I love?" It was said. Pedro searched Elizabeth's face for her response. It came slowly and was all the more precious because of it: from initial bafflement to gradual comprehension, and then, glorious unabated exultation.

"You will stay?"

"No, I will go."

"How can you go, if you love me," she retorted, her voice thick with accusation.

"It is because I love you, that I must go," he replied, simply.

He watched the delight drain from her face and then reached into the cabinet at the side of the bed. "Keep this," he said. "Keep this safe until I return."

Elizabeth's hand closed around the worn, leather pouch. The jewels inside jangled, sliding and shifting against each other. Pedro placed his hand over hers and, conscious of the open door, leant forward. "I will come back."

As she studied the dried, brittle drawstring, her head slightly bowed, he brushed her forehead with a whisper of a kiss. She raised her eyes and he spoke slowly and deliberately. "I will come back."

The following morning Pedro departed early, without seeing Elizabeth. He rode west, oblivious of the autumn beauty around him. He did not see the sun tinting the slopes, nor the will o' the wisp weaving ethereally through the vines, nor the couple on the track making their way to Caors for the market. His heart hurt, his stomach knotted, but he did not turn around. How could he? How could a man such as himself propose marriage to a woman of Elizabeth Gharsia's standing? He rode on until he reached the jetty. As he stabled the hired horse, he was silent and as he boarded the barge, the mariner who cast off grumbled about rude passengers. Throughout the river journey to Bordèu he was devoured by misery, and on the voyage to Holland, seasickness added to his wretchedness. Nevertheless, his spirits began to lift at the sight of the Dutch port.

He disembarked with a spring in his step, into the noise and bustle which was Amsterdam. A chill wind blew off the sea, but he was warm within his cloak. His doublet was slightly too large, but nobody would see beyond the richness of the cloth, and the new leather pouches were easily secreted within it. He held his head high as he wove his way through the crowds, marvelling at the waterways, at the diversity of the people he could see, and above all at the clamour of a city growing in confidence. What opportunities there would be for a man of aptitude and diligence; for a man from the shadows who had experienced persecution, and especially for a man who had a purpose and a quantity of Venetian gold ducats, in mint condition, ripe for investment.

EPILOGUE

Fort van Nassouwen, the North River, New Netherlands, Summer 1617

J ACOB EELKENS RESTED ON HIS SHOVEL HANDLE AND watched the canoes approach. He was unconcerned as they were few in number and totally unthreatening to his attachment of ten armed men. Around him, the others stopped their work, all involved in labouring to restore the damage wreaked by the spring thaw. The fort was vulnerable, situated as it was on an island at the confluence of the river flowing from the lands of the Mohawk and the great river recently explored by the Englishman, Henry Hudson. Each year the occupants had to cope with the effects of flooding as the melt water surged into the two rivers.

As the three canoes came nearer, Eelkens's first assumption was confirmed: these were not the usual tribe who came to trade, the Lenape, but were Mohawks, the most feared of the Iroquois. He ordered his men to reach for their arms although the presence of women and children ruled out a war party. In each canoe he could identify a warrior, their greased, muscled torsos catching the sun, a couple of youths, a woman and an assortment of very young children. Before he left the stockade to meet them, Eelkens checked that the two cannon and the swivel guns were manned.

The canoes came to a halt with a flourish and the warrior in the second canoe stood up. He was tall and broad-shouldered, every part of his strong body visible except for that covered by his breechcloth. Eelkens waited, curious to hear how the warrior would address him. Some of the traders had a smattering of Dutch but he doubted that the Mohawk would be able to communicate in that language.

"We come in peace, to trade," shouted the brave, in heavily accented English.

Eelkens replied, also in English, "What do you have?"

"Beaver."

"Leave any arms you have in the canoe."

The Mohawk spoke rapidly to his companions and removed his club from his waist. The others followed suit, except the warrior in the first canoe. He began gesticulating angrily, his face contorted with fury.

Worried, Eelkens demanded, "What ails him? He cannot come ashore."

There followed a quick interchange between the two Mohawks before the warrior stepped out of the second canoe. "He means no harm," he shouted. "He is upset because this trading post appears to be a fort."

Eelkens thought for a moment, his eyes sweeping across the three canoes. The bundles of furs were sizeable, there were only six men and youths who appeared capable of fighting, and although he had heard that squaws could be as fierce as their braves, the young woman in the second canoe was heavily pregnant, as was the one in the third. "You may come," he said to the Mohawk who was solicitously helping the woman from the second canoe. "Bring a bundle of skins so that I can check the quality."

Eelkens's nascent suspicion was reinforced when the woman appeared to reject the warrior's attentions whilst bestowing on him a look of such affection that it made a lie of her action. Once she was safely on dry land, a boy, of about seven years, jumped out and then carried a small child to the woman. There was some discussion between the adults before the warrior and the older boy walked towards the Dutchman.

The pelts were laid out and their quality was undeniable. Eelkens eyed the trader thoughtfully, deciding how few manufactured goods he could trade for the skins. The Mohawk waited perfectly still with arms crossed; the boy next to him, copying the warrior's stance. At last, Eelkens said, "They are of good enough quality. I have some fine knives, hatchets, and clothing."

"I will need more than a few pots and pans. These pelts will sell for a small fortune in Paris."

"Paris? What do you know of Paris?"

The Mohawk remained immobile; the only change, a slight challenge in his expression. The Dutchman scrutinised the warrior's face, especially his eyes, which were as black as obsidian, and the scars on his torso, which spoke of an eventful life, and experienced the uncanny feeling that he was being toyed with. "What do you want for your pelts?"

The Mohawk looked around, assessing the single building which acted as a trading post and warehouse, and the fortifications which included a moat the width of six strides.

"You are well-protected," he stated, "but your choice of site is questionable."

"Who are you?"

The Mohawk made no response. Instead he spoke to the boy, who lifted up a pelt and ran his hand across the soft fur before handing it to Eelkens. The quality was exceptional. The Dutchman's eyes glinted in the bright sunlight. "Tell me what you want."

"I want an honourable man. A man whom I can trust."

"You are an Englishman?"

"I am Mohawk. This is my son, Helaku. My wife sits by the canoe with my second son and soon I will have a third child."

"And I am an honourable Dutchman."

"Will you do me a favour, Dutchman? I will pay handsomely in pelts. What you see is beaver, but I have others, lynx and white fox, if you do as I ask."

"I am listening."

"Do you have pen and paper?"

"Of course."

"Will you, on your word, ensure that a letter reaches the Pays d'Oc?"

Eelkens clapped his thigh triumphantly. "You are French! You are some way south, my friend."

"It is my choice."

"I thought the French and the Mohawk were enemies."

"Do you have the pen and paper?"

"It might take months or a year to reach its destination."

"It does not matter, as long as it is delivered."

"When I next visit the coast I will talk to my contacts. It could reach Bordèu reasonably easily from Amsterdam."

"My family has trading links with Bordèu. It is a gamble, but it could work."

"Do you not want to return, yourself?"

For an instant, there is a flicker of yearning in the Mohawk's eyes, a longing which Eelkens recognised, and then it is gone. "I have a wife," he stated proudly, "and two sons." Then he pointed to the warrior still gesticulating and shouting in the first canoe. "And a brother, Matwau, who would die for me."

Eelkens nodded in understanding. "Come, I will find some paper."

It did not take long for the letter to be written, nor for some of the pelts to be exchanged for good iron tools. Eelkens held the sealed epistle in his hand and noted the fine hand, albeit slightly shaky, which had addressed it. He watched the Mohawk and the boy return to the waiting woman. She smiled a greeting and struggled to her feet, refusing the offered hand. It was only when she started to walk that Eelkens realised she was lame.

As the three canoes glided into the river, he could just make out the Mohawk's mien. Preoccupied, the man's face was an inscrutable mask and the Dutchman wondered what he was thinking as he paddled away, the Mohawk who was a Frenchman. Had he already forgotten the letter or had his encounter with another white man stirred long suppressed emotions? It was neither. With each stroke of the paddle, the warrior imagined himself as the letter. It would travel to New Amsterdam, and from there to Holland, the trade routes eventually taking it to Caors.

Its arrival would be announced by a knock on the door. The old oak, swollen if it was winter, would grate across the uneven slabs, grinding the rushes into dust. It would be carried across the hall, whose lofty roof revealed the original beams, to the small chamber at the back of the house. There his aunt would gaze at his handwriting in disbelief and turn to his grandfather. No, it cannot be his grandfather. The warrior remembers the moth: his grandfather is dead. He shakes his head, misses his stroke and silently curses. He sees his aunt try to open the letter but her hands tremble too much. He hopes she is not alone. Perhaps her brother is with her, when she finally unfolds the paper and finds he is alive? He is alive.

What he cannot imagine is the man who rises from his seat and stands next to his aunt. He is about the same height, his colouring testament to his heritage, and his clothes a declaration of his success. As she passes the letter to him, her face diffused with relief, the firelight glints the gold on her finger. The ring which proclaims her a wife.

ABOUT THE AUTHOR

Barbara Greig was born in Sunderland and lived in Roker until her family moved to Teesdale. An avid reader, she also discovered the joy of history at an early age. A last-minute change of heart, in the sixth form, caused her to alter her university application form. Instead of English, Barbara read Modern and Ancient History at Sheffield University. It was a decision she never regretted.

Barbara worked for twenty years in sixth form colleges, teaching History and Classical Civilisation. Eventually, although enjoying a role in management, she found there was less time for teaching and historical study. A change of focus was required. With her children having flown the nest, she was able to pursue her love of writing and story-telling. She has a passion for hiking, and dancing, the perfect antidotes to long hours of historical research and writing, as well as for travel and, wherever possible, she walks in the footsteps of her characters.

Discovery is Barbara's second novel. Her debut novel *Secret Lives* was published in 2016 (Sacristy Press).

 Matador

For exclusive discounts on Matador titles,
sign up to our occasional newsletter at
troubador.co.uk/bookshop